AZUELA AND THE MEXICAN UNDERDOGS

Published for the
UCLA Latin American Center
as Volume 48 in the
UCLA Latin American Studies Series
Series editor: Johannes Wilbert

Books published by the University of California Press in co-operation with the UCLA Latin American Center

1. Kenneth Karst and Keith S. Rosenn, *Law and Development in Latin America: A Case Book,* Volume 28, Latin American Studies Series, UCLA Latin American Center.

2. James W. Wilkie, Michael C. Meyer, and Edna Monzón de Wilkie, eds., *Contemporary Mexico: Papers of the IV International Congress of Mexican History,* Volume 29, Latin American Studies Series, UCLA Latin American Center.

3. Arthur J. O. Anderson, Frances Berdan, and James Lockhart, *Beyond the Codices: The Nahua View of Colonial Mexico,* Volume 27, Latin American Studies Series, UCLA Latin American Center.

4. Stanley L. Robe, *Azuela and the Mexican Underdogs,* Volume 48, Latin American Studies Series, UCLA Latin American Center.

(Except for the volumes listed above, which are published and distributed by the University of California Press, Berkeley, California 94720, all other volumes in the Latin American Studies Series are published and distributed by the UCLA Latin American Center, Los Angeles, California 90024.)

AZUELA

and the
Mexican Underdogs

by

Stanley L. Robe

UNIVERSITY OF CALIFORNIA PRESS

Berkeley   Los Angeles   London

University of California Press
Berkeley and Los Angeles, California
University of California Press, Ltd.
London, England
© 1979 by The Regents of the University of California
ISBN: 0-520-03293-4
Library of Congress Catalog Card Number: 76-20031
Printed in the United States of America

1 2 3 4 5 6 7 8 9 0

A tres finas personas que no alcanzaron a ver los frutos de estas labores:

Sturgis E. Leavitt (1888-1976)

José de Jesús Loera Rivera (1903-1976)

José Cornejo Franco (1900-1977)

Preface

Two years stand out from all others in the long life of Mariano Azuela. The years of crisis of the Mexican revolution—1914 and 1915—differ sharply from the writer's first forty years of comparatively tranquil existence, which were spent in the provinces in his native Lagos de Moreno and in Guadalajara. From an interested spectator, Azuela overnight turned into an active participant in the revolution during its most turbulent period. The activities and experiences of these months left an enduring stamp on his future novelistic output. The immediate product of this period is his masterpiece *Los de abajo,* which broke away from previous traditions of the novel in Mexico and affected prose writing in that country for decades to come, despite the novel's lying unnoticed for nearly ten years following its publication late in 1915. The pages that follow here trace the events of those two years and Azuela's participation in them as these bear upon the writing and eventual publication of *Los de abajo.*

Los de abajo came to the attention of a critical audience and the reading public when it was finally "discovered" in late 1924 and early 1925. Critics and professors of Spanish American literature examined and interpreted the novel throughout the 1930s and 1940s but lost interest in it thereafter. In large part the shift in interest derived from the emergence of younger writers who have changed or modified the course of the novel in Mexico, in particular Agustín Yáñez and Juan Rulfo, who, like Azuela, are also from the state of Jalisco.

The critics of the 1930s and 1940s recognized that in order to grasp Azuela's intent in the novel, it was indispensable, without slighting considerations of artistry and style, to approach his creation from a historical point of view. To a degree they accomplished their purpose and at the same time provided a number of well-prepared basic guides to Azuela's works and the literature of the Mexican revolution. But the task undertaken by the older critics was never completed. They were unable to fill in the entire story of the writing of *Los de abajo,* and they left editions of the work still to be discovered. The outlook of these scholars, however, is still fundamentally valid, and it is the one called for here, although it perhaps has gone out of vogue with those who are concerned with Mexican writers of the contemporary scene.

The tracing of the creation, development, writing, and publication of *Los de abajo* clearly belongs to the realm of literary history. Within the relatively narrow confines of this domain, the main consideration must be Azuela's personal contribution to the creative process. One cannot overlook, however, the political and military events that determined Azuela's course of action in 1914 and 1915 and shaped his personal view of the revolution. The succession of revolutionary governments and the ups and downs of the fighting cannot be disentangled from the thread of the novel as Azuela put it together. These nonliterary proceedings were part of the intricate panorama of figures, movements, and ideas that formed the revolution. Those who have written about *Los de abajo* have had a relatively firm grasp of the predominantly literary features of the novel but have been somewhat less effective in dealing with the detailed historical, geographical, and social forces that were equally significant in the writing of the novel.

A useful backdrop for keeping track of Azuela's deeds in the revolution would have been a history of the Villista movement in the state of Jalisco. Unfortunately no such work exists, despite the strong sympathy of the *jaliscienses* for Francisco Villa and the rousing welcomes that they gave him and his *dorados* when they appeared in Guadalajara. José Guadalupe Zuno has attempted to cover the activities of various factions in his *Historia de la Revolución en el Estado de Jalisco* (1964), which is one of a series of volumes dealing with the Mexican revolution state by state.[1] Zuno, a governor of Jalisco in the 1920s, has covered his subject only sketchily and is highly favorable to the Carrancista element. Thus the Villistas, with whom Azuela was affiliated, are given short shrift.

In order to provide some sort of perspective to Azuela's role in these two years in the revolution, I have drawn upon a variety of sources. The novelist's own statements have been indispensable. These are found mainly in the memoirs and reminiscences that have been included in the third volume of his *Obras completas,* although it has been necessary to determine their chronological order and identify more precisely many of Azuela's associates and friends. These pieces are supplemented by the compilation of much of Azuela's personal correspondence in Beatrice Berler's arrangement of his *Epistolario y archivo* (1969). There he answers specific questions put to him by scholars and admirers. Azuela's replies are authoritative and to the point.

There are rare glimpses of Azuela in the memoirs of jaliscienses who went through the revolution. Julián Medina, Azuela's immediate superior in military service, because of his dashing figure and participation in daring enterprises, is frequently remembered in these memoirs and in local histories of Jalisco and communities of that state. There is no lack of books written around the figure of Francisco Villa, but most authors have been attracted by the man's legendary features and his more spectacular exploits. Relatively few have taken notice of his two brief appearances in Guadalajara and his meetings with Medina and other sympathizers.

Two collections of contemporary newspapers gave a feeling of immediacy to news reports of events of 1914 and 1915. The move-

ments of Villa and Medina were followed closely in the columns of the *Boletín Militar,* published in Guadalajara during those hectic years. This extremely partisan sheet was subsidized by the Carrancista general Manuel M. Diéguez and apparently was printed in a railway car that accompanied his army. I was extremely fortunate in being able to examine also a lengthy file of *El Paso del Norte,* another Carrancista daily, which appeared in El Paso, Texas. This long-sought newspaper, which heretofore has not been consulted, was indispensable in determining at long last the early text and dates of publication of *Los de abajo,* which first appeared in its columns. Likewise it has shed light on the first volume of the novel, when it was published, and its reception by those who first read it.

Narrated accounts of incidents of the revolution in Jalisco supplied personally by eyewitnesses have supplemented the published material. Their refreshing comments have been of a kind not usually found in more formal sources and give popular rather than official views of the conflict. Few witnesses of events of sixty years ago are still alive. Throughout more than three decades of inquiry I have interviewed a number of residents of Jalisco and southern Zacatecas who related their experiences during the revolutionary period.

I have relied somewhat less on works of criticism relating to Azuela's writing. The thrust of the present study is not along these lines, although it should certainly lay the foundation for analysis and evaluation of the early editions of *Los de abajo,* a task that has not been undertaken because of the unavailability of these printings. Nevertheless, I have made use of Luis Leal, *Mariano Azuela, vida y obra* (1961), which provides insights into Azuela's biography at a number of points during the revolutionary years. Ernest R. Moore's "Biografía y bibliografía de don Mariano Azuela" has been my bibliographical guide to the early printed versions of *Los de abajo.*

The recent centenary of the author's birth did not bring forth a rash of studies; only one has come to my attention—*Mariano Azuela y la*

---

[1] I refer to the Biblioteca del Instituto Nacional de Estudios Históricos de la Revolución Mexicana.

crítica mexicana (1973)—a collection of pieces written by Mexican critics throughout the years and edited by Francisco Monterde. Examination of the historical and critical sources considered above suggests that the time is again appropriate for devoting attention to Azuela and in particular to *Los de abajo.* Despite the interest of the older generation, there has been but one published book-length study of Azuela and his writing, Luis Leal's *Mariano Azuela, vida y obra.* There is room for further serious treatment of Azuela's work.

In more than one sense, a literary era is coming to an end. The ranks of the remaining revolutionaries are thinning with each passing year, and before long those who can give direct testimony concerning their experiences in the throes of the conflict will have left this earth. Their passing will mean an end to the stream of personal reminiscences of military and political events as well as of literature and literary figures of those years. In a parallel situation, many of the older generation who have studied Azuela's work have already departed.

There is a more optimistic side of the picture, however. In their mature years, various participants in the revolution have written down their memoirs in detail. A number of these appeared in the 1950s and 1960s. At the same time there have been other careful historical studies of aspects of the revolution that have not been treated previously, with thoughtful organization and presentation. These and improved bibliographical tools will certainly make the work of the literary historian and critic easier in the future than it was for those pioneers who undertook the early pronouncements on Azuela's work.

The most optimistic note of all has to be the appearance at long last of the serial edition of *Los de abajo* which dates from the fall of 1915 when Mariano Azuela had fled to El Paso, Texas. The quest for the numbers of *El Paso del Norte* that contain his novel has been a long one, with many disappointments and blind alleys. It has had, however, its pleasant surprises and the success of the enterprise has been well

worth the time and effort devoted to tracking them down. There have been occasional "near misses" in the search. One of these involves Mariano Azuela's own proximity to the El Paso newspaper. For years a collection lay in the private library of Carlos Basave del Castillo Negrete in Mexico City. Azuela knew Carlos Basave and credited him with having provided background material for one of the short pieces contained in *Precursores.* He numbered Basave among "distinguidos amigos míos."[2] One wonders if the novelist was aware that his friend possessed the numbers of *El Paso del Norte* with the text of *Los de abajo.* If Azuela knew, he did not pass on that information to those who interviewed him in the 1930s. Had such been the case, the missing *folletines* would have turned up years ago.

I must acknowledge my indebtedness and appreciation to colleagues and friends who have given encouragement and invaluable assistance. Sturgis E. Leavitt has for years shown unflagging optimism in the pursuit of the early El Paso editions of *Los de abajo.* His words of support have in large part given me the persistence to bring to light the collection of *El Paso del Norte.* My colleague John E. Englekirk generously gave me access to his personal copy of the 1916 edition of *Los de abajo* and shared with me details of his quest for that work. The contribution of Antonio Loera has been unique and indispensable. He visited the Fondo Basave of the Biblioteca de México and confirmed the presence of *El Paso del Norte* on its shelves. My profound thanks go to him and to his father J. J. Loera Rivera, who as a boy worked in the shop of *El Paso del Norte.* He provided a rare view of the operation of the newspaper during the period when Azuela was in El Paso. Lic. Miguel Palacios graciously extended to me the use of the Biblioteca de México, and Concepción Alonso was most helpful and cordial in making my visit to the Fondo Basave a memorable one. Throughout the years many others have helped to piece together the background of *Los de abajo,* and the reader will find them cited

[2]*Precursores* (Santiago de Chile, 1935), p. 7.

frequently. To them and to those whom I have
mentioned above, I express my deepest gratitude.

An explanation of the arrangement of the
book is appropriate at this point. I treat in
Chapter 1 Azuela's early participation in the
local politics of Lagos de Moreno during the
early stages of the Mexican revolution and follow this with an account of his service with the
military forces led by Julián Medina and Manuel
Caloca. The latter is significant in that it has
provided the direct experience that has served
as grist for Azuela's novelistic mill. Chapter 2
takes up Azuela's experience as an exile in El
Paso and the form that *Los de abajo* took there.
The original *Los de abajo,* the text that was
first published in *El Paso del Norte,* is contained
in Chapter 3. Chapter 4 is a translation of that
text into English. The Appendix is an eyewitness view of one of the exploits of the men of
Medina and Caloca, very much in the spirit of
Los de abajo, which corroborates many of
Azuela's own observations of the revolutionists
and their military deeds.

                                                S.L.R.

Contents

Contents

ILLUSTRATIONS

MAPS

Illustrations are by Robert C. Robe.

Abbreviations

(Used in notes)

Almada	Almada, Francisco R. *La Revolución en el Estado de Chihuahua.* Biblioteca del Instituto Nacional de Estudios Históricos de la Revolución Mexicana. 2 vols. Mexico, 1965.
Calzadíaz	Calzadíaz Barrera, Alberto. *Hechos reales de la Revolución.* 3 vols. Mexico: Editores Mexicanos Unidos, S. A., 1965.
Davis	Davis, Will[iam] B[rownlee]. *Experiences and Observations of an American Consular Officer during the Recent Mexican Revolutions.* Los Angeles: Wayside Press, 1920.
Epistolario	Azuela, Mariano. *Epistolario y archivo.* Recopilación, notas y apéndices de Beatrice Berler. Mexico: Centro de Estudios Literarios, Universidad Nacional Autónoma de México, 1969.
Leal	Leal, Luis. *Mariano Azuela, vida y obra.* Mexico: Ediciones de Andrea, 1961.
Monterde	Monterde, Francisco, ed. *Mariano Azuela y la crítica mexicana.* Estudios, artículos y reseñas. Mexico: Secretaría de Educación Pública, 1973.
Moreno	Moreno Ochoa, J. Ángel. *Semblanzas revolucionarias. Compendio del movimiento de liberación en Jalisco.* Guadalajara, 1965.
O.C.	Azuela, Mariano. *Obras completas.* 3 vols. Mexico: Fondo de Cultura Económica, 1958–1960.
Páez Brotchie	Páez Brotchie, Luis. *Jalisco. Historia mínima.* 2 vols. Guadalajara, 1940.
Quirarte	Quirarte, Clotilde Evelia. *Nochistlán de Zacatecas. Cuatro siglos de su vida.* Mexico, 1960.

Mariano Azuela and the Villistas in Jalisco

Lagos: The Revolution Begins

Lagos de Moreno is a proud old town, given to contemplating itself frequently and expressing approval, for the most part, of its citizens, their accomplishments, and their manner of life. For some time, perhaps during most of the nearly four centuries since its founding, the residents of Lagos have been accustomed to focus upon themselves. Events that have occurred in the town are more significant than what has taken place elsewhere. There has been an unexpressed but plain feeling of self-sufficiency in regard to the tangible needs of the community as well as matters of the spirit and intellect. The *laguenses* have no crisis of identity.

Lagos and its hinterland in the Mexican state of Jalisco are a distinct *patria chica,* the community or province which one identifies as one's homeland, as contrasted with a feeling for the larger national entity. The latter is taken for granted, but the *laguense* steadfastly asserts his spiritual loyalty to the town of his birth, whether he is blessed by fortune and still resides there or whether through necessity he has been forced to dwell in a distant realm. No one can accuse him of a lack of devotion to his native town.

Mention of revered local heroes will cause chests to swell in Lagos. Among these the outstanding figure is Pedro Moreno, from whom the town has taken the second portion of its name. Moreno took up arms in the cause of Mexican independence in 1814. He harassed the Spanish forces in the vicinity, later successfully escaped their siege of him and his followers at the nearby Fuerte del Sombrero, but was pursued and captured near Guanajuato in October, 1817. After having Moreno executed, the Spanish commander severed his head and exhibited it impaled on a spike in the town square of Lagos. But patriotism has not been the only source of pride among those of Lagos. They attribute to themselves a reputation for progress, in material and in cultural matters. This spirit gained strength notably in the nineteenth century, but it was nurtured and guided under terms laid down by the community. Progress tended to serve the traditional way of life and traditional needs of the townspeople. It did not stray far outside those limits.

Solid advances had been made in the last half of the century. The imposing parish church, under construction for more than ninety years,

1

Mariano Azuela in 1911

was finally completed in 1873, and the graceful, slender spires, tastefully decorated and well proportioned, dominated the entire town and could be seen from miles away. After what seemed centuries of patient waiting, the last two spans of the stone bridge across the Río de Lagos were finished in 1870, and residents and travelers could cross over them on the way to outlying haciendas and farms, perhaps even to the city of León. These two monuments to progress, significant as they were to the residents of Lagos, had become the targets of irreverent barbs and coarse jests when the citizens of neighboring towns turned to consider these structures.

The old convent of the Mercedarios maintained a school for more than a hundred years, but it was sold in 1857 and the building was allowed to go to ruin. In the late 1860s the structure once occupied by the Capuchins as a convent was refurbished, and in it was installed a school for the youth of the community, endowed by a bequest from Father Miguel Leandro Guerra, a parish priest of the first half of the century. In 1914 Lagos would see no more of Father Agustín Rivera y Sanromán (1824–1916), who had in recent years moved away to León. Father Rivera kept his fellow laguenses well supplied with reading matter on religious, philosophical, and historical themes, and the local printing presses were constantly turning out his pamphlets and books. During his ninety or more years he had published 157 works, but by 1914 the stream was nearing its end.[1]

[1]Alfonso de Alba, *Antonio Moreno y Oviedo y la generación de 1903* (Mexico, 1949), p. 100.

Until 1914 the people of Lagos for the most part continued to pursue their normal activities. The rancheros, owners of small farms who had gained a degree of economic independence, tended their fields of corn and vegetable gardens and milked a few cows. From the more than two hundred small ranchos, they continued to bring their milk, grain, and produce to sell in Lagos. On the more than two dozen haciendas, herds of cattle fattened, and the hacendados continued to ship their animals to the Bajío area of Guanajuato where the beef was consumed and the hides supplied material for the shoe manufacturers in León. This pattern had existed without major changes for over three hundred years. Other hacendados had found that it was profitable to grow wheat on the level fields of the cool highlands. Everywhere the traditional food staples, corn and beans, were the basis of agriculture on both a large and a small scale and were in demand by the total population, including the peones and sharecroppers, who were landless and thus worked the lands of others.

Those who owned land strongly favored maintaining things as they were. The hacienda owner, usually of a traditionally wealthy family, sought to protect his social and economic position. This position was a significant factor in the life of Lagos, for this type of property was concentrated in the municipality to a much greater degree than in the neighboring territory of Los Altos to the southwest. The haciendas of Lagos were known far and wide, Ciénega de Mata, San Cristóbal, La Troje, Estancia Grande, Moya, Betulia, and El Puesto, plus a number of others. At the same time, the rest of the municipality was divided into more than two hundred parcels. The carving up of the land into small farms reflected the ranchero's search for security through the ownership of property. He had acquired his modest holding by dint of hard work. His economic security had been hard won, and he was reluctant to endanger it in any way.

The town of Lagos was originally settled by Spanish families in the 1560s to serve as an armed outpost to control the marauding tribes to the northeast of Guadalajara. Once this goal

Parish church of Lagos

was achieved, Lagos became a trading center where cattle raisers and farmers came to buy supplies and to sell their surplus grain and cattle, but the town never actively sought to extend its trade much beyond the immediate surrounding area. Thus the laguenses traded among themselves and with the nearby hinterland. In early 1914 it was still business as usual, quiet rather than brisk, and restricted in the main to the usual local pattern.

In 1914 Lagos had a small group of professional men. They were those who ministered to the physical aches and pains of the local population and those who through knowledge and use of the law either sought to bring about justice or to thwart it. Of these doctors and lawyers, most had gone away to study in Guadalajara, the state capital. A lesser number had been as far away as Mexico City. After receiving their professional degrees, these local youths had come back to Lagos, where most of them settled down into the familiar pattern of things.

But they were the ones in the town who maintained the intellectual and artistic spark. For the most part they wrote poetry, much of it incredibly romantic; a few tried their hand at prose. They printed their compositions locally on a modest press and distributed copies to their friends in Lagos, and a few, very few, copies reached Guadalajara, Mexico City, and provincial capitals elsewhere in the country. For years they had met regularly in congenial circumstances to read or declaim their compositions and discuss news of literary events elsewhere that had filtered through to Lagos. These lawyers, doctors, and a few alert political functionaries were among those in Lagos who shared an awareness of events that had been under way in other parts of Mexico since 1910 or 1911. Their repercussions were soon to be felt in Lagos.

Even in the twentieth century, the religious life of the laguenses remained but little altered since the centuries of Spanish dominion. Townspeople and ranchers retained their traditional devoutness, which was translated outwardly into formal religious observance, with regular attendance at mass in the parish church, La Merced, the Templo de la Luz, Santuario de Guadalupe, El Rosario, El Refugio, or one of the outlying places of worship. But the church's influence was not always formal. It served as an arbiter of social approval or disapproval. In this respect, the church could exert pressure equal to that of the civil government, although in Lagos the two institutions cooperated and strengthened one another. The people of Lagos were more eager to obtain the approval of the church, however, than that of the political authority. Thus the members of the clergy were looked up to and revered, and they enjoyed a high degree of prestige in the community. At the same time the church and the clergy did not encourage the local flock to extend its outlook beyond its immediate confines. Thus the church contributed largely to the inward-looking vision of the resident of Lagos upon his town and its hinterland. In this respect he resembled closely his neighbors in the towns of Los Altos of Jalisco. They and the laguenses still lived enclosed within their own communities, facing inward upon themselves rather than assuming a role in a much larger scene.

All this is not to say that the laguenses have hesitated to introduce innovations of a material nature. The late nineteenth century saw the construction of a textile mill that produced unbleached muslin, which was the type of cloth most used by the rancheros and those with limited resources. In connection with this mill, a small foundry produced simple machine parts and decorative ironwork for the public buildings and the more pretentious homes of the town. The increased acreage of wheat grown on the large haciendas of Lagos justified the building of a flour mill across the river from the town. These installations were on a rather modest scale, and through those who were employed there, Lagos derived some economic benefit, although that income was slight in comparison with that from agriculture and cattle. Furthermore, all three were the property of the influential Rincón Gallardo family. The steam plant that generated electricity had been installed in 1903, and the town replaced its streetlamps that previously had burned either animal fat or kerosene. By the same period, Lagos had its first telephone network that served the towns and the nearby rural areas. The material innovations made life more comfortable for some segments of the local population and likely brought some financial gain. They had little effect, however, upon the attitudes of the townspeople and their intellectual and cultural horizons.

The hermetic existence of Lagos nevertheless was shaken by the arrival of the Ferrocarril Central late in 1882. Its tracks snaked to the northwest from Mexico City across the plains and between the low hills of the Bajío region, past the provincial town of Celaya with its *cajeta* candy, the strawberries of Irapuato and Silao, the leather sandals, shoes, and belts of León, and then to San Francisco del Rincón, from where they climbed up to the plateau of Los Altos and into Lagos. The daily train became the major contact between Lagos and the rest of Mexico and eventually the world. It brought back townspeople who had visited other cities of Mexico and even the capital city of the republic. It also brought to Lagos visitors from those places and, with the completion of the railway line to Ciudad Juárez in 1884, even from the United States.

Equally significant was the increased availability of news through access to newspapers and periodicals for those who could read. These media and books exposed at least a number of laguenses to the writings and thought of other Mexicans and Europeans. The minority group made up of professional people welcomed the greater ease with which they could share the ideas and literary creations of their contemporaries. But the motivation behind the construction of the railroad was hardly that of promoting the spread of ideas. It benefited the hacendados of Lagos, who began to ship out their cattle and wheat by rail, in greater quantity and to more remote points. The telegraph system that accompanied the railroad served to regulate rail traffic and to convey official government messages. For the national government and the hacendados, the latter in particular, the

new railroad brought clear economic advantages and both parties profited from its use during the thirty years or so following its completion until the onset of the Mexican revolution in the twentieth century. At that time the function of the railroad changed radically. The railroad thus broke into a relatively stagnant social picture in Lagos and pointed to a developing conflict between traditional views and a changing social order in the twentieth century.

By June, 1914, that conflict had cast a shadow over Lagos, but culturally and materially the military activities that were under way elsewhere in Mexico had affected the life of the town to only a slight degree. Up to this time, fighting that could have disturbed the daily routine of living had been confined to the north of Mexico. The few battles that toppled old president Porfirio Díaz in 1911 took place along the boundary with the United States. Although in Jalisco there had been a few Maderista bands, they engaged in little or no fighting. The presidency of Francisco I. Madero was calm, but his forcible removal from office and his execution by army forces commanded by General Victoriano Huerta in February, 1913, set off a new series of revolutionary explosions in widespread areas of Mexico. Their purpose was to overthrow General Huerta, who by force had assumed the presidency. The opposition movement was most successful in the northern states of Sonora, Chihuahua, and Coahuila.

There were isolated uprisings in Jalisco and a few armed bands penetrated into Los Altos. Crispín Robles and his men were frightened off when they attempted to take Nochistlán, a large town in southern Zacatecas,[2] but were more successful when they attacked Yahualica.[3] In the spring of 1913 Leopoldo Arenal and seven others met death when attempting to enter Nochistlán.[4] There were no disturbances of this nature in Lagos, and generally the local political bosses were able to maintain their hold

[2]Quirarte, p. 177.
[3]Agustín Yáñez, *Yahualica* (Mexico, 1946), pp. 132-133.
[4]Quirarte, pp. 178-180.

on the town. The basic emotional and ideological attitudes in Lagos were the same as during the old Díaz regime. The principal changes had been in the faces of a few political leaders. In this respect Lagos was not unique. Except in the north, nearly all of Mexico's towns and villages had the same political bosses as before the revolution of 1910.

There were dissidents in Lagos, however, but in mid-1914 they were quiet. The events of 1910 and 1911 brought a number of them to light during Francisco I. Madero's campaign for the presidency of Mexico. Two of these were Dr. Mariano Azuela and his close friend José Becerra. Azuela had been practicing medicine in Lagos for some fifteen years, and Becerra was trained as a lawyer and had occupied minor political posts. Azuela and Becerra shared a common interest in literature, Azuela as a novelist and short story writer and Becerra as a poet. They attended regularly the literary gatherings in Lagos sponsored by Antonio Moreno y Oviedo, another of the town's lawyers, but kept their political beliefs to themselves in order to discuss literature freely.

During the final years of the presidency of Porfirio Díaz, Dr. Azuela and Becerra became ardent supporters of Francisco Madero. They were active propagandists for him when he announced his candidacy in opposition to Díaz. Becerra was at that time secretary to the Jefe Político, the local political authority, of the canton of Lagos. In his fervor for Madero, he converted his office into a Maderista propaganda center. His activities eventually became known to the Jefe Político, who dismissed him from his post. Becerra had to leave Lagos and find work where he was not known.

At the same time Dr. Azuela incurred the enmity of Díaz's Jefe Político, but because he did not hold public office, he was able to continue his activity in favor of Madero. Despite strong popular support throughout Mexico for Madero, the country's Congress declared Porfirio Díaz reelected, and he took office for a final presidential term on October 4, 1910. A day or two later, Madero issued his Plan de San Luis Potosí and called for an uprising against Díaz. Madero was jailed but managed to escape in San Luis Potosí and made his way to the United States.

In November, 1910, Díaz's police executed Aquiles Serdán, a senator from the state of Puebla and a staunch supporter of Madero. This event had repercussions throughout Mexico and gave impetus to Madero's drive to overthrow Díaz. In Lagos de Moreno, for example, Mariano Azuela brought together assorted groups of city residents, farmers, and young people and organized them in support of Madero.

These events and Madero's growing support were reflected in events that affected the state government of Jalisco. In early 1911 the governor was still Colonel Miguel Ahumada, a peripatetic politician who began his career in Colima, was sent by Porfirio Díaz to be governor of Chihuahua, and then in 1903 was brought back to assume the governorship of Jalisco. Ahumada was one of the most trusted subordinates of Díaz, but he decided not to complete his term. On January 25, 1911, he was granted a leave by the state legislature and handed over his office for an interim period to Dr. Juan R. Zavala. These moves may have accompanied what otherwise would have been a normal change of command according to Porfirista rules. During the interim period, elections for governor were held and the winner was declared to be Manuel Cuesta Gallardo. He took office March 1, 1911, for what was expected to be a four-year term. He was the last of Jalisco's governors of the Díaz regime.

In the north, however, the rebellion continued and reached its climax on May 10, when Francisco Villa and his men took Ciudad Juárez. It soon had repercussions in Jalisco. On May 23 there were riots and shootings in Guadalajara, and the following day Governor Cuesta Gallardo resigned. He was succeeded by Lic. David Gutiérrez Allende, who as president of the state supreme court was supposed to be a political neutral. President Díaz resigned on May 25 and a few days later in Veracruz boarded the *Ypiranga* for exile in Europe.

These were heady days for the Maderistas throughout Mexico. The departure of Porfirio Díaz had spectacular effects at the national level, but at the same time these filtered down to local politics. Shortly after the ouster of Governor Cuesta Gallardo, local elections were called throughout the state of Jalisco. In Lagos de Moreno Dr. Mariano Azuela was encouraged by the support for Madero which he had been able to arouse late in 1910 and offered himself as a candidate for the office of Jefe Político. This was his first attempt of any kind to seek a public office. Heretofore in Lagos, and throughout the country, the successful candidates were not determined locally but rather by the state or even the national political machine. Azuela was elected almost by acclamation amid the jubilation of sizable groups of townspeople. His success was almost beyond his expectations. For the first time since anyone could remember the local authority had been chosen completely by his constituents rather than handpicked by a higher-up. For Azuela and for *los de abajo,* the underdogs, it was a triumph of idealism.

The longtime political figures in the community had little difficulty in adapting to the new situation. Those who outwardly had been firm supporters of Porfirio Díaz took the line of least resistance and with unexpected ease declared themselves for Francisco Madero. Some of them became guerrilla leaders and organized bands of so-called Maderistas. Azuela has reported that early in the summer of 1911 when he went to his office in Lagos to assume his post as Jefe Político he found his way blocked by a group of these false Maderistas under the command of a self-styled colonel, Manuel Rincón Gallardo.[5] In order to assume the post to which the townspeople had elected him, Dr. Azuela found it necessary to seek help from the detachment of federal soldiers stationed in Lagos. These were held in contempt by genuine Maderistas and hardly to be trusted in view of their being holdovers from the Porfirista army. They responded to Azuela's appeal nevertheless, ousted Rincón Gallardo and his men from the building, and permitted the new Jefe Político to enter his office. The procedure was repugnant to Dr. Azuela in that he had to make use of the hated Porfirista soldiers in order to be installed as a legitimate Maderista official. But this was only the beginning of his disillusion with the Mexican revolution.

In succeeding years Mariano Azuela said little concerning the specific problems that he had to face during his tenure as Jefe Político. He and his supporters were little experienced in the tactics of political infighting, which unfortunately did not cease when Porfirio Díaz and Manuel Cuesta Gallardo left the political scene. The presence of political opportunists and their machinations affected Dr. Azuela deeply. In his retrospective writing he later referred to them constantly as *tejones* 'badgers.' The term is used in contempt and obviously refers to the qualities of craftiness and cunning shared by these animals and politicians who take advantage of every possible opening.[6]

According to Azuela, the activities of the species were not confined to Lagos de Moreno. In Guadalajara the state legislature deliberated and then voted to replace Lic. Gutiérrez Allende. In his place it elected Ing. Alberto Robles Gil as interim governor of Jalisco. Dr. Azuela interpreted the elevation of Robles Gil to the governorship as an act contrary to the interests of Francisco Madero, who was still engaged in his campaign for the presidency. Immediately after the new governor took office on August 1, 1911,

---

[5]*O.C.,* III, 1069–1070. Rincón Gallardo belonged to an aristocratic family of Lagos that numbered among its members the Marqués de Guadalupe. His guerrilla activities did not end with his ouster by the federal soldiers in Lagos. A few weeks later, on July 26, 1911, at the head of a band of 205 guerrillas he entered San Miguel el Alto, a large town in the Los Altos area to the southwest. There he was taken for a Maderista. No questions were asked and no resistance was offered (Francisco Medina de la Torre, *Apuntes estadísticos e históricos del Municipio de San Miguel el*

Alto, Estado de Jalisco, México [3d ed.; Guadalajara, 1935], p. 135).

[6]Apparently *tejón* is not widely used in Mexico with this meaning. Francico J. Santamaría in his *Diccionario de mejicanismos* (Mexico, 1959), p. 1023, gives only the zoological definition.

Azuela denounced him and in protest resigned his post as Jefe Político of Lagos. He had been in that office approximately two months.[7]

His protest was really against the tejones, those who switched allegiance from the old Díaz regime to the incoming Madero administration and would then abandon it at the first convenient moment. Their aim was to remain on top, regardless of who was president. Azuela was indignant because he observed that these people existed at all levels of Mexico's government. An extreme idealist and a sensitive man, he reacted to these people not as a politician but as a moralist. Thus he had become embittered with Mexico's long-awaited revolution barely two months after the departure of Porfirio Díaz for Europe.

Certainly Azuela's tejones did not cease their activities during the remainder of 1911 and the years immediately following. Madero and Pino Suárez were elected to the presidency and vice-presidency, respectively, and assumed their offices in November, 1911; but in Jalisco Alberto Robles Gil remained in office until October, 1912, when he gave way to José López Portillo y Rojas, candidate for the Catholic Party and winner of the governorship in the state elections. López Portillo, a lawyer and writer (the author of the novel *La parcela*), continued as governor even after Madero and Pino Suárez were liquidated by Victoriano Huerta in February, 1913, and finally ended up as a minister in the latter's cabinet a year later. His successor as governor was General José María Mier, who was to be the last Huertista authority in the state of Jalisco. Azuela's evaluation of Robles Gil was sound. When Victoriano Huerta formed his cabinet in February, 1913, his first Ministro de Fomento was Robles Gil. Other figures from Jalisco turned up in the entourage of the dictator, notably José María Lozano and Rodolfo Reyes. Both served as cabinet ministers. Reyes later became a deputy from Jalisco and finally split with Huerta after the latter dissolved the Chamber of Deputies and imprisoned its members.

[7]*O.C.*, III, 1070.

Following his resignation as Jefe Político of Lagos, Mariano Azuela resolved to refrain thereafter from political activity. After August, 1911, he scrupulously avoided any political role. Developments in local and state politics and the tragic ten days in February, 1913, when Victoriano Huerta grabbed the presidency, served only to strengthen his resolution. In Lagos Azuela had made enemies of the local caciques, who again were in control of the local government, and his tenure in any political office was sure to be shaky.

First of all, he returned to the medical practice that he had established in 1899 upon his graduation from medical school in Guadalajara. Azuela's practice was that of a general physician, providing treatment for the townspeople and the farmers and ranchers from the outlying areas. He had long shown a personal and professional sympathy for these people, most of whom were from the less affluent levels of society. From his earliest years Azuela had enjoyed their company; his family origins were modest, springing from farmers and small shopkeepers, and he was comfortable when he was with them.

Freedom from political activity made it possible for Azuela to turn again to his writing. He had taken up this activity upon his return to Lagos after finishing his medical training, although he had already turned out several brief prose items during his student days. In Lagos he varied his production among short stories, essays, and brief notes, but in 1907 he shifted his attention to the novel. By 1910 he had produced three: *María Luisa* (1907), *Los fracasados* (1908), and *Mala yerba* (1909). They accurately depicted Mexican society in the years immediately prior to the revolution. *Los fracasados* and *Mala yerba* in particular were based on life in and around Lagos as Azuela observed it.

While the events of mid-1911 were still fresh in his memory, Azuela sat down and wrote *Andrés Pérez, maderista,* which is perhaps the earliest novel written on the theme of the Mexican revolution. Its action parallels in several respects the author's experience as a campaigner for Madero, his tribulations as Jefe Político of

Lagos, and his almost immediate despair, when it became evident that the idealistic hopes of the genuine Maderistas were not to be realized. The novel seems to have been Azuela's way of unburdening himself following a moment of political and ideological crisis. In any case, *Sin amor* (1912) betrayed a much calmer spirit and little of the revolutionary activity of *Andrés Pérez, maderista*. Any effect of the new Madero government on the small Mexican town of this novel is scarcely discernible. When Azuela set to work on another new novel, he returned to the theme of subversion of the revolution, in this case by small-town capitalists who have become pseudo-revolutionaries. This was to be *Los caciques*.

The meetings of Moreno y Oviedo's literary group became a casualty of the political situation during the dictatorship of Victoriano Huerta. Most of those who formerly attended still remained in Lagos, but even the discussion of literature became difficult. Thus Azuela's association with Lic. Moreno y Oviedo, Dr. Bernardo Reina, the poet and druggist Francisco González León, and Lauro Gallardo was interrupted.

One member of the literary group had already left the town. José Becerra, who distributed propaganda for Francisco Madero while serving as secretary to the Porfirista Jefe Político, was in Tequila, a small town in western Jalisco forty miles northwest of Guadalajara. There Becerra was the prosecuting attorney for the municipality. He had long been Azuela's closest friend in Lagos. The separation did not affect the friendship between the two men, for they continued to exchange ideas, but now through correspondence. Azuela and Becerra shared the same idealistic political view—both had been ardent Maderistas—but in other respects were an improbable pair. Becerra was eight years older than Azuela; he was forty-nine when he went away to war in 1914. He was a restless person whose romantic nature and attitudes were constantly expressed in his poetry. In personality he contrasted sharply with the more deliberate Azuela. Furthermore, the latter as a writer concentrated all his attention on prose. In his reminiscences Dr. Azuela refers on

more than one occasion to Becerra's fondness for alcohol. Such was the novelist's admiration for him that Becerra inspired some of Azuela's more admirable characters of this period: the lawyer Reséndez in *Los fracasados*, Toño Reyes of *Andrés Pérez, maderista*, and Rodríguez in *Los caciques*.[8]

In addition to their personal and literary interests, José Becerra had something else to write about from Tequila. In 1913 and early 1914 the general political climate in western Jalisco was in much greater ferment than in Lagos. The take over of the presidency by Victoriano Huerta in February, 1913, was the signal for a series of local uprisings. These began in the spring of that year, and scattered bands of armed men still operated throughout the mountainous areas to the west and south of Guadalajara. For the most part, these uprisings were isolated and not carried out in coordination. A few names have survived here and there but the leaders and their ranchero followers have been largely forgotten. Few were able to affiliate with nationwide movements or cooperate with other armed groups or formal trained armies. They were unable to organize to exert significant pressure on the Huerta government, although its officials certainly increased their vigilance because of these men. There was clearly a growing restlessness among a significant element of the population.

As early as June, 1913, groups of men who called themselves Carrancistas took up arms in the mountainous western municipality of Santa Rosalía.[9] The Zúñiga brothers of Tlajomulco were active with anti-Huerta groups that ranged across southern Jalisco from the border with Michoacán as far as the Sierra de Tapalpa.[10] Julián del Real, his father, and his brothers had difficulties with the Porfirista authorities in Tlajomulco and left the community, moving to Ameca in the western section of the state. Del Real early began operations against Huerta's

[8]Leal, p. 103.

[9]Alberto Brambila, *Detalles de mi vida íntima* (Guadalajara, 1964), pp. 258-259.

[10]José G. Zuno, *Historia de la Revolución en el Estado de Jalisco* (Mexico, 1964), p. 79.

government, confining his activities to Ameca and the towns to the west.[11] In Etzatlán Crescencio Amaral Meza led a group of miners in revolt against Huerta.[12] One of the most active and perhaps the most celebrated of these guerrilla chieftains, whose exploits have been sung in ballads and recounted in literature, was Pedro Zamora, who took advantage of the rugged terrain between Tapalpa and Ayutla to harass the Huertistas in those sections.[13] As 1913 passed into 1914, these men became increasingly aware of the Carrancista army under General Álvaro Obregón, who for nearly a year had been advancing southward along Mexico's Pacific coast.

José Becerra wrote to Mariano Azuela concerning one of these regional leaders. Becerra had met Julián Medina, the most active anti-Huertista operating in the vicinity of Tequila. Medina, who was a native of a little town with a long name, Hostotipaquillo, had a background in mining activities, first at Etzatlán in western Jalisco and later at La Yesca across the state line in Nayarit. Becerra was favorably impressed with Medina, with his personality and his ability. Azuela has not revealed what Becerra told Medina about him, yet in the light of Medina's subsequent actions, Becerra must have convinced Medina of Azuela's profound political convictions and his worth as a human being. As Obregón's army marched into Jalisco from the west and north, Becerra became a member of Medina's band of revolutionaries. Medina made contact with Obregón's Constitucionalistas and operated with them in their drive on Guadalajara, which was held by Huertistas commanded by old General Mier in June and early July of 1914.

In contrast with the unrest of western Jalisco, Lagos had remained relatively quiet. An occasional troop train passed through carrying soldiers to combat the dissidents who were operating in the north of the country. Civilian

passenger trains continued to move northward, but their run was shorter, ending at Zacatecas by May and June. Throughout, Dr. Azuela continued to treat his patients and to compose his novels. He had nearly finished *Los caciques* and was putting the final touches on the manuscript when the tranquillity of Lagos was broken. Groups of dejected soldiers straggled through the town, downcast, weary, physically exhausted. Many were crippled or wounded. Their uniforms were tattered and ragged. This was an event of magnitude in the normally tranquil life of Lagos. Dr. Azuela observed them as they limped through the town, moving to the south in retreat, perhaps to rest or to regroup.

They were the remnants of Huerta's *federales,* of the twelve thousand men who served under the command of General Luis Medina Barrón in the defense of the city of Zacatecas. This was Azuela's first news of the bloody fighting and the utter rout of the federales, although in later weeks and months he would hear again and again eyewitness accounts from his revolutionary comrades in arms until he knew the details of the action as thoroughly as if he had been there in person. It was one of the decisive battles of the revolution. The Constitucionalistas had by that time established firm control over northern Mexico but found that their major obstacle to a southward push was a large defending force of Huertistas who held a strong position in Zacatecas. First, the Primer Jefe of the Constitucionalistas, Venustiano Carranza, ordered an assault by Pánfilo Natera, but he was repulsed. Felipe Ángeles then prepared a new plan of attack. Francisco Villa arranged his forces and began his advance on the morning of June 23, taking first two elevated positions on the northern edge of the city, Loreto and La Sierpe. The defenders were driven in retreat in the direction of the town of Guadalupe but were set upon by reserve troops of the Constitucionalistas. La Bufa, the mountain that dominates Zacatecas from the east, was the final point of resistance of the defending Huertistas, but by seven in the evening the city was in the hands of the attackers. The operation was brilliantly planned and dar-

[11]Páez Brotchie, II, 119. Also in Jesús Gerardo Villegas G., *Cosas de Tlajomulco* (Guadalajara, 1965), p. 139.

[12]Zuno, *Historia de la Revolución*, p. 73.

[13]Páez Brotchie, II, 118–119.

ingly carried out. The backbone of Huerta's resistance was broken, and the way was open for the revolutionary armies to enter the very heart of Mexico.

The victory was a shot in the arm for the revolution, and its effect upon the entire country was electric. It was significant as a decisive military engagement, yet its bloody and spectacular action accompanied by individual deeds of daring and bravery gave each revolutionary soldier something to recall and discuss for months and even years to come while sitting around fires or in barracks during the pauses between periods of fighting. The battle enhanced the personal prestige of Francisco Villa and added to the legendary qualities that already surrounded his figure. These were the circumstances under which Dr. Azuela acquired his vision of the taking of Zacatecas and was able to re-create the details and the spirit of the action for the depiction of the battle in *Los de abajo*.

Zacatecas was but one of the victories which opened up the center of Mexico to the revolutionary armies. The Sonorans of General Álvaro Obregón pushed into Jalisco from the northwest in late June, 1914, and joined forces with local guerrillas for an advance on Guadalajara. Rancheros of Jalisco under the command of Julián Medina and Julián del Real combined with the Yaquis led by General Manuel M. Diéguez, one of Obregón's subordinates, and took Guadalajara on July 8. The disaster here was every bit as serious for the federales as it had been at Zacatecas. Their commander General Mier was killed in the fighting, and they lost to the revolutionaries a half a million pesos that they had just extracted from the banks of Guadalajara. The daring cavalry sweeps of the young Sinaloan Rafael Buelna and the bloodthirsty infantry charges of the Yaquis were every bit as thrilling as the events at Zacatecas, but for some reason these exploits have appealed little to Mexicans generally and have received minor attention in the annals of the revolution. The methodical and efficient General Obregón could create no image that could compete in the popular mind with the figure of Francisco Villa.

Dr. Azuela was not on hand to see the fighting at Guadalajara nor did he witness its effects. Presumably José Becerra participated with Medina's forces and entered Guadalajara with the Constitucionalistas.

Azuela remained at Lagos throughout the summer. The town lay in the backwash of military operations, for the campaign against Huerta had passed on to the heart of Mexico. It ended finally on August 15, when the federal army surrendered to the Constitucionalistas, although Huerta had resigned a month previously before leaving for Europe. His departure brought a lull in the fighting while the Constitucionalista leaders sought to reconcile their differences. These existed principally between Venustiano Carranza and Francisco Villa and began to heat up when Villa disobeyed the orders of Carranza and undertook the successful capture of Zacatecas himself. The split widened dangerously in the late summer months. Finally, on September 22, 1914, Villa declared publicly that he no longer recognized Carranza as the Primer Jefe of the revolution.

In an attempt to patch up the deteriorating political and military scene, Carranza called for a convention of the leaders of all factions. It first convened in the capital on October 1, but Villa refused to attend. Subordinates of both generals sought some sort of compromise and succeeded in having it transferred to Aguascalientes, situated approximately midway between Villa's base of operations in Chihuahua and the capital, where Carranza had his headquarters.

The sessions got under way again on October 10. Carranza did not appear at the sessions at Aguascalientes. Villa did and kept his army nearby. Villa and Carranza each offered to remove himself from the political scene, but only if the other would do so first. Neither one was willing to take advantage of this reciprocal offer. After considerable deliberation, the delegates to the convention established a government for Mexico and elected General Eulalio Gutiérrez as provisional president. The followers of Villa and Emiliano Zapata affirmed their support of the new government but Carranza refused. The efforts to unify the Constitucionalistas had failed. The division was now wider than ever.

When Eulalio Gutiérrez designated Francisco Villa the commander of the military forces of the Convencionista government, the stage was set for fighting to resume. The enemy was no longer the federales of the hated Huerta but the Constitucionalista forces of Venustiano Carranza. Unfortunately Gutiérrez had no power in his own right, and he held the post only by the whim of Villa. The sessions of the convention continued until November 9, but all the real decisions had long since been reached. Each revolutionary chieftain had cast his lot with the Convencionistas or with Carranza. With the military support of Villa, Eulalio Gutiérrez prepared to move his government to Mexico City.

One of the military figures in Aguascalientes was Julián Medina, who by this time had become a general. Medina had on occasion cooperated with the Carrancistas, as during Obregón's drive on Guadalajara, but the two men did not get along well and Obregón reprimanded Medina.[14] As a consequence, when the moment of decision came at the convention, Medina threw his support to Villa. At Aguascalientes he coordinated his men with Villa's forces, and when Villa prepared to move south into central Mexico, Medina accompanied him. At the same time, Medina received the appointment as governor of the state of Jalisco under the Convencionistas. The rub was that the Carrancistas occupied the greater part of the state, and Carranza's appointed governor, General Manuel M. Diéguez, was holding firm in Guadalajara.

Lagos de Moreno lies only a little more than fifty miles to the south of Aguascalientes. Medina remembered well his conversations with José Becerra in Tequila, and when the Medinistas passed through Lagos, Major Francisco M. Delgado stopped off to visit with Dr. Azuela. Major Delgado was Julián Medina's private secretary and closest confidant. This was Mariano Azuela's first direct contact with any of the revolutionists.

Through Delgado, Medina invited Azuela to join him and to accept a post in the state government of Jalisco that he was in the process of organizing. Azuela was reluctant to accept such an invitation. His preference was still to remain outside all political and military activity. Medina's government still existed only on paper, and to bring it into being he must drive the Carrancistas from Guadalajara and establish an effective government there. A formidable task!

Major Delgado was a persuasive man and Azuela surely must have considered his own circumstances carefully before arriving at a decision. He had more than adequate reasons for turning a deaf ear to Delgado's arguments and remaining in Lagos. Dr. Azuela was the head of a rapidly expanding family. He had seven children, the oldest of whom was twelve, and another child was on the way. Were he to leave, who would provide income and care for them? In Lagos he had built up a medical practice over the preceding fifteen years and he consequently had obligations to his patients. Furthermore, an interruption in his practice would mean a loss of income and the problem of reestablishing himself whenever he should return. Finally, the doctor had resolved to refrain from political activity and had succeeded in doing so since August, 1911. The damage to him from his first foray into revolutionary politics had been ideological and emotional. Should Azuela abandon his resolution, he would run the risks of being burned again and of experiencing added disillusion with the course of the revolution.

There were, nevertheless, some attractive features to be considered. In Lagos the doctor had made political enemies as the result of his activity on behalf of Madero and his brief tenure as Jefe Político. These people were still influential in the community and made Azuela's existence there uncomfortable if not difficult. This consideration was probably not so forceful as the urging of José Becerra. Becerra, who was nearing fifty in late 1914, had already committed himself to future campaigns with Medina and sought to have his friend do the same. One further thought certainly appealed to Dr.

[14]Obregón, p. 136.

Azuela. By this time, the revolution had been under way for four years, including the period of Madero's presidential campaign against Porfirio Díaz. Heretofore the doctor's participation had been strictly political, and only this aspect of the conflict showed up in his novels. He still had no direct knowledge of the revolution's soldiers and their individual and collective exploits. Major Delgado's invitation offered the novelist an opportunity to gain firsthand experience with the soldiers of a revolutionary army.

Azuela at first politely refused the major's proposal, citing his professional obligations as a doctor in Lagos and also his position as the head of a growing family. These arguments did not deter Major Delgado, who accepted the doctor's excuses. He agreed, saying that Azuela could serve Medina equally well by remaining in Lagos, where he could proceed to divide and redistribute the lands of the large haciendas in the vicinity. Azuela was hardly prepared to undertake a task of that nature. Notwithstanding his family situation and his profession, the doctor decided to accept Medina's invitation to serve in the Convencionista state government of Jalisco.[15]

Under the circumstances of the moment, Azuela could have avoided the forthcoming conflict, as did many of his professional colleagues in Lagos, or he could have chosen between the Carrancistas on the one hand and the Convencionistas on the other. One wonders why Azuela, who was a sober, thoughtful person given to considering the moral consequences of his characters' actions when he wrote, should decide to cast his lot with Villa. His reminiscences give no indication of ideological considerations that might have attracted him to the Villista camp.[16] Rather than these considerations, José Becerra prevailed in the making of the doctor's decision.

Thus the revolution came to Azuela. The tranquil small-town life was now gone, as were the periods of writing and the leisurely discussions of literature with kindred spirits. With the exception of Francisco González León, the poet and druggist who remained in Lagos, the group was scattered. Lic. Moreno y Oviedo and Dr. Bernardo Reina sought refuge from revolutionary strife in the capital. José Becerra was already with the Villista army, and Mariano Azuela would soon join him.

In October, 1914, Dr. Mariano Azuela was forty-one years old. He was approximately five feet eight inches tall and stockily built, with light brown skin that revealed some Indian ancestry but a greater Hispanic contribution. His broad rectangular face was topped by dark, almost black, hair, and his neatly trimmed moustache was of the same color. His dark eyes peered intently from beneath thick eyebrows.[17] He was ready to leave Lagos to join the army. For the time being his wife Carmen Rivera and his seven children would wait until he could send for them.

Irapuato: October–December, 1914

During the last days of October, 1914, Mariano Azuela joined Julián Medina, who was in Irapuato, some seventy miles to the southeast of Lagos. Medina had with him only a part of his following and was waiting for the rest of his men, who had accompanied the main Villista

---

[15] *O.C.*, III, 1079.

[16] Ibid., pp. 1079–1081.

[17] Several photographs of Mariano Azuela taken around 1915 or some years earlier have been reproduced in Monterde, pp. 165, 167, 169. A group picture of the members of the Generation of 1903, including Azuela and José Becerra, can be found in de Alba, *Antonio Moreno y Oviedo*, preceding page 11. Note also the photograph of the author that appears on the title page of Azuela's *Andrés Pérez, maderista* (Mexico, 1911).

army to the east. He immediately appointed Azuela the head of his medical service with the rank of lieutenant colonel.[18]

There was not much to do at Irapuato. Military operations had to be undertaken in western Mexico but they could not proceed until the situation of the armies in and around the capital could be cleared up and the government set up by the convention at Aguascalientes given some sort of order. Medina could only wait until these questions were resolved. He waited at Irapuato, in central Guanajuato state, because of its strategic rail position, at the junction of the Ferrocarril Central and the important branch line that connects with Guadalajara, one hundred sixty miles to the west. There General Manuel M. Diéguez was bottled up, without rail communication with the main Carrancista army commanded by Obregón, who was engaged in central and eastern Mexico. Diéguez's only other rail connection was with the Pacific port of Manzanillo.

This was Azuela's first contact with military life. His situation was much like that of any soldier who spends relatively long periods of in-activity while waiting between spurts of fighting. The wait at Irapuato, however, provided him with the opportunity to become acquainted with his fellow soldiers and with Medina in particular. Azuela learned to respect him for his sincere revolutionary beliefs, his bravery, and his ability to handle his men. In his *Obras completas* Azuela has provided a physical description of Medina:

> Still young, around thirty years old, tall, well built, of ruddy complexion, his eyelids slightly drooping, thick lips, with little facial hair, with slow but expressive and sure gestures, he wore tight-fitting trousers and a deerskin jacket trimmed with braid and without a necktie; his shirt, which was open to reveal his bull-like neck, was puckered at the waist and showing outside his cartridge belt, which was completely full of cartridges. Despite his uncouth rusticity, he carried out discreetly and prudently the duties of the

high position that he occupied without failing to be witty, cheerful, optimistic, and willing to talk.[19]

At least one photograph taken of Medina during this period has survived and it confirms amply Dr. Azuela's description.[20]

Azuela has reported that during his stay at Irapuato he was able to talk at length with Medina almost daily. In those conversations Medina enjoyed telling his experiences and thus gave the novelist his first intimate contact with a man who had mounted a horse, fired a rifle, and fought in the revolution instead of merely talking and speculating about it. This was a completely new experience for a professional man like Azuela. As a writer, he was alert to the potential of these officers and soldiers for the creation of figures in a literary work, yet he later confessed that at this early stage he had no idea as to what kind of novel he might write about the revolution.[21] Nevertheless, Azuela listened carefully to Medina, particularly to the latter's accounts of his initiation into revolutionary activity. Evidence of these recollections showed up later in *Los de abajo,* and if he did not reproduce Medina's narrative verbatim, he was able to re-create his commander's initiation when he referred to Medina by name in the novel. There Anastasio Montañés comments: "Julián Medina in Hostotipaquillo with a half a dozen fellows with knives sharpened on a metate stood up against all the police and soldiers in the town, and he beat them. 'What do Medina and his men have that we don't have?,' said a man who had a very black beard and thick eyebrows to go with his kindly look. He was a strong, well-built man.[22]

Azuela's account, phrased in popular Mexican Spanish, is extremely succinct, yet it manages to condense into a few words all the spirit

[18]*O.C.,* III, 1079.

[19]*O.C.,* III, 1080.

[20]*La voz del pueblo.* Semanario político de información (Guadalajara). Época primera, Tomo I, Núm. 14 (February 6, 1939), p. 1.

[21]*O.C.,* III, 1079.

[22]*Los de abajo* (Mexico: Fondo de Cultura Económica, 1958), p. 11.

Julián Medina in 1913

and verve of a daring operation, typical of Medina's deportment as a soldier. It reveals nothing about Medina's political convictions, however, or what motivated his assault upon the police barracks in Hostotipaquillo. The antecedents of this event are known, as are its details. In the matter of political conviction, they reveal a man very similar to Azuela, yet in other ways they place the two men at opposite poles. Medina was disposed to take direct action and had an ability to organize and lead others in that action. He had a jovial, outgoing manner that contrasted sharply with the quiet, introspective personality of Azuela, who was deeply concerned with the moral aspect of things.

During the early months of the presidency of Victoriano Huerta, Julián Medina visited Mexico City in order to make contact with certain elements of the dictator's opposition. There he was able to convince the latter of his sincerity and his effectiveness as a leader, receiving

the promise that a quantity of weapons would be shipped to him. Not long after returning to Hostotipaquillo, he received a message informing him that the arms were to be addressed to a merchant in the community of La Yesca in nearby Nayarit and that they would be labeled as mining machinery. Medina was instructed to pick them up at La Quemada, the nearest railway station.

Huerta's secret police soon got wind of the shipment, however, and caused a warrant to be issued for Medina's arrest. In Hostotipaquillo his friends learned of the warrant and warned Medina, who had not confided his plans to even his closest friends. Medina then consulted with his brothers Jesús and Juan as well as his friends Leocadio Parra, Zenón Vallarta, Miguel López Aguilera, Emilio Herrera, Tomás Ojeda, Martiniano Hernández, Anacleto López, and Salvador López, all of whom were members of an anti-Huerta political club named after the nineteenth-century president Benito Juárez. All agreed that they had but one course of action, to use force of arms against the local authorities in Hostotipaquillo. The latter had been reinforced by eight federal soldiers who had arrived in the small town a few days previously. Medina and his companions proceeded to make plans for a concerted attack upon the barracks where the soldiers were quartered.

At nine o'clock on the morning of May 11, 1913, Medina and his men began their assault. They attacked the barracks that were in an inn owned by Arcadio Rosas in the Barrio known as El Rincón del Diablo. Their onslaught was so fierce that all eight federales died in the fighting. For weapons, Medina's men had only four Remington rifles and three pistols. The rest were armed only with knives. By the time the barracks were taken, they also had possession of the eight rifles taken from the dead soldiers, plus a quantity of ammunition.[23]

Thus Julián Medina began his military

[23]*La voz del pueblo*, pp. 1-2. In *Epistolario*, p. 128, Prof. L. B. Kiddle asks in a letter to Azuela dated April 16, 1939: "Parece que Medina, el líder revolucionario, tuvo un encuentro con la policía y los federales en Hostotipaquillo,

career. He was at the time thirty-three years old, having been born November 29, 1879. His previous experience had been with mining concerns, first with a mine owned by the Jiménez family at Etzatlán, Jalisco, and later with another mine at La Yesca.[24] Medina's family background was relatively humble; his parents had been farmers or laborers and Medina himself had worked as a mechanic.

Several of Medina's companions were still with his forces at the time that Mariano Azuela arrived at Irapuato. The most prominent of these was Leocadio Parra, who had accompanied the troops of Lucio Blanco to Mexico City and had not yet rejoined Medina. Azuela later learned to admire the bravery of Parra, who held the rank of general, and a few years later, after Parra's death, wrote a short story called "Cómo al fin lloró Juan Pablo," which was based on the last days and the execution of Parra.[25] Azuela does not mention all the other companions by name, although he characterizes them generally as rancheros of Jalisco, farmers or men of rural background, manners, and looks. Certainly Medina's brother Jesús was there; his brother Juan died while fighting against Huertistas at Pinos Cuates in Zacatecas in April, 1914. Likewise Captain Martiniano Hernández Montero was still with Medina as was Crescenciano Amaral Meza, who also had been a friend of Medina since the days in Hostotipaquillo.[26] Other men of similar background had joined Medina in the year and a half since he first set out on a military career.

These were the men closest to Medina, as members of his staff and in the conduct of the fighting. Rank meant little. Although one of them might boast the rank of an officer, he was

in the thick of the fighting and was usually at the head of his troops. They were countrymen, much like the rancheros whom Azuela had known around Lagos, with rustic speech, rural attitudes and interests. The difference was that these men were engaged in war, not in peaceful agricultural pursuits.

Their reasons for joining the revolution were varied. Some, like Medina, held strong political convictions, involving a commitment to Francisco I. Madero or more likely a hatred of Huerta. But many reasons were based on local politics or the harsh measures of a local cacique taken against his enemies. The motivation frequently was strictly personal: the simple desire to exact revenge for real or fancied wrongs. Certainly the revolution was the greatest adventure on which any of them had ever embarked.

Practically all the men gathered around Medina were younger than Azuela. Various of these people inspired the creation of the followers of Demetrio Macías in *Los de abajo*. In his *Obras completas* Azuela stresses their youth on more than one occasion. Pedro Montes, his model for Anastasio Montañés, was "a strapping young fellow of thirty years" (III, 1083). Medina's medical practitioner, who was the inspiration for Venancio of the novel, was "of average age" (III, 1084), but Bárbaro, the principal executioner of the band, was "25 years old, tall, strong, without expression in his face . . ." (III, 1085). Colonel Manuel Caloca, whom Azuela later accompanied for several weeks during the most difficult period of his military service, was a "youth less than twenty years old" (III, 1080). With José Becerra, Azuela in later months went to San Miguel el Alto to visit with Baca, whom he affectionally called "Baquita," "an eighteen-year old colonel" (III, 802). Their youthful nature is less apparent in *Los de abajo*, where Azuela was not so concerned with matters of age in the depiction of his characters and treated them, implicitly at least, as adults. The matter of youth was not peculiar to Medina's men; rather it was characteristic of participants in the revolution, of both Villistas and Carrancistas, but hardly of the followers of

---

Jalisco. ¿Me puede decir el año en que se verificó dicho encuentro?" Azuela answers in substantially the same terms as his corresponding passage in *Los de abajo*. The detailed account in *La voz del pueblo* should answer Prof. Kiddle adequately.

[24]Moreno, p. 114.

[25]This story was first published in 1918.

[26]J. Jesús León, "Vida y hazañas de Julián Medina" (Guadalajara, 1939).

Victoriano Huerta. Azuela was to be with them during the next seven or eight months, usually during the lulls between fighting, observing them during their periods of rest and waiting and listening to endless accounts of their exploits.

Julián Medina derived from the same origins as these men and understood them. They respected his ability and accepted his leadership. At the same time he had to deal with other men who were at his own level in the military hierarchy or even at a superior level. Azuela has stated clearly that Medina's opinions were also respected by men of that category. He was of a much higher level of ability than a mere ranchero and acquitted himself creditably.

Mariano Azuela had ample time to become acquainted with Irapuato. He said little or nothing about the town in *Los de abajo* but saved his observations for *Las moscas*. The latter scenes of that work are set in Irapuato. There is abundant detail of the town, the railway station, and the movement of the long trains that arrive and leave, jammed with human beings and their belongings, but the circumstances were different. In *Las moscas* the feeling of imminent disaster pervades the revolutionary mob, but in October and November there is still hope that something good can come out of the forthcoming campaigns of Francisco Villa and Julián Medina.

Irapuato was not a large town. With its twenty thousand inhabitants it was somewhat larger than Azuela's Lagos, but it was hardly a city. It had a few imposing buildings, including some that were constructed during the colonial period but none that could match the beauty of nearby Celaya and Guanajuato. Otherwise it was not particularly attractive nor did it have much that was distinctive. It had long been important as a commercial center and, with the completion of the Ferrocarril Central de México in the 1880s it became an extremely important railway point. In Mexico Irapuato is known as a center of fruit production, particularly of strawberries, a fame that it shares with nearby Silao. At the time of Azuela's stay in Irapuato, there was little available in the line of diversion for a large body of unattached men.

Azuela has said nothing about his living conditions in Irapuato, but it seems doubtful that the Villistas were quartered in the town itself, which was relatively small for sheltering a large body of troops. The standard practice in 1914 was to use military trains as barracks that could be moved from place to place as military needs required. Villa's army normally moved in this fashion, transporting men, horses, and equipment on the trains. Medina's men seem to have been lodged on one of Villa's trains left standing in the railway station at Irapuato, and if a man wished to visit the town, he boarded the trolley car that ran between the station and the nearby town, or, if he was affluent, he rented an automobile. Mariano Azuela's surroundings in Irapuato certainly were exclusively military.

Julián Medina's wait in Irapuato was determined by events that were occurring elsewhere in Mexico. Following the selection of Eulalio Gutiérrez as president by the convention in Aguascalientes, it was decided to set up his government in Mexico City. To the military and political leaders the move meant more than being installed in the largest city in the country. Its possession was highly necessary, for all the outward trappings of government were present there—the national palace with the elegance left over from the Porfirista period, its salons and even its furnishings—and it was of the utmost significance to have them at hand, regardless of what the circumstances might be or what needs had to be met before the country could be governed in an orderly manner.

The Carrancista forces were reluctant to leave the capital but finally evacuated it in late November. Villa's División del Norte camped outside Mexico in its trains at Tacuba, along with others that had brought forces of Eulalio Gutiérrez, José Isabel Robles, and Eugenio Aguirre Benavides. The Zapatistas, who did not possess such an advanced means of transport, pressed in on the capital from the south. The Convencionistas finally entered Mexico City early in December and on December 6 held a massive military parade on the Zócalo, with Villa, Eulalio Gutiérrez, and Emiliano Zapata standing on the balcony of the Palacio Nacional reviewing the might assembled below.

The Convencionista government encountered grave difficulties at its very beginning and ultimately succumbed to them. There was little trust among the titular leaders, who were intimidated by the presence of Villa and his army. There was much shadowboxing in the process of establishing a government suitable to Villa, Zapata, and Eulalio Gutiérrez, and this activity consumed several days following the parade and military review. During that time the Convención could undertake no military operations and the Carrancistas took full advantage of the lull to organize their new headquarters in the state of Veracruz and to reinforce as best they could their other precarious positions on the periphery of Mexico. During all this maneuvering Julián Medina was waiting at Irapuato with his men.

Guadalajara: December, 1914–January, 1915

On December 9, 1914, Francisco Villa in a press interview gave an idea concerning the military campaigns that the Convencionistas had in mind. At the same time he delivered himself of other statements that actually weakened the government that he was pledged to support and maintain. Particularly he expressed his disenchantment with the residents of the capital and a desire to leave it as soon as possible. At the same time he undercut the position of Eulalio Gutiérrez, the Convencionista president.

Specifically he spoke of the course that he planned to take against the Carrancistas: "I am going to Guadalajara to take possession of the capital and to exterminate General Diéguez and his forces in the state of Jalisco. Probably Pablo González will have joined Diéguez; at least I hope so. If they are there we shall kill two birds with the same stone. We shall overthrow President Gutiérrez more easily than when he was made the head of the executive branch of the nation."[27]

Villa let it be known that he was the power of the Convención and that Gutiérrez was sub-servient to him. Certainly Villa took personal charge of the military campaigns. He planned also to send troops against the Carrancistas who were holding out in Monterrey and Tampico. The latter points, especially Tampico, turned out to be much more strategic locations than Guadalajara, but apparently Villa was not aware of their significance in the developing campaign. The Carrancistas in the center of Mexico commanded by General Pablo González had been dispersed and for the time being were no threat to the Convencionistas.

Early in the morning of Friday, December 11, Villa's División del Norte began to load its men, horses, arms, and ammunition on the cars of the long trains that were waiting in the Buenavista station in Mexico City. Various of Villa's brigades were destined for Irapuato, which by rail was not more than ten or twelve hours away, even for the slow moving and heavily laden troop trains. In Irapuato Villa would establish his base of operations for the advance on Guadalajara, which would be under his personal command.

Mariano Azuela has noted that some of Medina's followers were among the Villistas on

[27]From *Vida Nueva* (Chihuahua), December 10, 1914, cited in Almada, II, 196.

these trains. One of them was Leocadio Parra of Hostotipaquillo. While drunk he became involved with another officer and commiteed a serious infraction of military discipline. Apparently Parra killed the officer, because he was subjected to a summary court-martial. Only the eloquent intervention of the poet José Becerra was able to save Parra from execution.[28]

In Irapuato there was a feeling of expectation and excitement over the approach of Villa. After weeks of inactivity and boredom for the soldiers waiting there, at last there was a realization that action was imminent. Nothing had happened for over six weeks. It had been nearly a month since the last train was permitted to go through to Guadalajara.[29] The excitement derived not entirely from the prospect of renewed conflict. In large part there was expectation of seeing Villa himself. The fame of his invincibility preceded him, and there was tense anticipation of the arrival of this legendary figure. Mariano Azuela had not seen Villa before. In his reminiscences and in *Los de abajo* he hardly expresses a direct judgment of the general or his reaction to him.[30] One can only assume that Azuela was as eager to catch a glimpse of Villa as were his fellow soldiers and officers who had been camped in Irapuato.

On Saturday, December 12, Irapuato's railroad yards were jammed with long lines of trains crowded with men, their arms, and their mounts. Much of Villa's military strength was concentrated here, but not all of it was to be thrown against Guadalajara. Three of Villa's brigades plus the men commanded by Medina were selected to take part in the operation. Their trains had to be sorted out and routed in se-

quence on the branch line to Guadalajara. Parts of the brigade commanded by Rodolfo Fierro took the lead, followed by a contingent of soldiers from Chihuahua led by General José Valles. Next came the Brigada Contreras and finally the Brigada Villa. The drive on Guadalajara exemplifies the dependency of the contending armies on the country's railroad system. In 1914 there was no other way to move large numbers of men and their impedimenta. Even the cavalry depended on the trains to carry its horses to the point where they could be brought into use against the enemy.

In all, some eleven or twelve thousand troops set out westward along the line toward Guadalajara in a stream of long trains, past Abasolo, Pénjamo, and La Piedad. At La Barca, the first town in Jalisco, just seventy miles from Guadalajara, they came into contact with Carrancista soldiers of General Enrique Estrada. The latter could only delay the Villista advance and give General Diéguez a little more time to evacuate his men from Guadalajara. There was little more than a skirmish at La Barca, nothing that resembled a battle. Actually Villa was engaged in a formidable offensive campaign and his forces and arms were superior to the resources of the Carrancistas.[31]

On December 12 Diéguez issued a decree ordering the removal of his capital from Guadalajara to Ciudad Guzmán in the southern part of Jalisco. He judiciously withdrew his troops before superior numbers and left the way free for Villa to enter Guadalajara with hardly a fight. This was on December 14.

The seemingly interminable trains of Villa's expedition moved into the railway station at the southern end of the city. There they lined up under the corrugated metal roofs of the sheds that covered the tracks of the station.

It was only appropriate that a parade should mark the entry into the second city of Mexico. It took place on Thursday, December

[28]*O.C.*, III, 1093.

[29]Davis, p. 61.

[30]Not so, however, in the closing scene of *Las moscas*. Azuela is more willing to discourse on Villa in the first redaction of *Los de abajo*. In the chapter in which Demetrio's men are waiting for Villa outside Zacatecas, Azuela stresses the legendary nature of the general and his publicized largesse to the poor and humble (*Los de abajo* [El Paso, 1916], pp. 67–70). In later redactions, Azuela's early reaction to Villa is toned down and several references have even been removed.

[31]Leal, p. 18, notes: "Perseguidos por los carrancistas, se ven obligados a retirarse hacia Guadalajara, a donde llegan en diciembre (1914)." This is a moment of triumph for the Villistas, not a defeat.

17, and for the Villistas must be considered one of the high spots of the revolution. It began at the railway station and made its way up the Calle de San Francisco (now known as 16 de Septiembre), past the churches of Aranzazú and San Francisco and the United States consulate at the corner with López Cotilla, through the business district, and finally into the central plaza, which is bordered by the state capitol building and the cathedral. Villa was the center of attraction, but he was preceded and followed by impressive contingents of his soldiers and accompanied by numerous brass bands contributed by the brigades. The display of military might and music drew an enthusiastic response from the *tapatíos*. They packed the balconies overlooking the parade route and choked all the side streets at the intersections. The central plaza was literally packed tight with human beings. Some had come out of sheer curiosity but most were there to express their support of Villa.

Will B. Davis, the consul of the United States in Guadalajara, was an eyewitness of this event:

> The entrance of General Francisco Villa into Guadalajara was a march of triumph. He, with his advance guard, progressed from the railroad station to the palace with all the glamour of a conquering hero—not omitting a profusion of brass band accompaniments.
>
> All Guadalajara was out to welcome him, the proletariat along the streets and the upper classes from their balconies kept up a continual din of "Viva México," while literally covering General Villa and staff with confetti and vari-colored serpentines all along their way of march. Every church bell in the city (and there were hundreds) intoned welcomes—men, women, and children of all classes seemed beside themselves in giving expression to their ecstasies of joy. Hardly a building but displayed national colors in profusion—no one was ever more universally, unreservedly, enthusiastically and demonstratively welcomed to a community than was General Francisco Villa on this, his first entrance into Guadalajara.[32]

[32]Davis, p. 69.

At the state house, Julián Medina, accompanied only by his chief of staff Francisco Delgado (who had been promoted to colonel), was waiting for Villa. They appeared together on the balcony of the building and received the cheers of the multitude below. In a speech filled with brilliant rhetoric the engineer Jiménez Loza presented Villa to the people of Guadalajara. Villa then spoke, but without the elegance of Jiménez Loza. He professed no other ambition than to achieve peace for the nation, adding that it was time to put an end to dictatorships in Mexico, whether they were "científico-porfirista" or "ignorante-carrancista."[33]

This has to be one of the high-water marks of Villismo in Mexico, emotionally and militarily. The enthusiasm of the welcome given by the tapatíos surpassed by far the one that greeted Villa in Mexico City.

Julián Medina, who had been the nominal governor of Jalisco since October, was installed as de facto governor in Guadalajara with the backing of Villa. Thus far Mariano Azuela's service had been exclusively military, as the chief of Medina's medical service, but with the organization of the state government in Guadalajara, Medina appointed him the head of public education for the state of Jalisco. Thus for the time being he was no longer a military doctor; his duties in his new post were of a civilian nature.

Azuela has not explained how he made the trip from Irapuato to Guadalajara. In view of the availability of Villa's trains, it is probable that he accompanied the main body of Villista soldiers. Neither has he referred to the ovation that Villa received in the streets of Guadalajara. It would seem strange if Azuela were not present to observe it. If he were not, the occasion was certainly the subject of discussion in later conversations in barracks and bivouacs. In later years other oldtime Villista soldiers held fond memories of this their first stay in Guadalajara.[34] One of the officers of Villa, General César Felipe Moya, was married to a young

[33]Páez Brotchie, II, 155.
[34]Calzadíaz, III, 102.

lady, a resident of the city, a few days after the occupation.[35]

After the shouting and the cheers had died down, Villa and his officials found it necessary to get back to the prosaic business of conducting a government and a war. On December 20 Villa informed the people of Guadalajara that he wanted a contribution of one million pesos. To that end he designated a committee whose function would be to interview various of the wealthier residents for the purpose of exacting contributions. It was headed by Dr. Ramón Puente, who often accompanied Villa for this purpose, Colonel Candelario Cervantes, one of his generals, and two officers from the staff of General Medina. They were only partially successful. One of the reluctant contributors was Joaquín Cuesta Gallardo, brother of the last Porfirista governor. A Lic. Pérez Rubio complained vocally concerning the amount of money that he was requested to contribute and went directly to General Villa in his railroad car to register his dissatisfaction. Villa did not make an immediate decision concerning Pérez Rubio or Cuesta Gallardo.

Two figures of Huertista fame fell into the hands of Villa in Guadalajara. One was General Antonio Delgadillo, governor of the state of Colima during the early months of 1914. Another was Colonel Tomás Bravo, the son of General Ignacio Bravo, defender of the city of Torreón against Villa's attempts to take it in 1913. These men were taken outside the city along with the Pérez Rubio brothers, one of whom was a priest who had taken up arms in support of Villa, and were shot by Rodolfo Fierro's men. Joaquín Cuesta Gallardo was executed in one of the military barracks of the city.[36]

Despite the enthusiasm shown for Villa, many residents of Guadalajara took advantage of the situation to lodge complaints against their personal enemies. The prominent motive was a desire for revenge. Executions arising out of the occupation were carried out in places removed from the public gaze, either in barracks or in outlying towns, such as Zapopan, Poncitlán, or Ocotlán. Generally the public reacted more favorably to the Villista administration than it did to General Diéguez and his Carrancistas, despite the executions ordered by Villa.

The civil government of Jalisco was installed and began to function to the best of its ability, considering the circumstances. The various branches of the state government and the municipal government of Guadalajara were staffed. Mariano Azuela's office, in which several employees worked, was in the state capitol, and José Becerra had a post in the state library two blocks away.

Will B. Davis, the consul of the United States, kept in touch with the new regime in Jalisco. Shortly after Julián Medina took office, Davis went to visit him and reported his impressions in a letter sent to his daughter in the United States:

I have had occasions to meet General Medina with frequency since my letter of December 19. Of people whom I have known to have been elevated to positions disparagingly beyond their merits—and I have seen many such examples in my country as well as in Mexico—this General Medina is the freak of them all.

Heavens!—the change from the old Díaz regime to the Carranza hoodlums was bad enough but we have to treat with this thing—this ignoramus—this untutored Indian—how can it be done?

General Medina had formerly been a mechanic. But when speaking of tradesmen, in Mexican parlance, one must not think to compare them with the intelligent American craftsman—oh, no, that would never do.

General Medina looks the Indian—General Medina acts the Indian—General Medina is an Indian—and, worst of all, an untutored Indian.

But I will say for General Medina that I believe his intentions are good—that if he knew how, he would do better—but he doesn't know how to conduct the affairs of State. He doesn't fit. He could not rise to the office, and to bring the office to his level would be like

[35] *Ibid.*, p. 104.
[36] *Ibid.*, pp. 103–104.

unto a return to the times of the North American aborigines, with their moccasin and teepee settings and tom-tom accompaniments — figuratively speaking.[37]

Davis's attitude is not surprising. He had been in his Guadalajara post for six or seven years and had become accustomed to the outward niceties of the officials of the Díaz period. He found it extremely difficult to adjust to those who were called upon to hold public office without having had training in how to act in a drawing room. One wonders also if the Villistas were as docile toward the representative of the United States as the Díaz officials had been. Davis expressed sympathy toward Medina as a person but was critical of him in the conduct of the office that he held. Mariano Azuela in his comments was aware of his leader's humble background but was not sarcastic when speaking of his lack of social graces. Davis frequently comments on Medina in later weeks.

Villa could not delay long in Guadalajara. Once his military hold on the city had been established and a semblance of government had been organized, he needed to attend to pressing business elsewhere in Mexico. He prepared to leave Guadalajara after spending approximately one week there. He left General Calixto Contreras in command of military forces in Jalisco and Rodolfo Fierro as commanding officer of the military garrison of the city of Guadalajara. Villa returned to Mexico City where Eulalio Gutiérrez was still struggling with the formation of the Convencionista government.

The long trains remained behind in the station, serving as headquarters for Generals Contreras and Fierro and as living quarters for their troops and women followers. The residents of Guadalajara came to see the trains and marvel at the powerful locomotives brought from the north, as well as the coaches of the high Villista officials, which were luxuriously furnished. They also admired the good looks of the women who accompanied these officers, also the women's expensive jewelry. They held a clear-cut advantage in these respects over the women who accompanied the Carrancista officers.[38]

With the prospect of a relatively stable period during which he would hold his position as director of public education, Dr. Azuela brought his wife and children from Lagos to Guadalajara. He rented a house on Avenida Madero, which until a year or two previously had been called Placeres, at No. 596, near the corner of Parroquia.[39] Certainly a concern of Azuela at this point was his wife, who was expecting their eighth child. Both husband and wife could now breathe easier. Azuela had been absent from her side for over two months. José Becerra resided with the Azuelas during this stay in Guadalajara.

It is not easy to determine who were Azuela's associates in December, 1914, and January, 1915. He still retained many friends from sixteen years previously when he was a medical student in Guadalajara. Also a number of employees worked under his direction, clerks and schoolteachers, although he was not always sympathetic to these people, who were subject to the stresses and whims of the revolutionary political administrations. Nevertheless in Guadalajara there were many who were interested in literature and art. The city has a long tradition in these areas, one that was evident even in those turbulent days. Certainly for Azuela it was a welcome change after spending two months with Medina and his soldiers. Two younger men whom Azuela met in Guadalajara were José Guadalupe Zuno and Manuel Martínez Valadez. They were both to be heard from politically and artistically in later years and during the novelist's stay in the city.

Azuela's existence in Guadalajara was not to be a tranquil one, but the circumstances were well beyond his control. General Álvaro Obregón had as one feature of his Carrancista strategy the need to keep the army of Francisco Villa occupied on its right flank. Following his retreat

[37]Davis, pp. 71–72.

[38]Páez Brotchie, II, 135.

[39]In a letter to his godfather, José María Azuela, dated January 5, 1915 (*Epistolario*, p. 22).

southward from Guadalajara to Ciudad Guzmán, Diéguez was joined in southern Jalisco by another Carrancista force under General Francisco Murguía, who led his men on a tiring and dangerous march overland from Toluca through the state of Michoacán to Ciudad Guzmán. Murguía's men strengthened the army of Diéguez, who lost no time in reorganizing his forces and began to push northward toward Guadalajara. Following fierce fighting around the communities of San Agustín and Santa Ana some ten miles to the south of the city, the Carrancistas prepared for a concerted attack with a view to gaining control of the railway line to Irapuato. Thus began the only real fighting for Guadalajara during the Villa-Carranza differences.

The Villista reaction to the advance of Diéguez was one of indecision. Some, who were fearful of the Carrancista generals and the severe measures that they might impose should they gain control, decided to flee. Consul Davis reported that the train leaving on the evening of January 15 was packed with private citizens who were seeking refuge in Irapuato or Mexico City.[40] Others were planning also to evacuate the city, but the defenders could not coordinate their efforts. Some blamed the worsening military situation on Rodolfo Fierro, who was said to have disobeyed Villa's personal instructions to avoid battle with Diéguez; rather, he drew the Carrancistas into combat.

Skirmishing on the southern environs occupied much of Saturday and Sunday, January 16 and 17, 1915. By Monday, January 18, the Carrancistas were able to implant their artillery on the heights of the Cerro del Cuatro, clearly visible to the south, and begin a bombardment of the rail lines leading to the south and east. There were also fierce ground fighting in this area but at midday the shelling suddenly ceased and the Carrancista infantry moved in. The defenders still outnumbered the forces of Diéguez; they were in strong positions and were well supplied but these factors seemingly caused them to

be overconfident. Their defense was inept and their command was divided. General Melitón Ortega of the Villistas was wounded in the heel during the fighting on the Cerro del Cuatro. He was brought into Guadalajara but the flow of blood from his wound could not be stopped and he died during the day. Julián Medina ordered his burial in the municipal cemetery.

By midafternoon the Carrancista infantry had reached the southern edge of the city and there was fierce fighting south of Agua Azul park. One of the witnesses was José G. Zuno, an employee of the municipal slaughterhouse who viewed the approaching battle from the roof of the building where he was working. The Villistas, sensing defeat, abandoned the fight and fled toward their trains, which were waiting to carry them to safety. At the slaughterhouse, workmen, clerks, customers, and businessmen hurriedly cleaned up their work as quickly as they could, fearing that they would fall into the clutches of the oncoming Yaquis, thoroughly dreaded by the tapatíos for their bloodthirsty habits.

The streets and roads leading from the south were jammed with civilians fleeing into Guadalajara. Zuno joined them but took the time to report a scene that the horde viewed as it passed by the city's parks. Zuno observes: "From the trees in Agua Azul and El Deán had been dangling for months the hanged soldiers of one faction or the other, who could be distinguished by their uniforms: the Villistas, rancheros with caps woven from reeds and red, white, and green ribbons, and the Carrancistas, with khaki uniforms, Stetson hats, and red ribbons. Buzzards added a black note to the macabre scene."[41]

Zuno pedaled his bicycle as fast as he could to the central plaza, where he met Martínez Valadez, to whom he explained the critical situation. Martínez Valadez was concerned for the safety of Mariano Azuela and suggested to Zuno: "Come, let's go see if don Mariano is in his

---

[40]Davis, pp. 73–74.

[41]José G. Zuno, *Reminiscencias de una vida* (Guadalajara, 1956), p. 82.

office. . . . Like as not he doesn't know about it and the Yaquis can grab him unawares. . . . Let's go see him."[42]

They found Azuela in his office. Zuno then reports on their flight to safety:

There was Dr. Mariano Azuela, Director of Public Instruction under Julián Medina, quietly working away on behalf of popular education. Because he knew we were jokers, he didn't want to believe us, but I convinced him with my story and then he ordered his employees to leave. We left the capitol building. We went to the library to pick up José Becerra, a poet from Lagos and a close friend of don Mariano. The four of us took a carriage and we went as fast as we could to the Colonia Seattle where my house and the Centro Bohemio were. Manuel remained with them constantly while I continued to work at the slaughterhouse, until Julián Medina made his famous dawn attack.[43]

Medina was able to extricate most of his men from Guadalajara. He loaded them on two long trains and they pulled out of the station, braving Carrancista artillery fire to the south and west. They headed for Tequila and Ameca, where Medina was familiar with the territory, where he had friends and could reorganize his troops.

By late afternoon the Carrancistas had entered the streets near the railroad station. There was gunfire all over the city, and columns of Carrancista soldiers filled the streets searching out any Villista stragglers they could find. Consul Davis estimated that one hundred fifty dead were lying on the streets.[44] That number seems extremely conservative in view of the sharpness of the fighting within the city itself. Neither does it take into account losses by the Villistas in the fight for control of the railway line.

At five in the afternoon General Diéguez reentered Guadalajara and proceeded to the state capitol where he addressed the citizenry from the balcony. Consul Davis reports on the general's feelings:

General Diéguez is now back and full of ire at the manner of General Villa's reception. He is wrathy at the preferences which were shown for Villa and is putting into effect the threats he made against all who manifested same. He is visiting vengeance upon the heads of everyone who had worked in any way under the Villistas. All employees who had served in any of the Government departments are marked for execution.[45]

On January 20 Diéguez ordered the execution of two employees of the Secretario de Gobernación during his own administration. They had refused to accompany him when he ordered the evacuation on December 12. They chose instead to remain in Guadalajara. They were shot at midday.[46]

Martín Luis Guzmán, who was on his way to Aguascalientes to see Villa, who had moved his headquarters there, encountered some of the consequences of the Villista defeat in Guadalajara:

At the station in Irapuato we waited more than twelve hours. The troops of Rodolfo Fierro and Calixto Contreras were returning from Guadalajara, defeated by Diéguez and Murguía: every half hour a train. The endless string of trains filled with men, horses, and artillery pieces blocked our way and the breakdown of the telegraph line to the north slowed down our movement still more.[47]

Fierro and Contreras had to proceed to Aguascalientes to account personally to Villa for their loss of Guadalajara. He listened to their embarrassed explanations at his new headquarters and began to make plans for the recovery of the city.

Julián Medina gathered his soldiers together to the west of Guadalajara and began to formulate his own plans. If Zuno's statement is accu-

[42]Ibid.
[43]Ibid.
[44]Davis, p. 80.
[45]Ibid., p. 81.
[46]Páez Brotchie, II, 138-139.
[47]Martín Luis Guzmán, *El águila y la serpiente* (4th ed.; Mexico, 1941), pp. 441-442.

rate, Azuela and Becerra, after escaping from the Yaquis, did not immediately make contact with Medina and rejoin his army. Neither could Azuela remain with his family because Diéguez and his men had a firm hold on Guadalajara. Apparently Mrs. Azuela and the children stayed behind in the house on Avenida Madero. The doctor says nothing in later years about their stay during his absence, but one can imagine that their situation was precarious to say the least. They apparently were without financial support in a city controlled by a hostile political faction. Mariano Azuela in his reminiscences makes no specific mention of his flight with Zuno and Martínez Valadez nor does he explain where he spent the period when he was away from the city.

During the second occupation by the Diéguez army, there occurred one of those events of the revolution that acquired legendary proportions because of its spectacular features, the danger involved, and finally the scar that it left on a city landmark. The incident remained in the minds of the tapatíos for years to come, but as often is the case, the details vary, depending on who is telling the story, even among those who claim to have been eyewitnesses. It has to do with the *albazo* of Julián Medina early Saturday morning, January 30, 1915, twelve days after he and his army were driven out by the Carrancistas.

Medina planned a bold maneuver in the best tradition of Villa himself. Under cover of darkness he brought his men unnoticed to the very edge of Guadalajara. In the early morning hours they quietly entered the northern and western portions of the city while most of its residents were asleep, including the Carrancista garrison. They succeeded in penetrating almost to the center of the city before they were finally discovered by the drowsy Carrancistas. Amid the clatter of Medina's cavalry on the cobblestones, rifle and machine gun fire resounded in the streets of the business district. The soldiers of Diéguez finally succeeded in putting together their defenses and began to present effective resistance to the Medinistas. Some of the latter were able to reach the central plaza but could not take possession of the statehouse where the government of General Diéguez was centered. During the struggle for the statehouse, the story has it, one of the Medinistas fired a shot at the face of the large clock that stands atop the main entrance. Calzadíaz Barrera asserts that it was Medina himself: "In a display of suicidal bravery, he moves in as far as the main plaza and, to prove that he has been there, he fires a shot with his pistol at the public clock. It was twelve o'clock midnight.[48] The hour of midnight seems quite early when compared with other accounts of the action. In any event, the fighting was bloody, with the Carrancistas admitting that the men of Medina were "penetrating into our barracks and fighting hand to hand in the arcades of the plaza of Guadalajara."[49]

Consul Will B. Davis provides a fairly dispassionate account of the events of January 30:

> I was awakened at 5 A.M. on the morning of the 30th of January, and at first thought that the discharges which I heard were being made by the explosions of fireworks from the roofs of the various churches of the city — a thing formerly not very uncommon in the early morning hours — but when I began to note the reports of rapid-fire guns and musketry within a half-block of my hotel — men, women and children — began pouring into my room — all in sleeping apparel, and in as complete a state of terror as could be imagined, each pleading, as in one voice, "Socorro! — amparo!" (succor — protection). . . . After about two hours of active fighting, during which time an incessant rattle of musketry and gatling guns could be heard as coming from every district of the city, the Villistas began to lose ground, and by 8:30 had been driven beyond the city limits. Cannon fire succeeded, and continued at intervals until about 1:30 P.M.[50]

---

[48]Calzadíaz, II, 128.

[49]Ignacio Muñoz, *Verdad y mito de la Revolución* (2 vols.; Mexico, 1960), II, 337.

[50]Davis, pp. 93–94.

The State House, Guadalajara

The Carrancistas reported to General Álvaro Obregón that the Medinistas lost 450 dead in Guadalajara and many prisoners plus 500 saddled horses. General Murguía declared that his cavalry pursued the dispersed Medinistas until none were left within the state of Jalisco.[51] It is true that Medina's surprise attack failed and his men were driven out, but Murguía's claims were highly exaggerated.

During the height of the battle Father David Galván braved heavy rifle fire in order to administer the last rites to soldiers who had been mortally wounded. While risking his life to do so, Father Galván was captured by a Carrancista named Vera, the brother of a Colonel Vera, a member of the staff of General Diéguez. Vera then had the priest executed. Father Galván's death caused considerable indignation in the city, and long after the Medinistas and the Carrancistas had left Guadalajara, Galván was still remembered.[52] Also, the inhabitants point to the hole left in the face of the statehouse clock. Agustín Yáñez has synthesized their feelings:

> . . . revolutionary epilepsy leaves a lasting wound, the one most pointed out among many, in the very eye of the city. It occurred at the time of the surprise attack of Julián Medina — with his moustache, robust, his slender hand on his pistol — who comes up in front of the statehouse, fires a shot at the face of the clock, and then moves away. That day the dead were carried away in cartloads.[53]

The spectacular intrusion and battle seem to have left no mark on Mariano Azuela, either in his fiction or in his memoirs. Azuela is hardly the type of man who would participate actively in a surprise raid like the one of January 30. Zuno has stated that the novelist rejoined Medina at the time of the raid, but neither Medina or Azuela has gone into detail.

Guadalajara: February–April, 1915

Following their recapture of Guadalajara on January 18 and their repulse of Julián Medina's surprise raid on January 30, 1915, the Carrancistas of generals Diéguez and Murguía managed to hold the city and the towns along the principal rail lines to the south and east. They were still unable to establish overland communication with the main body of Carrancistas in Veracruz and eastern Mexico. Diéguez sent General Murguía along the main line of the Mexico City railroad in an attempt to secure it for their use. Murguía moved eastward from Guadalajara as far as Yurécuaro in the state of Michoacán but there encountered stiff resistance from the Villistas. He then saw that it was useless to attempt to reestablish rail service and returned to Guadalajara.

The Villistas, however, were divided. Julián Medina and his followers held towns in northwestern Jalisco and could move without opposition through those areas that were isolated from the railroads. In those places public sympathy

[51]Obregón, p. 371.

[52]P. J. Camacho, *Breve narración de los datos recogidos acerca del fusilamiento del sacerdote D. David Galván* (Guadalajara, 1927).

[53]Agustín Yáñez, *Genio y figuras de Guadalajara* (Mexico, 1942), pp. 62-63. None of the photographs of Medina dating from the period of the revolution or later show Medina with a moustache and Azuela's description of him does not include one.

lay strongly in their favor and the Carrancistas could not operate effectively there. The Villistas enjoyed sympathy but derived little military support other than food and shelter from the countryside. The small local bands were not disciplined or coordinated with one another and could not unite to exert pressure on the Carrancistas at a given point.

Following the arrival of the defeated units of Rodolfo Fierro and Calixto Contreras at Aguascalientes, Francisco Villa reorganized his staff and the brigades that made up the División del Norte. At the same time he prepared a new advance on Guadalajara. General José Rodríguez led a column overland by way of Lagos, Jalostotitlán, San Miguel el Alto, and Atotonilco el Alto to La Barca, where they joined a large convoy that had traveled from Aguascalientes by rail. In the face of the new Villista advance, on Saturday, February 6, General Diéguez ordered the state capital transferred again to Ciudad Guzmán but did not completely move his soldiers out of Guadalajara until February 12. In the meantime, contingents of Villistas made up of men from Chihuahua pushed back the thin lines of the defending Carrancistas until they reached Las Juntas, a rail junction on the southern outskirts of Guadalajara.

Along the railway line they could still find evidence of the fierceness of the battle of January 18, in the form of numerous corpses that lay where they had fallen. One of the participants later described their find:

> When headquarters arrived, several squads of the ambulance service, helped by us, were ordered to proceed to clean up the countryside that was literally strewn with corpses in a state of putrefaction, with their stomachs swollen by the bloating that developed in the dead bodies, for because of the haste with which the attack on Guadalajara and its capture took place, Generals Contreras and Fierro did not have time to pick up the dead and wounded. Nevertheless, all the bodies lay barefoot, undressed, and covered with maggots. The sight could not have been more

horrifying. They had been lying exposed to the sun for weeks.[54]

When at last Villa's convoy reached Guadalajara, he ordered his troops to wait at Las Juntas. He entered the city accompanied only by an escort of one hundred of his famous dorados. They marched from the railway station up the Calle de San Francisco along the same route that they followed on December 17. It was now Friday, February 13. The tapatíos were as enthusiastic about Villa as they had been in December. They cheered wildly when Villa and his mounted dorados passed by. Luis Páez Brotchie presents a vivid picture of the reception by the people of Guadalajara:

> It was in the afternoon. A general ringing of bells deafened the city and everyone rushed to the Calle de San Francisco or 16 de Septiembre. Accompanied by an escort of one hundred men, General Villa made his entrance along this street, in the middle of an oppressive throng that applauded and acclaimed him, cheering him frenziedly. Then the multitude invaded the bandstand, lawn, benches, and sidewalks of the main plaza. The general, as soon as he arrived at the state capitol, came out on the main balcony and, after having ordered the cathedral bells silenced, spoke to the people, letting them know that this time he came with victory assured and that with no further delay he would leave on the following day for the country to the south; that his cavalry was skirmishing with the enemy rear guard. He promised all kinds of security and also to punish by all means the assassins of the people (referring to the Carrancistas for the deaths of January 18). He was applauded furiously.[55]

Consul Davis reported substantially the same scene, but added an opinion or two of his own:

> General Villa arrived at the Palace at 4 P.M., from the balcony of which he addressed the

----

[54] Calzadíaz, II, 129–130.
[55] Páez Brotchie, II, 140.

largest concourse of people that I had ever seen gathered in the plaza and street in front. People of all classes were out, and rejoicing as if they felt their d[e]liverer had come. Women and children of many of the best families—who had not been on the streets since General Medina's defeat by Diéguez on the 19th of February [January]—were seen in large numbers.[56]

Julián Medina again appeared on the balcony with Villa and with the latter's return resumed his post as governor of Jalisco. At the same time Mariano Azuela renewed his labors as director of public education for the state. They had been away a little less than four weeks. For the time being, Francisco Villa took personal charge of military activities in the state. Thus Medina was relieved from these responsibilities and could devote himself largely to civil matters. With the organization that he and his subordinates had been able to set up during their first occupation of Guadalajara, the civil government was able to function somewhat more smoothly than in December and January.

Villa did not want to repeat the errors of the month before that had permitted Diéguez and Murguía to retake Guadalajara. With the main body of his army he set out in pursuit of Diéguez and his Carrancistas. He caught up with them on the heights just south of Sayula and routed them in some of the bloodiest fighting of the whole revolution. The enemy held strong positions on the heights which the Villistas stormed and took. Both sides sustained heavy casualties. In addition, the dispersed Carrancistas lost many of their men as prisoners. A good proportion of these were executed by the bloodthirsty Rodolfo Fierro until Villa issued an order forbidding any further executions of prisoners. Diéguez and his shattered army retreated into the state of Colima behind the shelter of the rough barranca country and thus left the entire state of Jalisco under the control of Villa's armies.

The last days of February, 1915, are without a doubt the period of greatest optimism for Villismo in Jalisco. Dr. Ramón Puente, a close confidant of the general, has noted that Villa was deeply moved by the enthusiastic and sympathetic reception by the tapatíos upon his second entry into Guadalajara. He was encouraged and held hopes of realizing positive goals for Mexico: "Truly, Villa's hopes were high before suffering his first military disaster [at Celaya]. The way in which he is received by the city at Guadalajara, which is the second in importance in the Republic, causes him to consider the possibility of accomplishing in the not too distant future a goal that would not be factional but genuinely Mexican."[57]

At the same time, Dr. Puente was well aware of Villa's weaknesses, in particular the instantaneous brutal reaction toward anyone who approached him with a complaint. He was not without such moments during his stay in Jalisco. They contributed to his undoing and he was unable to take advantage of this spontaneous display of good will.

Many of Julián Medina's soldiers went on to southern Jalisco to participate in the campaign against Diéguez but Medina himself remained in Guadalajara. There he devoted much of his time to finding means of financing his government. A member of consul Davis's staff went to the capitol one day during the second occupation of Guadalajara and found Medina in consultation with Dr. Puente, Villa's principal fund raiser. Revolutionary financing was accomplished in two ways: first, by means of the *préstamo forzoso*, the forced loan exacted from the total population of the city, although various wealthy citizens hostile to Villa were singled out as the principal contributors, and second, by the generous issuance of paper currency, primarily in the form of bank notes known popularly as *de dos caritas*, because they bore the portraits of Francisco I. Madero and Abraham González each within an oval frame and signed

[56]Davis, p. 114.

[57]Ramón Puente, *Villa en pie* (Mexico, 1937), p. 125.

by Manuel Chao. This money, which was issued in Chihuahua, was the only currency allowed to circulate in areas dominated by Villa and it replaced the Carrancista *bilimbiques* used by Diéguez. Ricardo Delgado has estimated that the public debt attributable to the Villistas alone amounted to several million pesos, without taking into account the "loans" exacted by the Carrancistas and the paper money that they issued.[58]

Mariano Azuela tried to maintain the functioning of the state's public school system under these unsettled circumstances, although it is unlikely that his effective jurisdiction extended much beyond the city of Guadalajara. For other reasons, however, Azuela's return was significant. It marked the beginning of the longest period of repose that he was to enjoy during his attachment to the Villistas. Even so, it lasted only slightly more than two months. He would have a little more time to devote to his growing family. His daughter Esperanza was born during the family's residence in Guadalajara.

This stay in Guadalajara needs to be examined in regard to Azuela's experiences and their significance to him as a writer. Except for the two or three weeks of enforced absence from the city, since arriving there he had had relatively little contact with actual fighting men of the revolution. In fact, despite his proximity to fierce and bloody fighting, he had observed little or none of it. In December and again in February Villa's armies were able to take Guadalajara without having to fight for the city. Through an unusual combination of circumstances which caused Azuela to appear as an extremely ingenuous person, he was not a witness to the sharp fighting of January in which the Villistas suffered heavy casualties. The only engagement that he may possibly have observed was Medina's albazo of January 30. Even that is unlikely, for he was not the bold, daring type of soldier who would take his life into his own hands in the lair of the enemy. Nor does one

find the slightest allusion to this spectacular foray into Guadalajara in any of his writings.

Azuela seems to have decided to write a novel during the time he was with Medina at Irapuato. In his *Obras completas* (III, 1080) he notes that he had not yet decided what he would write about but that he had hit upon a title, *Los de abajo*. After he reached Guadalajara he decided to call his protagonist Demetrio Macías. There is evidence that Azuela had been considering a model for Demetrio from among his associates in the revolution. Julián Medina seems to have been his first thought, as stated by José María González de Mendoza in his introduction to the third edition of Azuela's *Mala yerba*.[59] Since the move to Guadalajara, Azuela had not seen as much of Medina. The two men did not have the time to converse together, as they did at Irapuato, and Medina found it necessary to devote his time to administrative duties rather than fighting. This type of activity is hardly appropriate to an attractive hero for a novel, especially when other and more dashing heroes are available. There was a clear need for a more appropriate model for the future Demetrio Macías.

Following his return to Guadalajara, Azuela had more time to think about his novel. He later admitted that he then abandoned the idea of a Demetrio Macías developed along the lines of Julián Medina. He turned to another figure from among Medina's associates, who appealed to him for his daring and bravery, as Leocadio Parra had already gained his admiration. He has reported on this young man in typical Azuela fashion, in the form of a succinct physical description and a synthesis of his background:

> Manuel Caloca, the youngest member of a family of revolutionary figures from El Teúl, of the state of Zacatecas, a youth less than twenty years old, tall, lean, olive complexioned, somewhat oriental in his countenance, cheerful and intrepid, recklessly brave in battle, replaced Julián Medina in the formation of my character. He had fought with valor

[58] *Las monedas jaliscienses durante la época revolucionaria* (Guadalajara, 1938), p. 127.

[59] (Mexico, 1937), p. 14.

and he had conferred on himself the rank of colonel, which Medina confirmed upon receiving him and taking him in as a member of his forces.[60]

When Manuel Caloca first came to Azuela's attention cannot be easily determined. Azuela has shed little light on the subject. He does not refer to this man among Medina's associates at Irapuato. He certainly was far from being a major figure of the revolution and was not in the forefront of campaigns and movements. Caloca is a much more obscure figure than Medina and his name appears infrequently in accounts of the fighting in Jalisco. The first clear notice has come from General Álvaro Obregón in reporting Julián Medina's albazo of January 30, in which Caloca is listed as one of the officers who led the invaders.[61] The style of the albazo, with its dependence upon surprise and daring execution, is clearly in accord with the spirit of both Medina and Caloca.

Other members of the extended Caloca family had already distinguished themselves in the Mexican revolution. As early as 1911, another Manuel Caloca had organized forces in southern Zacatecas in support of Madero.[62] General Pedro Caloca cooperated with the armies of Villa and Pánfilo Natera at the defeat of the Huertistas at Zacatecas in June, 1914.[63] A Colonel Caloca was the chief of staff of General Pérez, one of the characters of *El águila y la serpiente* of Martín Luis Guzmán.[64] Probably the best known of them was Lauro G. Caloca (1884–1956), who took part in the revolution both with Villa and Zapata and later assisted José Vasconcelos in setting up Mexico's system of rural schools. Lauro Caloca later became known as a journalist and a writer.[65] There is no evidence that any of these men served with

Julián Medina. The Manuel Caloca of Azuela's acquaintance was younger than any of these and at the time that Azuela knew him he was a youth of twenty years or less. At one point Azuela considers him to be only fifteen years old.[66]

The Demetrio Macías that Azuela eventually created is a much less sophisticated figure than either of the models that the novelist admits having used. The political awareness of Caloca and Medina, the latter in particular, has escaped Demetrio completely. It would be difficult to conceive of Demetrio as participating in a political club like the one that Medina formed in Hostotipaquillo.

Azuela's statements permit one to see the process through which he created Demetrio Macías. At Irapuato he decided upon the title *Los de abajo*. Having made that decision, Azuela then needed a protagonist appropriate to that level of contemporary Mexican society, culturally, economically, and politically. These were guidelines that he must maintain for a faithful portrayal of his view of the revolution.

During his service with revolutionary armies, Azuela would seem to have followed his frequent practice of modeling his characters on people whom he observed directly in life. This practice would account for his initial consideration of Julián Medina as a prototype for a protagonist. Medina was a brave soldier and a genuine revolutionary, desirable qualities in such a figure, yet he possessed other features that Azuela could hardly attribute to his protagonist. Although he could handle himself among rancheros, Medina was born in a small town and had lived there most of his life. He could read and write and normally used these skills in his daily activities. Furthermore Medina was knowledgeable and alert concerning the national political situation: his horizons extended far beyond the realm of the local cacique. It would appear that Julián Medina got too far away from Azuela's concept of his hero.

Yet Manuel Caloca's background was not greatly different. Some of the Caloca family

---

[60] *O.C.*, III, 1080.

[61] Obregón, p. 271.

[62] Quirarte, p. 172.

[63] *Diccionario Porrúa de historia, biografía y geografía de México* (2d ed.; Mexico, 1965), p. 1738.

[64] Pp. 214–215.

[65] J. Jesús Figueroa Torres, *Biografía de Caloca. El cuentista parlamentario* (Mexico, 1965).

[66] *O.C.*, III, 1268.

even attended the Liceo de Varones in Guadalajara in the years immediately preceding the
revolution and were politically active there.[67]
His family's participation in the revolution from
its earliest period is indicative of constant political activity and awareness. The Demetrio Macías
that eventually evolved is a much less enlightened
figure than either of the models that the novelist
has admitted using. Demetrio resembles more
the little-known leaders of small rural revolutionary groups, who were restricted in their
motivation, political outlook, and general capa-
bilities. Demetrio, it would seem, could have
been created without the benefit of specific
models. To a large degree, he is an ideal figure
who reflects Mariano Azuela's own outlook on
the revolution.

Demetrio Macías does have one clear debt

to Medina and Caloca. Through Azuela from
them he inherited his death-defying bravery in
battle, likewise his almost intuitive knowledge
of military tactics and prowess against the
federales. These qualities Demetrio used to advantage. Azuela could hardly have become
familiar with them without having known
Medina and Caloca intimately and listened to
their exploits.

By February, 1915, Dr. Azuela had begun
to form in his mind an image of Demetrio
Macías. He had hardly proceeded, however,
beyond the stage of taking notes, and many of
these at this stage must be considered only as
mental notes. The actual composition of the
novel and the preparation of a first draft would
not come until several months later under the
most trying of circumstances.[68]

To Lagos: April–June, 1915

Francisco Villa moved on to Ciudad Guzmán after his brigades routed the Carrancistas
on the slopes south of Sayula. He was quite
aware of the danger that the remnants of the
enemy forces still represented to the right flank
of his extended armies and he personally conducted the campaign against generals Diéguez
and Murguía in the hope of liquidating them
for good.

In Ciudad Guzmán Villa conferred with
the leaders of scattered bands from southern
and western Jalisco that supported him, at least
nominally. The residents of the town were sym-

pathetic to Villa and, as in Guadalajara, he
addressed them, this time from the bandstand
in the town's main square. In addition to the
Carrancistas, the general had another matter on
his mind. He was concerned over the instability
of the Convencionista government and the performance of its executives. In his remarks, he
directed his anger against Eulalio Gutiérrez,
whom he considered a traitor for having abandoned the government established by the Convention. He also accused Gutiérrez of having
appropriated for himself the funds of that government. Without Villa's knowledge, Gutiérrez

---

[67]Zuno, *Historia de la Revolución,* p. 57.

[68]In *Los de abajo* there is almost no reflection of the
author's presence in Guadalajara. The urban element scarcely appears in the novel, yet one does note a reference to the
old prison built by Governor José Antonio Escobedo in 1843
at the western end of the Calle del Carmen (now Avenida

Juárez), a massive building which occupied an area of three
hundred by one hundred fifty meters (F. L. y D., *La reina
occidental. Guía del viajero en Guadalajara* [Guadalajara,
1900-1901], p. 20). There Anastasio Montañez and El
Güero Margarito spent a year of confinement together (*Los
de abajo* [Mexico, 1958], p. 75).

and several of his ministers had fled the capital, abandoning their posts, on January 16, 1915.[69] Villa spoke in Ciudad Guzmán on February 19.

He then dispatched Rodolfo Fierro and Pablo C. Seáñez[70] with several brigades in pursuit of the Carrancistas, but Diéguez and Murguía slipped through the railroad tunnels with their battered forces past Atenquique into the safe area around Colima. The Villistas could not easily follow them through the deep canyons of the border country between southern Jalisco and northeastern Colima and established their headquarters at Tuxpan, while waiting to renew the pursuit. Thus far, Villa's campaign had had indecisive results. He had defeated the enemy in battle and driven them from territory that they had once held, but he had not been able to destroy them. Until they were disposed of, they would return to haunt Guadalajara.

At Tuxpan Villa received an urgent plea for reinforcement from the north. General Felipe Ángeles in Monterrey reported that he was being attacked by Carrancistas led by General Pablo González and was fearful of being overrun. Villa's plan had been to move southward to capture the port of Manzanillo and thereby completely bottle up Diéguez and Murguía but Ángeles continued his entreaties. Unwillingly Villa acceded to them and withdrew a portion of his forces, leaving Fierro and Seáñez to hold some nine thousand Carrancistas at bay in Colima. Francisco Villa then headed northward leaving a task unfinished.[71]

In Guadalajara Villa stopped to confer with Julián Medina. He also found there Duval West, a personal envoy of President Woodrow Wilson of the United States. They sat down to discuss various problems that Villa faced in future months. These were mainly financial and revolved around Villa's ability to obtain funds for continuing his military campaigns and financing the normal functions of government.[72] Still resounding in Villa's ears were the shouts,

plaudits, and the *vivas* of the tapatíos as they welcomed him on his second arrival in their city. Their hopes were on Villa and he in effect was the government, notwithstanding the Convención that was attempting to function in Mexico City under its new president Roque González Garza. Villa, however, held the physical power through his military might. He issued currency which circulated by his decree, he controlled the communications in the vast sections under his dominion, and although nominally he was subject to the Convención, his word was law. These were the circumstances under which Villa left Guadalajara. He would never return. These aspects of the revolution were on the level of *los de arriba* and not on that of *los de abajo*, which was of concern to Mariano Azuela.

Several thousand Villistas remained in Jalisco, almost all of them in the south, leaving Guadalajara in relative quiet. In Tuxpan in addition to the Brigada Fierro, commanded by Rodolfo Fierro, and one of the Brigadas Villa under Seáñez, there were 5,400 men from Jalisco from the troops of various local commanders, including those of Julián Medina, Pedro Zamora, Julián del Real, Teófilo Sánchez Aldana, and others.[73] Jesús Medina, Leocadio Parra, and various others of Julián Medina's trusted military staff were with the main body of the Villistas.

At first the Carrancistas were in difficult straits in Colima. They lacked weapons, ammunition, and especially money. By an accident of geography and because of the decision of the Villista high command, they were safe for the time being. From Colima, Diéguez communicated immediately with the Primer Jefe in his distant headquarters in Veracruz. Diéguez fortunately remained in control of the port of Manzanillo, which was his only point of contact with the rest of Mexico. Within a few weeks he received a shipment of arms and military equipment sent by sea from Salina Cruz and with them he could begin anew a drive on Guadalajara. The picture began to brighten for the Carrancistas, for they were able to survive one

[69]Calzadíaz, II, 138.

[70]John Reed gives an account of this young officer in *Insurgent Mexico* (New York, 1914), p. 44.

[71]Calzadíaz, II, 138.

[72]Puente, *Villa en pie*, p. 125.

[73]Moreno, p. 92.

of their darkest hours. At the same time, Villismo in Jalisco passed its peak and would soon begin its decline.

The renewed strength of Diéguez's army in Colima was not the only threat to Villa and Medina in Jalisco. General Álvaro Obregón had been able to penetrate into central Mexico with a sizable army, well equipped and experienced. He was able to entice Villa and the greater part of his forces out of the north. The two armies collided at Celaya in the Bajío region some thirty miles to the west of Querétaro and engaged in a series of clashes. The battles began on April 6 and 7 and continued again on April, 13, 14, and 15, 1915, along the main line of the Mexico City-Ciudad Juárez railroad. The styles of the combatants contrasted sharply. Villa's cavalry made headlong charges in an attempt to overrun the positions of Obregón's men. The latter held firm and the methodical Obregón made effective use of his infantry supported by artillery.

The first series of battles was intense but inconclusive. In the second series, a week later, Obregón gained significant victories over the Villistas, forcing them back to the west and north. The plains of the southern Bajío gave the latter no natural defensive position, and they could foresee the imminent loss of Irapuato, which was in an indefensible position thirty or forty miles to the west. Because it was a key rail connection with points to the west, all their forces in Jalisco were thus in jeopardy.

In Guadalajara life had proceeded more or less quietly during these developments. Even the local government had managed to conduct itself in a manner approaching normality. Diéguez and Murguía had been active and had begun to move toward the north, but they had not affected greatly the city's tranquillity. The calm was suddenly broken on Friday, April 16, when the Villista authorities ordered the transfer of the seat of the state government of Jalisco from Guadalajara to Lagos de Moreno, which at that time was still safely within Villista territory. Evacuation of all the state offices began that

same day. The Villistas had not lost Guadalajara in battle, but because of strategic losses elsewhere they could no longer hold it.

The sudden turn of events threatened disastrous consequences for the officeholders of the state and municipal governments. Guadalajara and the state of Jalisco generally were still ardent and enthusiastic supporters of Villa. It dawned on them that he was no longer in a position to protect them and that they could well be caught up in the wrath of General Manuel M. Diéguez, the vindictive Carrancista governor who was waiting to move in as soon as the Villistas could evacuate the city. This possibility caused consternation in their ranks and their first thought was flight. The only sure means of avoiding the approaching Carrancistas was to take passage on one of the long trains that was preparing to move the Villista government and its soldiers out of the city.

As soon as decree ordering the transfer was made public, the officeholders began to move aboard trains that were made ready in the railway station. The platforms under the long corrugated metal roofs swarmed with humans who were loading the contents of the government offices into railroad cars. These were jammed with furniture, office equipment, archives, and human beings. The majority of the rolling stock consisted of freight and cattle cars, but the higher officers and officials would travel in greater comfort. They had passenger coaches outfitted with the conveniences of the times. Throughout the day the movement aboard the trains was characterized by an air of great haste and urgency. The task was completed by nightfall and the trains were ready to leave Guadalajara for the safety of the main Villista army in Irapuato and Lagos de Moreno.

Consul Will B. Davis, who was one of those who could afford to remain behind, reported on April 18 that the previous evening four thousand Convencionista troops evacuated the city. He added that they were accompanied by all the employees of the state and municipal governments, the post office and the telegraph services, and many private citizens.[74] This was a sizable number, amounting to as many as seven or eight thousand persons, who all attempted to crowd into the limited space aboard the trains. They filled not only the interior of the passenger and freight cars but also all available space atop the latter, in a desperate attempt to leave the city. All this came to pass a bare two months following Villa's second triumphal entry into Gudalajara. Sweet victory was fleeting and short lived.

On one of those trains, almost lost in the multitude of anxious, uprooted humanity, was Dr. Mariano Azuela. Abruptly he was forced to abandon his labors as director of the public school system of Jalisco and was on his way back to Lagos de Moreno. He could not expect to continue in that post when Diéguez moved in again. Neither could the schoolteachers and inspectors who had been working under him. Various of these subordinates accompanied him in his flight.

Dr. Azuela had an additional preoccupation. He was leaving behind his wife and family in Guadalajara. They were thus separated from him again and apparently were without immediate means of support. Azuela did not explain in later years why they failed to accompany him, but the reasons are not hard to find. His family was large; he had a new daughter who was but a few weeks old. They could not travel comfortably on a revolutionary train of this type. The urgency of the evacuation of Guadalajara may well have been another reason for leaving his family behind. It simply had not been possible to make all the members ready in the time available before the trains had to leave.

At last the locomotives managed to pull the long strings of cars out of the station and head for Irapuato. Most of the journey had to be made at night because it was imperative to arrive at that junction while it was still under the control of the Villistas. Otherwise all would be trapped, with the advancing troops of Álvaro Obregón in front of them and Manuel Diéguez and his Yaquis from Sonora at their rear. The

line was cleared of all other traffic; nevertheless it was a relatively slow trip, for there were several trains and the locomotives and rolling stock were not of the best. They carried a heavy human load in addition to all the paraphernalia of government and war. Villa fortunately had among his followers a corps of expert railroad men who were thoroughly familiar with the operation of equipment and its maintenance. Without them he would not have been able to mount an effective campaign. In this case they succeeded in extricating his army from a difficult predicament with the added human baggage of *soldaderas*, politicians, officeholders and assorted hangers-on. It was essentially a salvage operation but a spectacular one. Unlike the advances on Guadalajara in December and February, which were almost exclusively of a military nature, the exodus of April was largely civilian. The soldiers in this multitude were outnumbered. Whereas they could be confident and occasionally even optimistic concerning the future, the bureaucrats could not. Their future was uncertain if not precarious, and they had nothing comparable to military weapons with which they could defend themselves.

The trip out of Guadalajara and the circumstances under which it was accomplished were an unusual event in the life of Mariano Azuela. Not necessarily so for others who had had long experience in the revolution. For many this kind of movement had been a fairly frequent occurrence since 1913 and the early campaigns against Huerta's federales. For the novelist it was still something of a new experience. There are clear reflections of this withdrawal from Guadalajara in his literary production. In *Los de abajo* in a similar scene aboard a crowded train Demetrio Macías and his staff were on their way to Aguascalientes to attend the sessions of the convention of October, 1914. In many respects the scene resembles those that Azuela observed on this journey to Irapuato and Lagos de Moreno, above all in regard to the popular types who are traveling, but the spirit is not the same, for in the literary work there is not

[74]Davis, p. 206.

the common bond of fear of impending disaster awaiting the passengers fleeing from Guadalajara.

The retreat to Irapuato is depicted most vividly in another of Azuela's works. The retreat carries forward the action in the early chapters of *Las moscas,* to which he assigned the extremely appropriate subtitle "Views and Scenes of the Revolution." In *Las moscas* the reason for the evacuation of the army and civilians is the same, the defeat of Villa's armies at Celaya and the imminent approach of the Carrancistas. Azuela clearly states the trains' destination, Irapuato, but he does not identify the provincial capital that the Villistas are forced to leave. In the opening chapters, or scenes, of *Las moscas,* which was not published until 1918, Azuela attempted something that he had not done before, the handling in prose of a tremendous crowd of people. He was able to capture the general features and the mood of the fleeing mass by using an economy of words, and at the same time he focused upon various of its members who possessed some individuality. Years later Azuela used the same process again in *Nueva burguesía* in presenting to his readers the rally in the Zócalo in Mexico City for the presidential candidacy of General Juan Andrew Almazán. He was equally adept there.

Memoirs of revolutionary figures and histories of the various factions tend to offer little more than the bare statements of the major events. To the historian, the departure from Guadalajara simply obeyed a demand of military strategy. It remained for Azuela to provide the human dimension in *Las moscas.* His "views and scenes" are admirable but unfortunately his sense of moral indignation took charge, and he leaned too heavily on sarcasm to condemn the various categories of opportunists who populated his train. He has been excessively harsh with most of them and although he is generally truthful to reality and faithful in his depiction of his fellow Mexicans in the revolution, in *Las moscas* he has shown true sympathy for very few of those who were accompanying him.

But Mariano Azuela had something else in his favor here, a condition that sets this work apart from his others, even his yet unborn *Los de abajo. Las moscas* has a ring to it that comes from Azuela's own participation in the events he is writing about. He was there, as the doctor in charge of his *carro sanitario,* invaded and practically overwhelmed by those who had been caught up in the revolution and were unable to flee from it. This was not vicarious experience, acquired in conversation with acquaintances who had experienced danger and hardship, leaving Azuela once or twice removed from the events themselves. This was direct observation and even personal participation, experiences that Azuela himself had realized as lacking in his preparation as a novelist before he left Lagos de Moreno in October, 1914.

The human cargo of the trains literally inundated Irapuato. Azuela had been there before, during the month and a half when he was waiting with Medina for the campaign against Guadalajara to develop. But now there were so many long trains in the railroad yards that there was no more room for them and they spilled out onto the incoming tracks. They had to remain parked there temporarily, waiting until they could move on to the north to escape the advance of the Carrancistas from the east and south. The civilian passengers from the recently arrived Guadalajara train swarmed through the streets of the town. They were nearly famished and their first concern was to find something to eat. That was not easy, for Irapuato was but a small provincial town, much smaller than Guadalajara, and it could not easily cope with invaders in such numbers. Another concern was to purchase items for future use while such articles were still available in order to dispose of the paper money issued by the Villistas. It would be worthless if one held it in Carrancista territory, and there was no certainty that everyone could crowd aboard the northbound trains with Villa's army.

Azuela has said little about the writing of *Las moscas.* It was not to see publication until

Medina's troops in southern Jalisco

several years had passed, following *Los de abajo* and a year and a half after the appearance of *Los caciques,* which Azuela had completed in June, 1914. The actual composition of the work must have been accomplished after the writing of *Los de abajo.* One may conjecture that Azuela made careful notes on the events of the journey and the people with whom he traveled, the scenes of the departure and then the arrival in Irapuato, conversations, and the general kinesthetic impressions of the experience, made perhaps during his stay of six weeks or so in Lagos de Moreno. Clearly *Los de abajo* was foremost in his mind at this time. *Las moscas* gives evidence of having been written somewhat later, when Azuela had had time to dwell upon his disenchantment with human beings who were caught up in the revolution either through their own choice or against their will.

At noon on Sunday, April 18, Guadalajara changed hands. Two thousand Carrancista troops led by Manuel M. Diéguez entered the city. As Villa had done, Diéguez proceeded directly to the state capitol where from the balcony he again addressed the tapatíos as a part of the standard operating procedure. Diéguez showed vexation over the second tumultuous reception given to Villa. He angrily remarked: "I will see (pointing to the cathedral towers) that those bells will never sound again!"[75] The memory of Villa lingered on, to the discomfort of Diéguez, who was unable to inspire enthusiasm among the populace as Villa had done.

The Carrancistas installed David Aguirre Berlanga as their governor of Jalisco. After a few days' rest, General Diéguez and most of his soldiers moved on to central Mexico in the pursuit of Villa, leaving a few hundred men as a garrison for Governor Aguirre Berlanga. In the first weeks following the departure of the Villista brigades, Guadalajara was actually very lightly defended. Those days and the months to come brought hardship to the people of Guadalajara and the state of Jalisco. There was very little

food, and at the same time an acute shortage of money plagued the state, a condition that was reflected in the scarcity of currency. Despite control of the rail lines by the Carrancistas, little or no rolling stock was available, there were no trains and the city was almost completely cut off, isolated from the rest of the country. These constant concerns were expressed in the dispatches of Consul Will B. Davis throughout the remainder of 1915. The Carrancistas were worried by the proximity of the enemy and the decided preference of the residents of the city of Guadalajara and the entire state of Jalisco for the Villistas.

In Irapuato one by one the trains that were moving Villa's army and his government began to head northward. Finally the last one was able to leave, that of Villa himself, and Obregón's army moved into Irapuato on April 21.

Julián Medina moved his military and civilian staff as far as Lagos de Moreno, where he established a nominal state government for Jalisco. Lagos was practically the only remaining site that could serve as a state capital for there was no other city of any consequence along the line of the Central Railway of Mexico as it curved and twisted across the northeastern arm of Jalisco. Considering the predicament of the Villistas, any regional government that they established could only be of a nominal nature. Lagos had never been the state's definitive capital, and it did not have adequate facilities for operating statewide functions. Furthermore, there was no hope for any degree of stability or of governmental effectiveness in view of the increasing tempo of military operations.

Mariano Azuela then was back in Lagos with Medina. He has not commented on the nature of his duties during this interlude, but certainly there was little to be done in the line of public education, considering the precarious existence of the state government. In any case, Azuela was with friends and relatives, although his wife and children had had to stay behind in Guadalajara. In Lagos he need not fear his political enemies. Dr. Azuela was a Villista and Villista forces were in full control of the town.

[75]Ibid., pp. 132-133.

The novelist's thoughts seem to have turned again to *Los de abajo* during the weeks that followed. These apparently offered a period of relative calm and repose that provided an opportunity to write. He later remarked concerning the novel *Los de abajo:* "Carefully documented, I began my notes." He noted cryptically that he was able to complete two chapters there.[76] One wonders which two chapters of *Los de abajo* these might have been, for by far the greatest part of Azuela's activity with the military that is reflected in the novel still lay ahead of him. They were, perhaps, tentative versions that he later chose not to include in the texts that he published. It seems more likely, however, that Azuela's writing consisted of extensive note-taking of materials that he could utilize in the future. The experience of the memorable train ride from Guadalajara remained with him in sharp detail. It is not out of order to consider that he also made use of his time to prepare notes that would be invaluable when he sat down to write *Las moscas* after the days of fighting were over.

After the battles at Celaya and his occupation of Irapuato, Álvaro Obregón methodically began his pursuit of Villa. During the hot month of May, Obregón slowly pushed forward. Villa was full of fight and gave ground only grudgingly. It was a month of maneuvering and probing to seek out the enemy's weak spots. Obregón was more successful at this than was Villa, and his autobiographical volume *Ocho mil kilómetros en campaña* reveals the careful planning that had gone into the campaign, the attention devoted to logistics and supply. The fighting of the Bajío campaign was exceedingly fierce and bloody, especially in the area north of Silao, Guanajuato. The Carrancista generals were not immune from the scars of battle. General Manuel Diéguez was seriously wounded, and at Santa Ana del Conde, General Obregón lost an arm when a Villista artillery shell exploded in a position from which he was observing the fighting. Santa Ana and Trinidad were the scenes of

the fiercest conflicts and at each point Villa and his men were forced to withdraw to the northwest.

Julián Medina's troops do not appear to have taken part with the other Villista brigades in the Bajío campaign along the line of the Central Railway of Mexico in Guanajuato and northeastern Jalisco. Most of Villa's men were *norteños,* principally from the rural sections of Chihuahua. Medina remained in Lagos as the nominal governor of Jalisco. His followers were still under his command, some in Lagos and others in the area of Los Altos to the southwest, where they were garrisoned.

The decision to leave Guadalajara brought about a change in military tactics for the Medinistas. As long as Francisco Villa held direct control over vast stretches of Mexico's rail system, his armies and those of his affiliated leaders conducted their campaigns along the principal rail routes, moving great numbers of men, arms, ammunition, and equipment by train. With the loss of Irapuato and the Guadalajara line, Villista movements were more restricted and the use of trains lost much of its significance. The effect was noticeable in the activities of the Villistas of Jalisco, who had operated largely within their own state. As rancheros and villagers, they were not accustomed to movement by train. Rather, their battle techniques were based on the horse. In the early months of the revolution, Medina and his companions from Hostotipaquillo depended almost exclusively upon this animal for getting around. It almost had to be this way. Rural Jalisco had no roads worthy of the name. Medina and his soldiers operated in remote sections of the state, far from the railroads and the few usable roads. During the Huerta administration the railway system was in the hands of the hated federales and was not available to the revolutionaries, but when the Constitucionalistas moved into the state in June, 1914, the latter controlled all train travel, the locomotives and the rolling stock, and made extensive use of them.

In April and May, 1915, the situation reverted back to the pre-1914 period. Medina's

[76]*O.C.,* III, 1268.

subordinates, Leocadio Parra, Manuel Caloca, and others, turned back to rely again on their horses and they again became a unit that stressed the use of cavalry. One might wonder about the role that the automobile played in the general picture of transport and movement. In 1915 few if any rancheros and villagers of Jalisco had yet owned one or gained experience in the operation and repair of an automobile. Neither were the roads between towns conducive to travel by this means. In Guadalajara, however, Consul Will Davis made use of them in the conduct of his business within the city itself. The Carrancistas of General Diéguez seemingly had one or more vehicles at their disposal. The Villistas who were pursuing the retreating Carrancistas southward from the western end of Lake Chapala in February, 1915, reported that several Dieguecistas slipped away from them by fleeing in an automobile.[77] In Irapuato General Malacara of *Las moscas* escorted young ladies around the town in a vehicle, but he, of course, was a general. The Villistas from Jalisco still stuck with their horses. Mariano Azuela would soon switch to this mode of travel.

Early in May, 1915, contingents of Medina's Villistas occupied San Juan de los Lagos and San Miguel el Alto. Militarily these were not important points except that they protected the Villista flank and precluded any advance overland by the Carrancistas from the direction of Guadalajara. These small towns were quite conservative in their political and social attitudes and the Villistas encountered little or no opposition, either from the Carrancistas or the townspeople. Rather, they were warmly welcomed and were given a cordial and ardent reception by the residents. Medina dispatched Leocadio Parra and Manuel Caloca to the village of San Miguel el Alto, some thirty miles to the southwest of Lagos de Moreno, where they arrived on May 5, Julián Medina did not accompany them.

Fortunately it has been possible to record some of the events and details of their stay in San Miguel and thereby shed light on the man-

ner of operation of the Villistas, what their members were like, their relations with the townspeople, on fighting that took place within the town itself, and a visit to San Miguel el Alto by Mariano Azuela and José Becerra. The late José de Jesús Delgado Román, then a young man, was a resident of San Miguel in 1915 and a witness to the presence of the Villistas and events involving them and their Carrancista foes. He has provided many of the details that follow, which were recorded during an interview granted in San Miguel in July, 1960.

The Villistas entered San Miguel during the first week of May. The town had little in the way of facilities for quartering troops, but their officers, at least, were housed in various *mesones,* or small inns. In addition to General Parra and Colonel Caloca, Delgado Román has identified three other Villistas. They are a Colonel Baca, a Lieutenant Colonel Avilés, who was an aide to Colonel Caloca, and an aide to Colonel Baca identified only as Coquito, rank unstated. Colonel Caloca was the same Manuel Caloca whom Mariano Azuela had taken as his model for Demetrio Macías, in substitution for Julián Medina. Delgado Román has provided a brief word picture of him: "Caloca was a very tall young fellow, extremely tall, thin and bent over. Even in a corral he could be seen because, well, he was of extraordinary height."

The only other officer about whom he has given physical details is Colonel Baca, who also was of interest to Azuela. Delgado Román said of him: "Colonel Baca had a limp in one leg. It may have dated from years back or perhaps from the time of the revolution itself. He was already somewhat gimpy."

There was relatively little for the soldiers to do in San Miguel el Alto. There were no Carrancistas in the immediate vicinity, which was at peace. The Villistas soon became acquainted in the community. They behaved themselves properly and soon gained the respect and sympathy of the townspeople, winning their confidence and social acceptance. During the month of May various residents of San Miguel prepared a performance of a short comedy entitled *Juan soldado.* The Villista offi-

[77]Calzadíaz, II, 132–133.

cers were invited to the performance, which took place in the large salon of the parish house. They attended willingly as did Benito Retolaza, the parish priest, and the other priests of San Miguel.

The theme of the play was appropriate to the military occupation of the town and the youth who played the principal role of Juan Soldado interpolated remarks which he directed to the officers in the audience and gave rise to a good-natured banter that was the subject of conversation in San Miguel for several days. The incident served to cement the good relations between the citizenry and the soldiers.

Delgado Román mentioned in passing the performance of a circus for the town's schoolchildren, but because he had not thought about the function during the intervening forty-five years, he was unable to recall details or the exact date. The circus in itself was not of great importance, but it has been well documented by Mariano Azuela in his *Obras completas*.[78] The novelist, accompanied by José Becerra, spent at least one day in San Miguel during this period:

One day he [Becerra] invited me to visit Baquita. Baquita was an eighteen-year-old colonel who was garrisoned in the town of San Miguel el Alto—in Los Altos of Jalisco. Whether he was fighting off a swarm of wasps out of the brush or a swarm of bullets in combat, his cheerful laugh and his personal charm won over all those who knew him. He received us with great displays of attention and tried to entertain us in a suitable fashion, but since in the town there was only a wandering circus and it was Wednesday, in his youthful mind he decided to turn it into Sunday, and he ordered his soldiers to take all the children out of the school and all the bricklayers, carpenters, and laborers off their jobs. Between ranks of soldiers more than a hundred upright but frightened workmen were escorted to the bullring. A draft! And with the schoolchildren all the seats were filled up.[79]

The circus performance was marked by an exchange of verses and outlandish comments between the circus clown and José Becerra. The latter, Colonel Baca, and others shared the contents of a bottle which must have contributed to the gaiety of the occasion. When the function had finally ended and the visitors were leaving the bullring, Becerra demanded that the local band play the national anthem. It complied and, made patriotic by the music, Becerra pulled out his pistol and fired shots into the air, to the general consternation of the townspeople. In the confusion, one of the shots struck a small dog, who began to spout blood from a paw. Becerra picked up the wounded creature and rushed him to a pharmacy, where he attended to the wound. Animals were one of Becerra's weaknesses.

Delgado Román could not supply such detail. Azuela did so to provide an insight into the personality of José Becerra. By this time Azuela's comrade-in-arms was no longer a young man. Azuela was already forty-two but Becerra was at least fifty, which was hardly the age at which one left home to go off to the revolution. He does not seem to have possessed any specialized ability, such as Azuela's medical background, that would make him valuable to the Villistas. In his poetry Becerra constantly expressed his clearly romantic outlook on life, which was the motivation for his choosing the life of a revolutionary soldier. He was old enough to be the father of Manuel Caloca or Colonel Baca, whom he affectionately addressed as Baquita. The events of this visit to San Miguel form the basis of Azuela's short story "José María," which first appeared in the regional literary journal *Bandera de Provincias*.[80] Azuela has said nothing about San Miguel el Alto other than the exploits of Becerra and Baquita there. Apparently he returned to Lagos de Moreno after the circus performance, which took place on one of the three Wednesdays following May 5, that is, May 12, 19, or 26. General Leocadio Parra remained in charge of the Villista detachment in San Miguel.

[78]*O.C.*, III, 802–803.

[79]Ibid., p. 803.

[80]*Bandera de Provincias* (Guadalajara), I, 7 (August 15, 1929), pp. 3, 5.

Francisco Villa was having mixed success in maintaining his positions in the Bajío. Throughout May and into the first days of June the Carrancistas forced him to withdraw slowly toward León, in northwestern Guanajuato. He was still able to cause considerable mischief in the rear of Obregón's armies and succeeded in retaking the city of Guanajuato and also Silao, a rail junction, which broke Obregón's communications and supply lines with central Mexico. This threat was serious enough to cause concern among the Carrancistas, who felt that it was necessary to dispatch relief forces to reconnoiter the area and, if possible, to regain these points from the Villistas, who were commanded by Pánfilo Natera and Santos Bañuelos. From Guadalajara General Enrique Estrada sent out a column of two hundred fifty men under the command of Colonel Miguel Guerrero with instructions to reach the railway line between León and Lagos de Moreno and to distract the Villistas, who were still offering stiff resistance to Obregón's northward thrust. Colonel Guerrero and his men began their overland journey on horseback with this destination.

On June 5 Leocadio Parra and Manuel Caloca were warned of the approach of Colonel Guerrero and his column of cavalry. Although Parra and Caloca had three hundred men under their command and were superior numerically, they ordered the evacuation of San Miguel and withdrew to San Juan de los Lagos without offering resistance. The Carrancistas entered San Miguel and took up quarters. Delgado Román, with justifiable pride in the saddle animals that had long been available in the town, supplied another possible reason for the expedition to San Miguel. He noted the presence among the Carrancista soldiers of Colonel Silverio López, a native of San Miguel, who reportedly persuaded Miguel Guerrero to visit the town for the purpose of replenishing the mounts of his troops with some of the fine specimens available there. The local explanation, however, does not coincide with the tactical one.

In San Juan de los Lagos, Parra and Caloca

reported the arrival of Guerrero and his cavalry. They picked up reinforcement so that their ranks swelled to over a thousand men. They immediately returned to San Miguel, arriving either late in the evening of June 5 or early the next morning. The stage was set for a battle that well could have been taken from *Los de abajo*. The combatants on the Villista side are the same as Azuela's models and from their accounts, if not from the position of an eyewitness, the novelist puts together Demetrio's assault on the village in Chapters XVI and XVII of the Primera Parte of *Los de abajo*.

The first skirmishes occurred at approximately eight o'clock on Sunday morning, June 6. Some of the Carrancista soldiers went to the river bank on the northern edge of San Miguel to gather fodder for their horses. The approaching Villistas fired a few shots at them, more to frighten them than anything else. The Carrancistas dropped their fodder and ran. The main body of the Carrancistas heard the shots and thought that they marked the beginning of a general attack on the town. The signal was given to take up battle stations. Most of the Carrancistas took shelter behind the stonework surrounding the atrium of the parish church while Colonel Guerrero and a number of his men climbed into the church tower, which dominates the town and the surrounding terrain.

The Villistas reacted, dividing their men into columns that encircled the town on all sides, leaving no escape routes for the Carrancistas. They then began to tighten the ring around San Miguel. If the soldiers were concerned over the imminence of battle, the noncombatants were in a predicament. They had not been involved in armed conflict during the revolution and in the face of danger expected the worst. The ferocious reputation of the Carrancistas had preceded them, and the townpeople feared reprisals for having sheltered the Villistas should the Carrancistas emerge victorious. The residents of San Miguel responded to their religious convictions and called upon God, the Virgin Mary, and the Archangel Saint Michael, the patron saint of the town, to protect them from harm during the impending combat. The sympathies in San Miguel were with the Villistas, and Delgado Román reported that some residents had seen Saint Michael in the form of a youth mounted on a white horse who appeared among the ranks of General Parra's soldiers and gave them encouragement before the engagement got under way.

After the Villistas had assumed their battle posts, they began their assault on the center of the town. Because the Carrancistas held the church towers and strong surrounding positions, General Parra and his men could not advance along the town's streets and attack them directly. This difficulty was one that the attackers had faced many times before and it was not insurmountable. General Parra stationed a complement of soldiers on the northern edge of the town where they could distract Colonel Guerrero and his men in the church towers. Parra began to approach the church atrium by perforating the walls of the intervening houses. By using a *barretón*, a bar with a sharpened blade of metal at one end, he was able to cut through the soft adobe walls, opening in each case a hole through which he could lead his men. In this fashion he was able to keep them concealed from the view of the defending Carrancistas in their advantageous position.

Parra finally perforated through an entire city block of houses and his men reached the halls of the parish primary school for girls, but they found the door heavily barred. The maid of the parish house heard the voices of the invaders and ran off to warn Father Retolaza, who feared that they were the dreaded Carrancistas and was on the verge of hurrying into his chapel to pray for safety. When he finally learned that they were Villistas, he gave them permission to enter. The primary school gave them direct access to the atrium, where the defenders were crouched behind the protection of the stone railing, awaiting an attack from those Villistas who were still visible on the northern edge of San Miguel.

Delgado Román, who witnessed much of the combat, narrates what happened next in the center of the town:

Once they had all entered the main room of the school, general Parra then gave commands to his soldiers: "A number of soldiers will be stationed at each window. When I give you the order, then open all the windows at the same time and then (as they put it in vulgar speech) get them in your noose and wipe them out."

Then when the soldiers were in position, the general gave the order. They opened the swinging windows of the schoolroom and then, aiming their rifles, those Villista soldiers dislodged the Carrancistas who were stationed along the stone railing of the churchyard. Once they had been driven out of that position, discipline began to break down in the ranks of the Carrancistas. Because they saw they were set upon fiercely, they began to shout, "We are in trouble."[81]

In the meantime the Villistas had stationed two sharpshooters hidden in the foliage of a mesquite tree on the western edge of the town. From there they observed Colonel Guerrero in his church tower, moving back and forth, giving orders to his men. One of these sharpshooters aimed at Guerrero and fired a shot that wounded him and caused him to fall from the tower to the church roof below. It is not clear whether Guerrero was killed or merely wounded following the fall, but in any case he was incapacitated and could no longer direct his men. The unexpected volley from Parra's soldiers in the rear and the loss of Colonel Guerrero to the sharpshooters brought panic to the Carrancistas. Their buglers called them together so that they could begin an orderly retreat. Those who were still physically able mounted their horses and galloped away in headlong flight toward the east. The direction in this case was not important. The fugitives were concerned only with saving their lives. Delgado Román and

---

[81]From a taped interview with Delgado Román in San Miguel, July, 1960. See Appendix.

his father watched the slaughter and confusion through a crack in one of the windows of their home.

The Villista cavalry entered the center of San Miguel and set out in pursuit of the harassed enemy. The Carrancistas, some of whom had just managed to escape from one trap, shortly found themselves in another. On the outskirts of the town, the pursuing Villistas succeeded in driving them into a corral where another body of Villistas was ready and waiting. The Carrancistas were caught in fire from their adversaries on two sides and suffered heavy casualties. A very few managed to escape and they fled as best they could to the south along the road to Atotonilco. After these Carrancistas were killed or dispersed, Colonel Caloca and Colonel Baca returned in triumph to the center of the town. There, various of their followers had liquidated the few stragglers who had been left behind in the town plaza and the arcades that surrounded it.

Others climbed to the church towers and rang the bells in glee. The rank and file of the Villistas gathered in the churchyard below and demanded that the body of Colonel Guerrero be thrown down. He was seized by the arms and legs and tossed from the roof of the parish church to the pavement below. The bodies of several of his comrades followed. The towns-people, despite their general inclinations toward the Villistas, thoroughly disapproved of this treatment and felt that the victors should have shown respect to their defeated enemy, even in death. Following this gruesome incident there occurred a scene that has become a legend in San Miguel; it has also been reported by residents of other towns in Jalisco. Delgado Román narrates it:

> They picked up Guerrero and then, according to a number of persons, they say that General Parra stood at the feet of Guerrero when he was laid out there in the arcades. He stood looking at him and he said: "I look at you, my dead fellow, and I respect you."
> That was the sentence that General Parra supposedly uttered. There the story ended be-

cause we were left alone with the dead, and we were in fear for some time afterward.[82]

Martiniano Hernández Montero, another participant in the combat on the side of the Villistas, has reported essentially the same incident with only slight differences in detail:

> As a matter worth mentioning I shall say that a great number of dead bodies had remained on the flat roofs of the houses and in the church tower. These were thrown down from these elevated places when General Leocadio Parra was passing in front of the church. He saw a body that fell awkwardly and recognized that it was General Guerrero, a worthy fighter in the revolution, brave to the point of being reckless, who had been in command of the opposing forces, having been killed in the church tower. General Parra immediately got down off his horse and put his arms tightly around his friend and fallen comrade (since only the differences among leaders at the top level had divided us into two opposing camps), shouting to him in despair: "Miguelito!" Then he ordered the men to place him on the saddle of his horse so he could be taken to San Juan de los Lagos, where he was buried with all the honors corresponding to a general and a hero. . . .[83]

Colonel Guerrero, who was twenty-eight years of age at the time of his death, was a native of Baja California. For his bravery in fighting, his fellow soldiers dubbed him "The Tiger of Tijuana." Around 1957 his body was removed from Jalisco and taken to Baja California, where it was buried again with appropriate honors.

The battle in San Miguel lasted exactly three hours, ending at one-fifteen in the afternoon. General Parra then ordered that all the dead bodies be gathered up and buried. Soldiers and townspeople together engaged in the task and lined up the bodies in one of the arcades facing the town square. After this chore was completed, late in the afternoon of June 8 Parra ordered the evacuation of his one thousand troops and they all left, heading for San Juan de los Lagos.

[82]Ibid.
[83]Moreno, pp. 116-117.

Delgado Román expressed the feelings of the people of San Miguel when all had become quiet again:

> When the soldiers had all gone, the town was left, so to speak, as if Judas had dragged it around. Then a breeze came up, a strong one, and that wind whistled through the cracks in the windows, adding to the macabre spectacle presented by all those dead men stretched out in the arcades, men who were buried on the following day, all in a common grave because it was not possible to bury each one of them individually.

The victory for the Villistas was a single bright spot in their almost uninterrupted string of defeats that had begun in March in southern Jalisco and continued in Celaya in early April. Certainly the thrust of the Carrancista diversionary column was stopped, and its men were killed or dispersed. Despite the clear victory, it was not a significant one. San Miguel was small and far removed from the main lines of transportation, and it was of no strategic importance to either side. The Villistas, apparently realizing this, immediately pulled out of San Miguel. They returned to San Juan de los Lagos where they would be closer to their commander Julián Medina. His post as governor of Jalisco was becoming increasingly precarious as the forces of Álvaro Obregón and Manuel M. Diéguez advanced on Lagos de Moreno from the south.

The spirit of the battle in San Miguel is reminiscent of earlier battles of the revolution, in the verve of the Villistas, in the ingenuity of their leaders in battle, and the moral and material support provided by the townspeople. Without a doubt it served to raise considerably the morale of the Villista officers and soldiers of Jalisco who served under Leocadio Parra.

In his autobiographical notes, Mariano Azuela has made no reference to having been in San Miguel el Alto at the time of the battle. The details, however, resemble those of the early fight in *Los de abajo,* in which Demetrio Macías and his soldiers take a village in the canyon of the Río de Juchipila from the federales, in the device of perforating the adobe walls of the houses to avoid detection by the enemy, in the use of the church towers for observation and defense, and the throwing of the dead and wounded defenders from the roof to the church-yard below (Primera Parte, Chapters XVI through XVIII). During Azuela's tour of duty with the Villistas, up to this time they had not participated in battles of this nature, although the same tactics had been employed elsewhere earlier in the revolution. Clotilde Evelia Quirarte has recorded similar procedures in an attack by a revolutionary group on Nochistlán in July, 1913.[84] The only real battles of the Villistas when Azuela possibly was present had been their loss of Guadalajara to the Carrancistas of General Diéguez on January 18 and their albazo on January 30. On each of these occasions the battle situations had differed considerably from what happened in San Miguel.

Azuela was with Parra, Caloca, and their associates soon after the fighting in San Miguel. If he did not witness the fighting, he was able to hear the vivid details from those who routed the Carrancistas there.

The overall situation of the Villistas in Jalisco began to worsen rapidly. On June 5 Villa was forced to surrender León, Guanajuato, to the Carrancistas. Álvaro Obregón, the commanding general of the latter, lost an arm in an engagement at the hacienda Santa Ana two days previously. Villa fell back to Lagos de Moreno, but he was unable to hold that town. Early in the morning on June 11 the Villistas exchanged shots with the approaching Carrancista cavalry of General Cesáreo Castro but made no attempt at a serious defense. Castro's men occupied the town at 11:00 A.M. Later in the day the main body of troops under Benjamín Hill entered Lagos.

Villa's armies, who were retreating along the railroad line in northeastern Jalisco, no longer held any major town in the state. He withdrew his forces northward to the city of Aguascalientes. As a result of this move, Julián Medina lost a base from which to operate the government of Jalisco as its chief executive.

[84] Quirarte, pp. 178-179.

The Rift: June, 1915

Inevitably there had to be a split between Julián Medina and Francisco Villa. It seems to have come about at the time when Villa and Medina had to evacuate Lagos de Moreno. There was a difference of opinion between the two men, determined by the concept that each one held of his role in the revolution. Basically Medina was devoted to Jalisco, his native state, of which he was the governor. His entire revolutionary career had taken place there, he knew its terrain and its people, and he felt an obligation to remain among them. Villa felt no such obligation, and he operated upon a much broader military base. Military necessity forced him to leave Jalisco, which had received him enthusiastically, but he was not tied to the state. He would retreat to the north, continuing to harass the Carrancistas there and in the center of Mexico.

In Aguascalientes Villa and Medina discussed what their next moves would be. There is more than one version of this conversation and the words that gave rise to Medina's forthcoming campaign. Martiniano Hernández, one of Medina's subordinates, claims to have been present at a meeting between Villa and Medina, where Villa asked his subordinate to collect his scattered troops in Jalisco and accompany them to Torreón in northern Mexico, where they would continue to participate in the campaign against the Carrancistas. Medina objected strenuously to this suggestion, claiming that as governor of Jalisco he should be the one to direct the Villista campaign in that state. Villa reacted as he frequently did when someone crossed him. He became angry but could not enforce his wishes. Medina got his way and remained as governor, but Villa cut off all military aid to him.[85] Thus Medina was strictly on his own thereafter.

[85]Moreno, p. 87.

The *Boletín Militar,* a highly partisan Carrancista newspaper published by adherents of Governor Aguirre Berlanga in Guadalajara, certainly did not wish to present Medina in anything approaching a favorable light. Its writers made the most of the differences between Villa and Medina:

The coward Julián Medina practically sentenced to death by Arango.

In Aguascalientes it is publicly and widely known that Villa commanded Julián Medina, accepting the wish of the latter to return to his home state to operate by treachery since he would be permitted to do such a thing, but with the condition that in order to obtain [Villa's] consent, he had to promise to come and take Guadalajara. After that he must continue as far as Manzanillo, which he must reach and then return again to Guadalajara, burning bridges and tearing up the railroad track.

The price: his life. He must never again appear before Villa if he did not want to be shot, if he did not report having carried out the orders of the bandit.

This is simply sentencing Medina to death, because it seems to us that it is going to take a lot of effort—certainly he won't succeed—to satisfy the destruction and absurd whims of Villa.

Those . . . are still hard to reach![86]

Mariano Azuela has certainly been more charitable than either Martiniano Hernández or the nameless Carrancista of the *Boleín Militar.* He was well aware of the friction between Villa and Medina: "General Medina certainly did not feel comfortable in his relations with Villa and promised him that he would retake Guadalajara with his handful of men."[87] Azuela did note,

[86]*Boletín Militar,* Tomo III, Núm. 203 (Saturday, July 3, 1915), p. 6.
[87]*O.C.,* III, 1190.

however, that Villa supplied weapons and ammunition for Medina's projected thrust into central Jalisco. Each of the three writers just noted has contributed something to the total picture of the predicament that confronted Julián Medina. His was far from an enviable position, since he had to deal with Francisco Villa on the one hand and the Carrancistas of Jalisco on the other.

In Aguascalientes he gathered his men together in order to plan and organize them for an operation directed against Guadalajara. He had at his disposal the thousand or more men who participated in the action at San Miguel el Alto. To them he added another thousand drawn from other garrisons and those who were with him during his seven weeks as governor at Lagos. In all he had over two thousand men under his command.

Some degree of planning should have gone into the forthcoming operation. In the event that the campaign turned out to be a long one, Medina would be completely cut off from the main Villista armies, who could not be any closer than Aguascalientes or the southern reaches of the state of Zacatecas. From them he would be unable to obtain supplies for his men. If Medina expected to achieve any real or lasting success, he had to take Guadalajara quickly. Otherwise he would have to feed and supply his men from the land where they operated, and they would be dependent for ammunition on what they could wrest from the Carrancistas. Under these circumstances the use of heavy weapons would be limited or perhaps absent entirely. The only means of transportation was by horseback and weapons were restricted to those that the men could carry by this mode of transport. There were no rail lines along the route between Aguascalientes and Guadalajara.

Fortunately the Medinistas could still count upon a sympathetic reception from the residents of Guadalajara, if they were able to gain control of the city. The people of the smaller towns and the ranchos of northeastern Jalisco definitely preferred the Villistas to the Carrancistas, who, because of their anticlerical attitudes and ac-

tivities and their reputation for growing wealthy at the expense of the areas that they controlled, were certainly feared if not actually hated by the residents of widespread sections of Jalisco. Consul Will B. Davis has confirmed the pro-Villista inclination of the jaliscienses and quotes from a letter that he received from an unnamed North American: "The Villistas are well liked by the common people, and I have personally seen a peone [*sic*] go hungry to give his dinner to some Villista soldier. . . . When it comes to wanton destruction, none of them compare with the Carrancistas."[88] Medina counted on assistance of this type in carrying out his move on Guadalajara, with the expectation that the civilian population would supply him not only with food but also information. The series of defeats suffered by the Villistas up to this point had had but slight effect upon their continuing support from the population at large.

Medina's scheme was a daring one, conceived in the tradition of Villa's dazzling cavalry moves of the early period of the revolution and entirely appropriate to Medina's own concept of battle, much like the daring action of January 30 when he took the Carrancistas by surprise in their barracks in Guadalajara. In June he counted on the Carrancistas' maintaining only a minimum garrison in Guadalajara. They had committed all available troops to the Bajío region to support Álvaro Obregón in his campaign against the main forces of Villa. Outside Guadalajara there were only scattered groups of nominal Carrancistas and bands of unaffiliated irregulars, but large areas still remained under the control of chieftains who considered themselves Villistas, for example, Julián del Real in Ameca and Pedro Zamora farther south in the Sierra de Tapalpa. Medina did not indicate whether he planned to cooperate with those men.

Mariano Azuela felt an obligation to Medina and his colleagues, and he also preferred to remain in Jalisco. There was no way by which he could return to Lagos de Moreno and resume his prerevolution manner of life.

[88]Davis, p. 206.

As a doctor he was well known there, and his commitment to the Villista faction following the convention of Aguascalientes was a matter of common knowledge. To go back to Lagos would be to place himself in the jaws of the lion. The Carrancistas were notoriously vindictive toward their enemies, and the people of Jalisco felt that they were at the same time uncharitable toward neutrals in the conflict. Azuela, then, stayed with Medina. Perhaps he really had nowhere else to go. Thus he played a role in Medina's advance on Guadalajara and at the same time began intensive composition of *Los de abajo*. He turned from contemplation of the novel to actual writing.

Medina made no changes in his personnel. He would be accompanied by the same soldiers who had served him faithfully in his campaigns for at least two years, ever since their first slaughter of the Huertistas at their barracks in Hostotipaquillo. His right-hand men were General Leocadio Parra and Colonel Manuel Caloca, each in charge of a column in the advance. Not many others can still be identified. One was Colonel Ricardo Macháin, whose name does not occur frequently in the annals of the period; another is Martiniano Hernández, who has reported on several of his military experiences with Medina.

The prospect of renewed action stirred up considerable enthusiasm on the part of Medina and his followers when they set out on this adventure. Nevertheless the whole enterprise shows signs of having been put together in extreme haste, with little real thought being given to possible alternatives should the expedition fail to achieve its aims. One wonders also how much thought had been devoted to the tactics to be employed once the Villistas reached Guadalajara; how they would go about taking the city and how they would hold it should they succeed in capturing it. It appears also that the two thousand men were provided with very little ammunition and almost no provisions. In view of Lagos's having fallen to the Carrancistas on June 11 and Medina's planning to be at the gates of Guadalajara on June 15, not more than

a few days could have been given to planning and preparation for his move to recuperate the state capital. The nature of the scheme and the way in which Medina went about making ready betray the impulsive motivation behind it. The preparations were makeshift and were a portent of the disaster that awaited the Villistas in Jalisco.

The route to be followed lay straight through the heart of Los Altos. Cutting to the southwest of Aguascalientes, the column struck the old route of the stagecoaches, following it from San Juan de los Lagos through Jalostotitlán, Valle de Guadalupe, and Tepatitlán. These were old towns, attractive in many ways and relatively isolated in those days, preserving old manners and attitudes. The Mexican revolution had paid them little attention, and they were still practically untouched by its conflicts and battles. The warring factions had settled their differences elsewhere, and each town had remained for the most part self-sufficient in questions of economics, food, and self-defense.

June, 1915, was no time for an unaccompanied traveler to undertake a journey through this section of Jalisco. There was no authority of any kind in the rural areas. These were still overrun with stragglers, many of whom had been soldiers cut off from Villa's army who were working their way northward along back roads, hoping to reach their homes in northern Mexico. At the same time, armed bands of irregulars prowled the roads. They were not driven by political convictions or affiliations but merely sought to rob the unprotected traveler, seeking money, pack animals, mounts, and even food. In those times one still traveled by horseback or by burro, and goods and freight hauled into Los Altos must be carried by the traditional *arrieros* and their pack trains. They were able to keep business operating in the towns but were frequent victims of robberies on the roads. The Carrancistas were hardly in evidence and maintained no regular force in the area. Medina and his men need have no fear of Carrancistas, irregulars, stragglers, or bandits. In Los Altos they outnumbered by far all these people combined.

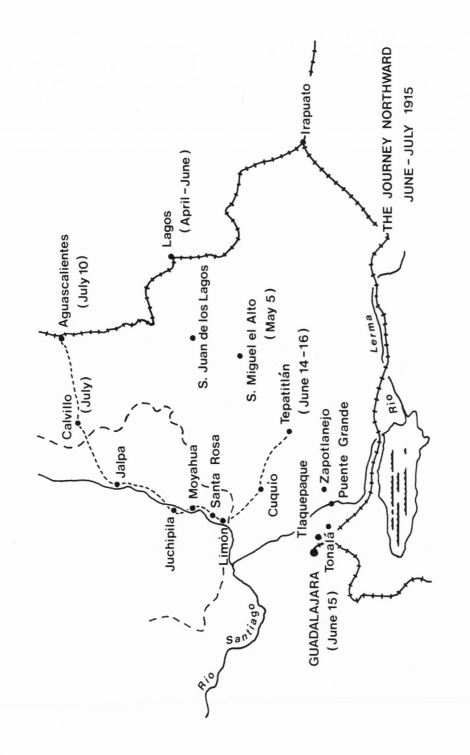

THE JOURNEY NORTHWARD
JUNE – JULY 1915

Irapuato

Lagos
(April – June)

Aguascalientes
(July 10)

S. Juan de los Lagos

S. Miguel el Alto
(May 5)

Tepatitlán
(June 14 – 16)

Calvillo
(July)

Zapotlanejo
Puente Grande

Jalpa

Moyahua
Santa Rosa

Cuquio

Tlaquepaque

Juchipila

Limón

GUADALAJARA
(June 15)

Tonalá

Lerma

Rio

Rio Santiago

Rio

In the center of Los Altos the columns of Medina approached Tepatitlán, the largest town between Lagos and Guadalajara. It lay in an attractive setting, on a long slope that trailed off to the south, a town of whitewashed walls, red roofs, and green foliage placed atop the reddish earth that underlies much of Los Altos. The towers of Tepatitlán's four churches dominated the town, thrusting through the mass of buildings and foliage into the sky above. Tepatitlán was a convenient place to pause. The people were congenial, and the town offered more conveniences than its neighbors, including a small hospital. Medina's troops rode up the narrow cobblestone streets to the town's main plaza. On one side stood the eighteenth-century parish church with its twin towers, still unfinished. In the center was the ornate bandstand with its fancy ironwork, a leftover from the epoch of Porfirio Díaz. Julián Medina dismounted and entered the *presidencia municipal,* the equivalent of the city hall, passed through the arcades beneath, and proceeded to the second-story balcony. There, cigar in hand, he addressed his troops and the townspeople.[89]

Following the brief pause in Tepatitlán, the column continued on to the southwest in the direction of Guadalajara. Azuela did not continue the march, however. Arrangements were made for him to remain behind, with the idea that he would be on hand to care for the wounded at the hospital in Tepatitlán. The Medinistas expected to encounter opposition from the Carrancistas as they approached Guadalajara, fifty miles away. They were especially concerned about the possibility of a clash with the enemy at Puente Grande, where they would have to cross the Río Santiago on the old stone bridge built in colonial times. The river lay between them and their goal, and there was no other bridge on their direct route.

Azuela could well have continued on toward Guadalajara with the main body of the Medinistas if their goal was to take that city and if they really had expectations of capturing it. Certain-

ly it possessed medical facilities infinitely superior to those available in Tepatitlán and much closer to the scene of the expected battle. Were such the case, there would be no point to Azuela's waiting in Tepatitlán. He would have proceeded with the rest of the troops. One suspects that Medina had doubts concerning his ability to take Guadalajara, despite the sizable army that he had assembled for the attempt. The doubts, however, may have been the property of Azuela, who, discouraged by the decline of the fortunes of Villa and Medina, did not believe that the latter was capable of retaking Guadalajara and was being cautious so as not to expose himself to inordinate danger. In any case, Azuela and Medina did not see one another again during the years of the revolution.

In Tepatitlán Mariano Azuela met a priest, apparently a Father Varela, whom he had known in Lagos de Moreno in his youth. The priest was quite solicitous concerning Azuela's safety, because the people of Tepatitlán had learned that he was a doctor for Medina's soldiers, and a report was circulating that a party of Carrancistas was approaching from the direction of San Juan de los Lagos. The doctor did not know how reliable the report was. The father offered to hide him on his nearby ranch, but Azuela was reluctant to leave the town for fear that he would not be on hand should wounded men in need of attention be brought in during his absence. Azuela decided to accept his invitation when the priest promised to notify him as soon as his medical services were required. He dismissed his two assistants, who disguised themselves as mule drivers and left for Encarnación de Díaz, a town in northern Jalisco just south of Aguascalientes. Azuela then proceeded to the ranch.

The brief interlude in Tepatitlán and vicinity was significant literarily. While waiting at the ranch, Azuela met several rural types of interest, but more unusual was the setting: "It was a poor adobe house with three *tepozán* trees in the patio, on a broad plain where not even shrubs grew."[90] It is the scene of Chapter X of

---

[89]Reported orally by the late J. de J. Reynoso, parish priest of Tepatitlán, in August, 1938.

[90]*O.C.,* III, 1086.

the Segunda Parte of *Los de abajo*, where Demetrio Macías stopped to spend the night before moving on to Tepatitlán. Azuela filled out the scene with more detail in the novel: "Demetrio went out with Camila to take a walk through the encampment. The level plain, with golden-colored stubble, completely shorn of shrubs, stretched away in its immense desolation. The three big ash trees in front of the poor houses seemed almost a miracle, these trees with their greenish black tops, round and waving, their abundant foliage that flowed down until it nearly kissed the earth."[91]

The stay on the ranch provided Azuela with further material which he retained for use many years later. In the notes that shed light upon various of his works, he has commented: "During the period of our recent revolution I had the opportunity to become acquainted at first hand with where the famous guerrilla leader from Jalisco Antonio Rojas was born and grew up, a man well known for his cruelty and his capacity for plunder."[92] This visit provided Azuela the setting for "El hombre masa," one of the three short pieces that make up the volume *Precursores*.[93] There he refers to El Buey, a rancho at the foot of the Cerro Gordo. This landmark, which is clearly visible from Tepatitlán and many points of Los Altos, has long been a refuge for *guerrilleros*, from the savage *indios chichimecas* of the sixteenth century to the dissident *cristeros* of the 1920s. Azuela shook the hand of Mónico Velázquez, known as El Güero Mónico (*güero* 'blond'), a little old man who, with a few comrades who possessed intimate knowledge of the terrain, was able to hold off a superior number of *federales* on many occasions.

Tepatitlán figures prominently in *Los de abajo*, especially in the Segunda Parte. The town is presented attractively, both as to its appearance and to its people. Azuela elsewhere refers in passing to his having completed two more chapters of *Los de abajo* there.[94] Again he

must be referring to notes for two chapters, for his stay in the vicinity hardly lasted more than three or four days at the most. Neither does the sequence of events of the novel permit the writing of two chapters at this juncture. Certainly Azuela did not use in the novel all the notes that he made during his stay there. Many of them did not see the light of day until years later when he told his readers how he came to write *Los de abajo*.[95]

Detailed accounts of life in Los Altos have never been particularly common and are even more scarce in the period of the revolution. By mere coincidence, I have been able to consult a chapter of personal reminiscences which coincides remarkably with the passage of Julián Medina through Los Altos and the stay of Mariano Azuela in Tepatitlán. Ana María Cornejo y Mejía, a resident of Teocaltiche, decided to leave her home to seek refuge in Mexico City not long after Villa's defeat at Trinidad in El Bajío.[96] Because of the danger of attack and robbery during those unsettled times, she traveled by a roundabout route, from Teocaltiche to Yahualica, Cañadas, Mexticacán, Acacico, and finally to Tepatitlán. After resting there for several days and being treated by a doctor (who was not Dr. Mariano Azuela), she started out again for Guadalajara.

Miss Cornejo, who was accompanied by two of her servants, followed the route to Guadalajara taken by Julián Medina and his two thousand men and apparently stayed close on their heels. As she and her servants approached Zapotlanejo, twenty-seven miles to the southwest of Tepatitlán, they were warned that a large number of revolutionary soldiers was in the vicinity and that they should proceed with caution. When they arrived at the edge of the town, they heard firing that indicated that a battle was in progress. At that very moment revolutionaries were attacking the town. She was given shelter in one of the first houses on the eastern edge of the village and waited there

[91] *Los de abajo* (Mexico, 1958), p. 105.
[92] *O.C.*, III, 1109.
[93] "El hombre masa," in *Precursores*, pp. 111-125.
[94] *O.C.*, III, 1268.

[95] Ibid., pp. 1077-1099.
[96] "Un viaje en el año de 1915." This typed manuscript of 18 pages was written in 1963.

The bridge at Puente Grande

while the battle continued. The few police protecting Zapotlanejo tried to prevent the attackers from entering, but they were outnumbered and overcome. The firing finally died down, and soon columns of smoke rose over the center of the town from the government offices and business establishments that had been set afire. From the timing of the trip and from these and other details, the attacking soldiers can be identified as those of Medina. Martiniano Hernández Montero, who was with Medina, has reported "light skirmishes with the enemy in Zapotlanejo."[97] Later Miss Cornejo visited the center of Zapotlanejo where she viewed the charred ruins and the looted stores, then continued on to Guadalajara the next day after resting overnight.[98]

The anticipated battle at Puente Grande did not materialize. The Medinistas encountered no opposition there and easily passed over the old stone bridge across the river choked with water lilies.

Miss Cornejo was again on the heels of the revolutionaries. She continued on to Arroyo de Enmedio where she found that they had just left, taking with them all the horses they could find as well as any other objects of value. Miss Cornejo prudently remained there for several hours, then traveled on to San Pedro Tlaquepaque by way of little-traveled roads and was able to avoid further contact with the traveling band of soldiers. Luis Páez Brotchie in telling of Medina's approach to Guadalajara has recorded that the general called Governor Aguirre Berlanga in Guadalajara by telephone from Arroyo de Enmedio, demanding of him the surrender of the capital and threatening to take the city by force if he did not cede it willingly. Aguirre Berlanga, of course, refused the demand.[99]

The reason behind this telephone conversation is hard to determine. By calling Aguirre Berlanga, Medina tipped his hand and thereby removed entirely any advantage that he might have obtained through the element of surprise. General Enrique Estrada, the Carrancista military commander of Guadalajara, made ready to resist Medina. If his telephone conversation had been pure bravado for the purpose of bluffing the Carrancista defenders, it had failed.

Hernández Montero complained that Medina's soldiers were short of ammunition. They stopped on the hill overlooking the town of Tonalá, where they distributed it, allotting five shells to each man.[100] The Medinistas arrived outside Guadalajara on the morning of June 15, 1915. There they organized the two thousand men into three columns. One under Julián Medina himself planned to attack from the direction of Zapopan on the northwest. Another, headed by Leocadio Parra, made ready to strike from the southeast from the direction of San Pedro Tlaquepaque, and a third, under the command of Manuel Caloca, prepared to approach from the park of Agua Azul on the southern fringes of Guadalajara.[101] This was exclusively an engagement that involved Medinistas against Carrancistas. There is no evidence that Julián del Real and Pedro Zamora took any part in this action, as Jesús Romero Flores has asserted.[102]

The advance on the city did not begin until afternoon. Medina's battle style resembled closely that of Villa. In open terrain he relied heavily upon dashing cavalry charges. Azuela in *Los de abajo* constantly mentions the superior horsemanship of the *serranos*. His other effective device had been that of surprise, which he used effectively in the early morning attack of January 30, but he had already disposed of it here. The attackers were able to reach the fringe of the city without difficulty. Initially they

[97] In Moreno, p. 117.

[98] See also Emilio Guevara, *Historia particular de Zapotlanejo* (Guadalajara, 1919), p. 26.

[99] Páez Brotchie, II, 141.

[100] Moreno, p. 117.

[101] Hernández Montero indicates that General Pedro Caloca commanded one of these columns, but other reports of the battle do not confirm his presence.

[102] Jesús Romero Flores, *Anales históricos de la revolución mexicana* (3 vols.; Mexico, 1959), I, 394.

achieved some success on the south and east. The Carrancistas at first did not present an effective resistance; in fact, they were probably outnumbered. General Enrique Estrada then took personal charge of the operation and organized his defenders, who not only stiffened their resistance but put together and executed a counter attack. This was directed against the Medinistas on the south and east, where the soldiers of Parra and Caloca carried the brunt of the fighting. Hernández Montero has noted the impressive casualties suffered by the men of Caloca's command.[103] For some time Medina's men had not participated in fighting as heavy as this and apparently were unable to penetrate the enemy's lines.

The decisive fighting took place at the Garita de San Pedro, the tax-collecting station on the southeastern edge of Guadalajara, near what is now the intersection of Calle de Analco with Avenida Porfirio Díaz, well within the built-up area of present-day Guadalajara but on the outskirts of the city in 1915. The Carrancista counterattack cut off the Medinistas at this point.[104] The defenders took advantage of the separate emplacement of the forces of Parra and Caloca, and General Estrada was able to divide them. By this move he was able to inflict heavy casualties on the attackers, push them back, and disorganize them. That was the beginning of the end for the Medinistas. By late afternoon the battle had resolved itself into isolated skirmishes in various suburbs and to all intents it had ended.

Consul Davis sums up the situation:

On the afternoon of the 15th of this month,

General Medina, former Constitucionalista Governor of this State, with a force of some 2,000 soldiers attempted to retake Guadalajara, beginning the attack at 3 P.M., and continuing a sort of running fight until 5 o'clock.

The Medina forces did not come nearer than the suburbs of the city—they were repulsed by the Constitucionalista forces.[105]

When it appeared that the battle was lost, Medina's men retreated westward to the area of Tequila and Ameca, where they rested and regrouped. The Carrancistas pursued the remnants of the columns of Parra and Caloca across the barranca to the east of the city and dispersed them. Many of these stragglers, including Leocadio Parra himself, made their way to western Jalisco where they rejoined Medina's main forces. They continued to operate there, centered around Tequila and Hostotipaquillo, but never again were they able to threaten Guadalajara seriously.

The Carrancistas were jubilant and gloated over Medina's defeat in the *Boletín Militar:*

Guadalajara has fallen!
According to a sheet published by a scoundrel in this land of the tapatíos, the city of Guadalajara has been in the hands of Jolián [*sic*] ever since this coward tried to visit us, being received in a suitable fashion by our brave soldiers.
The handbill says that Jolián was received here with bouquets and cheers and that immediately he set about to impose order.
You couldn't even see Jolián's dust after the first shots fired by the Carrancista rifles.[106]

---

[103]Moreno, p. 117.
[104]Páez Brotchie, II, 142.

[105]Davis, p. 142.
[106]*Boletín Militar*, Tomo III, Núm. 201 (Thursday, July 1, 1915), p. 7.

Flight: June–July, 1915

Colonel Manuel Caloca was wounded in the action. Mariano Azuela has declared that he was wounded at San Pedro Tlaquepaque, perhaps during the withdrawal from Guadalajara. The afflicted man was forced to retreat with the other stragglers from the dispersed Medinistas on the southeastern approaches to Guadalajara, through the rugged hills around Tonalá and then across the Río Santiago. With his painful wound Caloca was forced to travel over rough terrain. Furthermore, he had to keep on the move in order to stay out of the clutches of the Carrancistas who were on his heels. The joyless state of Manuel Caloca was comparable to that of many of Medina's followers.

The journey to Tepatitlán took at least one full day. Caloca arrived accompanied by eighty men. Immediately a messenger was dispatched to the rancho where Mariano Azuela was waiting. The messenger arrived there in the evening. It could have been no sooner than June 16, the day following the battle, but it might have been even June 17, another day later. Azuela hurried to Tepatitlán, where he examined Caloca. In his memoirs and reminiscences he has given no information concerning the nature of the wound. It must have been fairly serious, for Azuela determined that he could not treat it adequately in the little hospital in Tepatitlán. He proceeded to give the wound preliminary treatment and then he and Caloca considered what they should do. Their decision was to leave Tepatitlán. Either the wound was such that it required treatment as soon as the patient could reach adequate medical facilities, or Carrancista troops were approaching and presented a threat of capture. In view of the desperate military situation of the Villistas, the latter factor seems to have carried weight in deciding what to do.

Manuel Caloca could not walk; neither could he ride normally on horseback. Probably the wound was in his leg, as was Demetrio's in the early chapters of *Los de abajo*. In order to travel at all, Caloca would have to be carried on some kind of litter or stretcher. Among the eighty or so men who had slipped away from the Carrancistas outside Guadalajara was a core of expert cavalrymen who were intensely loyal to him. It was their concern that he should be transported with care and as comfortably as possible under the circumstances. The Caloca family had won widespread respect and sympathy throughout southern Zacatecas, and those feelings in that area extended to its youngest member, whom Mariano Azuela characterized as "a youth of fifteen years who had earned his rank of colonel as other he-men had earned theirs."[107]

Without delay the column got under way from Tepatitlán. Its purpose was to remove Caloca to safety where he could be operated upon. As a destination Guadalajara was clearly out of the question because it was in Carrancista hands. The next largest city within reasonable traveling distance was Aguascalientes, which was the residence of the Ávila family, whose members were related to Caloca. Among their numbers were surgeons who could operate on him. Fortunately the city was still under the control of Villa. A direct route would be extremely risky because Carrancista columns had begun to fan out westward from Lagos de Moreno and other points along the central railway line that was in their hands. Caloca and his men elected for a westerly route that would keep them away from well-traveled roads and take them through communities where Villistas friendly to his family still held most of the territory. It was longer, more circuitous, and would take much more time, but it would avoid major contact with the Carrancistas.

[107] *O.C.*, III, 1268. A contemporary photograph of Julián Medina and a number of colleagues in arms shows Caloca in civilian attire (Monterde, p. 169).

The next few weeks were the making of the real *Los de abajo*. Despite the adversity of recent weeks, the novel had become foremost in Azuela's mind. He had begun to devote much more attention and time to it since Villismo went into its decline than he ever did during the period in Guadalajara when it was still a force to be reckoned with in the future of Jalisco and Mexico. The novelist's note-taking and the formation of characters for the work had speeded up in recent weeks. The changing nature of the revolution accounted in large part for the intensification of the writing process. As long as Azuela was with Medina's government and was amply protected by an effective military power, he could feel some sense of security. He had been able to extricate himself from a difficult situation in Lagos de Moreno by electing to serve with Julián Medina. In June, he found himself in the same dilemma from which he had tried to escape back in October, 1914. The Villista revolutionaries in Jalisco, deprived of the military support of Francisco Villa, were fragmented and could be hunted down, as the noncombatants of the revolution had always been. Azuela was aware of the increasing enmity and bitterness among the contending factions and the intensification of the hatred that had arisen between one Mexican and another. Azuela would continue to experience a conflict of this type during the weeks and months to come. The pages of *Los de abajo* will reflect it faithfully.

Little of Azuela's earlier period in Irapuato and then in Guadalajara has been carried directly into the pages of *Los de abajo*. From that period, however, derive various of the minor characters of the novel, for example, the companions of Demetrio, and perhaps some of the features of Demetrio himself for which Azuela had taken Julián Medina as a model. Hereafter Manuel Caloca was Azuela's major concern both in life and in the unfolding novel. The remainder of Azuela's days as a Villista in Jalisco have been poorly documented or not at all, for the people with whom he was traveling, while they were

admirable grist for Azuela's literary mill, were unknown to compilers of histories of the period. In his reminiscences Azuela has thoughtfully given his readers a view of these people and his experiences with them.

Azuela has never stated when the band pulled out of Tepatitlán or under what circumstances. Their first destination was Cuquío, a village mentioned frequently in *Los de abajo,* which was only twenty-five miles away in a straight line to the northwest. The first few miles of the journey were over the relatively level terrain of the plateau of Los Altos, but then as they moved westward it began to be more broken until they came upon a formidable barrier, the barranca of the Río Verde. At its confluence with the Río Santiago forty miles downstream, its canyon is all of eighteen hundred feet deep, but here it could not have been more than half that. Even so, it had to be traversed with the aid of guides, for there were no well-defined roads that crossed it, only trails that could be traversed by horseback or afoot, and then with the assistance of guides who were familiar with every inch of the terrain. It would be necessary to carry Manuel Caloca across on a litter.

There was little time to contemplate the awesome scenery. Caloca was lowered down the precipitous walls of the canyon, slowly and gently in order not to cause him excessive pain and discomfort. At the bottom he was eased across the river, whose waters fortunately were not high, for in mid-June the summer rains had scarcely begun. It was warm on the floor of the canyon, where there was no wind and the lower altitude was perceptible in the temperature and the lush vegetation. Then they had to begin the laborious ascent up the opposite canyon wall. It was a painstaking, slow process to lift Caloca up the rough path foot by foot. The horses also found the climbing tough, but finally the task was completed. No Carrancistas had penetrated into this corner of Los Altos, and it was possible to accomplish the crossing without interference. As far as their travel was concerned, this was the most rugged country that Caloca and Mariano Azuela would have to cross. It seems to have made little impression on the novelist. It is not reflected in *Los de abajo* nor in his non-novelistic comments. It is a bit hard to imagine Camila and La Pintada making the crossing in *Los de abajo* without some appropriate comment concerning its difficulty.

On the northwestern side, *la otra banda,* as it is called locally, the travelers came out on an extensive plain. The level country was welcome because the wounded men could travel much more comfortably. As they moved toward Cuquío, the land began to rise slightly, and the fields were fairly free of stones and planted with wheat. The group could not travel much farther in one day, considering the slow pace made necessary by the concern for Caloca. Although it is an old town with roots deep in the colonial period, Cuquío is little more than a village. An undistinguished church with a single slender spire dominates the low adobe buildings of the settlement. Cuquío lay on the route followed by Dr. Azuela and he certainly must have stopped there. The town figures in *Los de abajo,* but the novelist goes into no details. When Demetrio and his men are there, Azuela is more concerned with the conduct of La Pintada and how Demetrio will finally manage to get rid of her.

At an earlier period in Mexican history, Cuquío was a point of transit for another figure who had just suffered a humiliating defeat. In January, 1811, the royalists under Viceroy Calleja threshed the insurgents of Father Miguel Hidalgo at the bridge across the Río Calderón on the main road between Tepatitlán and Zapotlanejo. Father Hidalgo had made arrangements to retreat to northern Mexico in the event of a defeat at Calderón, so he took a direct route, leading his army across the barranca of the Río Verde, in some disorder, and then proceeded to Cuquío, where he arrived at night. As he passed by the village church, he observed that services were going on inside. When he stopped to make inquiry of a bystander, he was told that the townspeople, who had learned of the defeat of his army, had gathered together to pray for his safety.[108] Cuquío has had few such historic moments.

After Caloca and his escort had passed Cuquío, they veered to the north. This section of Jalisco was still relatively free of Carrancistas. Soldiers of Villista affiliation still held the northern approach to the Puente del Arcediano in the barranca of the Río Santiago just north of Guadalajara, and the Carrancisas found it hard to penetrate into deep canyons of the area to the north of the river. As Caloca moved northward, he approached the country where he and his family were known and respected and, fortunately for him, forces loyal to Francisco Villa were still the dominant faction there. In his mind at least, Caloca could rest more easily, knowing that the danger of attack was diminishing. His wound, however, was painful, but Azuela treated it with the means he had at hand. Still, the group could not travel very fast. Although the men stopped to rest and spend the night at various points, the novelist has not identified these places.

Beyond Cuquío the plain continued to rise gradually. At its northern edge is a range of low mountains that marks the political boundary between Jalisco and Zacatecas. Caloca's party ascended it, then moved down the northern slope of a chain of hills. But the terrain in itself was not significant. It became so only as the men neared El Limón. It consisted of a dozen houses or so, scattered over rolling land nestled among jumbled mountains. These were humble farmhouses, of adobe or stone walls, usually the latter, and with thatched roofs that betrayed the poverty of those who lived in them. Fences made of boulders neatly piled in lines five or six feet high swept up the slopes until the latter became too steep for cultivation. To the south and east were high hills, mountains perhaps, with rocky slopes in the upper reaches and covered with low trees. El Limón itself is on slightly rolling terrain, neither level nor broken. Its few houses were not placed closely together. One

[108]Pedro Garcia, *Con el cura Hidalgo en la Guerra de Independencia* (Mexico, 1948), pp. 149–150.

would be hard put to determine the center of El Limón, for the community has no square and no formal arrangement of streets. Its houses are concealed, blending in with the stone fences and hidden by occasional clumps of trees. Neither does it have a church or anything in the nature of a store or a business establishment. This was strictly a rancho, in Mexican terminology, and the people who lived here were rural in manners and attitudes. This place was poor and remote. Its lack of wealth and solidity of construction were in sharp contrast with the communities that Azuela had just seen.

In the winter and spring El Limón is rocky, dusty, and bleak. In the summer months it is fairly attractive, for there is more vegetation, and it is lush and green. Thus it was when I saw it in July, 1966. Except for the paved highway that curves down the hillside and loops through the settlement, it has changed little since Mariano Azuela passed through in June, 1915. It may now have fewer than the 176 inhabitants attributed to it by the Mexican census of 1921.[109]

This is the spot that Mariano Azuela chose to be the home of Demetrio Macías. One might say that he had Demetrio with him in El Limón, for he was accompanying Manuel Caloca, who here was obviously his model for the protagonist for the novel. From his presence there Azuela was able to determine the principal character and the physical setting for the opening of *Los de abajo*. He could not have written the initial chapter of the novel before his arrival at El Limón. He has stated in his recollections that he was in the habit of taking notes during his travels with Caloca. Certainly he wrote down notes concerning El Limón, either while he paused there or immediately afterward, and possibly he even began tentative composition of the novel at that time.

Azuela has indicated that there have been many Demetrios in Mexico. Certainly he felt

that such was the case at the beginning of the revolution. Likewise there have been many Limones. This specific rancho was the one that he chanced to visit, and from it he derived Demetrio's residence in his novel. It could have been, however, any one of the numerous ranchos or small communities touched upon by Azuela during his revolutionary travels. Other factors and experiences contributed to the selection of El Limón, but those that are linked intimately with this journey ultimately decide the direction of the novel, its plot, and the identity of the principal characters.

Certainly the party paused to rest there, perhaps even to spend the night. Beyond El Limón the terrain is more broken. There are canyons, then one strikes the lower reaches of the Río de Juchipila. At various points the river passes through chasms whose walls are of sheer solid rock, and there is scarcely room for the water to make its way between them. These are perhaps five or six miles to the north of El Limón. At this point on their journey, Caloca and his band were spotted by an isolated party of Carrancistas. At least Azuela labeled them as such, but he did not say how many they were or who their commander was. The following is his version of the incident:

> With Caloca on a stretcher, a band of Carrancistas surprised us in the bottom of the canyon, but since all of the colonel's men were made up of mountaineers and excellent horsemen, they easily took possession of the vantage points and quickly put the enemy to flight. In the meantime, protected by a small cave that opened in the solid rock, I made notes for the final scene of the novel that I had scarcely begun.[110]

This is a vivid real-life incident that can easily be transported to the pages of a novel. Caloca's men were in the bottom of the canyon when they were suddenly set upon from above by the enemy. The surroundings approached the spectacular. The setting, then, was made to order for the heightened effect desired in a

[109]Santa Rosa, a hacienda, had 554 inhabitants (Estados Unidos Mexicanos, Departamento de la Estadística Nacional, *Censo general de habitantes. 30 de noviembre de 1921. Estado de Zacatecas* [Mexico, 1928], p. 90).

[110]*O.C.*, III, 1087.

novel. Azuela was instantly cognizant of the fact and set to work taking notes on the spot. He did not, however, transfer the scene directly to the novel without modification. As an artist, he arranged and transformed the participants and the sequence of events in order to fit the scheme of the work that he was devising.

The encounter was an exciting one for Azuela, whether it was a battle or a skirmish, however one wishes to characterize it. There seems to have been an exchange of shots with the enemy, but it could not have been of great duration because the serranos, as Azuela called them, were able to gain control of surrounding heights and drive off the attackers. Azuela and Caloca were relatively safe in their depression in the canyon wall. In all Azuela's writing concerning the revolution, there is scarcely mention of his personal involvement in a battle or actual combat. He perhaps had seen some shooting at Guadalajara when he escaped from the Yaquis of General Diéguez. He saw none at Lagos and none at Tepatitlán while Medina was trying to take Guadalajara, and he has not mentioned having been present at the fighting at San Miguel el Alto. On only one other occasion did Azuela admit his presence during a military conflict, that when he and José Becerra took refuge in a corral while fleeing from the Carrancistas.[111] The skirmish in the canyon was indeed a minor one in the eyes of the soldiers, yet the doctor attributes considerable importance to it, because it is one of the very few that he actually witnessed. Azuela was not a fighting man. There was no real need for him to become involved with the fighting itself, and most of his material concerning battles and warfare came from conversations with others who had actually fought. But here the situation was quite different, and the difference was carried over into *Los de abajo*.

The band of Carrancistas encountered in the canyon of the Río Juchipila was well within territory held by Villista sympathizers and was far from any Carrancista base. Azuela has made

no statement concerning casualties on either side.

A few miles farther on, at the hacienda Santa Rosa,[112] Caloca's party stopped to rest in the afternoon. Since the departure from Tepatitlán, Azuela's assistant had been a youth who formerly had been a clown in a circus. He confessed to Azuela that the skirmish in the canyon had been too much for him and that he had decided to leave the group. In his place, Azuela took on another man who also joined the party at Tepatitlán. He had formerly been a sacristan in a church.

Late in the afternoon of the same day, the group started a long descent and could see below to the north the loops of the Río Juchipila and on its eastern bank the town of Moyahua. The road descends here into the broad valley of the river. Gone were the sheer canyon walls between which the river had to force its way. At Moyahua the valley floor is broad and flat, with imposing mountain ranges rising both to the east and west. Moyahua was the first settlement of any size in southern Zacatecas, although it was hardly more than a village. Here Caloca and Azuela and their men prepared to rest and spend the night. Apparently Moyahua was not held by Carrancista forces or these men would not have been able to enter it without putting up a fight. Certainly it was not the base for the Carrancistas encountered in the canyon of the Juchipila. That group looked increasingly like a party either of independents or lost Carrancistas.

When Caloca arrived, Moyahua was in the hands of Villista sympathizers. It had supplied leaders at all stages of the revolution, however, beginning in its earliest period. Roque Estrada, a native of Moyahua, was the secretary of Francisco I. Madero during the latter's election campaign as early as 1909. A brother, Enrique Estrada, took up arms against Victoriano Huerta and joined Álvaro Obregón in his push on Guadalajara in June and July, 1914. In June, 1915, he was the Carrancista general charged with the defense of Guadalajara. It was he who

[111]Ibid., pp. 801–802.   [112]Ibid., p. 1087.

repulsed on June 15 the attack led by Julián Medina, Parra, and Caloca in which the last named was wounded. The very first revolutionary chieftain who visited Moyahua was Luis Moya, who came through in 1910 seeking recruits for the Maderista cause. Later Moyahua was constantly visited by the leaders of one faction or another, accompanied by their followers, some of whom were welcome in the community and some who were not. The townspeople were frequently torn between the contending revolutionaries, and feelings on occasion ran high.

In Moyahua until recent years there have been residents who were present during the years of the revolution and could recall events involving figures of that period. One of those who was still alive in 1966 when I visited Moyahua was Víctor Hernández, then eighty-five years of age. Hernández had the dark skin, the prominent cheekbones, and the scrawny black moustache of an Indian. He was short and delicate of build. He was talkative and anxious to converse concerning the years immediately following 1910. Hernández had been a personal friend of Enrique Estrada, the Carrancista mentioned above, who later became governor of the state of Zacatecas. When Luis Moya entered Moyahua late in 1910, he asked Hernández to join his armed band and to accompany him throughout the state. He offered Hernández a good post, that of paymaster, but he refused to join that band or any other. He explained to Moya that he did not know how to handle weapons or ride a horse. That was not true, he commented, but it served as an excuse for not going off to fight. "The others are stirring up the dirt [i.e., dead]," he observed.

Later, in 1914, Hernández learned how to operate the electric light plant at Moyahua. Whenever it ran out of fuel, he had to make the trip all the way to Guadalajara to bring back fuel oil, obtaining it from Enrique Estrada when he was in military control of the city. In that period or slightly earlier, the Medinas and the Calocas came to Moyahua from time to time. Víctor Hernández met these men at dances

that they organized in Moyahua. One of the Medina brothers, Juan, died fighting the Huertistas at Palos Cuates, a point west of Moyahua in the direction of El Teul. Later, he recalled, one of the Caloca brothers passed through Moyahua on the way north. This Caloca, he added, had been seriously wounded in battle. He referred here to Colonel Manuel Caloca, whom Mariano Azuela was accompanying in late June, 1915.

Although it was far removed from the principal military operations of the revolutionary years, Moyahua saw its share of disturbances, hard feelings, and privation. In the later years of the revolution, a soldier was wounded in a skirmish at Juchipila and was able to travel only as far as Moyahua, but with great difficulty, unable to rejoin his unit. Víctor Hernández found him and hid him in a dugout cave across the river from the town. He remained there for several days while Hernández swam the river each day to take him food. In this period the troubled conditions brought about a scarcity of food staples in Moyahua, and Hernández found it necessary to forage in order to feed this soldier. Like Manuel Caloca, this man was a native of El Teul. He recovered from his wound and continued on southward, where he rejoined his company. Later Hernández met him in Ixtlahuacán del Río in northern Jalisco.

The Estrada, González, and Reynoso families have been the most prominent in Moyahua. These have all intermarried and are the most numerous in the town, although there are other surnames. Of these people Azuela later commented: "I was in Moyahua only once and I have never known anyone from that town."[113] According to his testimony, the characters of *Los de abajo* who supposedly resided in Moyahua were exclusively of his own creation. He commented that he spent only a part of one late afternoon and the night there before proceeding northward. Apparently the cacique of Moyahua, the don Mónico of *Los de abajo,* thoroughly hated by Demetrio Macías, was fictional. One

[113]In *Epistolario,* pp. 122-123.

native of Moyahua and a member of a family that still resides there, considered the person of don Mónico for a few moments, then remarked to me that the town did have a *cacique político* at the outbreak of the revolution. His name was Melquíades Reynoso.

In Azuela's time Moyahua was extremely remote and transportation was exceedingly difficult. Whereas one now makes the trip to Guadalajara by automobile over a paved highway in the space of two hours or so, in past years the trip took three days and one went on horseback or burro. Until the late 1950s one traveled as the arrieros did. Leaving Guadalajara, the arrieros started before dawn in order to descend into the barranca, cross the Río Santiago, and make the laborious climb up the other side of the canyon before the day became warm. The crossing of the Río Santiago was at the Puente del Arcediano, upstream from the present highway bridge at a point where the canyon walls are much closer together. The old bridge charged no toll for humans, but it did exact one centavo for each animal. From the bridge, the arrieros and their human and animal companions climbed to Ixtlahuacán del Río, where they spent the first night. Beyond Ixtlahuacán, the modern highway generally follows the route of the old road of the pack animals and their drivers. They spent the second night at El Limón, although there the accommodations were even more primitive than at the mesón in Ixtlahuacán del Río. At El Limón one slept on the ground in the open or under a thatched shelter. If the traveler was fortunate, he had a petate underneath him but this was not always possible. Then he had to sleep directly on the hard ground. El Limón, then, was a stop on the main route between Guadalajara and Zacatecas.

Residents of Moyahua simply refer to El Limón as "un ranchito," located on a *bajío*, the local designation of a relatively level area between *serranías*. The old road followed by the arrieros when Azuela passed through keeps farther to the east along the base of the mountain range, away from the modern highway. Prominent stone fences still mark the line followed by

the old dirt road. The houses of El Limón today are of stones or adobe bricks, dull gray in color, without a coating of plaster, and a roof of red tile. Farther to the north, near the Cuesta de Santa Rosa, one begins to see houses that have walls of adobe brick or occasionally wattle, with steep pitched roofs of thatch that come to a peak at the top. These resemble more closely the house of Demetrio Macías as described by Azuela in the opening scene of *Los de abajo*. Perhaps more houses of this humble style were evident in the time of the revolution than now.

The travelers reached their destination, Moyahua, on the third day. Despite the physical discomforts of the journey, it was not considered unpleasant. The company of the arrieros was enjoyable, for these men possessed an inexhaustible supply of stories, jests, news items, and interesting bits of information with which they kept their traveling companions amused. Although Caloca's band was still stinging from its defeat and Caloca himself had a painful wound, the spirit of the arrieros was not entirely absent during their journey through the canyons.

Moyahua may well have been Azuela's idea of the town that Demetrio and his men first took in *Los de abajo*. It is the nearest town of any consequence to El Limón. Azuela, however, does not specify his model. As did that town, Moyahua has a modest parish church that seems to have been built in the nineteenth century. It also has, across the street to the south, a *parián,* a kind of enclosed plaza where business establishments open outward on the street and inside is a small tree-shaded park with tables and benches.

The town and its surroundings were attractive to Mariano Azuela and made a remarkable impression on him. Although he was hastening to remove Manuel Caloca to safety, he found time to make extensive notes on the physical aspect of these places. Many of these are identifiable in *Los de abajo*, but he later peopled them with characters from elsewhere. The latter came principally from among his previous revolutionary acquaintances in Jalisco and were no longer with Caloca but with Julián Medina, holding out against the Carrancistas in the western part of the state. But for _Los de abajo_ southern Zacatecas had become significant because Azuela had recently chosen it for his initial and final settings. In regard to the combat with the Carrancistas in the canyon, the doctor has indicated that he had scarcely begun to write the novel. Perhaps he began it during the stop at El Limón, for the initial episode of the novel occurs there.

After a night's rest at Moyahua, Caloca and Azuela continued their journey northward up the valley of the Río Juchipila. As they ascended, the valley became wider. Imposing mountain ranges on both the east and the west gave the impression, which may have been erroneous, that the valley was shallow. Beyond the small village of Contitlán, the Cerro de las Ventanas rose on the east, and as they approached Juchipila there was an impressive mountain to the west, the Cerro de la Santa Cruz, whose outcroppings of red stone were capped by the vivid green foliage of the rainy season. Its prominent rounded sides loom over the valley and are visible for miles.

As the day progresses, it becomes hot on the valley floor. Its altitude is lower even than that of Guadalajara, and consequently its climate is much warmer. Fields of sugarcane appeared just north of Moyahua and continued, watered by the river, until the travelers reached Juchipila. Sugar dominates the agriculture of these places.

These are the Cañones de Juchipila, for thus is the region known in southern Zacatecas and northern Jalisco. The valley and the surrounding country was the residence of the valiant Caxcanes at the time that Europeans first arrived, in 1530. Their centers were at Nochistlán to the east, at Juchipila, and at El Teul, across the mountain range to the west. With difficulty the Spaniards put down their well-organized rebellion in the 1540s and pacified and area by settling some of the Indians elsewhere and forming the others into controlled villages whose names appear frequently in documents of the colonial period. Later, in the seventeenth and eighteenth centuries, there was a heavy influx of Spanish colonials, who were attracted by the fertile soil and the opportunities for agriculture. They came in such numbers that they far outnumbered the original inhabitants and their descendants. In Moyahua, for example, there are many people of fair complexion and light skin. The Spanish element seems quite strong. One inhabitant reported: "There has not been much crossbreeding here." Yet there are some mestizos in the population. Mauricio Magdaleno also has observed the predominantly Hispanic cast of the people of the canyons. He has visited Juchipila and has said of its inhabitants: "The people are all white, with beards, of undeniable Spanish origin. . . . Good-looking girls and sturdy youths. Many light-colored eyes and much chestnut brown hair."[114] The rancheros of northern Jalisco and southern Zacatecas are much more likely to be of Spanish descent than mestizos and rarely can be considered as Indians.

Azuela has mentioned passing through Juchipila on his journey, but he has not provided details concerning his stay there. The third part of _Los de abajo_, however, reflects faithfully Azuela's experiences of this period. There he has painted an extremely dreary picture of the town, parts of which had been burned and were in ruins. Only with difficulty and at considerable expense could the soldiers find anything to eat. The weariness of the inhabitants and their lack of food was translated into an openly hostile attitude toward the outsiders.[115] Azuela has mentioned the lack of food on this long journey. He has spoken of eating the flesh of a cow roasted over a fire in the open and consumed without salt. Instead of coffee they had only a substitute made from toasted garbanzos. The scarcity of food was not limited to the valley of the Río Juchipila but extended to much of Mexico. Consul Will B. Davis was constantly

---

[114]Mauricio Magdaleno, _Ritual del año_ (Mexico, 1955), p. 48.

[115]_Los de abajo_ (Mexico, 1958), pp. 135-136. The colonial church mentioned by Azuela (p. 134) has been replaced by a modern structure completed in 1930.

concerned over the difficult situation of the residents of the state of Jalisco at this same time.

In contrast with the somber appearance of Juchipila, Demetrio's men were cheered by the religious celebration the women were holding in the parish church. It turned out to be for the Sacred Heart of Jesus, and the ringing of bells cheered up the dejected men, reminding them of the early period of the revolution, when they were still optimistic concerning the future and the residents gave them a rousing welcome when they entered a village. Someone in the band recalled that it had been just a year since the resounding victory over the federales at Zacatecas. That battle occurred June 23, 1914. If such was the case, Azuela passed through Juchipila one year later, in the neighborhood of June 23, 1915. This is highly likely, because Caloca's party left Tepatitlán on June 17 or 18, and they had been on the road approximately one week.

In one of the towns of the Juchipila valley (he does not specify which one), Azuela encountered the physical model for La Pintada of *Los de abajo*. She was the companion of Colonel Maximiano Hernández, the commander of the Villista detachment there. Azuela has said of her:

He had as his companion a dark little girl, with her mouth, eyes, and cheeks all painted up. She was wearing a short dress of a bright color that was almost dazzling, a hat trimmed with braid, and a blouse that was crossed in front with two cartridge belts loaded with rifle shells. Seated on a rough pine table with her legs dangling, she was wearing blue cotton stockings with bluish purple garters below the knees. She had a reputation for being lewd and it was told about that she had been the cause of many bloody quarrels. She was the only woman among all those soldiers. In *Los de abajo* she bears the name of "La pintada."[116]

The trip northward was not really productive of characters of *Los de abajo;* La Pintada was apparently the only one decided upon by

Azuela during the journey. His presence was more productive of landscapes, settings, and the broad sweep of action and plot.

To the relief of Caloca and Azuela, the communities of southern Zacatecas were still in control of Villa sympathizers. The birthplace of Caloca, San Juan Bautista del Teul, to the west of Juchipila across the mountain range, was the strongest Villista center of the whole area. The danger from Carrancista attack was reduced at this point, not just for Caloca and Azuela, but for their escort also. The marches were long, and there was little opportunity to stop to rest. The weariness and the lack of food caused many to leave the party, because they could not continue or because they were near home and its attraction was strong after years of absence. It would seem that the departures had been particularly frequent in the valley of the Río Juchipila. The towns themselves were largely abandoned. Their former inhabitants, who could no longer remain there in safety, had left for Zacatecas or Aguascalientes, hoping to avoid misfortunes by banding together.

From Juchipila the wounded man and his escort moved on northward to Jalpa, a town that was larger than Juchipila and located in the same river valley. Jalpa normally was important agriculturally, especially for its sugarcane, but in June, 1915, food was as scarce there as in other areas of Jalisco and Zacatecas. In *Los de abajo* there are references to this town and to an image of the Virgin that is supposed to be venerated there. In the initial scene of the novel, as soon as the federal lieutenant and his men have left Demetrio's house, his wife exclaims: "Holy Virgin of Jalpa! How they frightened me! I thought it was you they were shooting at!"[117]

If the reference is to the town of Jalpa, she has in mind an image of the Virgin of Guadalupe who is venerated there. The latter is not the patron saint of the town but has her own chapel. The townspeople celebrate her feast nine days after the usual feast day of Our Lady of Guadalupe, which is December 12. In Jalpa

[116]*O.C.*, III, 1084.

[117]*Los de abajo* (Mexico, 1958), p. 8.

the local feast is December 21.[118] The reference to the Virgin is slightly different in the 1915 and 1916 editions of *Los de abajo,* but it is not without significance. Azuela originally wrote the phrase "—¡Qué susto, madre mía de Talpa!" and it appeared in this form in the El Paso editions.[119] The slight difference in the name of the town is probably not the result of a typographical error. Talpa is a small town situated in the mountainous country of western Jalisco and is the seat of one of the three famous religious shrines of that state. The image is of Nuestra Señora del Rosario, visited by pilgrims from all the west of Mexico, and her name is a household word throughout Jalisco and the other western states of the country. A church has even been dedicated to her in Los Angeles, California. In literature, she is the motivation for the pilgrimage in the short story "Talpa" of Juan Rulfo.[120] The reference is highly appropriate in the early editions of *Los de abajo,* although elsewhere in the same editions Azuela refers to the Virgin as being from Jalpa. In printings of the novel that have appeared since 1920 he has used only the latter toponym.

At Jalpa Caloca and his men were almost due west of the city of Aguascalientes. At that point they left the Juchipila valley and turned to the east, following a route that took them up a tributary of the Río Juchipila to Calvillo, Ojo Caliente, and from there to Aguascalientes. Mariano Azuela has furnished little or no information concerning the events of this final leg of their journey. Were they able to travel a normal day's journey, they could have traversed it in two or three days, but with the injured Caloca it must have taken a week or more. The valley of the Río Juchipila and its people had aroused Azuela's creative spirit, and he had already committed the novel to that setting. Therefore the towns of western Aguascalientes did not excite his attention. Furthermore the urgency of reaching the city of Aguascalientes with Caloca was foremost in their thoughts.

When they left Tepatitlán in mid-June, Villa had just retreated to Aguascalientes, and Obregón's men had not yet advanced northward beyond Lagos de Moreno. In the weeks following, the Carrancistas continued to press forward, taking next the small town of Encarnación de Díaz. Early in July Obregón began operations directly against the city of Aguascalientes. Villa's positions in and around the city were fairly strong, and he still retained intact the main body of his División del Norte, despite the defeats at Celaya, Trinidad, and León. Heavy fighting began to the south of Aguascalientes near Peñuelas on July 6. At that time General Obregón received a substantial shipment of arms, ammunition, and food supplies and brought in reinforcements from the state of Guanajuato which he planned to use as reserves in the developing battle. Fighting was particularly bloody on July 7 and 8. Obregón then shifted his approach from the south to the east and northeast, and by July 9 the situation of the Villistas had become difficult.

At that point Manuel Caloca and Mariano Azuela finally reached Aguascalientes. Upon their arrival, their escort, which had consisted of eighty men upon their departure from Tepatitlán, numbered a mere fourteen. The others had melted away along the route, because of fatigue, hunger, and sheer dejection with the worsening situation of the Villistas and in particular with their band.

In Aguascalientes Azuela took Caloca to be cared for: "I operated on him in that state capital, in the clinic of his relatives the Doctors Ávila, and that very afternoon we took the train for the north, already being able to hear the cannonading of the Carrancistas who a few hours later would take the city."[121] Azuela notes that they spent but a few hours in Aguascalientes. He did not divulge the nature of Caloca's

---

[118]Reported by María Teresa Venegas, members of whose family have resided in Zapotlanejo, Jalisco, and Jalpa, Zacatecas.

[119]Folletín Núm. 1 of *Los de abajo* in *El Paso del Norte* (Wednesday, October 27, 1915), p. 3. Also in *Los de abajo* (El Paso, 1916), p. 9.

[120]In *El llano en llamas* (Mexico, 1953), pp. 62-75.

[121]*O.C.,* III, 1080.

operation, but one may conjecture that it involved the extraction of a bullet from the body. Neither did the doctor specify the date of the operation or that of their departure from Aguascalientes.

On the morning of July 10, the Carrancistas of Álvaro Obregón began a determined and effective attack on the city from the north and northeast. They were able to drive the Villista infantry from its positions, and their cavalry broke through the defenders' lines, leaving the way open to the center of the city. At that point Villa ordered the city evacuated. The removal of the army and its impedimenta was a matter of extreme urgency for if the main railway line to the north should be cut, neither men nor their equipment could be removed. Villa in person, accompanied by a number of the dorados, assumed charge of the evacuation of his artillery, which had to be used first to protect the removal of the long military trains to the north.[122] The trains carrying the infantry were ordered to depart first, and they were followed by another train that transported the general headquarters of the División del Norte. The Villistas took special pains to gather their wounded aboard a hospital train, called the *servicio sanitario,* which left for the north while the city was under attack by the Carrancistas.[123] Apparently Azuela and Caloca were aboard that train. They had barely caught it in time. Had they arrived one day later, Aguascalientes would have been completely in the hands of the Carrancistas.

Thus the long trek from Tepatitlán came to an end. Caloca and Dr. Azuela had traveled for twenty-four days through backwater areas of the revolution. Although the struggle between Villistas and Carrancistas continued in the remote areas of northern and western Jalisco and western Zacatecas, what occurred there was of secondary importance in the ultimate outcome of the revolution. That situation has made it extremely difficult to document the background of *Los de abajo,* for Mariano Azuela's concern was with the effect of the revolution on the little man, whether he was in the mainstream of events or was relatively remote from them.

Caloca was operated on successfully in Aguascalientes, yet in other respects the journey seems an almost futile one. He and Azuela were united again with the main Villista units, but the future of these was dimming in view of their forced departure from Aguascalientes. The string of Villa's defeats showed no signs of ending. For the time being, however, it meant continued personal safety for the two men. As it turned out, their approach to Aguascalientes from the west had been after all the safest and wisest one. The western approaches to the city were those that Villa held longest and were the most protected.

In the departure of the trains from Aguascalientes there was considerable confusion, and in the urgency of the situation at least one train was lost. From their positions on the hills to the northeast of the city the Carrancistas were able to train their artillery on the departing trains. Calzadíaz Barrera has explained the predicament: ". . . when the train carrying the supplies and ammunition, under the command of Major Luis Escárcega, got ready to leave, another of the trains of the Medical Corps cut in front of it and Major Escárcega could no longer move forward, and by that time the Carrancistas had already severed the line."[124]

The army of Villa thus lost approximately one million rounds of ammunition, which was of immediate use to the soldiers of Obregón, whose supplies had been seriously depleted by the prolonged and hard-fought battle for the city. Villa managed to extricate his army only with great difficulty.

Aguascalientes was the last center of any importance held by Villa in the center of Mexico. Rather than attempt a defense of the city of Zacatecas, Villa decided to retreat still farther to the north and ordered a concentration of all his forces in the Laguna section

[122]Calzadíaz, III, 49.
[123]Ibid., p. 50.

[124]Ibid.

around Torreón, Coahuila. He brought all his trains together there, including the main body of his army that had been holding large portions of the states of Guanajuato and San Luis Potosí in the central area of Mexico. In Torreón Villa expected to regroup his military resources and make plans and preparations for another campaign.

Manuel Caloca and Mariano Azuela did not remain in Torreón with the main body of the Villista army. Perhaps they paused there but Azuela has not gone into that matter. He continued northward with Caloca and eventually delivered him to the military hospital of the Villistas in the city of Chihuahua. The long flight had ended or at least had been interrupted. It had been difficult and tiring.

Azuela has not specified when he arrived in Chihuahua. It could not have been before mid or late July of 1915. Neither has he explained what he did there, whether or not he still performed any duties for the Villista government. From scattered clues that he has provided concerning his friends and associates there as well as his precarious economic situation, it is evident that he had no medical or educational assignments such as those that occupied him during the period when he accompanied Julián Medina in Guadalajara.

Chihuahua in that period sheltered a number of intellectuals who, like Azuela, had been pushed to the north of Mexico along with Villa's armies. During the preceding months, certainly since the withdrawal from Guadalajara in April, he had had practically no contact with intellectuals, only with rancheros and soldiers. In Chihuahua he met Enrique Luna Román, whom he esteemed highly and has mentioned frequently. There were others whose acquaintance he made in the city, then encountered again when he was forced into exile in El Paso, but Luna Román liked Azuela and did all that he could to ameliorate the doctor's desperate financial condition. Following the organization of the Convencionista government, Luna Román participated in framing the governmental structure of the state of Chihuahua and occupied a

post of some responsibility and influence there throughout much of 1915.[125] In that capacity he was in a position to be of assistance to the stranded doctor.

Some of Azuela's recollections of his stay in Chihuahua have to do with food. It was extremely scarce during the flight from Tepatitlán to Aguascalientes and was hardly abundant during the train ride north with Caloca. He has spoken of the "tremendous hunger of Chihuahua and the meals prepared by the Chinese that only served as appetizers, because one came out of the restaurant hungrier than when he went in."[126] Although food was available again, he had no resources with which to purchase it. It is not surprising that Azuela's writings composed during that period have a bitter taste.

The novelist arrived at Chihuahua with a bundle of notes. Amid the privations of hunger and the turmoil of a mass of uprooted people, he prepared at last to write *Los de abajo:* "With my notes in my breast pocket I reached Chihuahua and began to put them in shape."[127] He must have begun them at the time of his first arrival in Guadalajara with Julián Medina in December, 1914, or perhaps even earlier. He had continued to add to them in Guadalajara, in Lagos, in Tepatitlán, and more intensively during the flight from Tepatitlán, through the canyons of Juchipila, to Aguascalientes. Most of them date from this last leg of the journey, and they certainly were the most fresh in his mind.

Throughout his lesser writings, Azuela has made scattered references to the process of putting his novel together, in Irapuato, then Guadalajara. He adds later: "With excellent documentation I began my notes. Two chapters in Lagos, two more in Tepatitlán."[128] Concerning the escape through the Juchipila area, he commented: "The novel wrote itself."[129] In these cases, which the novelist recalled at a much later period of his life, he seems to have had in mind only the making of notes, mental or written, but in a letter to Professor L. B. Kiddle,

[125]Almada, II, 226.	[126]*O.C.*, III, 1089.
[127]Ibid., p. 1087.	[128]Ibid., p. 1268.
[129]Ibid.

written more than twenty years later, he remarked that he had actually written the first chapter during his stay in Guadalajara early in 1915.[130]

The author's specific procedure in putting his work together must be taken into consideration here, whether he wrote isolated chapters of interior sections of the work and later inserted them into the novel in their definitive order, or whether he sat down and wrote the novel through from beginning to end in the order that it finally took. If Azuela employed the latter procedure, he could not have begun composition until he reached Chihuahua. Those sections of the novel that are intimately related to El Limón, Moyahua, and Juchipila are based on his experiences of June and early July, 1915, and were obviously written after that time. Some of these occur at the very beginning of *Los de abajo*. In any case, by that time he had decided upon the final form that the first edition of his novel was to take.

The composition of *Los de abajo* occupied Azuela in Chihuahua during August, September, and part of October, 1915. He did not have access to a typewriter so he had to write out his chapters in longhand. After he had completed a draft of the Primera Parte he showed it to his friend Lic. Enrique Luna Román. The latter read it, liked it, and became enthusiastic. Shortly afterward, Luna Román left Chihuahua, probably when the military position of Villa began to deteriorate, and moved on to Ciudad Juárez. He continued to write to Azuela, however, and his enthusiasm for *Los de abajo* did not diminish. After Luna Román's departure, the novelist continued his writing and during October, at a time that he has not specified, he finished the Segunda Parte. By that time his funds were dwindling, and he could no longer remain in Chihuahua.

Dr. Azuela left for Ciudad Juárez in the hope of finding a publisher for his manuscript. Luna Román had written to him, assuring him that he had found one. Azuela could not prac-

tice medicine in Chihuahua or in El Paso, the border city on the North American side. When he arrived, he and Luna Román made the rounds of several publishing houses: "We visited several agents of publishing concerns, and they asked me for the original manuscript to send it in. But since I was in urgent need of money, I had to accept the offer made by *El Paso del Norte:* a thousand copies of the offprint and three dollars a week in cash during the time that the novel was being printed as a serial."[131] Thus he was able to find a publisher, one who was hardly known outside El Paso and Ciudad Juárez. The novel would get no promotion whatever, and Mariano Azuela would not become famous from it. The three dollars weekly would at least allow him to eat in a time of great hunger.

During those fall months of 1915, Dr. Azuela lived in both Ciudad Juárez and El Paso and was familiar with both cities. He has mentioned eating in the Delmónico restaurant in Ciudad Juárez, where he found a haughty waiter, a man who was to him extremely disagreeable, and pressed him into service as a model for El Güero Margarito. This repugnant character thus entered into *Los de abajo*, which the novelist had not yet finished.[132]

Azuela evidently moved into El Paso, where he was closer to the offices and printshop of *El Paso del Norte*. Furthermore, food was more abundant there and was inexpensive. In later years he recalled those days: "I even remember fondly those five-cent loaves of bread and those pints of refrigerated milk as a blessing from heaven in El Paso, Texas, after my journey through mountainous areas of Jalisco and Zacatecas, eating roasted cow's meat with no salt. . . . El Paso endures in my memory as a paradise for gluttons."[133]

Publication of *Los de abajo* in the daily *El Paso del Norte* began late in October. Azuela

---

[130]In *Epistolario*, p. 139.

[131]*O.C.*, III, 1088.

[132]Ibid., p. 1083. In *Los de abajo*, however, the restaurant is noted as being in the city of Chihuahua rather than Ciudad Juárez.

[133]Ibid., p. 1089.

later recalled that the editor Fernando Gamiochipi placed a typewriter at his disposal, and he
set to work writing the Tercera Parte in the
printshop where the newspaper was set up and
printed. That section of *Los de abajo* began
with the letter from Luis Cervantes, who supposedly was in El Paso, to Venancio, who was
still in Mexico with Demetrio and his soldiers.
The letter reflected to some extent Azuela's own
surroundings of the moment, his state of mind
at the time he was writing that portion of the
novel, his lack of funds, his preoccupation with
food, and a biting irony that supposedly hides
things as they are but at the same time reveals
them to the reader.

Azuela was not alone in El Paso. He met
Lic. Luna Román again and shared portions
of *Los de abajo* with him and various compatriots who also were in exile. The novelist has
mentioned some of them by name:

> One November night in 1915 I read it to a
> group of friends and acquaintances, all of
> them exiles, in one of the rooms of the hotel
> where we were staying. Among them were the
> *licenciados* Enrique Pérez Arce, Abelardo
> Medina, Enrique Luna Román, and several
> other professional people. When I reached
> the part where Demetrio Macías was carried
> on a stretcher through the canyon of Juchi-
> pila, Manuel Caloca, who also was among my
> listeners, recognized himself immediately.[134]

Caloca apparently had recovered from his
wound in the military hospital in Chihuahua
and had made his way to El Paso, where he rejoined Azuela. This reference is his last mention
of Caloca. Following the informal gathering in
El Paso he dropped out of sight, and Azuela
has given no more news of him. Neither is he
cited in other postrevolutionary documents and
histories.

Not so with Pérez Arce and Medina. Both
were young men from the state of Sinaloa who
had studied at the Liceo de Varones in Guadalajara at the time that Francisco Madero began
his campaign for the presidency in 1909, and

both had campaigned for him. Pérez Arce, at
least, had declared himself for Villa when the
Convencionista government was established
late in 1914. With the decline in Villa's fortunes he had decided to go into exile in El Paso.
Following the revolution, both men were prominent in the life of their native state, Medina as a
poet and a literary figure[135] and Pérez Arce in
the political life of Sinaloa. He was govenor of
the state from 1950 to 1953.[136]

In El Paso Dr. Azuela devoted himself almost exclusively to literary pursuits. There he
found even less opportunity to practice medicine
than he had encountered in Chihuahua. His
only assets were his novels. In a letter written
to his wife Carmen in Guadalajara on November 10, 1915, he asked her to mail to him copies
of all his works, that he had nothing else that
could possibly provide him with any funds.[137]
Given the almost complete absence of editorial
facilities in El Paso and the little regard for
Mexican literature in that period, Azuela's hope
of supporting himself from his writing was a
forlorn one. He had begun to consider returning
to Mexico, for in the same letter he informed
his wife that he had written to the government
of the state of Jalisco asking that he be granted
the normal constitutional guarantees so that he
could return there. If they were not forthcoming, he would not risk the return. His economic
situation was desperate, and the paltry income
from the serial publication of *Los de abajo*
would continue for only ten or eleven days
more.

If Azuela's position was worsening, so was
that of Villa within Mexico. Following the retreat from Aguascalientes, his armies were able
to hold Torreón for barely two months. They
relinquished that city on September 19 and
moved their headquarters to the city of Chihua-

---

[134]Ibid., pp. 1081–1082.

[135]The principal public library of Culiacán, Sinaloa,
bears the name of Lic. Medina (Amado González Dávila,
*Diccionario geográfico, histórico, biográfico y estadístico del
Estado de Sinaloa* [Culiacán, 1959], p. 367).

[136]Ibid., p. 241. Also in Héctor R. Olea, *Breve historia
de la Revolución en Sinaloa (1910–1917)* (Mexico, 1964),
p. 77.

[137]Monterde, p. 168.

hua. Azuela was in Chihuahua at that time and must have witnessed the transfer. The city was aswarm with Villa's disheartened soldiers and hangers-on from his armies in addition to numbers of refugees from points south who had been evacuated. Azuela left this confused scene and moved on to El Paso in October. Despite the concentration of his army in Chihuahua, Villa was unable to hold it for long. His troops were unable to hold back Obregón's Carrancistas, who continued to press northward from the direction of Coahuila. In the face of pressure, the Villistas evacuated the city of Chihuahua on December 20. Villa retreated with a body of his forces to the western part of that state, but the rest of his army underwent defections and desertions. General Jacinto B. Treviño approached from the south and occupied Chihuahua on December 23.

Almost simultaneously negotiations were undertaken for the surrender of Ciudad Juárez. Various members of the Villista garrison there and civilians of the city entered into negotiations with Venustiano Carranza. The Carrancista consul in El Paso aided in the transfer of messages and in the negotiations. Without much fanfare and practically no military activity a surrender was arranged, and on December 20 control of the city was handed over to the Carrancistas. Thus the Villistas lost possession of their largest city and their most important port of entry into Mexico. The disaster was thus complete. Francisco Villa's activities hereafter were to be largely of a guerrilla nature and these, although they were occasionally spectacular, could have but little effect on the future of Mexico.

Following the arrival of the first Carrancista detachment in Ciudad Juárez, there was a degree of confusion when the Villista border guards were removed and replaced by Carrancistas. At the same time the latter assumed control of the city police. Azuela, who had been aware of the impending surrender of Villa's garrison, took advantage of the situation and during the first few hours following the changeover slipped across the bridge back into Mexican territory.[138] One of Azuela's worries was removed when General Elizondo, the commander of Carranza's army in Chihuahua, arrived in Ciudad Juárez. Upon orders of the Primer Jefe, General Elizondo granted amnesty to those Villistas who were caught in the city. Only Francisco Villa and his brother Hipólito were excluded from it. General Elizondo began the process of granting individual amnesties shortly after he reached the city, and the practice was continued by General Gabriel García, who arrived from Hermosillo, Sonora, on January 1, 1916, to be commander of the military sector in Ciudad Juárez.[139]

Villa's loss of Chihuahua and Ciudad Juárez brought about a significant change in Mexico's internal communication system. For the first time since April, 1915, the main railway line that leads south from Chihuahua through Torreón, Zacatecas, and Aguascalientes had come under the control of a single faction. The development was highly significant for Dr. Azuela because it meant that it was now possible, although with restricted speed and little regularity, to travel all the way to Irapuato and from there by the branch line to Guadalajara. Train departures were infrequent, the equipment had not been maintained, and the track itself was in wretched condition. Furthermore, food was extremely scarce. Traveling was inconvenient and highly uncomfortable, but at least travel in some form was possible again. Without delay, Azuela sought a way to rejoin his family, whom he had not seen since the preceding April. In Ciudad Juárez he found a soldier who was willing to sell his railroad pass. From his slender savings, Azuela took money and bought it. His plan was to use it to return to Jalisco. He has noted that his traveling companion on this journey was José G. Montes de Oca.[140]

The trip was not without its anxious and exasperating moments, particularly at its beginning. When he got on the train, he encountered

[138]*O.C.*, III, 1088.   [139]Calzadíaz, III, 193.
[140].*O.C.*, III, 1088.

a sympathetic human being who took compassion on him because of his impoverished condition, recognizing that he was not a soldier. The novelist has expressed his thankfulness to that man:

> The train's conductor did not want to honor the pass. "You are not soldiers," he said. "You are farm workers going to pick cotton in the Laguna area." His keen perception saved us because he took pity on us because of our impoverished condition and permitted us to go on, without asking us for our tickets again. The trip lasted a week, with periods when we could not sleep, tribulations, and unexpected incidents.[141]

Azuela thus made his way to Guadalajara. It was January, 1916. His family had been there for over a year, since December, 1914, shortly after his first arrival there with Julián Medina. The novelist has not commented specifically on the circumstances in which he found his wife and children. He had not been able to provide for them since April, 1915, and their financial situation, like his, must have been desperate. But the returning man of the family had little to offer them. He was without funds and with little clothing other than what he was wearing. Given this economic predicament, it was necessary to make a decision as to how to provide for the family. For at least two reasons Dr. Azuela was extremely reluctant to return to Lagos de Moreno. In the first place, the medical practice he had built up over the years was no more. He had left it in October, 1914, and should he move back, he would have to start again in the same financial straits as when he began in 1899 just after finishing medical school. Secondly, he obviously did not care to live again among those who had been his political enemies since the days of Madero.

Azuela's determination was to establish a practice in completely new surroundings. In March, 1916, he left his family in Guadalajara and moved to the capital, where he began anew

as a doctor in the Peralvillo section. His family followed him to Mexico City in July of the same year. During those early months following his return from exile he had no clientele, and the surroundings were strange. It was a brave new start for a man of forty-three, yet this time he was not going off to war, and the future, although it was admittedly bleak, especially in regard to Azuela's ideological position, at least was not beset by the likelihood of further fighting, and his family was finally reunited with him.

The establishment of his residence in the capital is a convenient point to mark the end of Azuela's active participation in the Mexican revolution. The doctor's first interest in the revolution had been exclusively political. After his early disillusion in that area, the entreaties of José Becerra and Colonel Francisco Delgado induced him to leave his medical practice and his family and embark upon a most unlikely career for a basically peaceful man.

The consequences of that decision were varied and turned his personal and literary lives in directions that he had not anticipated before the revolution. Affecting the doctor and all the members of his family was the economic disaster that began in April, 1915, and that continued for several years after they moved to the capital. The political and ideological disillusion was equally painful for Azuela. The complete military and political defeat of the faction that he had supported was particularly hard on his ego. With that defeat came the final destruction of the ideals that he had hopefully nurtured during Madero's campaign, only to see them frustrated even before Madero could take office. The victory of Carranza over the Villa faction ended any shred of hope that might have remained and brought complete disillusionment. *Los de abajo* is the story of this process.

From this series of afflictions Azuela nevertheless acquired a store of experiences and observations that otherwise would not have come his way. He had gone into the great adventure precisely for the purpose of acquiring that fund. The decision had been deliberate and

---

[141]Ibid.

was made with clear knowledge of the hazards that it might entail. The fund was put to immediate use in the writing of *Los de abajo,* and in that sense the experience must be entered on the credit side of Azuela's ledger.

The last consequence has to do with *Los de abajo* itself. The novel, which to the literary world is an undeniable accomplishment, could hardly have been achieved without the physical hardships, the political reverses, and the ideological catastrophe that only its author could have experienced. These, then, constitute the price that Mariano Azuela has had to meet in order to create his masterwork.

CHAPTER 2

Los de abajo in El Paso, Texas

The Elusive Novel

Los de abajo is the most esteemed of Mariano Azuela's novels and has been acclaimed as the novel par excellence of the Mexican revolution. Its fame, however, rests not on the versions that Azuela hastily put together to be published in *El Paso del Norte,* either in serial form or as a paperback. Those editions have been nearly forgotten. After all, the novelist spent only eight or nine weeks in El Paso. He set no roots there, and he had no reason to return there after the fighting of the revolution had ended. The literary public has known of those editions only through what the author has said about them in his reminiscences and what literary historians have drawn out of him in interviews and have published in their studies.

Later events have tended to overshadow the early redactions of *Los de abajo.* Azuela seems to have left them abandoned as orphans in El Paso. After his return to Mexico he again turned his attention to his novel, for which he expressed a certain affection,[1] and prepared a completely new text, following in general the early editions but adding a character, modifying and rearranging numerous passages, and introducing countless replacements of vocabulary items. These innovations were first introduced in the 1920 edition, which Azuela has reported having paid for himself.[2] It is extremely unlikely that the author could have afforded a large printing if the cost came out of his own pocket.

Los de abajo lay practically forgotten for nine years, known only to the author, his friends, and one or two critics. It emerged finally in 1924, when Francisco Monterde brought it to public view. Late in December of that year, Mexican writers at last turned to an assessment of the revolution in terms of its literary production. It got under way with an article by Julio Jiménez Rueda entitled "El afeminamiento en la literature mexicana," which appeared in *El Universal* on December 20 of that year. The spark that set off a spirited discussion were these words of Jiménez Rueda: ". . . there has not yet appeared the poetic, narrative, or dramatic work that compiles the deeds and analyzes the turmoil of the people during all that period of bloody civil war, a vehement struggle of interests. The people have dragged their wretchedness before us, without claiming from us even one brief moment of contemplation."[3] Monterde's reply, "Existe una literatura mexicana viril," mentioned specifically Mariano Azuela

---

[1]Mariano Azuela in a letter to L. B. Kiddle dated April 13, 1951 (*Epistolario,* p. 142).

[2]*O.C.,* III, 1112.

[3]Cited in F. Rand Morton, *Los novelistas de la Revolución Mexicana* (Mexico, 1949), p. 54.

and considered *Los de abajo* as a "faithful reflection of the flames of our recent revolution."[4]

John E. Englekirk has told the story of the
resulting controversy and identifies the roles
played in it by the principal participants, Julio
Jiménez Rueda and Victoriano Salado Álvarez
on the one hand and Francisco Monterde on the
other, with a supporting cast of other critics who
engaged in the debate, Carlos Noriega Hope,
Manuel Martínez Valadez, Eduardo Colín, José
Luis Velasco, Rafael López, Gregorio Ortega,
and others.[5] Their search for literature of the
revolution brought belated but deserved recognition to Azuela and placed him in the forefront of Mexican novelists.

A tangible consequence of the controversy
of 1924-1925 was a flurry of new editions of
Los de abajo. The first of these was prepared
by *El Universal Ilustrado,* authorized by its edi-
tor Carlos Noriega Hope (1896-1934) to meet
the demand stirred up by the discussion among
the critics. The novel appeared as a serial in the
Suplemento Semanal between January 29 and
February 24, 1925.[6] In 1927 the state government of Veracruz prepared an edition, and in
the same year two more appeared in Madrid.
On the heels of these came three editions in
Spanish from Argentina, Spain again, and
Chile, followed by translations into French,
English, German, Czech, and other languages.
These versions of the 1925-1930 period are the
basis of almost all the early scholarship relative
to *Los de abajo,* but the texts of all of them,
with minor modifications, are derived from the
revised form that Azuela first published in 1920.
To all intents and purposes the primitive edi-
tions from El Paso remained unknown.

The "discovery" marked the beginning of
true criticism regarding *Los de abajo*. Once the
controversy brought the novel to the attention of
Mexico's reading public, the stature of *Los de
abajo* became evident. Since that time nearly all
aspects of the novel have been of interest to

someone or other, as the bibliographies of
Manuel Pedro González, Ernest R. Moore, and
Luis Leal clearly demonstrate.[7] Mexican critics
have long concerned themselves with Azuela's
novel as an artistic product of the Mexican
revolution, the novel's reflection of the political
and social causes of the turmoil, and the average
Mexican's reaction to the ideologies of the conflict. In line with the intellectual ferment of the
1920s, they quite naturally considered it an expression of national spirit, in the light of what
they regarded as Mexican. In later years the
scope of criticism broadened considerably as
Azuela's other works became known, and he felt
free to express his feelings and preferences concerning Mexican literature. A consistent concern was the role of Azuela in the Mexican
revolution and his contribution to the body of
literature that grew out of that conflict. The
emergence of *Los de abajo* gave clear impetus
to a whole series of works dealing with the revolution, whether these were autobiographies,
reminiscences, chronicles, or novels, that kept
students of Mexican literature busy for the succeeding twenty years. Only during the mid-1940s
when stylistic and technical innovations began
to appear in the Mexican novel did interest in
literature of the revolution show signs of waning.

News of the "discovery" reached the United
States and in succeeding years *Los de abajo*
became a standard item of fare in classes dealing with Spanish American literature. North
American professors became as excited over the
work as had their neighbors to the south. They
initiated correspondence with Azuela and expressed a desire to know him personally. They
sought to know the details of his life and background, his experiences in the revolution above
and beyond those expressed in his novels. They
were curious to know the factual background of
Los de abajo and the circumstances surrounding the novel's composition and publication.

---

[4]Monterde, p. 13.

[5]John E. Englekirk, "The Discovery of *Los de abajo*
by Mariano Azuela," *Hispania*, 18 (1935), 53-62.

[6]Leal, p. 135.

[7]Manuel Pedro González, "Bibliografía del novelista
Mariano Azuela," *Revista Bimestre Cubana,* 48 (July-
August, 1941), 50-72; Ernest R. Moore, *Bibliografía de
novelistas de la Revolución Mexicana* (Mexico, 1941), pp.
21-28; Leal, pp. 135-168.

Following up their correspondence, they sought him out at his residence in Mexico City to converse with him and to exchange opinions and ideas concerning literature. Specifically, Arturo Torres Rioseco has reported the details of a visit with Azuela in Mexico City in July, 1930.[8] Torres's colleague, Lesley Byrd Simpson, has recounted a visit to Azuela's home and clinic in the summer of 1931.[9] Others began to interview him during this period. Azuela received and patiently and amiably answered their questions and inquiries. With many of these people he formed friendships that lasted until his death. One might note here, among others, Manuel Pedro González, John E. Englekirk, Lawrence B. Kiddle, Sturgis E. Leavitt, and the late Ernest R. Moore. Various of these have provided accounts of their conversations with the author.[10]

In addition to their concern with *Los de abajo* against the background of the revolution and the novel's social and political implications, the North Americans were curious to know more about the early editions of the work. In that connection they also sought to construct bibliographies in order to gain a clearer picture of Azuela's development as a writer, but much of their interest was focused on his literary activity during the years of the revolution. Azuela reminisced concerning his political support of Madero in Lagos, in general terms of his experiences with Julián Medina, and finally of his residence in El Paso.

As a contribution to these bibliographies, Azuela recounted his adventures in the marketing of *Los de abajo* and its appearance as a serial in the columns of *El Paso del Norte*. From there he proceeded to details of the other early editions, until he reconstructed their sequence as best he could, although twenty years had passed since the events occurred. They can be sum-

marized as follows, using as a basis the carefully prepared bibliographies of Ernest R. Moore:

> *Los de abajo.* In *El Paso del Norte,* El Paso, Texas, October to December, 1915.
> *Los de abajo.* Cuadros de la revolución mexicana. Novel. El Paso, Texas: Imp. de "El Paso del Norte," 1916.
> *Los de abajo.* In the daily *El Mundo,* Tampico, Tamaulipas, Mexico, 1917.
> *Los de abajo.* Cuadros y escenas de la revolución mexicana. Tampico, Mexico: "El Mundo," 1917. 144 p.
> *Los de abajo.* Cuadros y escenas de la revolución mexicana. Mexico: Tip. Razaster, 1920. 126 + (2) p.[11]

In the light of Azuelan scholarship since Moore's time, several of his comments concerning these editions are subject to revision. Azuela was unable to produce copies of the first four. He possessed a copy only of the last, the rewritten version of 1920 that he had had printed after he settled down to practice as a physician in Mexico City. He also had in his personal library other Mexican editions that had appeared following the "discovery" of 1924–1925. But those volumes that dated from the actual period of the revolution were missing, and Azuela did not know where copies could be obtained. The absence of the earliest editions was a clear challenge and various of Azuela's new friends set out to meet and overcome it.

Outwardly, the search for the missing editions seems to have been almost, if not exclusively, a preoccupation of North American scholars. In the early years of Azuelan scholarship, they felt a need for a broad vision of Azuela the writer, which could be attained by means of a thorough acquaintance with his works and the manner in which they evolved. In Azuela's case, they attached a high value to the historical significance of these works, and they approached criticism with a historically oriented methodology. In doing so, they were deliberate and strove

[8] Arturo Torres Rioseco, *Grandes novelistas de la América Hispana* (Berkeley and Los Angeles, 1949), pp. 5–6.

[9] Mariano Azuela, *Two Novels of Mexico. The Flies. The Bosses,* Lesley Byrd Simpson, trans. (Berkeley and Los Angeles, 1956), pp. xi–xii.

[10] This writer has had access to fairly extensive manuscript notes taken by Moore during an interview with Azuela during the evening of August 1, 1935.

[11] Moore, *Bibliografía,* p. 22.

to be thorough. The quest for the *Los de abajo* editions clearly reflects this desire.

In all the criticism written concerning *Los de abajo* and the accounts of the quest for the early printings, there has been no documented indication that Mexicans have engaged in the pursuit. During those years when North Americans were attempting to track down long lost editions and rare bits of comment on Azuela in out-of-the-way publications, the revolution was still a live issue in Mexico, certainly in its social and ideological significance, and the critical concern of the day was to relate *Los de abajo* to these forces. Much of what was written there about Azuela was motivated by this concern. One also gains the impression that Azuela in the 1920s and 1930s was not greatly bothered by the fate of the El Paso and the Tampico editions of his novel. Their redactions had clearly been superseded by a version (the Razaster edition of 1920) that was more satisfying to Azuela in matters of style and character delineation. There seemingly was no urgency in unearthing earlier forms of the novel that did not meet their author's standards.

The North Americans, however, had an additional motivation. The initial publication of *Los de abajo*, through a historical accident appeared in the United States rather than in Mexico. Regional and national pride, if not geographical proximity, may have served to some extent as a stimulus. The absence of Mexican participation in the search seems to have been more apparent than real, particularly during the early years of the history of the novel. It looks increasingly as if Mexicans and North Americans were each going at the same task, with one group unaware of what the other was doing. The Mexican contribution is not yet clearly discernible, but in the long run it is likely to provide some surprises.

The search by the North Americans could not get under way until the mid-1930s. By that time several young professors had already interviewed Azuela and were ready to start looking, although twenty years had passed since the first printing of *Los de abajo*. The passing of time

in many respects had made their questions harder, especially in El Paso, where they concentrated their efforts. Nevertheless, they felt that the endeavor was well worth undertaking, and when one views their activities from the vantage point of the 1970s their venture was justified, despite the odds existing against them. The excitement of the revolution had long since turned to calm. The military actions between Villa and Carranza were only memories, and the factional and political differences that had divided Mexicans in 1915 were no longer significant. But, most important of all, the actors who had been present when *Los de abajo* first saw the light of day were no longer on hand to tell the story of how it happened.

John Englekirk, a young professor of Spanish at the University of New Mexico at Albuquerque, two hundred sixty miles up the Río Grande from El Paso, began inquiries in the mid-1930s. From Azuela he had learned of *El Paso del Norte,* the daily in El Paso that published *Los de abajo* in serial form. Englekirk undertook to find the newspaper in which it had been printed. There were other Spanish-language newspapers in the city but *El Paso del Norte* no longer existed. He sought out print-shops in El Paso, hoping that perhaps in one of them he might find someone who had worked on the newspaper or could tell him of other persons who had done so. Englekirk worked on the problem for several years. The nature and frustration of the search is revealed in a letter that he wrote to Mariano Azuela on October 23, 1940: "I am still continuing to look for the newspaper in which it first appeared. Recently I was able to make contact with a person who was well acquainted with the editors, but he is unable to tell me where I can lay hands on any numbers of *El Paso del Norte.*"[12] Clues concerning the newspaper were few and far between. Occasionally a resident had heard of its editor Fernando Gamiochipi, but the latter was no longer in El Paso and apparently no one there had bothered to retain files of the newspaper.

---

[12]In *Epistolario,* pp. 123-124.

If the serial version of *Los de abajo* still eluded him in El Paso, Mariano Azuela had mentioned to Englekirk that Gamiochipi had prepared a paperback edition, although Azuela did not own a copy. Gamiochipi had agreed to provide him with a thousand copies in payment for the novel, but Azuela did not know their fate.[13] Armed with this information, Englekirk began to visit book and magazine stores in El Paso, particularly those that catered to a Spanish-speaking clientele. He has reported to me orally that he visited several such establishments, one of which was La Ideal, a small but long-established bookstore, well supplied with older works in Spanish. There he browsed through the stock that was displayed on the ground floor and then moved upstairs where there were still more books, some of them in a multiple number of copies. There, among other older works, he found a small paperback, *Los de abajo,* bearing the subtitle "Cuadros y escenas de la Revolución Mexicana," and with a 1916 copyright. This, then, was the first edition in book form to which Azuela had referred, apparently unknown to scholars until that time.

Despite his find, Englekirk was in something of a dilemma. The bookseller had on his shelves a number of copies of what was obviously a rare item, at least to a scholar of Spanish American literature. Englekirk was anxious to buy as many copies as he could, but at the same time he wanted at all costs to avoid suggesting to the bookseller that he might have rare volumes in his stock. After some deliberation, Englekirk decided upon six or so copies, which he was able to purchase without any questions being asked of him. He wrote to Azuela: "A couple of weeks ago I had the pleasure of sending you a copy of the first edition of *Los de abajo* which I found in El Paso after several years of looking for it. If I remember, you did not have a copy, did you?"[14]

The copy sent by Englekirk seems to have been the first seen by Azuela since the paperback had appeared in El Paso nearly twenty-five years before. The fate of those early copies as well as the one that Englekirk forwarded to him remains a mystery. Luis Leal has reported that no copy was in the author's library after his death in 1952.[15]

By 1940 at least one other person had been in El Paso to look into the publication of *Los de abajo.* Ernest Richard Moore completed his doctorate at Cornell University in June, 1940. In the preparation of his dissertation "Studies in the Mexican Novel," he had interviewed practically all those Mexican prose writers who were still living, including Mariano Azuela, and had published in the United States and Mexico most of the results of his investigations. Moore was particularly adept at ferreting out unusual bibliographical items, and he traveled widely in search of works or figures to complete his studies on the novelists of the revolution. He insisted upon personal consultation of the works in their various editions and was thorough and persistent in this goal. In the summer of 1941 I accompanied him in travels over much of northern and central Mexico in search of hitherto unreported works by Mexican authors and we scoured libraries in Saltillo, Torreón, Durango, Zacatecas and nearby Guadalupe, Aguascalientes, Guadalajara, San Luis Potosí, and Mexico City, examining little-known editions and making copious notes. Of many writers we talked but for some reason, very little about Mariano Azuela.

That same year Moore published his *Bibliografía de novelistas de la Revolución Mexicana,* a listing that recorded many items for the first time. Obviously he had worked for several years in its preparation and had visited libraries and bookstores both in the United States and Mexico in far greater numbers than those we visited during the summer of 1941. In his bibliography he noted the 1916 edition of *Los de abajo* on page 22:

> *Los de abajo.* Novela. Cuadros de la revolución mexicana) [*sic*]. El Paso, Texas, Imp. de "El Paso del Norte, 1916. [*sic*] 143 +

[13]*O.C.,* III, 1088.

[14]In *Epistolario,* pp. 124–124.

[15]Leal, p. 33 n 33.

(1) p. (EM: parece ser el único ejemplar conocido).

This statement demonstrates that Moore owned a copy of this edition and clearly believed that it was unique. Yet he provided no details concerning the source of his copy, and I regret that I did not make inquiry of him during the period that we were colleagues. It also must have come from El Paso in view of that city's being the source of all other known copies of the edition referred to. It is clear that Moore's acquisition antedates Englekirk's, for Moore had already made substantially the same statement in his "Biografía y bibliografía de don Mariano Azuela." Had he stumbled across the stock that Englekirk reported finding in La Ideal, he would not have noted that it was the "único ejemplar conocido." Surely he would have acquired more than the single copy that he has reported, and others distributed by him would have come to light in the more than twenty-five years that have elapsed since his death.

During the years of the Second World War, Donald H. Walther, later of Purdue University, was a government employee stationed in El Paso. During his residence there, at one of the local bookstores he acquired a copy of the 1916 edition which he later presented to Sturgis E. Leavitt of the University of North Carolina. In all likelihood he retained also a copy for his own use.

The critical literature on Azuela and his works contains no other references to copies of the 1916 edition, and I have no personal knowledge of copies other than the ones mentioned. By the mid-1940s a new group of Mexican novelists had begun its entry on the scene, and attention turned away from Azuela, who had never regained the center of the stage which he had occupied since 1925. Likewise enthusiasm for the search for his early works has flagged. A few have kept it up, but it is no longer the intense concern of students of Mexican literature.

In the long run, the results of the quest have been clear and tangible in that copies of the 1916 edition of *Los de abajo* have been salvaged and made available for research. John Englekirk has reported that he presented copies to the libraries of the University of New Mexico and Tulane University. A copy given by him to the late Jefferson Rea Spell is now held by the University of Texas library. Professor Leavitt has presented his to the library of the University of North Carolina. Ernest Moore's copy is now in the Syracuse University library. Four or five copies must remain in private hands in the United States.[16]

Those who sought out the 1916 edition met with some degree of success, but when it came to tracking down the serial edition in *El Paso del Norte,* their efforts came to nought. Englekirk's letter to Azuela is typical of the experiences of those who sought to find it. In subsequent conversations Englekirk has related the difficulties that he encountered in attempting to locate the shop where it was printed or any trace of its files. Ernest Moore confessed ignorance of the existence of the serial edition. "No copies exist," he reports in his bibliography of Azuela's works;[17] he repeats this observation even more emphatically in his *Bibliografía de novelistas de la Revolución Mexicana* (p. 22): "It appears that no copies whatever of this daily newspaper are in existence." This statement strengthens the likelihood that Moore personally visited El Paso in his quest for early editions of the novel.

The most direct and detailed report of the futile search in El Paso is provided by Lawrence B. Kiddle, formerly an associate of Englekirk at the University of New Mexico and later a professor at the University of Michigan. In the

[16]I have not made a serious attempt to determine the number of copies of this edition that may be available in Mexico. Azuela has mentioned that from El Paso he sent one to Victoriano Salado Álvarez, but that copy later passed into other hands (*O.C.,* III, 1113). I have been informed that some years ago an autographed copy was in the possession of Fortino Jaime, a bookdealer in Guadalajara, since deceased. In El Paso Azuela presented copies to Enrique Pérez Arce and J. Jesús Valadez, reviewers of the novel for *El Paso del Norte.*

[17]Ernest R. Moore, "Biografía y bibliografía de don Mariano Azuela," *Ábside,* 4:2 (February, 1940), 55.

summer of 1950, Professor Kiddle made inquiries concerning *El Paso del Norte* at the El Paso Public Library. He passed on to Mariano Azuela the results of his investigation there and observations on local reactions to the initial publication of *Los de abajo* in that city:

> Apparently there is nothing left in the city of either the above-mentioned newspaper [*El Paso del Norte*] or the Gamiochipi family. . . . I explained to the librarian who was in charge of the newspaper collection what I was looking for, even if it were just a few numbers of the publication *El Paso del Norte*. She had heard of your novel and how it had appeared in the columns of a Spanish [*sic*] newspaper of her city. The two of us lamented the fact that no file had been preserved or obtained when it was possible to do so. It is amusing now to hear Texans speak, those who are professors of Spanish in the United States, when they exhibit great pride because *Los de abajo* appeared in Texas. They believe, therefore, that it is a Texan work.[18]

To one familiar with Azuela's life and *Los de abajo*, the characterization of the novel as a Texas work is amusing. It is hardly surprising that no copies of *El Paso del Norte* have been preserved in repositories in El Paso. The latter are oriented to the Anglo element of the population, and the newspaper was intended strictly for a Spanish-speaking Mexican population. Furthermore, *El Paso del Norte* existed for a well-defined purpose—to promote the military and political fortunes of Venustiano Carranza, a purpose that was not meaningful to the Anglo population generally. Carranza's moment on the scene had long since passed when someone finally became interested enough to come looking for *El Paso del Norte*.

For those who wanted to search out *El Paso del Norte*, the obvious approach was to attack the problem directly by going to El Paso and making inquiry on the scene. The city had a relatively stable Spanish-speaking population

with some tradition of journalism if not of book publishing. In the solution of a problem that involved essentially a process of detective work in tracking down a daily newspaper that circulated there for a period of six years or more or in locating its editors or employees, the method of the scholars was logical enough, but unfortunately it seems to have produced no tangible results. There were, at the same time, other available approaches that might have provided clues, and one wonders to what extent those were utilized, particularly the reference works and newspaper indexes normally employed by scholars. For example, since the early years of this century, N. W. Ayer and Sons, an advertising firm of Philadelphia, has prepared an annual listing of all newspapers published in this country, including those printed in a foreign language, providing information concerning their editors, frequency of publication, general contents, and circulation. The Ayers' listings are available at the larger research centers. The San Jacinto Museum of History Association has prepared *Texas Newspapers, 1813–1938*, a careful listing of holdings which it describes as "A Union List of Newspaper Files Available in Offices of Publishers, Libraries, and a Number of Private Collections."[19] The entry for *El Paso del Norte* (p. 7) is disappointing. The compilers have found but one number of the newspaper in the entire United States, that being the issue of July 28, 1917, which is held by the Library of Congress. It sheds no light on the serial edition of *Los de abajo*, which had appeared nearly two years earlier. The University of Texas Library lists no holdings of *El Paso del Norte*. Neither does the *Union Serials List*. To search further in the United States would hardly seem profitable.

During much of its life, and especially during the 1914–1916 period, *El Paso del Norte*, although it was published in the United States, reflected faithfully one aspect of the factionalism of the Mexican revolution. During that time (and perhaps for a longer period) the newspaper

---

[18]From a letter to Azuela dated April 13, 1951, *Epistolario*, p. 141.

[19](Houston, 1941), p. 72.

was subsidized by Venustiano Carranza and his Constitucionalista supporters. Given that situation, one might expect to find some reference to it in bibliographies that deal with the revolution. In fact, Mexican scholars have long been aware of the existence of a lengthy run of *El Paso del Norte,* but for some reason their North American counterparts have failed to take notice. In his excellent *Bibliografía de la Revolución Mexicana,* Roberto Ramos includes the following listing (item 2789):

> (El) PASO del Norte. Diario Político y de información. — El Paso, Texas, 3 de agosto de 1911 a 1º de noviembre de 1917. de la 2.ª Epoca, tomo V, Núm. 258 a la Epoca II, tomo IX, Núm. 2379. — El Paso, Texas (Talleres Gráficos del periódico El Paso del Norte.) 1911–1917.
>   10 v. 51 cm. C B y del C N.[20]

It would appear that Mexicans have been more concerned and more successful in preserving a set of the newspaper than have their North American neighbors. Those who have written on *Los de abajo* have overlooked this reference to *El Paso del Norte* or have failed to track it down. They have not noted it in their writings and apparently have made no effort to locate and consult it. Their attention has been concentrated almost solely upon the city of El Paso as the most likely location of a file and as a consequence have overlooked other possibilities.

The notation at the end of Ramos's citation indicates that in the 1930s the set of *El Paso del Norte* was in private hands. It was in the library of Carlos Basave del Castillo Negrete, upon which Ramos relied heavily as a source of his listings. During the period of the revolution and the years following, Basave was a functionary in the administration of president Venustiano Carranza, of whom he was a close affiliate. During those years he devoted himself to collecting and gathering printed documents and newspapers from the time of the revolution and accumulated a sizable library of that material. Although his own particular interest was the

agrarian program, he showed no favoritism in his collecting and acquired items dealing with a wide range of subjects. His library came to be known to Mexican historians of the 1930s, but literary critics apparently were unaware of its significance in themes relating to their interests.

In the 1940s the situation changed. During that decade Carlos Basave died. The federal government was aware of the wealth of the collection of newspapers and pamphlets and made available funds to purchase the library intact. One of the favorite projects of the late president Manuel Ávila Camacho was the establishment of a new public library in the center of Mexico City. In 1946 he organized an institution of this type under the directorship of José Vasconcelos and gave it the name Biblioteca de México. Its buildings are historic, for they are those of the old fortress and barracks known as La Ciudadela, located on the plaza of the same name in downtown Mexico City, where some of the bloodiest fighting of the Decena Trágica leading to the death of President Francisco I. Madero took place in February, 1913. These buildings also contain Basave's volumes, which have retained their identity, being known as the Fondo Basave, and are kept separately in the Salón Basave.

The set of *El Paso del Norte* described by Roberto Ramos is still contained in the Fondo Basave. In the Fondo's card catalogue is the simple notation: *"El Paso del Norte /* 10 vols. / C B C N." The run of the newspaper, although it is not complete, is significant because it does contain nearly all those numbers in which the serial edition of *Los de abajo* was printed late in 1915. In October, 1972, I was at last able to verify the presence of the run of *El Paso del Norte* in the Biblioteca de México and obtain a photocopy of those issues that contain *Los de abajo.* Thus Ernest Moore's statement of 1940 that "It appears that not a single copy of this newspaper exists" happily must now be rectified.

Mexico, then, has the honor of possessing the only known set of the serial edition of Azuela's novel. How the long run of the newspaper made its way from El Paso, Texas, into

[20](3 vols.; Mexico, 1931–1940).

the library of Carlos Basave del Castillo Negrete is a story of which only a few details are known.[21]

The accessibility of the serial edition makes it possible to fill in and clarify much of the early history of *Los de abajo* that hitherto has been known only imperfectly. The most significant development is the ability to establish the text of the novel as Azuela originally wrote it in Chihuahua and El Paso. That version until now has been denied to scholars of Mexican literature. Neither have they possessed a description of the serial publication suitable for bibliographical purposes. Before proceeding to other features of interest, I treat first the physical features of *Los de abajo* as it appeared in *El Paso del Norte*.

The following is printed as a brief announcement on page one of the October 27, 1915, issue of the newspaper. I reprint and translate it in its entirety:

LEA NUESTRO FOLLETIN

"Los de abajo," novela que hoy empezamos a publicar en forma de folletín, aparecerá encuadernada lujosamente y dentro de pocos días estará a la venta para el público.

READ OUR SERIAL

"Los de abajo," the novel that we are beginning to publish today in serial form, will appear in a luxurious binding and within a few days will be on sale to the public.

The edition promised in a "luxurious binding" is the one that Fernando Gamiochipi had agreed to print for Mariano Azuela in partial payment for *Los de abajo*.

The first installment or folletín appeared in No. 1763 of the Segunda época, or second period, of *El Paso del Norte*. This issue cor-

responds to Wednesday, October 27, 1915. The initial installment begins on the lower part of page three and bears the heading shown in the facsimile.

The text of the novel follows immediately. It is set in ten-point type with a two-point lead between lines, each of which is 3.3 inches long. The text is arranged in three columns that occupy the entire lower part of the page to a depth of 34 lines. The remainder of the folletín is contained in three more columns at the bottom of page four of this issue.

Publication continued through twenty-three folletines; the last one appeared on Sunday, November 21, 1915. The complete tabulation of these folletines appears below, arranged by calendar date during October and November. Immediately below the day of the month I have indicated the number of the folletín that corresponds to that date. It must be noted that *El Paso del Norte* did not appear on Mondays, being published only six days a week.

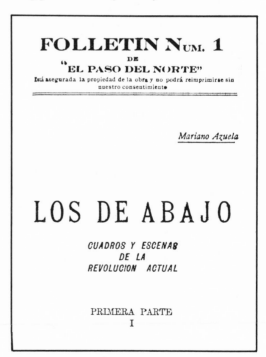

FOLLETIN Núm. 1
DE
" EL PASO DEL NORTE"
Está asegurada la propiedad de la obra y no podrá reimprimirse sin nuestro consentimiento

Mariano Azuela

LOS DE ABAJO

CUADROS Y ESCENAS
DE LA
REVOLUCION ACTUAL

PRIMERA PARTE
I

Initial installment of *Los de abajo* in *El Paso del Norte*, October 27, 1915

[21] Basave's collection was written up on at least one occasion. See Eduardo Enrique Ríos, "Don Carlos Basave y sus libros," *Todo* [Mexico], January 13, 1938, cited in Stanley R. Ross, et al., *Fuentes de la historia contemporánea de México. Periódicos y revistas* (Mexico, 1965), I, 961. Basave, who was a member of a family from Jalisco, was the brother of Agustín Basave, a native of Guadalajara but a longtime resident of Monterrey, where he taught literature and prepared a number of literary studies.

October–November 1915

Sunday	Monday	Tuesday	Wednesday	Thursday	Friday	Saturday
			Oct. 27	*28*	*29*	*30*
			No. 1	No. 2	No. 3	No. 4
Oct. 31	*Nov. 1*	*2*	*3*	*4*	*5*	*6*
No. 5	— —	No. 6	No. 7	No. 8	No. 9	No. 10
Nov. 7	*8*	*9*	*10*	*11*	*12*	*13*
No. 11	— —	No. 12	No. 13	No. 14	No. 15	No. 16
Nov. 14	*15*	*16*	*17*	*18*	*19*	*20*
No. 17	— —	No. 18	No. 19	No. 20	No. 21	No. 22
Nov. 21						
No. 23						

In the issue of November 6, folletín No. 10 is erroneously listed as No. 9. Thus there are two that bear the latter number. The numbering of the issues is not consecutive; the first installment appeared in No. 1763 on October 27 and the last in No. 1755 on November 21 of the Segunda época. At this point it must be noted that the file of *El Paso del Norte* is incomplete. The five issues between October 21 and October 26 are missing as are those for November 11 and 12. The latter two seriously affect the availability of the text of *Los de abajo* in that folletines 14 and 15 are absent. The bound files of *El Paso del Norte* show no signs of ever having contained issues of the newspaper for the dates indicated.

From the second through the twenty-second installment, the six columns of each folletín are divided equally between page two and page three of the newspaper and are placed at the bottom of those pages. The last installment of November 23 contains but two columns of text of the novel, divided between page three and page four. Each installment contains approximately 1,450 words; the novel itself has a total of over 33,000 words.

The text has been set completely by hand. It contains frequent typographical errors and shows little evidence of having been proofread. The impression of the type is not clear and sharp,

and the characters are often blurred where the shoulder has taken ink and printed because of the worn condition of the type. Occasionally a slug has worked loose in the chase with the same result. No illustrations or typographical ornaments of any kind accompany the text of the novel.

This, then, was the form in which Mariano Azuela first saw his creation. Aesthetically it was not much. The type face was undistinguished and of the style ordinarily used by newspapers of the period. It is decidedly not a book face and little care went into its composition. The typographical arrangement was unattractive and the paper was newsprint consisting largely of wood pulp. Fortunately, after sixty years it is still in good condition, although how long it will remain that way is doubtful if it is going to be consulted and handled frequently.

Examination of the files of *El Paso del Norte* has shed light on the specific dates of publication of this primitive edition of *Los de abajo*. Those who interviewed Azuela and later wrote about his work have had to rely upon the author's memory of events that had taken place twenty or twenty-five years previously. Moore, Englekirk, Leal, and others have consistently cited the dates of the serial edition of *Los de abajo* as October–December, 1915. Actually publication lasted a somewhat shorter time. The author has stated clearly that the editor Gamiochipi agreed to pay him on a weekly basis during the time that *Los de abajo* was to be published as a serial in *El Paso del Norte*.[22] The span of publication as indicated on the calendar shown above was but three and one-half weeks and after that period had ended, presumably Azuela received no further cash payment for his work. The lack of funds made the author's existence a precarious one.

In the pages that follow, the focus on the folletín edition will continue throughout the description of *El Paso del Norte* first and later in remarks concerning the first text of the novel.

El Paso del Norte

The daily *El Paso del Norte* at the time when *Los de abajo* was published in its columns was not a pretentious newspaper. It consisted of only four pages of six columns each, and each page measured 37 by 54.5 centimeters. It did not have a specially designed logotype across the top of its front page. Instead, the name of the newspaper appeared in large capital letters three-quarters of an inch high. In "ears" at either side were brief advertisements for local business firms. Immediately below the title is a statement of the newspaper's political position: " 'El Paso del Norte' es el único diario constitucionalista en El Paso, Tex., escrito por mexicanos."

Additional light on the paper and its position is shed by the masthead (here called the *indicador*), which appears on an inside page, sometimes on page two, at others on page three. It says in part: "El Paso del Norte / Diario Político y de Información / Se publica todos los días, con excepción de los lunes. / — / El mejor diario mexicano, más / antiguo y de mayor circula- / ción en más de la mitad / del Estado de Texas." The latter claim is an ambiguous one, especially in the limitation of the geographical area concerned. The address is stated as: "Calle Sur Oregon No. 609 / Teléfono 1255,

P. O. Box 297 / El Paso, Tex." Fernando Gamiochipi is listed as the "Editor Propietario." Oregon Street is located in the southern or "Mexican" part of El Paso not far from the international bridges. It runs north-south between Stanton and El Paso streets. This is the third location of the newspaper. From January, 1912 (and perhaps earlier), until mid-1913 its offices were at Calle Texas No. 315. They then moved to the "Esquina de las Calles Overland y Santa Fe No. 119," and finally to South Oregon Street. Between 1912 and 1917 the telephone number and the post office box always remained the same.

Frequently an advertisement for the newspaper and its printshop appeared on page three, just above columns four to six of the folletín of *Los de abajo* of that particular issue. The framework for the advertisement occupied the full width of the page and was imposing enough to substitute for the logotype on page one. The printshop, the Imprenta Moderna, claimed that it was the "Casa Editora del único Diario Constitucionalista / en ambas fronteras." It further noted that *El Paso del Norte* was founded in 1903, adding that "Su circulación es LA MAYOR ALCANZADA POR NINGÚN / OTRO DIARIO escrito en Castellano / en ambas Fronteras."

[22]*O.C.*, III, 1268.

INDICADOR

EL PASO DEL NORTE

DIARIO POLITICO Y DE INFORMACION

Se publica todos los días, con excepción de los lunes.

El mejor diario mexicano, más
antiguo y de mayor circulación en más de la mitad
del Estado de Texas

`Este periódico fué registrado
como artículo de segunda clase en
la Oficina de Correos de Ciudad
Juárez, Méx., el 9 de Mayo de
1914.

Entered as second class matter
November 20 of 1910 at the Post
Office of El Paso, Texas, U. S. A.
under the Act, of march 3 of 1879

Precios de subscripción:

Por un año $4.50
Por seis meses 2.75
Por tres meses 1.50

Oficina: Calle Sur Oregon No. 609
Teléfono 1255.   P. O. Box 297.
El Paso, Tex.

Editor Propietario,
FERNANDO GAMIOCHIPI

No se servirá ningún pedido
que no venga acompañado de su
valor.

The masthead of *El Paso del Norte*

Some of the statements are clearly factual, but others are open to doubt. In using the term "Constitucionalista," the newspaper clearly identifies itself with the forces and ideas of Venustiano Carranza. In this period Villa nominally supported the Convencionista government. Thus the opposing factions were Constitucional-istas and Convencionistas. That it was the only Constitucionalista daily in the El Paso-Ciudad Juárez area is hardly surprising. Until late December, 1915, Ciudad Juárez and Mexican territory across the Río Grande to the city of Chihuahua and beyond was in the hands of the Villistas, and one would hardly expect them to permit a Carrancista newspaper to operate in territory under their control. The question of circulation is open to question also. The *El Paso Morning Times* had long been established in the community, and its section in Spanish derived substantial support from it. I have been unable to check figures for the 1915 period in the annual directory of N. W. Ayer and Sons.

Because the file of *El Paso del Norte* is incomplete, the date of its first publication cannot be determined precisely. The available file is entirely of the second period of the newspaper. In his bibliography Ramos has noted that Basave's holdings consist of ten volumes. The card catalogue of the Biblioteca de México has retained the numbering system used by Carlos Basave del Castillo Negrete and lists these as volumes 19 through 28, as indicated by the call number in the card catalogue: "G - VII - 19 a 28 / 'El Paso del Norte' / 1911-1917. —El Paso, Tex. 10 vols." Of these, the library does not contain volumes 19 and 21. Volume 19 obviously began with the issue of August 3, 1911, as cited by Ramos. The earliest issue of the Biblioteca de México collection is Época II, Tomo V, Núm. 328, for January 5, 1912. The last issue is Época II, Tomo IX, Núm. 2308 [2380], for November 2, 1917. There is an obvious typographical error in the number assigned to that issue. There are numerous lacunae between these two issues. In addition to volumes 19 and 21, individual numbers are missing here and there. Despite these holes, the collection of

El Paso del Norte is both extremely valuable and highly useful to students of Mexico's revolutionary period.

Assuming that there were six issues per week, the Época II must have begun in late September or early October, 1910, when revolutionary activity against president Porfirio Díaz of Mexico following the ceremonies in commemoration of the centenary of the country's independence began to intensify. In view of the chronology of the Mexican revolution, the hypothesis would seem a sound one. Other than the reference in the house advertisement to the newspaper's founding in 1903, there is no evidence concerning an earlier period of publication. If it had actually been established in 1903, publication was not continuous from that time until 1911. Ayer and Sons do not report that the newspaper was in publication, yet there must have been an Época I. It would have been well before the beginning of the revolution, and in that case the newspaper could not have been supported by Venustiano Carranza.

Throughout the years of the revolution, page one was devoted largely to military news, although there was a constant interest in political items. For example, in the issue of February 10, 1913, headlines in large type announce the beginning of the revolt against Madero's government that was to turn into the Decena Trágica, with news of the plotting of Félix Díaz and the death of General Bernardo Reyes when he tried to attack the Palacio Nacional in the capital. *El Paso del Norte* on September 7, 1915, erroneously reported that Benjamín Argumedo and Higinio Aguilar had been executed by Villa. In October of that year the latter's military situation began to deteriorate rapidly, and the Carrancistas accelerated their northward movement along the principal rail line between Zacatecas and Ciudad Juárez.

The columns of *El Paso del Norte* made the most of this situation and pointed with glee to the difficult straits of the enemy, to the desertions of soldiers and their officers, and to real and alleged atrocities committed by Villa and his followers. They reported the surrender of officials in the Villista government and the flight northward of others. The number of Saturday, October 2, carried the headline on page one: "Nueve trenes de refugiados vienen en camino para la frontera" 'Nine trainloads of refugees are headed for the border,' and a subhead announced an "Enorme caravana a pie" 'An enormous caravan on foot.' Many of these sought refuge across the border in the United States. Page one of the October 13 issue announced the presence of "Miles de oficiales vi- / llistas en El Paso" 'Thousands of Villista officers in El Paso.' At approximately that time Azuela himself moved north from Chihuahua to cross the border into the United States. His friend Enrique Luna Román had preceded him by a few days.

The writers did not strive for objectivity in their reporting and the references to figures of the opposition were uncomplimentary and even offensive. The following quotations illustrate the degree of invective employed: " . . . se está formando un tren de provisiones que se va a mandar al traidor Canuto Reyes." '. . . a trainload of provisions is being put together to send to the traitor Canuto Reyes.' "Hablamos con algunos bandidos villistas sobre las últimas derrotas de los aranguistas." 'We have spoken with several Villista bandits concerning the recent defeats of Arango's [Villa's] followers.' "El asesino Villa se encuentra indeciso en Alamito." 'The murderer Villa is in Alamito, unable to make up his mind.' ". . . estuvieron al lado del bandolero Villa." '. . . they were at the side of the robber Villa.' ". . . se informa que Miguel Baca Valles, cobarde asesino de algunos niños parralenses, tutor y mentor de Villa, fue asesinado en Chihuahua. No se dan los detalles de la muerte de ese monstruo." '. . . it has been reported that Miguel Baca Valles, the cowardly murderer of a number of children from Parral, the teacher and guardian of Villa, has been assassinated in Chihuahua. The details of the death of that monster are not yet known.' *El Paso del Norte* reported on December 21, 1915, the surrender of Ciudad Juárez to Carranza's forces the previous day. The city was handed over without a shot being fired, after negotiations between the Villista garrison and various Carrancista functionaries.

Occasionally the columns were enlivened by contributions from well-known figures of the period. These in general were vocal in their support of Venustiano Carranza or their condemnation of Villa. Rarely did they display equanimity. Much of page three of the number for Saturday, November 27, 1915, is taken up by "Un discurso del Dr. Atl en Piedras Negras." Atl was, of course, Gerardo Murillo, a native of Jalisco and one of the artists and intellectuals who joined Carranza at the time of the break with Villa. Especially vitriolic toward Villa was Pascual Ortiz Rubio who published various chapters "de un libro en preparación." These he entitled "Pancho Villa, hijo adoptivo de la Casa Blanca." Six or seven sections appeared, beginning Saturday, August 14, 1915.

Fernando Gamiochipi made the most of a lengthy letter written by the Peruvian poet José Santos Chocano to Manuel Bonilla, a onetime supporter of Carranza and later of Villa. Gamiochipi printed a facsimile of the letter, seven pages long in Santos Chocano's handwriting on stationery of the Hotel Paso del Norte, dated August 30, 1915, and directed to Bonilla, who was in New York. The much publicized letter bore the imposing headline "Santos Chocano se dirige a Manuel Bonilla / 'Francisco Villa es un epiléptico' " in *El Paso del Norte* for Sunday, September 12, 1915. The letter appears prominently on page one and is continued inside on page three. The point here is that Santos Chocano, who once supported Villa enthusiastically, now refers to his former idol in the most uncomplimentary terms.

There was a strong patriotic note on the front page of the newspaper for Thursday, September 16, 1915. The borders for this Independence Day number were in red and green, with a portrait of Father Miguel Hidalgo and the Águila Mexicana in prominence appropriate to the occasion. In the lower corners were the poems "Campo de batalla" by Enrique González Martínez and "Soy mexicano" of Manuel Carpio.

If the first page was nonpartisan in its appeal to Mexican patriotism, the inside pages were not. They were devoted to highly laudatory biographies and photographs of Carrancista worthies of the moment, nearly all of them in military uniform. Mariano Azuela was understandably uncomfortable upon seeing his *Los de abajo* in columns adjacent to "news" stories of this nature. But only a Carrancista newspaper would pay him for his novel.

Frequently *El Paso del Norte* included news about other newspapers and journalists who were active in El Paso and northern Mexico. The blood pressure of Gamiochipi and his reporters rose several degrees whenever they mentioned the *El Paso Morning Times* and the editor of its Spanish section, Ramón Prida. The issue of October 27 said of him in its headlines: "El Reaccionario Ramón Prida E- / chado a Patadas del Mor- / ning Times / Lo Sustituye el Bilimbi- / que Tovar y Bueno." Naturally Prida and Tovar were Villistas. But Gamiochipi and Prida had not always been enemies. In 1914 *El Paso del Norte* printed a two-volume work by Prida, *De la dictadura a la anarquía. Apuntes para la historia política de México durante los últimos cuarenta y tres años.*[23] A long-time journalist, Prida (1862–1937) began to protest against Huerta. His differences with Gamiochipi in El Paso obviously are based upon the split between Carranza and Villa in the fall of 1914.

Another target of *El Paso del Norte* was Silvestre Terrazas, one of the officials of Villa's government in the state of Chihuahua. The newspaper identified him as a "santuchón degenerado" 'a sanctimonious degenerate.' Late in 1915 Terrazas fled Mexico to El Paso, where he later founded his own newspaper, *Patria*.

Each issue of *El Paso del Norte* contained

---

[23]Cited in Ramos, *Bibliografía*, I, 368, item 1385. Prida has commented on his stay in the United States in *Datos y observaciones sobre EE. UU. de Norte América* (Mexico, 1922), listed in Ramos, *Bibliografía*, I, 368, item 1384. Prida returned to Mexico late in 1915, approximately at the time that Mariano Azuela crossed the frontier into Chihuahua. See *Diccionario Porrúa* (3d ed., 2 vols.; Mexico, 1971), II, 1674.

an editorial on page two. Usually it supported some action or policy of the Carranza faction and was much more subdued than the news columns. Elsewhere on the interior pages Gamiochipi printed lengthy articles on various themes, reminiscences of the revolution, figures prominent in the revolutionary period, and arguments in support of revolutionary political or economic theory. The tone is frequently anticlerical. These articles are usually signed and are contributed by a variety of authors.

It is clear that *Los de abajo* was not the only literary work to be published in *El Paso del Norte*. On page one of the newspaper for November 23, 1915, one finds this notice: "Lea usted nuestro / nuevo folletín en / 3a y 4a páginas." This is the first number following the completion of the serial edition of Azuela's *Los de abajo*. On page three the new serial begins: "Folletín Num. 1 / 'VIDA Y HECHOS DE / PERIQUILLO SARNIENTO.' " In subsequent issues the same format is followed as for *Los de abajo*. Mariano Azuela has never commented on the sequence of the two serials in *El Paso del Norte* but for once, at least, *Los de abajo* was in good company.

In some numbers there is a Sección Literaria, which contains short items in prose or in verse. In the issue of November 21, for example, this section is made up of two poems, one by J. Jesús Valadez and the other by Felipe Guzmán Medina, the latter identified as a resident of El Paso. In the same number is a piece in prose, "Caín," by Miguel Ángel Fernández Ochoa, a short story based on an episode of the revolution.

Several sources of news are apparent. Frequently a reporter for *El Paso del Norte* interviewed travelers in El Paso or Ciudad Juárez from areas where Villa still was in control, for example, North Americans who had just arrived from the city of Chihuahua or Mormons who lived in Casas Grandes in remote western Chihuahua. There were correspondents, who were not identified, in Ciudad Juárez, just across the river from El Paso, and in other cities in central Mexico. Often a story from one of the latter points bore a name and the identification

"El Jefe de la Of[icina] de Inf[ormación]." These came from Guadalajara, Toluca, and Mérida, among other cities, and were put out by Carrancista press agents. Other stories from Mexico bore the notation "Por correo" and probably came from the same sources. Occasionally an item or article was reprinted from another newspaper or periodical. There is no indication that any of the stories were ever taken from a wire service nor are there many stories concerning domestic events in the United States that had little or no relation to Mexico.

If the news columns were restricted in large degree to subjects that bore some relation to Mexico, no such limitation existed for the advertisements, which were much more varied. They occupied at least half the space on pages two, three, and four and must have provided a consistent source of revenue for the newspaper. The goods and services that they offered appealed for the most part to Mexicans and Anglo-Americans alike, but because only the Spanish language was used, they consequently were directed toward a Mexican audience.

There were moving picture houses with Charlie Chaplin and Mack Sennett comedies and at the same time another theater with zarzuelas in Spanish. Dundee Woolen Mills offered men's winter suits for as little as $15. Doctors were prepared to treat a wide range of human afflictions, and dentists would make a *dentadura completa* at a price ranging from five to eight dollars. Victrolas cost as little as $16 and could be bought for two dollars down and one dollar a week in payment. Records, largely of band music, cost seventy-five cents each. The Carrancista *El Paso del Norte* advertised the recording "Francisco Villa—Paso doble." Lawyers and music teachers offered their services. Loans were available for buying property and residences, including adobe houses. An office supply firm was agent for the "máquina de escribir 'Oliver,' " one of which figures in an incident in *Los de abajo* preceding the attack on Zacatecas (Part I, Chapter XVIII).

Other advertisements tied in more closely with the place and the times: "A los refugiados.

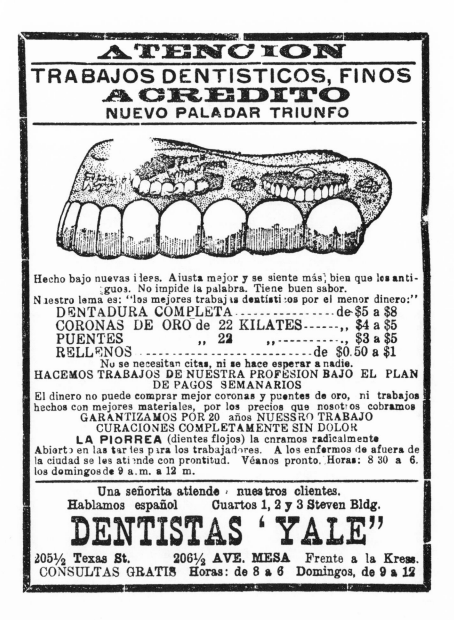

Encontrarán buenos cuartos de rentar en la línea de Highland Park. 2413 Copper Street."
The Restaurant México served *mole poblano* on
Sundays and enchiladas every evening. These
establishments could well have appealed to
Mariano Azuela, who has remarked in his *Obras
completas* on the cheap and abundant food in
El Paso.[24] For those who craved Mexican alcoholic beverages, there were numberous bars,
including the Cantina Tres Piedras. A professor
advertised evening classes for anyone who was
anxious to learn English. More closely con-
nected with the business community was the El
Paso Exchange System, which bought and sold
currency of the various political factions of
Mexico. The advertisement of the Compañía
Ensayadora Mexicana reflected the predomi-
nance of the mining industry of the area.

Extremely pertinent to the history of the
early editions of *Los de abajo* is the offering of
La Ideal. In practically every issue it informs
the reading public that it has a stock of "novelas
en español," magazines, picture postcards, and

stationery in general at its place of business at
Calle Overland No. 108. The owner of the firm
at that time was J. R. Díaz and Company, whose
mailing address was P. O. Box 38, El Paso.
Thus La Ideal was doing business at the time
when *El Paso del Norte* was printing *Los de
abajo* in serial form and Fernando Gamiochipi
was printing the novel in paperback. Certainly
a bundle of the latter, perhaps the bulk of the
printing, made its way on to the shelves of La
Ideal. There John Englekirk found a number of
them twenty-five years later. In the intervening
period there was ample opportunity for the purchase of other copies of *Los de abajo,* in addition to those bought by Moore, Englekirk, and
Walther. Did no one living in the El Paso area
buy copies between 1915 and 1940? This hardly
seems likely, and other copies may still be held
by private parties.

The printshop was an important factor in a
small operation such as *El Paso del Norte.* The
shop not only set up and printed the six issues
per week of the newspaper but also did extensive commercial printing for the local community, in addition to an occasional book. The job

[24]*O.C.,* III, 1089.

printing operation must have been a steady source of income over the years.

José Jesús Loera Rivera of Los Angeles, who as a youth worked in the printshop, has generously drawn upon his memory to provide details concerning its operation. Fernando Gamiochipi restricted his activities to the editing of *El Paso del Norte,* so that Loera had little opportunity to become acquainted with him. The operation of the shop was entrusted to a Mexican foreman who directed all its activities, which were organized according to the traditional Mexican *gremio* or craft system.

Much of the actual work was done by a crew of youths, really young boys, who were learning to be printers. Loera, who was born in 1903, worked on *El Paso del Norte* in 1914 and 1915. He was hired as a compositor, setting type by hand, for which he was paid one dollar for each galley. Other boys of Loera's age were hired for the same purpose and did the bulk of the typesetting for *El Paso del Norte.* The newspaper was printed on a flatbed cylinder press, of a type described by Loera as a "prensa de cilindro cuadruplo," in which the type lay flat, then was inked. The paper was placed over the type and then a heavy cylinder passed over it in order to make the impression. The press was fed by hand. The establishment did not possess a linotype machine, consequently all type was laboriously set by hand. Facilities for providing illustrations for the newspaper were extremely limited.

Throughout the five-year period between 1912 and 1917, *El Paso del Norte* retained practically the same format, except for special news events or patriotic occasions. There was an occasional "extra" when there was a resounding military victory for the Carrancistas or their government was recognized by a foreign power. The ink used was consistently black except for the issues for September 16. With constant use the type used in the news columns had become noticeably worn. This condition was particularly noticeable in the type of the masthead, which became blurred and hard to read. Apparently the masthead was set up and used for five years or more without change.

All staff members of *El Paso del Norte* and all employees of the printshop were Mexicans, residents of Ciudad Juárez across the river. There was not a single North American in the operation. Fernando Gamiochipi functioned as director and editor of the daily, apparently responsible for the editorials and the general policy of the newspaper. In 1912 Gamiochipi was identified as the "editor" and T. F. Serrano as "director" in that order. After that year, Gamiochipi held the post of "editor propietario." I have not yet been able to identify Serrano.

Immediately below Gamiochipi were several *redactores,* who did the major portion of the news gathering, interviewing, and writing of the stories that filled the columns of *El Paso del Norte.* One of the redactores was named Ugartechea (Loera does not recall his given name), a man of thirty or thirty-two, always very neat and well dressed. Ugartechea wrote many of the longer unsigned articles during 1914 and 1915. Two brothers named Calderón also worked as reporters. In 1915 or soon thereafter the brothers established their own newspaper in the border area, giving it the name *El Popular.* One of the brothers later moved on to Mexico, where he became associated with a longtime North American expatriate William O. Jenkins (1878–1963), who owned textile factories, sugar mills, and business enterprises in Mexico. Jenkins placed Calderón on the staff of *El Heraldo de México,* another of his properties, a daily newspaper that was being published in the capital in the early 1920s. Years later after the death of Jenkins, Calderón inherited certain concerns that Jenkins had owned.

The names of Gamiochipi and Ugartechea do not appear in records and Mexican reference works of the 1920s and later. Apparently they did not remain long in El Paso. Neither did Enrique Aguirre, who was a fellow worker with Loera in the printshop of *El Paso del Norte.* Aguirre moved to Los Angeles, where for many years he operated his own printing establishment on Alpine Street in the vicinity of Union Station.[25]

Aside from what I have been able to glean from the columns of *El Paso del Norte*, I have found but one reference to Fernando Gamiochipi. After the new Carrancista commander reached Ciudad Juárez early in 1916, he attempted to enlist public support for the purpose of cleaning up the city. He held a low opinion of Gamiochipi, which was based on the news-

paperman's performance or lack of it: "I appointed a Committee for Public Health, which failed because the demoralization of the people had reached such a degree that there was no one to call upon. Mr. Gamiochipi, the editor of the newspaper 'El Paso del Norte,' turned out to be so apathetic and useless that he did not get around to organizing the committee of which he had been named president."[26]

The El Paso Editions

In the issue of October 27, 1915, the day the first installment of *Los de abajo* was printed in *El Paso del Norte*, Fernando Gamiochipi announced that a separate edition of the novel would be forthcoming. During the weeks when the serial was appearing, advertisements for the promised edition appeared at intervals. The brief advertisement in the facsimile is from page three of the newspaper for Saturday, October 30.

The publication still was not ready when *Los de abajo* was completed with the installment of Sunday, November 21. Presumably the composition was not ready until that time or shortly before. Then it was necessary to rearrange the type of the text in new chases to conform to the pages of the book, to number these, and to prepare a cover and title page. Then the promised edition could be printed.

"LOS DE ABAJO"

Cuadros y Escenas de la Revolución Mexicana actual.
Por MARIANO AZUELA.
Novela de palpitante interés y de gran actualidad.
PRONTO ESTARA DE VENTA.

Advertisement for *Los de abajo* in *El Paso del Norte*, October 27, 1915

---

[25]There were other printing concerns in El Paso in 1914–1915. In one of these, owned by North Americans, the foreman was a German referred to as "Ike," his last name now forgotten. Loera remembers him with respect, for he encouraged the young Loera to attend school in El Paso, where he took courses that prepared him for the trade of printer, to which he devoted his adult life.

[26]Gabriel Gavira Castro, *General de Brigada Gabriel Gavira. Su actuación político-militar revolucionaria* (2d ed.; Mexico, 1933), p. 165.

This activity consumed a week or two. The first indication that it is at last ready comes in the issue of Sunday, December 5, 1915, when a new advertisement makes its appearance on page four:

"Los de Abajo"

Por Mariano Azuela

"CUADROS Y ESCENAS DE LA REVOLUCION MEXICANA"

Esta novela es el trasunto más fiel de la contienda civil en México. Su autor no adula a ninguno de los partidos políticos y con la verdad desnuda dolorosamente flagela el crimen y la injusticia en donde quiera que lo encuentra, sin restricciones ni piedad alguna.

Remita Ud. 30 centavos en giro postal, en timbres o por express, y recibirá un ejemplar de "Los de Abajo" franco de porte.

De venta en "El Paso del Norte."

Immediately below is a short advertisement printed from boiler plate in which a New York firm asks the reader "¿Es Ud. SORDO?" in an effort to sell him a cure for deafness. Below that was a three-column advertisement announcing a Sunday performance for children at the Teatro Estrella in El Paso.

The offering of *Los de abajo* continued in most of the issues for the rest of December, 1915. To all intents and purposes, however, the novel appeared on December 5. On the basis of what is presently known, the date cannot be fixed any more accurately than this, and it is highly doubtful that any evidence obtained in the future is going to change matters to any extent. The outside cover bears the statement "Copyrigth [*sic*] by Mariano Azuela November 1915." The title page reads "1916 / IMPRENTA DE 'EL PASO DEL NORTE' / EL PASO, TEXAS." The former of these is the more accurate.

When the volume became available, Azuela sent or presented copies to various of his friends. He mailed a copy to Victoriano Salado Álvarez, who at that time was residing in Mexico City.[27] The author has not mentioned others to whom he sent copies, but from another source we learn that he gave copies to at least two of his acquaintances in El Paso. It is opportune to mention them because they are the first Mexicans to record a reaction to *Los de abajo*.

In later years Azuela commented bitterly on the initial reception of his novel. He remarked that one month after it appeared in the bookstores of El Paso, only five copies had been sold.[28] He was not encouraged by the expression of Villista officers stationed in Ciudad Juárez who had read *Los de abajo* and advised him not to return to that city.[29] Azuela has never mentioned the commentaries published by his friends in *El Paso del Norte* in December, 1915. He has made known the touching scene in which he read the recently completed manuscript to a group of fellow refugees in a hotel room in El Paso.[30] One of those present, Enrique Pérez Arce, later wrote a brief review of the novel which was printed on page two of *El Paso del Norte* for Friday, December 10, 1915. It follows in the left-hand column below with its translation to the right.

[27] *O.C.*, III, 1112–1113.
[28] In "El novelista y su ambiente," *O.C.*, III, 1088.
[29] In a letter to L. B. Kiddle dated November 10, 1948 (*Epistolario*, p. 140).
[30] *O.C.*, III, 1081–1082.

LOS DE ABAJO

De puntillas, sin que nadie lo sienta, el Dr. Azuela llega a la ventana lírica del arte, deja ahí furtivamente un puñado de rosas frescas, y luego torna a su viejo retiro silencioso.

On tiptoe, without anyone noting his presence, Dr. Azuela approaches the lyrical window of art, lays there uneasily a bouquet of fresh roses, and then withdraws into his usual silent retreat.

Como de las nieves alpinas brotan flores de encanto, así del olvido (injusto olvido por cierto) en que labora Mariano Azuela, surgen libros perfumados y bellos que compendian el armonioso espíritu de la Patria.

Gráfica, como "María Luisa;" intencionada como "Los Fracasados;" pintoresca y sutil como "Mala Yerba," producciones pretéritas de su brillante péñola, aparece su última novela "Los de Abajo," que es la cristalización de las escenas más típicas de la actual Revolución Mexicana. Todo aquel que conozca de cerca los hombres (los de abajo) y las cosas de la guerra social que conmueve a nuestro país, podrá identificarlos en los capítulos de esta interesante obrita, llena de color y de vida nacionales. El soldado, el General, la muchacha raptada, el saqueo, el asalto, el cañón de la sierra, el villorio tomado a sangre y fuego, todas aquellas almas rústicas, todos esos episodios sangrientos, todos estos lugares comunes, están descriptos con galanura literaria y maravillosa observación.

Riscos de la montaña, donde los pinares gimen como apocalípticos violones pulsados por el viento!

Llanuras interminables y resecas, sobre las cuales mueren los hombres de insolación y los caballos de sed. Aquí rostros febriles, pañuelos blancos y húmedos que defienden las cabezas del sol, ánforas que se vacían desesperadamente, bestias que se cansan y bocas que blasfeman! Allá, el vivac en torno de una gran hoguera, donde el ocote chisporrotea, las "gordas" se calientan y la tropa charla animosamente al calor de las viejas y la lumbre!

Y, lamido por las aguas límpidas y azules del arroyo, al que bajan las mujeres con sus cántaros olorosos, el pueblo de casas de adobe, capilla descuartizada, vecindario medroso y huertos en flor, entre cuyas fragancias se madura "ella," la ranchera bonita de diecisiete años, la muchacha sabrosa de sangre cálida y diabólicas redondeces, trenzas sembradas de flores y pestañas chinas, pechos incitantes y ojos muy negros, que junto al comal se enamora del

In the same manner that delightful flowers spring forth from alpine snows, so do splendid, delicious books issue from the oblivion (certainly an undeserved oblivion) in which Dr. Azuela toils, books that distill the proper spirit of the country.

Vivid, like *Maria Luisa;* to the point, like *Los fracasados;* graphic and observant, like *Mala yerba,* past productions of his brilliant pen, so appears his most recent novel, which is the essence of the most typical scenes of the present Mexican Revolution. Everyone who knows at first hand the men (the underdogs) and all the details of the social war that is disturbing our country will recognize them in the chapters of this exciting book, charged with the color and the life of our nation. The soldier, the general, the kidnapped maiden, the pillaging, the attack, the gorge in the sierra, the little town captured with fire and sword, all those humble souls, all those bloody episodes, all these well-known places are described with a literary charm and expert observation.

Mountain crags, where the pine forests groan like fateful viols that are stroked by the wind!

Endless parched plains upon which men die of sunstroke and their horses of thirst. Here one glimpses feverish faces, moist white handkerchiefs that protect heads from the sun, canteens that are drained furiously, mounts that are exhausted and mouths that curse! There the soldiers camp at night around an enormous fire where the pine log crackles and pops, the tortillas are heated up and the fighting men chatter spiritedly warmed up by their women and the fire!

And, lapped by the clear blue waters of the stream, where women come down with their fragrant pitchers, in the village made up of humble houses of adobe, the little church with cracked, ruined walls, fearful villagers and orchards in bloom, among whose perfumes "she" comes of age, the seventeen-year-old-country girl, the alluring hot-blooded maiden with tempting roundness to her figure, with flowers in her hair and dark eyelashes, breasts that

sargento bizoño, quien en una noche de placer y de luna, se la roba en su caballo zaíno y va a tender el tálamo debajo del huanacastle del camino, a cuya sombra los besos y el mezcal hacen su fiesta, hasta que las dianas despiertan al campamento y el lucero del alba, como luminosa esfera de cristal lanzada por un malabarista caótico, va elevándose en el cielo rosado por los primeros rayos de la aurora.

Y en el fondo de todos los paisajes, como queriendo inluminar los corazones, la lucecita azul de ensueño patriótico, del ideal político, de la justificación de estas santas rebeldías del pueblo esclavizado, de estas benditas cóleras de la raza escarnecida y triste que en un día de admonición y de protesta, dejó el yugo del negrero y cogió el fusil revolucionario para irse al combate y buscar una revancha y un desquite!

Que plumas doctorales hagan la crítica literaria del libro. Acaso muchas páginas sean susceptibles de pulimento. Acaso algunos de los protagonistas sean, psicológicamente falsos. Tal vez la obra en general padezca deficiencias que deban corregirse. Pero quien glosa estas líneas es incompetente para hacer tal estudio y se reduce a dejar estampada aquí su impresión y como de todas maneras juzga que el esfuerzo es noble y bien logrado, y superior a todos los semejantes que han atestado los escaparates de folletos sin alma y sin arte, reciba un cordial y entusiasta aplauso el inteligente y modesto autor.

E.P.A.

Pérez Arce was somewhat younger than Mariano Azuela. When he was in El Paso, he could not have been more than twenty-five. He had much the same background as Azuela. He was a graduate of a secondary school in Guadalajara with which the novelist was familiar. When the revolution came, both had cast their lot with Villa and served with his armies during much of 1915. When his fortunes dropped late in the year, they fled Mexico and met in El Paso.

arouse thoughts, black eyes, who by the kitchen fire sets her affection on the greenhorn sergeant, who one pleasurable moonlit night spirits her away on his chestnut horse and spreads out the nuptial bed beneath the conacaste tree beside the road, in whose shadows kisses and alcohol come into play until the notes of the bugle arouse the sleeping soldiers and the morning star, like a shining crystal sphere tossed by a wild juggler, ascends into the rose-colored sky through the first rays of dawn.

And in the background of all these scenes, as if trying to bring some insight into human hearts, the little blue light of a patriotic flight of fancy, of a political vision, of an apology for these sacred uprisings of enslaved people, of the hallowed rage of the lowly scorned breed who one day of remonstrance and protest threw off the yoke of the slave driver and seized the revolutionary weapon to go off to war to seek revenge and retaliation!

Let learned pens undertake literary criticism of the work. Perhaps many pages are in need of polishing. Perhaps some of the characters are not psychologically true. It may be that the work in general has defects that ought to be corrected. But this writer is not qualified to embark upon such a study and limits himself to putting down here his impressions and in any case concludes that the attempt has been a noble one and well achieved, by far superior to all those others that have clogged the shop windows with lifeless and artless pamphlets. May the intelligent and modest author receive a hearty and vigorous round of applause.

E.P.A.

Unlike most of Azuela's associates in 1915, Pérez Arce was an intellectual. He was one of the few friends and acquaintances of the writer who was able to appreciate what he had done in *Los de abajo*. In addition to possessing a comparable military and political background, he had a certain flair for writing and particularly for stringing together a series of images. This he did in his commentary on *Los de abajo*, demonstrating an appreciation of the novel's plot, its scenery, and the outlook on the revolution that Azuela expressed. Of all this Pérez Arce approves. When it comes down to an evaluation of the novel on a purely literary basis, he evades the issue, taking refuge in generalities. He refers to characters who are not well drawn, to "deficiencias" that need to be corrected, and passages that need further polishing. Pérez Arce certainly was aware of the haste with which Azuela wrote his novel and in the absence of evidence to the contrary, one must consider that his remarks were directed toward flaws in the novel of which Azuela was already well aware.

By December 10, the date on which the commentary was printed, Pérez Arce surely had received from Azuela a copy of the paperback edition of the novel. Another commentary, written by J. Jesús Valadez, appeared on pages two and three of *El Paso del Norte* for Tuesday, December 21. Valadez declares that Azuela has already presented him a copy which the author had dedicated appropriately. The commentary of Valadez is as follows:

LOS DE ABAJO

El señor Doctor Mariano Azuela me ha hecho el honor de distinguirme, confiriéndome, con atenta dedicatoria, un ejemplar de su galana novela revolucionaria, la cual lleva el mismo nombre del epígrafe con que encabezo estas líneas.

La obra del señor Azuela es sencillamente magistral.

Escrito en estilo conciso, sencillo y claro, y en el lenguaje castizo de "los de abajo," ella es la interpretación genuina del alma popular.

Por ella pasan, como por una película fantástica, todas las peripecias de las guerrillas formadas por nuestros hombres del pueblo, los más perseguidos, los más explotados y escarnecidos por las pasadas y brutales tiranías, que por fin han logrado sacudir aquellos, a costa de tantos y tan cruentos sacrificios.

Ella nos trae en sus páginas aromas de la nativa tierruca lejanas, con sus bosques seculares y sus riachuelos murmuradores; con sus praderas olientes a tomillo silvestre, y sus campos exornados con el oro de las espigas; con sus montañas nativas de empenachados airones y de intricadas bifurcaciones, tras de cuyos riscos abruptos se parapeta el rebelde que, por medio de un certero dispara, hace rodar junto a la linfa del arroyuelo al infeliz "pelón," como les llama nuestro vulgo a los pobres ex-federales.

En ella campean descripciones y pasajes tan atrevidos y sugestivos como el siguiente:

Doctor Mariano Azuela has done me the honor of bestowing upon me, with a kind dedication, a copy of this splendid revolutionary novel, which bears the same name as the title that appears at the head of these lines.

Doctor Azuela's work is simply masterly.

Written in a concise style that is simple and clear and in the noble style of "the underdogs," it is the genuine interpretation of the popular spirit.

Through it pass, as through a fantastic film, all the ups and downs of the guerrilla bands formed by our common people, those who have been the most persecuted, exploited, and scorned by brutal tyrannies in the past, who finally have succeeded in shaking them off, at the cost of so many bloody sacrifices.

In its pages it brings us the distant fragrance of our native land, with its century-old forests and its gurgling streams, with its meadows smelling of wild thyme, and its fields adorned with the gold of the heads of grain; with its native mountains with spectacular crests and intricate patterns of spurs, behind whose sharp crags the rebel takes shelter and with an unerring shot causes the miserable *pelón* to tumble into the water of the stream, using the term that our common people apply to the wretched soldiers of Díaz's and Huerta's armies.

In it emerge descriptions and passages as bold and striking as this one:

.... "El humo de la fusilería no acaba de extinguirse.

Las cigarras entonan su canto imperturbable y misterioso; las palomas cantan con dulzura en las rinconadas de las rocas; ramonean apaciblemente las vacas.

La sierra está de gala; sobre sus cúspides inaccesibles cae la nieve albísima como un crespón de nieve sobre la cabeza de una novia.

Y al pie de una resquebrajadura enorme y suntuosa, como pórtico de vieja catedral, Demetrio Macías, con los ojos fijos para siempre, sigue apuntando con el cañón de su fusil....."

Ya quien me precedió opinando acerca del libro del Doctor Azuela, hizo muy acertadas y justas apreciaciones; por eso yo, como el primero, dejo a plumas mejor cortadas el juicio crítico de la obra, que quizá no carezca de ciertos defectillos, pero sí aseguro que ellos serán de muy poca monta.

De todos modos, la labor de mi estimado amigo Azuela, es laudable y merecedora de todo encomio, porque él no ha sabido encerrarse en ese indeferentismo criminal de los que injustificadamente se titulan "neutrales," ante los dolores de los que sufren por reconquistar sus perdidas libertades.

Esto pone de manifiesto una vez más, que no estamos solos, y que también en las filas revolucionarias militan hombres de reconocido talento.

Recomiendo, pues, a mis buenos amigos y correligionarios la lectura de tan interesante producción que, además de contener profundas enseñanzas filosóficas y sociológicas, proporciona al que la lee, ratos de verdadero solaz y de expansión, haciendo asomar más de una vez a sus labios, la risa inocente, franca y expontánea.

Vaya por ello mi más expresiva y sincera felicitación al ameno autor de "Los de abajo" cuya obra cierra con el final que he citado, verdaderamente digno de un canto homérico!

J. Jesús VALADEZ

El Paso, Tex., Diciembre 21–15

.... "The smoke of the gunfire has not yet cleared away.

The locusts chant their imperturbable and mysterious song; the doves sing softly in the nooks of the rocks; the cows browse peacefully.

The sierra is in all its finery; on its inaccessible peaks falls dazzling snow like a veil of snow upon the head of a bride.

And at the bottom of an enormous and gorgeous crack in the rock, like the portico of an ancient cathedral, Demetrio Macías, with his eyes fixed for eternity, continuous aiming the barrel of his rifle....."

The one who has already given an opinion concerning Dr. Azuela's work made very appropriate and correct remarks. Therefore I, as he did, leave to more qualified writers the critical evaluation of the work, which perhaps is not free from certain minor defects, but I can declare that they are of but slight significance.

In any case, the work of my esteemed friend Azuela is laudable and worthy of all praise because he has refused to take refuge in that criminal insensibility of those who without justification call themselves neutral in the face of the anguish of those who must suffer in order to regain their lost liberties.

This makes it still clearer that we are not alone and that in the ranks of the revolutionary armies one will find fighting men of recognized talent and ability.

I recommend, then, to my good friends and fellow believers that they read such an interesting creation which, in addition to containing profound philosophical and sociological teachings, will provide its reader moments of recreation and enjoyment and will cause innocent, frank, and spontaneous laughter to appear on his lips.

Therefore my most heartfelt and sincere congratulations are extended to the genial author of *Los de abajo* which closes with the passage that I have cited, one that is truly worthy of a Homeric poem!

J. Jesús VALADEZ

El Paso, Texas, December 21, 1915

The remarks of Valadez hardly differ from what Pérez Arce has already said. In fact, he refers to the previous observations on *Los de abajo* in the newspaper. Valadez uses a few less visual images strung together, perhaps, and he is certainly the first to comment in print on the effectiveness of the final scene of the novel. He was a fairly frequent contributor to the columns of *El Paso del Norte* and would seem to have been a resident of the Ciudad Juárez–El Paso area. I have found no reference to him in works dealing with the literature or the political situation of Mexico.

The December 21 issue of *El Paso del Norte* contains a highly significant news item concerning Mariano Azuela's stay in El Paso. It reports the take-over the previous day by Carrancista forces and the surrender of the Villista garrison in Ciudad Juárez. Azuela had left El Paso and crossed over into Mexico during the first few hours following the change. It is doubtful, then, that he saw what Valadez had written, since he was no longer in El Paso when the article appeared in print.[31]

This was the immediate reception of *Los de abajo* late in 1915. The relatively subdued remarks and their consequences differ markedly from the enthusiasm that Mexico finally began to show for Azuela following the "discovery" of 1925. El Paso was hardly the place that an ambitious author would have chosen for launching an epoch-making novel, certainly not in 1915. It boasted daily newspapers and several well-established magazines that appeared at regular intervals but no publishing concerns that could promote, publicize, and distribute their books and bring them to the attention of a sizable audience. No author of a truly significant novel would want to have his creation printed as a serial in the newspaper of a minority group in a foreign country which could not promote and sell the work and which lacked even adequate typographical facilities for printing a modest book.

[31]I have remarked further on the commentaries by Pérez Arce and Valadez in "Dos comentarios de 1915 sobre *Los de abajo*," *Revista Iberoamericana*, 41 (1975), 267-272.

The delayed appearance of the folletín edition has clarified many of the obscure points in regard to the El Paso publication of the novel. The most important of these is the revelation of the novel as Azuela delivered it to the printer. Thus at long last it provides a starting point for critical study of the text of *Los de abajo.* At the same time, a comparison of the text of the El Paso paperback with the folletín serial provides various clues concerning Azuela's editing of the novel. The combination of hasty writing and abominable typographical conditions in the printshop gave rise to a work that caused Azuela obvious dissatisfaction. This discontent is visible in Azuela's own statements concerning the early appearances of the work. It is clearly evident in the modifications, although they are relatively few and largely of a typographical nature, that were introduced in the paperback edition of December, 1915.

The text of the folletín edition was plagued with typographical errors, probably as a result of the system of hand composition by young boys. Proofreading did very little to remedy the misprints, for an average of two or three have remained in each short column of text. In some respects, the typographical presentation makes it difficult to ascertain how Azuela intended to arrange and divide his chapters. In the Primera Parte the last numbered chapter is XVI, yet there are actually eighteen, for there are two chapters numbered XV and two numbered XVI. The converse exists in the Segunda Parte, where XIV is the last numbered chapter, but there are actually only twelve because numbers VII and XI are omitted. The Tercera Parte has but three chapters of which none are misnumbered. In the Primera Parte of the paperback no rectification of chapter numbering has been made. In the Segunda Parte number VIII is inserted, with no modification of the text, but Chapter XI is still omitted. The Tercera Parte shows no changes.

Both El Paso versions are organized in three parts, a division that Azuela has retained in later redactions. In the table presented below, I have listed the number of chapters present as indicated by the numbering system employed in the corresponding edition. The figures in parentheses refer to the actual number of chapters irrespective of the numbered headings assigned to them. The last column refers to the stable arrangement present in the definitive text established in the edition published by Razaster in 1920.

	Folletín	*Paperback*	*Definitive*
Primera Parte	16 (18)	16 (18)	21
Segunda Parte	14 (12)	14 (13)	14
Tercera Parte	3 (3)	3 (3)	7

The insertion of the chapter heading VIII at the appropriate point in the text causes the paperback to have one more actual chapter than the folletín but gives rise to no appreciable difference between the editions. Both of these are considerably shorter than the rewritten editions that appeared in 1920 and later, not only in the number of chapters but also in actual wordage. Seymour Menton has commented upon the neat tripartite arrangement of chapters in the later versions and points out the proportion of twenty-one, fourteen, and seven chapters,

respectively, in the three parts.[32] Azuela's division in the El Paso editions, whether actual or intended, reveals no such balance, and the text gives no clues to his having had this thought in mind, certainly not in 1915. The typographical arrangement of that year, over which Azuela seemingly had little control, obscures the author's original intention.

It is clear that Gamiochipi utilized the same type that he had set up for the serial in *El Paso del Norte* to print the paperback edition. Not only is the type identical but also the length of the individual lines. Except for the division into folletines, the idiosyncrasies of composition present in the first printing are carried over into the paperback. The impression of broken and defective letters is repeated consistently.

There are, nevertheless, a few changes in composition that are not corrections of typographical errors. They are not the work of a proofreader but of a copyreader and perhaps even of the author himself. A number of these follow:

[32]Seymour Menton, "La estructura épica de 'Los de abajo' y un prólogo especulativo," *Hispania*, 50:4 (1967), 1004-1005.

Folletín	*Paperback*

no. 8, col. 5, line 9: era hombre sólo y tenía mujer y muchos hijos

p. 51, line 25: era hombre pobre y tenía mujer y muchos hijos

no. 8, col. 6, lines 31-33: tienen muy agraviado, me robaron una hija, y un oficialillo me quitó una mujer que yo tenía... ¡Hijos de .....!

p. 53, lines 21-22: tienen muy agraviado: un oficialillo me quitó una mujer que yo tenía.... ¡Hijos de .....!

no. 16, col. 16, lines 23-27: Un mozalvete, de los últimos reclutados, con algo / de aguardiente en la cabeza se ríe y avanza sin zo- / zobra, hacia la puerta. /

Demetrio con la pistola humeante en las manos, / inmutable, espera a que los soldados se retiren.

p. 100, line 26-p. 101, line 2: Un mozalvete, de los últimos reclutados, con algo / de aguardiente en la cabeza, se ríe y avanza sin zo- / zobra hacia la puerta. /

Pero antes de que pueda franquear el umbral, / un disparo instantáneo lo hace caer como los toros heridos por la puntilla. /

Demetrio con la pistola humeante en las manos, / inmutable, espera a que los soldados se retiren.

no. 2, col. 4, line 7: en el hierbazal

p. 14, line 9: en el herbazal

no. 3, col. 1, lines 5-7: —Ya me .... quemaron —gimió Demetrio y rechinó los dientes.

—Hijos de.....! Y con prontitud se dejó resbalar hacia un barranco

p. 17, lines 18-21: —¡Ya me .... quemaron! —gimió Demetrio y rechinó los dientes.

—Hijos de.....! / Y con prontitud se dejó resbalar hacia un ba- / rranco.

no. 6, col. 3, line 8: ¡Allí está otra infelizada más!

p. 37, line 17: ¡Ay está otra infelizada más!

no. 7, col. 22, line 31: Desde hoy vamos a seguir

p. 43, line 9: Desde hoy vamos a ir

no. 7, col. 3, line 1: lo hace Crispín Robles en Juchipila

p. 43, line 11: lo hace Crispín Robles de Juchipila

no. 7, col. 3, line 4: somos más de cien

p. 43, line 14: semos más de cien

no. 9, col. 3, line 25: para agujerear las paredes?

p. 56, line 7: para abujerear las paredes?

no. 16, col. 5, line 10: la equitativa repartición

p. 101, line 18: la equitativa partición

no. 16, col. 5, line 13: Hoy nos está dando de cerca

p. 101, line 21: Hoy nos está dando de cara

no. 17, col. 3, line 14: Yo te voy a sacar de esta agrupación.

p. 105, line 18: Yo te voy a sacar de esta apuración.

None of these differences reflects a major change in the novel, either in its style or structure. The first three differences noted above are of such a nature that they would seem to have been suggested by Azuela himself rather than by a proofreader. Various of the others, particularly where a completely new word has been introduced, also reflect Azuela's direct influence. Some reveal Azuela's preference for a popular form, which is closer to his concept of his character's manner of speech, rather than a standard item. When compared with later editions of *Los de abajo*, these early El Paso editions contain somewhat less use of the rural and popular speech for which the novel is noted. Still other changes are merely the correction of typographical errors that appeared in the folletín: the proper arrangement of transposed letters, the addition of exclamation marks, the capitalization of proper names, spacing between words where none had existed, and the replacement of mis-set characters. Such errors were frequent but less than half of them have been detected and corrected in the second or paperback edition. The printer's font of type did not possess the character *ü*, which occurs with some frequency in the novel. Consequently he substituted the combination *ii* for it, a practice found not infrequently in works set up and printed in Spanish America. For example, one notes in *Los de abajo* the proper name *el güero Margarito.*

Two full weeks elapsed between the last installment of the folletín on Sunday, November 21, and the announced appearance of the paper-

back on December 5. This was the time available for Azuela to correct the novel's text and introduce modifications, although the earlier parts of *Los de abajo* had been set up for the folletín since late October. The typography of the paperback gives evidence of having been prepared in considerable haste. The few modifications that appear to have been introduced by the author occur for the most part in the earlier chapters of *Los de abajo,* as though Azuela had been able to give it attention up to a point, in the time available to him. The text of the final chapters varies in few if any respects, and very few typographical errors present in the folletines have been rectified. The last changes of any consequence at all correspond to Folletín no. 18. Neither Azuela nor anyone else has done anything here to prepare *Los de abajo* for its appearance in book form.

In the haste, the "luxurious binding" that was promised with the first number of the folletín was overlooked, and in its place was substituted a paper cover with a cut based on the initial chapter of the novel showing Demetrio looking down from a height. In the canyon below his house is burning.

Had the El Paso versions of *Los de abajo* been the only ones published, the ultimate fate of the work would have been otherwise. They represent the initial redaction of the novel and, as an artist, Azuela was aware of their strength as well as their shortcomings. He had captured the immediacy of the events of the revolution, the involvement of the ordinary Mexican in a movement that he did not understand and whose direction was beyond his control, and his ultimate disillusion and death. The same circumstances that made possible this achievement did not permit Azuela to attain the artistic expression that he had anticipated. The versions that he produced seem almost improvised, written urgently in the confusion and uneasiness of the revolution, with little opportunity for attention to the work's formal aspects, to careful revision and rewriting. Their initial publication was beset by the same improvisation, haste, and even carelessness. Azuela clearly had envisioned something else and when more relaxed circumstances were at hand, proceeded to provide a version more satisfactory to him.

The Return Home

In the progression from the primitive editions to Azuela's revised text of the novel, the author's return from El Paso to Guadalajara is highly significant. One wonders what form of *Los de abajo* he carried with him. Both the folletín and the paperback editions were available and perhaps even the typed manuscript that he prepared in the office of *El Paso del Norte*. His departure from El Paso was precipitous, perhaps with little opportunity to bundle together his few possesions. Azuela was impoverished when he undertook the arduous southward journey, yet in this humble baggage he carried in some form his novel, practically the only tangible possession that he had acquired during his fifteen months as a revolutionary. The future of *Los de abajo* hung by this slender thread until he could rewrite and republish the work four years later. In the 1930s when scholars began to question Azuela, he no longer possessed the primitive redactions. They had been lost.

The process of seeking out these primitive texts has been a slow one. Not until now has it been possible to consult both El Paso editions of *Los de abajo*. Despite an arduous search in the late 1930s and the early 1940s, no one has yet reported having had access to the two editions of the novel that supposedly were printed in the seaport town of Tampico in 1917. These are generally considered to be the third and fourth editions, as listed by Luis Leal and others.[33]

Vicente Villasana, a fellow townsman and friend of Mariano Azuela during his youth, as an adult moved from Lagos to Tampico, where he became the editor of a daily newspaper, *El Mundo*. In some fashion Villasana came into possession of one of the El Paso editions of *Los de abajo*. The exact manner by which the novel passed to Villasana has not been explained. Without requesting or receiving permission from Azuela, he printed a serial version in the pages of *El Mundo*. The most careful listing of these editions is given by the late Ernest Moore, who was unable to determine the dates of publication even though he communicated directly with the editor of the newspaper. Moore has reported: "According to the editor of the daily, Vicente Villasana, the numbers that he owned and that contained the novel were lost in a fire; it is not known if there were other copies."[34] A paperback edition followed the Tampico folletín publication. In his description Moore has noted that this volume contained 144 pages but does not explain where he obtained

[33] Leal, p. 135.
[34] Moore, *Bibliografía*, p. 22.

this precise information because he again comments that "no copy of this work is known."[35]

In a communication to Lawrence B. Kiddle, Azuela has explained that Villasana's printings were made without his knowledge or permission. He answers a query concerning the texts of the Tampico folletín and the paperback, declaring that the only redaction available in 1917 was the one that had appeared in El Paso.[36] Consequently Villasana's editions could not have been based on a revision of the text, a project that Azuela certainly had in mind at that time if he had not actually undertaken it. Several years would pass before the rewritten version would see publication.

The challenge to scholars to locate copies of the Tampico printings is still present, but the likelihood of finding them is indeed bleak. Apparently none have come to light since Moore's bibliography appeared in 1941. There is no need to lose hope, for until recently the expectations of finding the El Paso folletín edition were certainly no brighter. The absence of the Tampico printings in any study of the development of the text of *Los de abajo* is not critical, in view of Azuela's nonparticipation in their preparation. Analysis can proceed without the benefit of their presence.

Following his return from El Paso, the novelist resolved to move with his family to the capital and to establish practice as a physician there. Azuela arrived in the capital in March, 1916, and set to work to begin a new medical practice. The first two or three years were precarious. He has reminisced concerning his economic difficulties during that period,[37] but at the same time there were satisfactions. Despite his straitened financial circumstances, which slowly began to improve, he had at last settled down in one place and knew where he would be from one day to the next. The medical practice soon gave him something of a routine, and Azuela again had some time that he could devote to writing.

The manuscript of *Los caciques,* which Azuela had completed in mid-1914, was instrumental in providing him a start in the capital. Shortly after his arrival, he submitted it to the editor of *El Universal,* Ing. Félix Palavicini, who not only accepted it but paid Azuela one hundred pesos.[38] Other publications came much more slowly. Azuela turned to writing about the revolution, his experiences, his associates, and his personal disillusion. He learned of the court-martial and execution of Leocadio Parra, who had served Julián Medina faithfully until the latter's surrender in western Jalisco early in 1916. As one of the terms of his amnesty, Parra agreed to join the Carrancista forces but was soon tricked into joining an apparent conspiracy, then tried and executed. The incident served as the basis for the short story "De cómo al fin lloró Juan Pablo," which was not published until 1918.[39]

From these same years dates the composition of *Las moscas,* a prose piece that Azuela labeled "Cuadros y escenas de la revolución," a subtitle that he had already assigned to *Los de abajo.* The events of *Las moscas* and *Los de abajo* are contemporaneous in that both are based upon Azuela's experiences with the forces of Julián Medina. In this sense the subtitle is highly appropriate; likewise it suggests the form of the work, for *Las moscas* is hardly a conventional novel. It can be considered an account of Azuela's flight from Guadalajara aboard one of Medina's military trains in April, 1915, with his observations on the variety of military figures, public employees, and hangers-on who are caught up in the hurried evacuation.

As soon as the short stories and *Los caciques* and *Las moscas* were out of the way, Azuela set about revising *Los de abajo.* None of the editions prepared prior to that time had received careful attention from an editor and obviously were of an improvised nature. If Azuela was able to exercise but little control over the El Paso printings, there had been none at all

[35]Ibid.   [36]In *Epistolario,* p. 141.
[37]*O.C.,* III, 1090.

[38]Ibid., p. 1076.
[39]Ibid., p. 1093.

over those from Tampico. The numerous misprints obviously displeased him, but it is clear that for some time he had felt a need for a general revision of the text of the novel. He gave the matter considerable thought before getting down to the actual work.

Lawrence B. Kiddle apparently was the first to observe the differences between the text of the El Paso paperback and those of the post-1920 editions. In a letter of April 13, 1951, he referred to the revisions and asked Azuela when they were made. Azuela dispatched a prompt reply on April 22 and devoted an entire paragraph to Kiddle's inquiry:

> The faith that I have always had in this brief work caused me to have prepared a second edition (I do not call an "edition" one that I have never seen) in Mexico in the print-shop of a friend (Razaster), and to this end I wrote some time before the changes that one finds in this edition as well as the later ones. The touches and additions that I made to it were only for the purpose of strengthening characters or scenes but not for reasons of style. I have been concerned with the latter only as it affects clarity and conciseness. When I achieve this, I am satisfied.[40]

In the brevity of his reply, he cannot specify persons and passages, but what Azuela has left unsaid is fully as significant as the words that he has put on paper, and some elaboration will be in order later. Azuela reveals, however, something that is equally as important in the process of revision. That is the matter of his own personal feelings toward the novel that account for his desire to rework it.

Obviously Azuela liked *Los de abajo*. He spoke of it with affection and was clearly pleased with his creation. Although Azuela expressed this feeling to Professor Kiddle at a point late in his life, his fondness was of long standing and existed during the first years of his residence in the capital. Had he not felt this fondness for his work, he would not again have directed his creative attention toward it. During the up-

heaval in Azuela's life following the El Paso editions, he had not forgotten *Los de abajo*. It remained in his thoughts, although the author's experiences in the revolution upon which the scenes of his novel were based were retreating into the past.

Azuela's statement to Kiddle is his only admission that he made substantial changes in the text of *Los de abajo*. He acknowledged that he had gone about his revision deliberately. He further noted that the initiative had been his own and, although he did not say so to Professor Kiddle, the printing was done at his own expense.[41]

Following his return to Mexico, the novelist had no stock of copies of the novel at hand. Fernando Gamiochipi had prepared the paperback edition in El Paso, but Azuela apparently was unable to bring a significant number of copies with him during the exhausting journey back to Mexico late in 1915 and early 1916. He received no copies from Vicente Villasana's unauthorized Tampico printings of 1917. Azuela thus possessed no copies of any edition of *Los de abajo* that he could distribute to his friends and acquaintances. In view of his general satisfaction with the novel and his liking for it, it was necessary to prepare a further edition to liquidate that need. It must have been acute, for to finance it he took funds from his precarious medical practice which was only beginning to get on its feet again. The new edition, listed as the fifth by Luis Leal, was printed by Razaster early in 1920. The press run could not have been great.

Azuela had two thoughts in mind in rewriting *Los de abajo*. Foremost was his desire to "strengthen characters and scenes." He did not specify to Professor Kiddle which characters of the novel and which scenes or landscapes were in need of strengthening, so that these features remain to be examined and analyzed. Azuela stresses in addition his constant preoccupation with "clarity and conciseness," a goal for which he constantly strived. To him, "style" was

---

[40]In *Epistolario*, p. 141.

[41]*O.C.*, III, 1112.

equated with this economy of expression. Consequently he has declared that "estilo" was not the motivation for the changes, for they in most cases lengthened the novel rather than making it more concise.

Modifications in theme and plot were not the novelist's concern. Even in his primitive redaction, he was interested most of all in the man who was inferior to the force of the revolution and who was propelled by it, a victim of its power. His destiny was beyond his control, and Azuela saw him in this light. Azuela does not lose sight of this regard when he reinforces various characters of *Los de abajo*. That action serves at the same time to sustain the already established theme.

A tight, well-constructed plot has never been Mariano Azuela's trademark. One could easily attribute the episodic, sometimes erratic progression of events in the novel to the sporadic note-taking during the journey with Manuel Caloca and the hasty composition of the text in Chihuahua and El Paso, but even in circumstances more favorable to contemplation and writing Azuela did not toil over this feature of his novels. The very nature of his theme, however, did not permit a neat design or a smooth development of the action. The novelist seems to have had a clear idea concerning the plan of the story and its structure, if one wishes to call it that, from a fairly early date. The design for the remainder of the novel was already in Azuela's mind when in October, 1915, he crossed the bridge into El Paso carrying the manuscript of the still unfinished novel.

The apparent untidiness of plot of the El Paso redactions has not bothered the novelist. All the episodes that Azuela originally included have been retained in the rewritten version, even those of a secondary nature that do not give impetus to the main current of the plot. The only reordering of events concerns the actions and conversations of some of the lesser characters. These are found in the Primera Parte whereas those of the Tercera Parte are aimed at a clearer purpose. In all redactions of *Los de abajo*, the Tercera Parte opens with a letter written by Luis Cervantes, who has made his way to El Paso where he has established himself by using the wealth that he accumulated during his months of activity in the revolution. In the primitive text Venancio reads the letter as the band of famished and weary soldiers approaches Juchipila, grumbling at their leadership, which is dominated by officers who formerly served under the hated Victoriano Huerta. The longest interpolation made by Azuela in his revision follows immediately upon the reading of the letter. The remainder of Chapter I is completely new, as are Chapters II and III. Not until Chapter IV does he revert to the events of the initial chapter of this section as found in the El Paso printings. He introduces new material that he interweaves with the incidents, the conversation, and the imagery of his initial invention.

Azuela has caused Demetrio to linger several days in the valley before moving on to Juchipila. The few days that he adds here are highly effective in that they permit him to use the valley as a backdrop for the rapidly deteriorating predicament of Villismo in general and of Demetrio's band in particular. Azuela passed through this valley but once, using it as a corridor for his retreat from Tepatitlán to Aguascalientes in June and July, 1915. On the basis of this single journey, he has been able to construct two contrasting periods of time in *Los de abajo*, and in each the valley and its people reflect the future course of events.

In early pages of *Los de abajo* the valley of Juchipila is hospitable. Its inhabitants are friendly, sympathetic, and willing to support the revolutionaries. Thus Demetrio is able to find refuge for his men, obtain food, and even pick up a few recruits among the more adventuresome souls and those who hold some grievance against the local Huertista authorities. As Azuela describes it, this was life in the valley before June, 1914, when the small band of soldiers left its refuge to take part in Villa's assault on Zacatecas.

The El Paso texts do not establish a notable contrast between these relatively easy circumstances and the hostile environment that Demetrio and his men encounter when they return. During their year of absence the fields have not been tilled. Cultivation has been neglected; the basic corn and beans have not been planted, so that little or no food is to be had. The ravenous soldiers who are in transit through the towns of the valley overburden an already inadequate food supply. The people of Moyahua and Juchipila are short-tempered and testy, hostile to their unwanted military guests.

The air of the inhabitants stands out against the magnificence of the landscape, the majestic configuration in the red stone and bright green foliage of the Cerro de la Santa Cruz and the imposing Cerro de las Ventanas, the expanse of the broad valley and its winding river, billowing cloud formations that darken and let loose a brisk shower, drenching the landscape and giving the atmosphere an unreal but fresh transparency. It is no wonder that Azuela speaks of "una verdadera mañana de nupcias."[42] Despite their rejection by the *serranos,* the mountain dwellers, the wandering soldiers (or their officers, at least) do have their occasional bright moments. In the revised text Azuela makes much of the finding of a barrel or keg of tequila by one of their number, an event that boosted morale in a period of severe depression, accompanied by the gaiety of music and cockfights.

In the haste of preparing the El Paso texts, Azuela was not able to highlight in the Tercera Parte the declining military fortunes of Villa. He rectifies this with a vigorous scene in the revised text, in which Demetrio confronts a group of Villista deserters who offer clear proof of the trouncing taken by Villa's armies at Celaya. There is no denying, then, in addition to the physical pangs of hunger and weariness of body, the hopeless military situation of Francisco Villa. This realization bursts upon Demetrio with startling suddenness in the isolated valley, cut off from communication with the main Villista forces. It ultimately filters down to every man in Demetrio's command and is in tune with their declining fortunes and morale.

In the period of which Azuela is writing, the northeastern portion of Jalisco, all of Aguascalientes, and southern Zacatecas have been overrun by deserters and stragglers separated from Villa's retreating armies, men who were making their way northward toward home and family. Their presence was far from unusual, for they were a highly visible feature of the landscape of the era. Azuela's use of these people in the interpolated Chapters I and II of the Tercera Parte is a clear forecast of Demetrio's rapidly approaching downfall and is highly effective in leading up to the final scene, which completes the circular nature of the action.

Azuela has devoted much more attention to his characters than to modifications in the plot. He has added one completely new individual and has made significant changes in the construction of several others. In the initial chapters of the Tercera Parte, without having been previously introduced, a man named Valderrama protests Demetrio's orders to seek out villagers who have fled their homes and to bring them to him. In his defense of the serranos, Valderrama's high-flown literary speech and his phrases in Latin are clearly out of place. After five or six brief moments before the reader, Valderrama makes a sudden unexplained exit.

Neither this man nor the relatively minor incidents in which he participates appear in Azuela's El Paso editions. The manner in which the novelist has introduced Valderrama into the narrative makes one suspect that his presence in *Los de abajo* is something of an afterthought. What, then, motivated Mariano Azuela to introduce the character of Valderrama into his novel? The explanation is to be found only partly in what Valderrama the character is and does there. He is clearly not of the same stock as the other soldiers, in his poetic manner of expression, his general philosophical outlook, and his view of the revolution.

In his "Letras de provincia" Azuela has stated explicitly that Valderrama is a representation of his lifelong friend and native of Lagos de Moreno, José Becerra: "Licenciado Reséndez of *Los fracasados* has a lot of him. He is

---

[42] *Los de abajo* (El Paso, 1916), p. 140.

Rodríguez in *Los caciques,* Valderrama in *Los de abajo,* and José María in the short story that bears that name, aside from several other characters in whom I put some of his features and manners."[43]

Becerra was influential in persuading Azuela to cast his lot with Julián Medina in October, 1914, and the two men remained inseparable throughout the rest of that year, during the occupations of Guadalajara by Medina and Villa. They were still together following Villa's defeats at Celaya in April, 1915, but the latest documentation of their presence together during the fighting of the revolution is from May, 1915, when the two visited San Miguel el Alto in Jalisco.[44] A month later, when Azuela left for the north escorting Manuel Caloca, Becerra was not with him. There is no word of Becerra during the trip by horseback to Aguascalientes and then by train to Chihuahua and on to El Paso, nor does Azuela mention Becerra among his exiled compatriots who had taken refuge in the United States.

Likewise, Valderrama is absent from Azuela's first versions of *Los de abajo.* His not being there is clearly related to the circumstances of the writing of the novel. Becerra did not participate in those events that Azuela witnessed during his journey from Jalisco to Chihuahua. These have been of the utmost significance in the inspiration for *Los de abajo.* The companionship of the two men in Jalisco, interrupted during the second half of 1915 by the downfall of the Villistas, was renewed after Azuela established his life anew in the capital. Azuela's piece, "El caso López Romero," a thinly disguised conversation between Azuela and Becerra, continues the novelist's bitter view of the revolution which he set forth in *Los de abajo,* intensifying the sarcasm that creeps into the novel. "El caso López Romero" is dated "Abril de 1916" and must have been one of the first of Azuela's compositions after he prepared the

El Paso text of *Los de abajo.* Certain of Becerra's phrases and sentences uttered as López Romero are repeated by Valderrama later when he speaks in *Los de abajo,* as, for example, when he speaks concerning the revolution:

> The glass sparkled as it came out of his pocket. He said to me, "Let's have a drink."
> And then he began to talk about Villa, Carranza, and Obregón....
> He exasperated me: "Villa? Carranza? Obregón? X... Y... Z...."
> "Doctor, I love the revolution like a volcano that erupts, the volcano because it is like the revolution. But the stones that are left on top after the cataclysm, what difference do they make to me?
> We drank in silence.[45]

Azuela modified this conversation slightly and inserted it into Chapter II of the Tercera Parte, where Valderrama utters the comments of both the doctor and López Romero in the section quoted above.[46] The corresponding statement is lacking in Azuela's El Paso redactions, either because at the time they were written Becerra had not yet uttered it, assuming that it was thus spoken, or the expression had not yet hatched in Azuela's mind, if this particular expression is his creation.

When Azuela decided to insert these episodes involving Valderrama into his novel, he endowed this man with a combination of unusual traits that set him apart from his companions in arms and probably from the real-life soldiers of Julián Medina. Valderrama is a "vagrant, mad, and something of a poet" (p. 126) or a "romantic poet" (p. 128). Demetrio calls him to sing "El enterrador" 'The gravedigger' and play the guitar and is so affected by Valderrama's eyes (pp. 130–131). He lapses into Latin (p. 125) and quotes verses from the Bible (p. 130) that are incomprehensible to Demetrio's unlettered soldiers. Unlike them, he

[43]*O.C.,* II, 799.

[44]In "Letras de provincia," *O.C.,* III, 797–807, and in "José María," *O.C.,* II, 1094–1097.

[45]Ibid., p. 1073.

[46]*Los de abajo* (Mexico, 1958), p. 128. Page references in parentheses will be to this readily available modern edition.

is unwilling to witness an execution (p. 128), and he is incensed by the brutality of the cockfight promoted by La Codorniz and El Meco and must sing in order to brush away his anger (pp. 130–131). But like the others, he is inordinately fond of alcohol. Azuela makes no bones of Valderrama's weakness in noting "the first period of the first drunken binge of the day" (p. 132) and "upon his brow the reflection of a white bottle of tequila" (p. 128). When Demetrio handed him a bottle, "Valderrama greedily gulped down half of it" (p. 131). Despite his uncommon characteristics, the soldiers and Demetrio express affection for him, particularly the latter, who remarks: " 'I am fond of that harum-scarum,' said Demetrio smiling, 'because some times he says things that set a person to thinking' " (p. 128).

As usual, Azuela does not sketch in carefully the features of his character. He says little that aids the reader to form a visual image of Valderrama, and where a physical feature is mentioned, its purpose is to suggest some emotional quality of the man which is either characteristic of him or pertinent to the scene of the moment. Azuela notes that Valderrama's eyes bear an indication of insanity: "His eyes shone like those eyes in which the glint of insanity sparkled" (p. 131). His lips reflect a desire to please: "And Valderrama, with his never-ending smile of satisfaction on his lips, came forward and asked the musicians to hand him a guitar" (p. 130). Again, facial expressions suggest an emotional state rather than defining features: "Valderrama's countenance was scornful and solemn, like that of an emperor" (p. 128), and "Valderrama, who had not held back a face showing violent indignation, began to tune up" (pp. 130–131).

Becerra's friends and contemporaries have left ample testimony concerning his literary interests and personal qualities. Mariano Azuela had no friend whom he admired and trusted more than Becerra, a feeling that he expressed by introducing him into his novels in recognizable roles and recounting their experiences to-gether in his "Letras de provincia." Becerra was active in several literary groups in Lagos in the years before the Mexican revolution. He and his brother Alfredo were associates of Ruperto J. Aldana, whose interests and activities have been noted by Alfonso de Alba: "All of them are romantics on both sides of the family. They call each other 'brothers' and at the tavern (although not all of them) drink wine 'because it enervates and kills, bearing in its bubbles poison and forgetfulness....' "[47]

Later Becerra joined with Dr. Bernardo Reina, Lic. Antonio Moreno y Oviedo, the poet Francisco González León, and his close friend Mariano Azuela to form what de Alba has called The Generation of 1903, so named because of their participation in the literary tourney in Lagos in June of that year. It is not strange that Azuela refers to Valderrama in *Los de abajo* as a "poeta romántico" (p. 128). In the Prólogo to Alfonso de Alba's volume, Azuela has more to say concerning Becerra's performance at the literary gatherings in Lagos:

> With the first sip of his aperitif, Becerra lost whatever discretion he had left. His ardent spirit burst into flame and the bright sparkle and color-charged talk provided the dominant note. Our great Pepe Becerra, effusive, warmhearted, sparkling in his expression, as violent and impetuous when he was praising someone as when he was insulting him, always thwarted by his own overflowing good will, preparing from the age of eight his play "The Big Prize," which he had not succeeded in finishing when he was eighty. With him fate was inexorable but, like Prometheus, he was able to face up to it and carve in his own flesh the most beautiful and intense tragic poem of his life as a poet.[48]

Valderrama is one of Mariano Azuela's tributes to Becerra. Neither in the words above nor in his novels does he speak as cordially of Becerra as in his "Letras de provincia." There he states plainly what Becerra has meant to him:

[47]de Alba, *Antonio Moreno y Oviedo*, p. 146.
[48]Ibid., p. 15.

Of three good friends that I had, none was as intelligent, as enthusiastic, and as generous as he was. He was the only one who was able to keep me going in the struggle and give me courage in times of boredom and disillusionment. With the stimulation of his warm, encouraging words, at the same time forceful and sincere, he made me keep up my fondness for writing, despite its being a silent and uncertain struggle, for more than twenty years.[49]

Becerra is one of those close friends who are possessed of faults of character whom Azuela preferred over people of more conventional traits. In Valderrama, Azuela has re-created his close friend José Becerra, with his faults, of which an addiction to the bottle is the most serious, and his eccentricities, including his inability to tolerate suffering among small animals, pets, and even less significant creatures. Some of these characteristics make for an unusual person even in real life. When Azuela transfers them to Valderrama in *Los de abajo* and places this lofty, emotional poet among a band of revolutionary soldiers whose main concern is killing, Valderrama loses still more in credibility and Azuela must thus intimate that he is insane, using the term "loco" repeatedly to characterize his creation. Either that or Valderrama is acting out a role.

There are problems, too, in working Valderrama into the stream of action of *Los de abajo*. His presence in the novel and the episodes in which he participates are an afterthought and Azuela, who is remarkably careless as a plot maker, does not take the necessary pains to justify logically Valderrama's entry into the novel and his departure later. He is reduced to noting these actions in a single long sentence: "Valderrama, the tramp of the highways who joined up with the band one day, without anyone knowing exactly when or where, managed to overhear what Demetrio was saying, and since there is no crazy person who enjoys eating fire,

that very day he disappeared in the same manner that he came" (p. 134).[50]

Unlike Valderrama, Luis Cervantes was one of Azuela's creations for the El Paso redactions. This individual has undergone extensive modifications in the Razaster and later editions of *Los de abajo*. In a sense this man is less important as a human being than for what he represents in relation to the Mexican revolution. Certainly this is one of Azuela's main concerns, and much of the expanded portion of the Primera Parte has to do with defining more clearly the role of Cervantes in the novel.

Mariano Azuela operates with a sure hand in the depiction of those men and women of a popular background, beginning with Demetrio and his ranchero companions, whom he has constructed from direct observation. With Cervantes he has been less sure, in part certainly because he has not made use of a specific model but rather has had to create him. The novelist has explained that in the formation of this character he has made use of malicious gossip circulating among Julián Medina's men around the figure of Major Francisco Delgado, private secretary to the general.[51] Azuela makes it clear that the qualities attributed to Delgado by his enemies were imaginary but nevertheless they suggested to him the traits and characteristics to be employed in the delineation of Cervantes. The problem was to combine them in a credible fashion in one individual who acts and interacts with other figures of varying motives and backgrounds in the dynamic stream of the revolution. After considering the personality and development of Cervantes in his original form, Mariano Azuela resolved to outline this man much more clearly in his new redaction of *Los de abajo*.

In the El Paso editions, Luis Cervantes personified the opportunism and greed of many leaders and participants in the revolution. Fol-

[49]*O.C.*, III, 798.

[50]The two El Paso editions carry no dedicatory note whatever. The first revised edition of 1920 bears the simple statement "A José Becerra" on p. [5]. It is repeated on p. [2] of the 1925 edition printed in *El Universal Ilustrado*.

[51]*O.C.*, III, 1082.

lowing his return to Mexico, Azuela's personal frustration and disappointment were intensified, and he felt increasing bitterness toward the administration of Venustiano Carranza and, in Azuela's view, its disregard of the goals of the revolution and the new politicians' concern with personal enrichment. The novelist obviously felt that in the 1916–1919 period when he set about to revise *Los de abajo* there was need to underline still more this quality of Cervantes. Azuela's righteous denunciation of greed and personal gain at the expense of the revolution was still as timely as it had been two or three years before. The rewritten text is certainly to the detriment of Luis Cervantes.

In Chapter V of the El Paso texts, Cervantes is introduced as a deserter from the federales, captured by Pancracio, who shoots him in the foot. Demetrio, whose wound has begun to pain him again, decides to postpone a decision about the captive and orders Pancracio and El Manteca to guard the prisoner overnight in a corral. The nocturnal thoughts of this man dwell almost exclusively upon the immediate circumstances, which Azuela summarizes in a single sentence: "Luis Cervantes, muy pensativo, se paseó toda la noche de largo a largo del corral." (Luis Cervantes, absorbed in his thoughts, spent the whole night pacing back and forth in the corral).[52]

Up to this point Azuela has divulged very little concerning Luis Cervantes other than that he is a city fellow entirely out of place among Demetrio's uncouth rancheros and is dismayed by their hostile reception of him and their lack of response to his revolutionary palaver. But there is still much unsaid concerning Cervantes's credentials as a revolutionary and his experiences as a federal prior to his desertion. Neither has Azuela gone into his human features, his personal traits, and those inner springs that push him forward and motivate him. The novelist is well aware of the qualities that he plans to attribute to Cervantes but in his original redaction chooses to reveal these through the man's partici-

pation in subsequent events. Consequently his development into the complete opportunist is a slow process and is not really complete until Venancio reads the letter from Cervantes in the opening lines of the Tercera Parte.

When Mariano Azuela sat down to prepare his new text of *Los de abajo,* he decided that merely the outward features of the man were not adequate as an introduction of Luis Cervantes to his readers. To that end he prepared a chapter that was completely new, Chapter VI of the Razaster and subsequent editions. He retained only the final paragraph of Chapter V of the original text, modifying it slightly and shifting it to the final position of his new chapter. There he gave it another setting, subordinate to the added material, where it serves to bring Cervantes out of the reverie of his political and military fortunes and back to the reality of his being a prisoner in a corral where Pancracio, El Manteca, and a hog are all snoring.

The function of the new chapter is to tip off the reader as to what he may expect from Cervantes. This the novelist does by revealing selected events from Cervantes's past and the attitudes that determined them. The hours when he could not sleep thus offer the opportunity for a flashback to the Luis Cervantes who not only castigated those in rebellion against Victoriano Huerta but later left his journalistic outbursts to become a soldier of the federales to seek them out in combat. Azuela thus gives the lie to the *curro* when he states to Demetrio that he had been conscripted against his will. Azuela is intent upon exposing this man personally as well as ideologically by writing from within Cervantes himself, for the man recalls his own ineptness as a soldier, his humiliation at the hands of his commanding officer, his half-hearted championing of the unfortunate and oppressed, and an early hankering for material gain.

These antecedents were not divulged to readers of the original version. The latter were required to undertake their own evaluation of Cervantes on the basis of his betrayal of Camila,

[52]*Los de abajo* (El Paso, 1916), p. 25.

his crafty weighing of his prospects in the revolution, his acquisition of money and jewels during Demetrio's campaigns, and his ultimate flight to El Paso, where he settled to live off the loot. The reader's decision has to be the result of an ongoing process throughout the novel. Azuela spares him this process in the revision. There he has decided to inform the reader immediately as to the nature and intentions of Luis Cervantes.

A few chapters later the novelist introduced additional modifications to the development of Cervantes. Already in the El Paso editions he had made use of a lengthy interior monologue to reveal this man's thought processes, which he has preserved in the middle of Chapter VIII of the revised version. While he is occupied in curing his foot, with Camila as an onlooker, the curro carefully weighs in his mind the reports of newspapers controlled by Victoriano Huerta against his own observation of the revolutionaries in order to determine if he has made the proper shift by deserting the federales. In Azuela's first presentation, Cervantes is still puzzled and interrupts his train of thought when he mutters aloud in the presence of Camila: "¿Si me habré equivocado de veras?" 'I wonder if I've really made a mistake?'[53] Azuela retains the monologue in his reworking, even the specific thoughts that run through the mind of Cervantes. The conclusion at this point, however, is a decisive one, in line with Cervantes's new image as determined by his monologue during the restless night in the corral: "No, lo que es ahora no me he equivocado—se dijo para sí, casi en voz alta." 'No, this time I didn't make a mistake, he said to himself, almost out loud.'[54]

By the time of Demetrio's return to Moyahua following the battle of Zacatecas, Luis Cervantes had accumulated a bag of gold coins and a medicine box crammed with rings, ear pendants, and assorted jewels and trinkets that he offered to share with Demetrio if the latter were willing to join him in exile. Demetrio, who was at heart a decent man, refused to enter-

tain the idea, to his eternal credit. Thus Azuela underscored the greed of Cervantes as the author originally depicted him, and despite considerable editorial revision, the incident has remained basically unchanged in the later versions (Chapter VI of the Segunda Parte).[55] As if this quality had not been expressed adequately, Azuela thought it necessary to insert a further sequence in the rewritten version, in Chapter XI of the Segunda Parte, during the approach to Tepatitlán. There Cervantes coveted a collection of watches and jewels accumulated by Codorniz, who perceived the curro's eagerness to acquire the valuable items and finally agreed to sell him only a watch in order to obtain cash to pay off a gambling debt. For once Cervantes was frustrated. The scene is hardly necessary to establish the more base features of Cervantes's character. Azuela had already done that. The new scene, which is absent in the primitive text of *Los de abajo,* is consistent, nevertheless, with the novelist's drawing of this man and confirms Azuela's existing creation.

Alberto Solís has expressed what some have considered Mariano Azuela's own outlook on the revolution during the last days of Villa's fighting forces: "—Yo pensé una florida pradera al remate de un camino … y me encontré un pantano." 'I had my heart set on a flower-decked meadow at the end of the road, and it turned out to be a swamp.'[56] Both Solís and Azuela were disillusioned over the conflict between the ideal, or what they expected from the revolution, and the real, or what they actually found in it. In both redactions of *Los de abajo,* Azuela considered Luis Cervantes the incarnation of those forces and human failings that prevented him from attaining his *florida pradera.* The novelist's feelings toward Cervantes became much more intense after the return to Mexico in 1916. His bitterness moved him to warn readers of later editions of *Los de abajo* about Cervantes, what he stood for and what they might expect of him.

Although Azuela's ideological position is

[53]Ibid., p. 30.
[54]*Los de abajo* (Mexico, 1958), p. 29.

[55]Ibid.
[56]Ibid., p. 62.

clearer, his anger has not necessarily improved the development of his novel or the depiction of Cervantes. There can hereafter be no doubt as to the character and role of this man, but Azuela has run the risk of turning Cervantes into a caricature. In the long flashback following the apprehension of Cervantes by Demetrio's men, he exaggerates the curro's humiliation as a federal. He makes excessive use of sarcasm there and in his recalled conversations with the three federales whom he supposedly championed. Their revelations sound much more Azuelan than Cervantine. Azuela has overstated their baseness and distorts them as credible human beings.

The third intellectual introduced by Azuela is Solís, the young officer on the staff of Pánfilo Natera. In the revised version Solís has not changed direction; he has remained much as he was in Azuela's original depiction of him. The conversations between Luis Cervantes and Solís are practically the only instances in the novel in which two articulate Mexicans converse. Solís is starved for intelligent conversation; Cervantes is likewise but is uncomfortable and squirms under the questions of his old friend who knows of Cervantes's Huertista affiliation as a journalist. The more loquacious of the two is Solís, in large part because the curro is embarrassed. Their conversation permits Azuela to express himself concerning the revolution in a manner more sophisticated than that employed by Demetrio and his fellow rancheros. The comments of Cervantes and Solís are philosophical, frequently poetic, and they view the revolution within a much larger framework. Only the eccentric Valderrama resembles them in this respect, and he met neither Cervantes nor Solís personally.

Azuela's presentation of the ideological positions of these two men shows two minor adjustments in the revised text, although their interaction is only slightly affected. Their observation of the battle of Zacatecas from the vantage point of the mountain overlooking the city elicits some generalizations that proximity would not have permitted. In these circumstances

Cervantes is moved and remarks: "How beautiful the revolution is, even when it is most barbarous!"[57] When he rewrote *Los de abajo,* Azuela took this quotation away from Cervantes and attributed it to Solís, as well as the expression of fears that now the revolution would produce monsters like Victoriano Huerta, rather than merely eliminate him, a thought that is clearly Azuelan.[58] This expression is much more consistent with the attitudes of Solís (and Azuela) than those of Luis Cervantes, whose incentive for being in the revolution would hardly permit him to produce a statement in those terms. Azuela thus clarifies in another respect the figure of Cervantes.

Solís, who comes as close as anyone to expressing the novelist's position, explains to Cervantes why he continues fighting in the revolution:

> "You may ask me," he continued, "why I keep on in the revolution in spite of everything. First, because the revolution is a hurricane and the man who is swept up in it is a wretched dry leaf.... Second, because a stubborn primitive attitude and my mental attitude of a confirmed idealist and a hopelessly sentimental person have caused me to believe with every ounce of my conviction that any Mexican who bows down to the government of the murderer Victoriano Huerta is despicable and contemptible! ...... Contradictions! .... Rubbish! What more do you want?"[59]

When Solís expounds his position to Cervantes in the revised version, he gives but one of these reasons, the first. Azuela's usual practice in rewriting is to expand the text, yet here he has pared it down, but probably not because he has modified the concept of Solís. The phraseology of the first statement is philosophical and poetic, in line with the novelist's use of imagery elsewhere in regard to man's role in the conflict. The remainder of Solís's discourse is not on this plane. Although the tyranny of Victoriano Huerta is opprobrious when considered strictly

---

[57] *Los de abajo* (El Paso, 1916), p. 73.
[58] *Los de abajo* (Mexico, 1958), p. 73.
[59] *Los de abajo* (El Paso, 1916), p. 62.

within the framework of *Los de abajo,* when Mariano Azuela was preparing his new text in 1917 or 1918, the subject was no longer as immediate as it had been during the period of actual warfare in 1914, or even in 1915. Furthermore, the second reason offered by Solís is more of a political statement, and Azuela, to maintain consistency in the character and ideology of Solís, has considered that the first of the two expressions is much more appropriate to this man.

The relatively brief appearance of Alberto Solís at the very middle of *Los de abajo* has more than ideological significance. Seymour Menton has referred to the role of Solís in the exaltation of Demetrio Macías to the position that Azuela clearly felt that he deserved in the novel.[60] Azuela has accomplished his purpose by an initial buildup of Villa by the soldiers of Pánfilo Natera prior to the assult on the city of Zacatecas. The latter attest to the glory of Villa, his prowess in battle, his magnificent equipment and abundant supplies, while Demetrio's men listen in amazement with mouths agape. To their credit, one of their number, Anastasio Montañés, punctures the inflated reports of Villa's prowess by determining that Natera's men have never fought alongside Villa's troops and that their reports are only based on hearsay.

If Anastasio contributes to the belittling of Villa, if that is the appropriate term, Solís is responsible for the exaltation of Demetrio Macías. The process begins upon their first meeting in Fresnillo with Demetrio's interruption of the uneasy conversation between Solís and Luis Cervantes. Solís's admiration of Demetrio is obviously genuine, in his greeting and in his description of Demetrio's exploits, to the considerable discomfiture of Cervantes. The process is concluded on the slopes of the mountain overlooking Zacatecas in Solís's recounting to the curro Demetrio's daring charge that decided the battle in favor of the attacking Villistas. Only through the words of Solís does Azuela inform the reader of Demetrio's heroism, for he does not focus directly upon this incident in the novel. His intent is to establish a valid contrast between Villa and Demetrio which will work to the decisive advantage of the latter, who has emerged as the protagonist of *Los de abajo.* In effect, Azuela modifies the figure and the exploits of Demetrio only slightly. The major changes affect his presentation of Villa significantly and open up another area of Azuelan speculation, namely, the novelist's evaluation of Villa in *Los de abajo* and elsewhere in his writings of the revolutionary period.

The scenes of battle and military life that Azuela depicts in *Los de abajo* are faithful to the actual events and vivid enough but are deceptive as a reflection of his personal involvement in the revolution. He was thoroughly committed to Villismo as represented by Julián Medina, but Medina operated almost exclusively in the backwash of the fighting, in areas remote from Villa's main north-south movement through the center of Mexico along the rail line that linked Torreón, Zacatecas, Aguascalientes, Lagos, Irapuato, and the capital. Even Guadalajara was off Villa's beaten path. Azuela's experience was limited almost exclusively to areas of Jalisco and western Zacatecas where Villa was rarely present. Villa made two triumphal entries into Guadalajara, first in December, 1914, and again in February, 1915, but Azuela has remained silent as to whether he was present or participated in them. Neither does he verify having seen Villa at Irapuato in April, 1915, following the withdrawal by Medina and Azuela from Guadalajara, although Villa appears prominently in the final scene of *Las moscas,* which pictures this hasty and confused retreat. Thus Azuela's sources of information are not greatly different from those available to Pánfilo Natera and his men.

Azuela characterizes Villa as he is introduced in the text of *Los de abajo:* "And the poor forge a legend around him that time will embellish so that it will live from one generation to another."[61] The novelist, even while he was engaged in the composition of *Los de abajo,*

[60]Menton, "La estructura épica de 'Los de abajo,' " p. 1005.

[61]*Los de abajo* (Mexico, 1958), p. 68.

was aware of the process by which legends were wrought around the figure of Villa. In his life with Medina's soldiers, he witnessed the formation of these legends and their adornment in the folk culture of these men. Azuela's presentation of Villa, accomplished through the accounts of Natera's soldiers in the novel, is entirely faithful in this respect. Their comments in the El Paso writing are cast in these terms but with one notable additional factor. Villa emerges as much more of a true legendary hero. His military victories are a marvel, but his appeal to the common soldier is greater in his role as a Mexican Robin Hood who befriends the poor. This type of legend has shown remarkable durability until this day.

Azuela stresses the force of legend that is dominant over actual facts in the formation of the ordinary soldier's attitude toward Villa: "But those deeds that have been seen and heard cannot compare with the fabulous. The ancient Mexican legend was reborn again: the unconquerable man of the mountain, pursued like a wild beast by the government,...."[62] Villa exacts ten thousand pesos from a wealthy industrialist or a hacienda owner, then thrusts a fistful of bank notes upon an old man riding a decrepit mule. He leaves a bag of coins with a widow who is so poor that she has only prickly pear leaves to feed her six children. "And thus the life of the bandit who is Providence is spent, robbing the rich to make the poor happy."[63] Azuela then launches into the scenes of horror wrought by Villa as revenge upon those who had thwarted or deceived him, a wealthy businessman whose head had been torn from his body, a banker found dead in office, disembowled and with his intestines strewn over the floor, an hacendado left dead in a pasture where he had been tortured and his body partly eaten by buzzards. "Proteus, who from what is sublime shifts abruptly to what is bestial. The Great Man of the mob!"[64] These are passages that Azuela has omitted in the Razaster and later

[62] *Los de abajo* (El Paso, 1916), pp. 67–68.
[63] Ibid., p. 68
[64] Ibid., pp. 68–69.

editions of *Los de abajo*, although he has retained with some modification the accounts of Villa's prowess, which follow immediately the passages just cited.

Even in the El Paso versions, Azuela has set up Demetrio Macías in competition with Francisco Villa. As long as the rivalry is strictly along military lines, Demetrio can hold his own, but Azuela has hardly made him into a "bandido-providencia." He has not surrounded Demetrio with a cloak of popular legendry that accompanies or even precedes him wherever he goes, and without this, Demetrio cannot compete successfully with the "Centaur of the North." Rather than endow Demetrio with such qualities, Azuela has decided not to bring them up in his depiction of Villa, leaving the comparison strictly on a military basis where Demetrio can hold an equal if not an advantageous position.

Thus the new text has affected one person or character who does not even appear in *Los de abajo*. That person is Francisco Villa, whom Azuela has set up as a measuring rod for enhancing Demetrio's prestige. Despite his absence from the novel, Villa was a spectacular and renowned (and even notorious) figure of the revolution about whom no contemporary Mexican, including Mariano Azuela, could fail to hold an opinion. His influence is felt throughout Azuela's book at many points and at more than one level. Demetrio and his close followers show constant concern for his fortunes and relate them to their own, on a clearly personal basis. The intellectuals, Cervantes, Solís, and perhaps Valderrama, aside from any selfish interests that they may have, view Villa within a broader perspective. Azuela, as the creator of these people, is involved at both levels, and his attitudes toward Villa are thus considerably more complex. He is decidedly more explicit in his reactions in the El Paso editions, less so in his later versions. Azuela's devotion was to a larger cause. He remained faithful to the Villista Julián Medina as long as the latter could operate effectively in Jalisco and was dismayed with Villa's ensuing defeats and Carranza's military and political ascendancy.

Azuela's attention was not directed exclusively toward strengthening the characters and clarifying the role of each. Many of his modifications are subtle and obey only artistic considerations. All chapters reveal a careful and thoughtful rewriting. Even the initial and final scenes of the novel, which seem to have been particular favorites of Azuela and more resistant to modification than the interior sections, have undergone various substitutions of phraseology and vocabulary. Elsewhere the revisions are frequently more extensive; in all chapters Azuela has considered carefully each word, each phrase and sentence, and the order in which he has put them down. He has left few if any of these identical with its primitive form, either as it stood in the folletín edition or the paperback published by Fernando Gamiochipi.

These are the "retoques y adiciones" that the novelist has referred to. They are the features of the later redactions of the novel that stand out when they are juxtaposed to the primitive El Paso texts. Each individual *retoque* in itself is slight—an inversion of word order, the addition of an adjective or brief phrase, the substitution of a more distinctive noun for one that is perhaps commonplace, or the insertion of a proverb or traditional saying. Even when Azuela has preserved his original words and phrases, they have often been given a new se-

quence, and despite the disclaimer that he is not concerned with "style," the cumulative effect is considerable. The combination of major and minor emendations is of such a magnitude that to all intents and purposes Azuela has prepared a text that is practically new. The work must have occupied him for several months, assuming that he devoted the greater part of each day to his medical practice and reserved a few precious hours for writing. The setting up of a routine with available time, coupled with relative peace of mind, made it possible to bring *Los de abajo* into line with the author's exacting artistic standards.

The alterations fall into several patterns. These can be discerned when the corresponding passages from the El Paso redaction are compared with those from the modern text. For this purpose, examples in the left-hand column below are from the El Paso paperback edition of *Los de abajo*, dated 1916 but actually published late in 1915; those in the right-hand column are from the 1958 edition published by the Fondo de Cultura Económica. The examples included here are only a representative selection from the many changes that Azuela wrought.

The most frequent modifications consist of a simple lexical substitution, which may involve a noun, pronoun, a verb, or a modifier, such as those shown below.

El Paso, 1916	*Fondo de Cultura Económica*
p. 7. —Se perdiera también, si viniera de borracho como nosotros	p. 6 —Se perdería, mi sargento si viniera de borracho como tú ...
p. 9 —¡Qué susto, madre mía de Talpa!	p. 8 —¡Madre mía de Jalpa! ¡Qué susto!
p. 14 ... el croar de las ranas en el río.	p. 12 ... el croar de las ranas en los baches.
p. 18 Ya no pudo subir a su caballo.	p. 16 Ya no pudo montar su caballo.
p. 20 Una moza muy amable se acercó con una jícara de agua azul.	p. 17 Una moza muy amable trajo una jícara de agua azul.
p. 21 —¡Con .... tal! Ya estás moliendo "Codorniz".	p. 19 —¡Con un...! ¡Ya estás moliendo! ...
p. 23 —¡Es federal!—interrumpieron algunos, mirándolo con admiración.	p. 20 —¡Ah, es federal!...—interrumpieron mirándolo con pasmo.
p. 59 ...se dedican a desbalijar a los que traen mejores ropas.	p. 60 ...se dedican a desnudar a los que traen mejores ropas.
p. 67 Y los sombrerudos de bufandas al cuello, de gruesos zapatos de baqueta y callosas	p. 68 Y los gorrudos de bufandas al cuello, de gruesos zapatones de vaqueta y encallecidas

manos de vaquero, comiendo y bebiendo sin cesar, sólo hablaban de Villa y de sus tropas.

p. 80 Demetrio no pudo sostener los ojos furiosamente provocativos de la muchacha y tuvo que bajar los suyos.

p. 126 ...y un billete de cinco pesos para la víctima.

manos de vaquero, comiendo y bebiendo sin cesar, sólo hablaban de Villa y sus tropas.

p. 76 Demetrio no pudo sostener la mirada furiosamente provocativa de la muchacha y bajó los ojos.

p. 119 ...y un bilimbique de cinco pesos para la víctima.

Frequently the author modifies the form of a word by the use of a different derivational affix, although the meaning is not affected:

p. 12 ...de cejas espesas y muy negras, de mirada dulzachona, hombre maciso y robusto.

p. 17 ...conservaba la expresión dulzona de sus ojos dormidos y su rostro barbado ...

p. 32 ...le metí un navajazo a un capitancillo faceto ...

p. 90 ...palmeando el cuello corvo del soberbio animal.

p. 128 El olor de las fritangas abrió el apetito de Demetrio.

p. 11 ...y cejas espesas y muy negras, de mirada dulzona; hombre macizo y robusto.

p. 15 ...conservaba la expresión dulzona de sus ojos adormilados y su rostro barbado ...

p. 39 ...le metí un navajazo a un capitancito faceto ...

p. 84 ...palmoteando el cuello enarcado del soberbio animal.

p. 121 El olor de las frituras abrió el apetito de Demetrio.

Azuela has been constantly aware of the use of popular speech in his revision. Already in the El Paso redaction it entered frequently into the conversation of the soldiers and rural people, probably to a greater degree than in later versions of the novel:

p. 19 Le llamaban el dotor ...

p. 56 ...algo así para abujerar las paredes?

p. 57 —¡Todavía no! Todavía no veo a mi hermano.

p. 66 "¿No quiere más?"

p. 78 ¡Ah, cómo traiba oro el condenao!

p. 89 ... hasta que lo eruto.

p. 64 —¿Quién me compra esta maquinaria?

p. 111 Dende qué ha que se metió el sol y él sigue sin parar.

p. 128 ... se removían como las moscas a la puerta de un panal....

p. 16 Le llamaban *el dotor* ...[65]

p. 58 ...algo así como para agujerear la pared?

p. 59 —¡Tovía no! ... ¡Tovía no! ... Tovía no veo a mi hermano.

p. 66 "¿No quere más?"

p. 74 ¡Ah, cómo traiba oro el condenado!

p. 83 ... hasta que lo eructo.

p. 65 —¿Quién me merca esta maquinaria?

p. 105 ¡Qué ha que se metió el sol ..., y mírelo, no pára todavía!

p. 121 ... se removía, como las abejas a la boca de una colmena....

The novelist retains a popular Mexican proverb in later redactions but follows the custom, common to conversational style, of stating only the first half of the proverb when the other half is well known to the listener:

p. 25 ¿pa qué hecha tantos brincos ... estando tan parejo el suelo?

p. 21 ¿Pa qué son tantos brincos? ...

Azuela's frequent use of similes was already established in the early versions of *Los de abajo* and was occasionally the object of modification:

p. 22 ... como una uña delgada, la luna ascendía.

p. 19 ... la luna ascendía como una fina hoz.

[65]Yet in *Los de abajo* (Mexico: Editorial Pedro Robredo, 1938), p. 26: "Le llamaban *el doctor* ...."

p. 59 Es el capitancito rubio de bigotes retorcidos, blanco como el papel ....

p. 60 Es el capitancito rubio de bigote borgoñón, blanco como la cera ....[66]

p. 67 ... el guerrero invicto que como boa fascina ya liebres y conejos.

p. 67 ... el guerrero invicto que ejerce a distancia ya su gran fascinación de boa.

p. 72 Demetrio lazó una ametralladora y la arrastró como quien tira un toro bravo.

p. 72 Demetrio lazaba las ametralladoras, tirando de ellas cual si fuesen toros bravos.

One notes on numerous occasions a simple inversion of word order. Most of these cases involve the position of a modifier in the sentence:

p. 11 ... salieron, uno tras otro, muchos hombres, de piernas y pechos desnudos, obscuros y repulidos como viejos bronces.

p. 10 ... salieron, unos tras otros, muchos hombres de pechos y piernas desnudas, oscuros y repulidos como viejos bronces.

p. 15 ... que sólo en los dientes y en los ojos tenía algo que blanqueara—

p. 13 ... que sólo en los ojos y en los dientes tenía algo de blanco—

p. 23 —Pues yo soy revolucionario también.

p. 20 —Pues yo también soy revolucionario.

p. 29 ¿Y por qué no le revolvió agua fría mejor? ......

p. 29 ¿Y por qué no le regüelve mejor agua fría? ...

p. 29 —"En dónde están esos hombres admirablemente montados y armados ...?

p. 29 "¿En dónde están esos hombres admirablemente armados y montados...?"

p. 42 ... no peleamos para derrocar a un miserable asesino....

p. 45 No peleamos por derrocar a un asesino miserable ....

p. 45 Y todo el mundo buscó a Camila con los ojos.

p. 48 Y todo el mundo buscó con los ojos a Camila.

p. 87 Era el giiero Margarito un hombrecillo gordo....

p. 81 El güero Margarito era un hombrecillo redondo....

p. 93 Le rodeaban el mismo Luis Cervantes, Anastasio, "El Manteca" y muchos otros.

p. 87 Le rodeaban Luis Cervantes, Anastasio, el Manteca y otros muchos.

Other examples involve the modification or expansion of a complete clause. I have noted only a few parallel passages here to give an idea of the nature of the rewriting:

p. 10 Clareó la mañana cuando Demetrio Macías comenzó a bajar al fondo de la barranca.

p. 9 Todo era sombra todavía cuando Demetrio Macías comenzó a bajar al fondo del barranco.

p. 50 A media noche, Demetrio Macías mandó ensillar.

p. 53 A medianoche, Demetrio Macías dio la orden de marcha.

p. 52 Sobre el caserío asomaba la ancha cúpula cuadrangular de la iglesia.

p. 54 Dominando el caserío, se alzaba la ancha cúpula cuadrangular de la iglesia.

The last-mentioned process entered frequently into the revision of the text, not to mention the author's restructuring of complete sentences and his interpolation of others that were absent in the initial text of *Los de abajo*.

Azuela's new version, beginning with the Razaster edition of 1920, is significant quantitatively. He has corrected the numbering of those chapters that in the El Paso printings were improperly labeled, he has rearranged the content of some chapters and modified the division points, and in the first and third parts has added completely new material. These modifications have increased the number of chapters in the three parts to twenty-one, fourteen, and seven, respectively. They likewise affect the actual number of words in the text. The El Paso printings each contain in the neighborhood of 27,600, whereas the Razaster and subsequent editions of the novel reach approximately 33,000 words, an increase of nearly one-fifth.

[66]The Pedro Robredo edition (Mexico, 1938) reads "de bigote borgoñonés" (p. 107).

Significance of the Two Versions

Los de abajo held a double significance for Mariano Azuela during the weeks that he spent in exile. He had left Lagos de Moreno with the thought of acquiring firsthand knowledge of the revolution. He had achieved that goal and his literary creation was the product of that experience, but the latter took its toll from Azuela in physical hardship and deep ideological disappointment and despair. At the same time, *Los de abajo* was seemingly his only source of income, temporary and precarious, during the weeks that he felt forced to leave Mexican soil.

Once these purposes had been fulfilled, it almost seemed that *Los de abajo* was destined to be cast aside. The work was born out of adversity, had struggled to see the light of day, and finally came forth in an obscure printshop in El Paso. Once the author was able to leave that city, no one was left to care for it, a stranger in a barren land. He left behind the copies that Fernando Gamiochipi had printed for him, and in El Paso no one seemingly bothered to put aside the numbers of the newspaper in whose pages the novel had appeared as a serial. Thus it passed out of sight, from Mariano Azuela, from literary critics, and the reading public. At this point, one might conjecture as to how scholars and critics would have evaluated Azuela's contribution as a novelist had he produced only the El Paso printings of *Los de abajo*.

But years later renown came to Azuela, and *Los de abajo* gained recognition as a masterwork of literature. After 1925 critical comment on this novel became abundant and widespread and elevated Azuela to eminence. Yet acclaim was based not on the printings left behind in El Paso but on a new text that the author had prepared shortly after he settled down in Mexico City following the revolution. That new text, with various modifications of vocabulary and spelling, has in effect been the only form of *Los de abajo* known to those who have felt moved to say something about the novel.

The long-delayed enthusiasm for *Los de abajo* finally brought to light the existence of Azuela's 1915 editions. They did not attract the attention of a wide group, however, and only a few of the more assiduous and persistent scholars attempted to track them down. Their success was not immediate. The paperback edition came to light around 1940 or slightly earlier, but the number of available copies was extremely small and their presence has made practically no dent in Azuelan scholarship and criticism. The folletín edition of the novel eluded scholars until the 1970s, and its availability has been made known only in the preceding pages of this study.

Azuela's El Paso editions are more than curiosities from a bygone period. They contribute to a critical focus on the novel using various techniques and from several points of view. Of basic significance is the availability of the folletín, which can now be described and recorded with accurate details. The folletín supplies a long-missing element in the bibliographical picture first traced by Ernest Moore and Manuel Pedro González. The establishment of this sound bibliographical foundation has long been a feature of Azuelan scholarship.

The series of folletines sheds considerably more light on the appearance of *Los de abajo* in El Paso than does the paperback. It owes this advantage to *El Paso del Norte*, whose columns not only carry the text of the novel but also sketch in the political, military, and social scene that surrounded it. These early printings must be considered and studied in their relation to *El Paso del Norte* and its role as a newspaper in the El Paso–Ciudad Juárez community.

Furthermore, the installments can be dated precisely by the issues of *El Paso del Norte* in which they appear. Advertisements and reviews that occupy its pages permit dating of the paperback volume with reasonable accuracy. The improvised typographical arrangements normally used by the newspaper carry over into the serial version of *Los de abajo* and from there into the paperback, and in both cases they do injustice to the aesthetic features of the novel. Certainly the typography did nothing to cheer Azuela during the difficult days of his exile. The newspaper also points up Azuela's impoverished state in El Paso. He has commented upon the slender weekly allowance furnished by Fernando Gamiochipi during the period that the installments of his novel were appearing. He has also noted the one thousand finished copies that were to be his as payment, but he did not report that these were to be sold for thirty cents each. Had Azuela been able to sell the total printing, he could never have cleared more than $300 from the sale of the edition.

But the true significance of these works lies elsewhere. Theirs is the first text that Azuela wrote of *Los de abajo,* no more than three months following the events that the author worked into his novel. This text, then, is the ancestor of the whole series that has followed. It has to be the initial stage in tracing the continuous development of Azuela's redaction of his creation. His second redaction, the one that Razaster published in 1920, introduced by far the most drastic modifications, but in later years he constantly substituted new lexical items, modified spelling and punctuation, and introduced new phraseology. This process complicated to a considerable extent the editing of the author's *Obras completas*. Alí Chumacero, who was charged with preparing the texts of Azuela's novels, has noted specifically the presence of these variant readings in his "Advertencia" that precedes them.[67] Chumacero gives no indication that he was aware of the contribution of these early versions to the formation of *Los de abajo*. These early printings do permit a clearer view of Azuela's technique of writ-

[67] *O.C.,* I, xxiii.

ing, of his practice of literary craftsmanship. They help point the way toward a more careful stylistic examination of *Los de abajo* and of Azuela's prose.

Along with his textual alterations, the novelist has introduced various innovations that affect the arrangement of *Los de abajo,* or its structure, if one wishes to call it that. In the primitive redaction the unity of the work is less apparent than after 1920 in Azuela's reworking. There he has pulled it together more and has produced a neater structural package. This structural contrast between the El Paso and later versions still merits a careful inquiry.

Those who have written about *Los de abajo* have concerned themselves mainly with philosophical and historical features of the novel. Accessibility of the folletines and the accompanying paperback edition will do little to change the direction of the comments. Although Azuela's political idealism is evident throughout *Los de abajo,* he provides his characters with little in the way of guiding philosophical concerns or moral principles. This feature is common to the El Paso texts as well as the revisions. Azuela has been concerned with a time span of only two years, from 1913 to 1915. In this sense the roots of his characters and their predicaments hardly go back to the brief government of Madero and rarely reach into the abuses prevalent under Porfirio Díaz. The novelist treats only that which is immediate, as if he wrote *Los de abajo* taking into account only what he had observed during his months with Julián Medina and Manuel Caloca. The sense of immediacy, if it is evident in later versions of the novel, is probably more intense in the text written in 1915 when Azuela's own existence was still guided by day-to-day considerations. These characteristics were all established when Azuela first wrote *Los de abajo* in Chihuahua and El Paso and, despite the extensive reworking, have been maintained throughout all subsequent editions.

The El Paso versions will not affect the prestige that *Los de abajo* has attained during the past half a century nor is Mariano Azuela's stature as a novelist at stake on the basis of these early texts. Rather, they pull back the curtain to reveal the genesis of *Los de abajo* and the initial state of the chronological development of that novel. After having eluded literary historians for sixty years, the pages of *El Paso del Norte* have now divulged what was in the manuscript that Azuela offered for sale to Fernando Gamiochipi. The quest for that precious creation, brought forth during defeat and hardship, has now ended.

CHAPTER 3

Los de abajo

The text that follows is that of *Los de abajo* as it appeared in the pages of *El Paso del Norte* between October 27 and November 21, 1915. It has not been republished until now. The purpose in presenting it here is to provide an accurate reproduction of *Los de abajo* as Mariano Azuela first saw it in print. It is not simply another edited or emended text.

In order to achieve this purpose, the format has been made to follow closely that of the folletín edition of the novel. The only difference is in the size of the type and the arrangement of the heading of each installment. The text is set line by line to correspond to the printed original. The *entregas* or folletines of *Los de abajo* are clearly identified and numbered as they were in *El Paso del Norte*. Numbers 14 and 15, however, are missing from the bound collection held in the Fondo Basave, and there is no other known collection that contains these portions. In order to provide a complete text of Mariano Azuela's first redaction, for these missing numbers I have substituted the corresponding sections from the paperback edition prepared by Fernando Gamiochipi. A comparison of the newspaper text with that of the paperback reveals very few differences, and those affect the course of the novel only slightly. The only problem involved in the substitution has been to

determine the dividing point between the two missing numbers. On the basis of the number of lines contained in the other installments, Numbers 14 and 15 have been made to correspond in length, and hopefully the division point has been located accurately.

One would normally expect the layout of the folletines to take into account the convenience of the reader. That has not been the case in determining the dividing points or breaks between installments. Obviously the printers themselves have decided where these breaks should occur and have considered only the space that was assigned to *Los de abajo* for each daily installment in the columns of *El Paso del Norte*. From the text of the novel which had been set up in type previously, each day the layout man judged the space available, then took only the number of lines of type that filled that space. As a result, none of the typographical breaks correspond to the ends of chapters in *Los de abajo*. In six cases, installments are broken off in mid-sentence, as between folletines three and four: "... pero en el combate de antier conseguí desertarme y / he venido caminando en busca de ustedes." The layout does not even respect the integrity of the word. On four occasions, words are divided between installments, for example, between folletines four and five, "Una

veintena de encuerados, pio- / josos y mugrientos ....," and again between twenty-two and
twenty-three, " ... y se queda tendido in- /
móvil. Venancio cae a su lado ...."

At the same time, other idiosyncrasies have
been retained here. These include Azuela's own
peculiarities of orthography, which in many
cases have been modified in subsequent editions.
Likewise the numerous typographical errors that
plagued both the folletín edition and the El
Paso paperback have been left in. The original
use of orthographic accents and capital letters
has been respected, likewise the digraph *ii* used
in place of the standard *ü*. Unfortunately these
typographical and stylistic features do not make
for an attractive edition, but they are indicative of *Los de abajo*'s lowly birth and unpromis-
ing future in late 1915.

The appearance of the long run of *El Paso
del Norte* and the republication of the El Paso
redaction of *Los de abajo* after a wait of sixty
years are in themselves significant events in the
novel's history, but the implications for future
critical study far outshadow these. With a careful version of the folletín edition as a starting
point, it is possible to view and study the total
sweep of *Los de abajo* from its humble origin
in El Paso through Azuela's major overhaul of
1920 and the subsequent minor alteration of the
text that continued even until his death. One
can now view the novelist's views and artistic
processes with a much clearer focus.

The Text from El Paso del Norte

FOLLETIN NUM. 1

DE

"EL PASO DEL NORTE"

Está asegurada la propiedad de la obra
y no podrá reimprimirse sin nuestro consentimiento

Mariano Azuela

LOS DE ABAJO

*CUADROS Y ESCENAS
DE LA
REVOLUCION ACTUAL*

PRIMERA PARTE

I.

—Te digo que no es animal... Oye cómo ladra el "Palomo".... Debe ser algún cristiano. ....

La mujer fijaba sus pupilas en la obscuridad de la sierra.

—¿Y qué fueran siendo federales?—repuso un hombre que en cuclillas yantaba en un rincón con una cazuela en la diestra y tres tortillas en taco en la otra mano.

La mujer no le contestó, sus sentidos estaban puestos fuera de la casuca.

Se oyó ruido de pezuñas en el pedregal cercano, y el "Palomo" ladró con más rabia.

—Sería bueno que por sí o por no te escondieras Demetrio.

El hombre, sin alterarse acabó de cenar; se acercó a un cántaro y bebió agua a borbotones. Luego se puso en pie.

—Tu rifle está debajo de la cuna— pronunció ella en voz muy baja.

El cuartito se encontraba alumbrado por una mecha de manteca. En un rincón descanzaban un yugo, un arado, un otate y otros aperos de labranza. Del techo pendía una cuerda sosteniendo un viejo molde de hacer adobes, que servía de cuna, y sobre mantas y desteñidas hilachas dormía un niño.

Demetrio ciñó la cartuchera a su contura y levantó el fusil. Alto, robusto, de faz bermeja, sin pelo de barba, vestía camisa y calzón de manta, ancho sombrero de soyate y huaraches.

Salió paso a paso, desapareciendo en la obscuridad impenetrable de la noche.

El "Palomo" enfurecido, había saltado sobre la cerca del corral.

De pronto se oyó un disparo, el perro lanzó un gemido sordo y no ladró más.

Unos hombres llegaron maldiciendo y vociferando. Dos se apearon y otro quedó cuidando las bestias.

—¡Mujeres!.... algo de cenar: blaquillos, leche, frijoles, lo que tengan; que venimos muertos de hambre.

—¡Maldita sierra! Sólo el diablo no se perdería!

—Se perdería también, sargento, si viniera de borracho como nosotros.

Uno lelvaba galones en los hombros, el otro cintas rojas en las mangas.

—¿En dónde estamos, vieja?... Pero, ¡con un tal! ¿Esta casa está sola? Y entonces ¿esa luz? y ese chamaco?.... ¡Vieja, queremos cenar, y que sea pronto! ¿Sales, o te hacemos salir?

—¡Hombres malvados, me mataron mi perro! ¿Que les debía, que les comió mi pobrecito "Palomo"?

La mujer entró, llevando a rastras el perro muy blanco y muy gordo, con los ojos claros ya, y el cuerpo suelto.

—¡Mira nomás qué chapetes, sargento! Mi alma, no te enojes, te voy a convertir tu casa en palomar y te voy a servir hasta de rodillas; pero ¡por Dios!.... "no me mires airada..... no más enojos....."

—Mírame cariñosa, luz de mis ojos.....'' cantó el oficial con voz aguardentosa.

—Señora. ¿Cómo se llama este ranchito?—preguntó el sargnto.

—La mujer que soplaba las brasas del fogón y ponía más leña, contestó hosca, pero sin miedo.

—¿Conque aquí es "Limón"? La tierra del famoso Demeterio Macías....¿Lo oye, mi teniente? Estamos en "Limón".

—¿En "Limón"?...... Bueno. ......para mí ¡plim! Ya sabes, sargento, si he de irme al infierno, me voy en buen caballo. Pero tú nos has visto cachetes como estos: sí parecen un peroncito en sazón..... para morderlos.

—Y usted ha de conocer al bandido ese....Hace mucho que yo lo conocí: estuvimos juntos en la Penitenciaría.

—Sargento, traeme una botella de tequila; he decidido pasar la noche en la amable compañía de esta morenita......¿El coronel?...que vaya mucho a... Y si el coronel se enoja..... pa mí ..... ¡plim! Anda, sargento, dile al cabo que desencille y eche de cenar. Aquí me quedo. Oye, chata, deja a mi sargento que fría los blanquillos y caliente las gordas; tú ven acá conmigo. Mira, esta carterita apretada de billetes es sólo para tí. Es mi gusto: figúrate.....ando un poco borrachito por eso y por eso también hablo un poco ronco: como que en Guadalajara dejé la mitad de la campanilla y por el camino vengo escupiendo la otra mitad... ¿Y qué le haces? es mi gusto. Sargento, mi botella de tequila. Chatita, estás muy lejos; arrímate a tomar un trago......¿Cómo que nó? ¿Le tienes miedo a tu marido. .. o lo que sea? Si lo guardas por allí oculto en algún agujero como las ratas, dile que salga.......pa mí ¡plim! te aseguro que no nos estorba siquiera.

Una sombra blanca llenó la boca obscura de la puerta.

—¡Demetrio Macías!— pronunció el sargento despavorido, dando unos pasos atrás.

El teniente se puso en pié y enmudeció, quedando inmóvil como una estatua.

—¡Mátalos, Demetrio!— exclamó la mujer con la garganta seca.

—¡Ah! dispénseme, amigo.... yo no sabía. Pero yo respeto a los valientes de veras....

Demetrio se quedó mirándolos y una sonrisa insolente y despreciativa plegó sus líneas.

—Y no sólo los respeto, sino que también los admiro y los quiero....Aquí tiene la mano de un amigo.....Está bien, Demetrio Macías, usted me desaira...... Es que no me conoce, es porque me ve en este perro oficio.. ¡Qué quiere, amigo, es uno pobre , tiene familia que sostener... Sargento, vámonos: yo respeto siempre la casa de un valiente, de un hombre de veras.......

Luego que desaparecieron, la mujer abrazó estrechamente a Demetrio.

—¡Qué susto, madre mía de Talpa! Creí que a tí te habían tirado el balazo!

—Vete luego a la casa de mi padre—dijo Demetrio.

Ella quiso llorar, detenerlo, suplicarle; pero él, apartándola dulcemente, agregó sombrío:

—Me late que van a venir todos juntos.

—¿Por qué no los mataste?

Demetrio alzó los hombros y con gesto fatalista, respondió:

—Seguro que no les tocaría.

Salieron juntos, ella con el niño en los brazos. Y en la puerta misma se separaron en opuesta dirección.

La luna poblaba la montaña de sombras vagas. En cada risco y en cada chaparro, Demetrio seguía mirando la silueta dolorida de una mujer con su niño en los brazos. Y cuando después de muchas horas de ascenso, volvió los ojos, en el fondo del cañón, cerca del río, se levantaban grandes llamaradas: ¡su casa ardía!....

II.

Clareó la mañana cuando Demetrio Macías comenzó a bajar al fondo de la barranca. El angosto talud de un cantil era vereda, entre el peñazcal veteado de enormes resquebrajaduras y la vertiente de centenares de metros, cortada como de un solo tajo.

Sosteniéndose de los ramajes echó su diestra hacia atrás, tiró del cuerno que pendía a su espalda, lo llevó a sus labios gruesos y por tres veces sopló, inflando los carrillos. Tres silbidos prolongados contestaron la señal más allá de la crestería frontera. Entonces siguió descendiendo con agilidad y rapidez.

"Seguramente—pensó—ahora sí van a dar con nuestro rastro los federales y se nos vienen encima como perros. La fortuna es que no saben veredas, entradas ni salidas. Sólo que alguno de 'Moyahua' anduviera con ellos de guía; porque los de "Limón," "Santa Rosa" y demás ranchitos de la sierra, son gente segura y nunca nos entregarán..... En "Moyahua" está el cacique que me trae corriendo por los cerros, y ese sí tendría mucho gusto en verme colgado de un poste del telégrafo y con la lengua de fuera."

Y llegó al fondo de la barranca cuando todo era sombra todavía. Se tiró entre las piedras y se quedó dormido.

El río se arrastraba, cantando en diminutas cascadas; pajarillos piaban escondidos en los pitayos, y las chicharras monorrítimicas llenaban de misterio la sombra y la soledad de la montaña.

Demetrio despertó sobresaltado, badeó el río y tomó la vertiente opuesta del cañón. Como hormiga

FOLLETIN NUM. 2

arriera ascendió la crestería, crispadas las manos en las peñas y ramazones, crispadas las plantas sobre las guijas de la vereda.

Cuando escaló la cumbre, el sol bañaba la altiplanicie en un lago de oro. Hacia la barranca se veían rocas enormes, rebanadas; prominencias erizas como fantásticas cabezas africanas; los pitayos como dedos anquilosados de coloso; árboles tendidos hacia el fondo del abismo. Y en la aridez de las peñas y de las ramas secas, albeaban las frescas rosas de "San Juan" como una blanca ofrenda al astro que comenzaba a deslizar sus hilos de oro, de roca en roca.

Demetrio se detuvo en la cumbre y sopló tres veces en su cuerno. A su señal contestó la señal. En la lejanía, de entre un cónico hacinamiento de paja podrida, salieron, uno tras otro, muchos hombres de piernas y pechos desnudos, obscuros y repulidos como viejos bronces.

Vinieron al encuentro de Demetrio.

—¡Me quemaron mi casa!—respondió a las miradas interrogadoras.

Hubo imprecaciones, amenazas, insolencias.

Demetrio los dejó desahogarse; luego sacó de su camisa una botella, bebió un tanto, limpiola con el dorso de la mano, y la pasó a su inmediato. La botella, en una vuelta de boca en boca, se quedó vacía. Los hombres se relamieron.

—Si Dios nos da licencia—exclamó Demetrio,—mañana a esta misma noche les hemos de mirar la cara otra vez a los federales. ¿Qué dicen, los dejamos conocer estas veredas?

Los hombres semidesnudos saltaron regocijados, dando alaridos de alegría. Y luego redoblaron las injurias, las maldiciones y las amenazas.

—No sabemos cuántos serán ellos,—observó Demetrio, escudriñando los semblantes.

—Julián Medina en Hostotipaquillo, con media docena de pelados y con cuchilos afilados en el metate, les hizo frente a todos los cuicos y federales del pueblo, y se los echó.... ¿Qué tendrán algo los de Medina, que a nosotros nos falte?—dijo uno de barba y de cejas espesas y muy negras, de mirada dulzachona, hombre maciso y robusto.

—Yo sólo les sé decir—agregó—que dejo de llamarme Anastasio Montañez si mañana no soy dueño de un mausser, cartucheras, pantalones y zapatos. ¡De veras! Mira, "Codorniz" ¿voy que no me lo crees? traigo media docena de balas adentro de mi cuerpo.... ¡Ai que lo diga mi compadre Demetrio, si no es cierto!.... Pero a mí me dan tanto miedo las balas como una bolita de caramelo. ¿A que no me lo crees?

¡Que viva Anastasio Montañez!—gritó "El Manteca."

—No—repuso aquél—¡que viva Demetrio Macías que es nuestro jefe y vivan Dios del cielo y María Santísima!

—¡Viva Demetrio Macías!—gritaron todos.

Encendieron lumbre con zacate y leños secos, y sobre los carbones encendidos tendieron trozos de carne fresca. Se rodearon en torno de las llamas, sentados en cuclillas, olfateando con apetito la carne que se retorcía en las brazas.

Cerca de ellos estaba, en montón, la piel dorada de una res, sobre la tierra húmeda de sangre. De un cordel, entre dos huizaches, pendía la carne hecha cecina, oreándose al sol y al aire.

—Bueno,—dijo Demetrio,—ya ven que aparte de mi treinta treinta, contamos no más con veinte armas. Si son pocos, les damos hasta no dejar uno; si son muchos, aunque sea un buen susto les hemos de sacar.

Aflojó el ceñidor de su cintura y desató un nudo, ofreciendo, luego, el contenido a sus compañeros.

—¡Sal!—exclamaron, tomando cada uno con la punta de los dedos, algunos granos.

Comieron con avidez y cuando quedaron satisfechos, se tiraron de barriga al sol y cantaron canciones monótonas y tristes, lanzando gritos estridentes después de cada estrofa.

III.

Etnre la maleza de la sierra durmieron los veinticinco hombres de Demetrio Macías, hasta que la señal del cuerno los hizo despertar. Pancracio la daba desde lo alto de un pico de la montaña.

—Ahora sí, muchachos, pónganse changos—dijo Anastasio Montañez, reconociendo las muelles de su rifle.

Pero transcurrió una hora sin que se oyera más que el canto de las cigarras en el hierbazal, y el croar de las ranas en el río.

Cuando los albores de la luna se esfumaron en la faja débilmente rosada de la aurora, se destacó la primera silueta de un soldado en la parte más alta de la vereda. Y tras de él aparecieron otro y otros diez y otros cien; pero en breve se perdían en la sombra. Hasta que asomaron los fulgores del sol, pudo verse el acantilado cubierto de gente: hombres diminutos en caballos de miniatura.

—¡Míralos qué bonitos—exclamó Pancracio.— ¡Vamos a jugar con ellos!

Aquellas figuras movedizas, ora se perdían en la espesura del chaparral, ora negreaban más abajo, sobre el ocre de las peñas.

Distintamente se oyeron las voces de jefes y soldados. Demetrio hizo una señal: crugieron las muelles y los resortes de los fusiles.

—¡Hora!—ordenó con voz apagada.

Veintiún hombres dispararon a un tiempo y otros tantos federales cayeron de sus monturas.

Sorprendidos, se quedaron inmóviles, como bajos relieves de las peñas.

Una nueva descarga, y otros veintiún hombres rodaron de roca en roca con el cráneo abierto.

—¡Salgan, bandidos, muertos de hambre!......

—¡Mueran los come-vacas!....

—¡Mueran los ladrones nixtamaleros!

—Los jefes federales gritaban a los enemigos que, ocultos, quietos y callados, se contentaban con seguir haciendo gala de una puntería que los había hecho ya famosos.

—Mira, Pancracio—dijo "El Moco", un individuo que sólo en los dientes y en los ojos tenía algo que blanqueara—ésta es para el que va a pasar detrás de aquel pitayo..... ¡Hijo de la.... insolencia!.... Toma... en la pura calabaza, ¿viste?... Ora al que va en el caballo tordillo...¡Abajo, pelón!

—Yo voy a darle una bañada al que viene por el filo de la vereda.... Si no llegas al río, mocho infeliz, no quedas lejos.... ¿Qué tal? ¡lo viste!.....

—Hombre, Anastasio, no seas malo; empréstame la carabina. ¡Andale, un tiro no más!

"El Manteca," "La Codorniz," y los otros dos que no tenían armas las solicitaban, pedían como una gracia suprema el que los dejaran hacer un tiro siquiera.

—Asómense si son tan hombres!

—Saquen la cabeza, hilachos piojosos!

De montaña a montaña, los gritos se oían tan claros como de una acera a la del frente.

"La Codorniz" surgió de improviso, en cueros, con los calzones tendidos en las manos y haciendo gesto de toerar a los federales.

Entonces comenzó una lluvia de proyectiles sobre los de Demetrio.

—"¡Codorniz" jijo de un .... tal!—gruñó Demetrio.

—Parece que me echaron un panal de moscos en la cabeza—dijo Anastasio Montañez, sin atreverse ni a levantar los ojos.

—A donde les dije—rugió Demetrio.

Y arrastrándose tomaron nuevas posiciones.

Los federales comenzaron a gritar su triunfo e hicieron cesar el fuego; pero una nueva granizada de balas los desconcertó.

—Ya llegaron más....—clamaban los soldados.

Y presa de pánico inesperado, unos volvieron grupas resueltamente, otros abandonaron los caballos y se encaramaron, buscando escondites entre las peñas. Fué preciso que los jefes hicieran fuego sobre los fugitivos para restablecer el orden.

—¡A los de abajo, a los de abajo!—exclamó Demetrio, tendiendo su treinta treinta hacia el hilo cristalino del río. Un federal cayó en las mismas aguas e indefectiblemente siguieron cayendo uno a uno a cada nuevo disparo. Pero sólo él tiraba hacia el río, y por cada uno de los que caían, pasaban intactos diez o veinte.

—¡A los de abajo, a los de abajo!—siguió gritando encolerizado.

Los compañeros se prestaban ahora sus armas, y, haciendo blancos, cruzaban nuevas apuestas.

—Mi cinturón de cuero si no le pego en la cabeza al del caballo prieto. Préstame tu rifle, "Meco."

—Veinte tiros de mausser y media vara de chorizo porque me dejes tumbar al de la potranca mora.

—Viste qué salto dió!..... ¡como venado!

—No corran, mochos...... ¡Vengan a conocer a su padre Demetrio Macías!

Ahora de éstos partían las injurias. Gritaba Pancracio, alargando su cara lampiña, inmutable como si fuera de piedra; y gritaba "El Manteca" contrayendo las cuerdas de su cuello y estirando las líneas de su rostro de ojos torvos, de asesino.

FOLLETIN NUM. 3

Demetrio siguió tirando y advirtiendo del peligro a los demás; pero éstos no oyeron su voz sino hasta que comenzaron a sentir el chicoteo de las balas por uno de sus flancos.

—Ya me…. quemaron—gimió Demetrio y rechinó los dientes.—Hijos de…..! Y con prontitud se dejó resbalar hacia un barranco.

IV.

Faltaron dos: Serapio el charamusquero y Antonio el que tocaba los platillos en la banda de Juchipila.

—A ver si se nos juntan más adelante—dijo Demetrio.

Volvían desazonados. Sólo Anastasio Montañez conservaba la expresión dulzona de sus ojos dormidos y su rostro barbado, y Pancracio, la inmutabilidad repulsiva de su duro perfil de prognato.

Los federales habían regresado ya y Demetrio recuperaba todos sus caballos, escondidos en la sierra.

De pronto "La Codorniz," que marchaba adelante, exhaló un grito. Acababa de descubrir a los compañeros perdidos, pedientes de los brazos de un mezquite.

Eran ellos, Serapio y Antonio. Los identificaron y Montañez pronunció en voz alta:

—Padre Nuestro que estás en los cielos…..

—Amén—contestaron todos con la cabeza inclinada y el sombrero sobre el pecho.

Y apresurados tomaron el Cañón de Juchipila, rumbo a Moyahua, caminando sin descansar hasta ya muy entrada la noche.

"La Codorniz" no se apartaba un instante de Anastasio. Las siluetas de los ahorcados con el cuello flácido, los brazos pendientes, rígidas las piernas, suavemente mecidos por el viento, no se borraban de su memoria.

Otro día, Demetrio se quejó mucho de su herida; no pudo subir a su caballo. Fué preciso conducirlo desde allí en una camilla improvisada con ramas de roble y haces de yerba.

—Sigue desangrándose, compadre Demetrio—dijo Anastasio Montañez, y de un tirón arrancó una manga de su camisa y la anudó fuertemente al muslo, arriba del balazo.

—Bueno—dijo Venancio—eso le para la sangre y le quita la dolencia.

Venancio era barbero y en su pueblo sacaba muelas y ponía cáusticos y sanguijuelas. Gozaba de cierto ascendiente porque había leído "El Judío Errante" y "Sol de Mayo." Le llamaban el doctor, y él, muy pagado de su sabiduría, se había hecho "hombre de pocas palabras."

Turnándose de cuatro en cuatro, condujeron la camilla por mesetas calvas y pedregosas y por cuestas empinadísimas.

Al medio día, cuando la calina sofocaba y se obnubilaba la vista, con el canto incesante de las cigarras se oía el quejido acompasado y monocorde de Demetrio.

En cada jacalito, escondido entre las rocas abruptas, se detenían y descansaban.

—Gracias a Dios que en todas partes hemos encontrado un alma compasiva y una gorda copeteada de chile y frijoles—decía Anastasio Montañez.

Y los serranos, cuando los miraban alejarse, después de estrecharles fuertemente las manos callosas, exclamaban:

—"¡Dios los bendiga! ¡Dios los ayude y los lleve por buen camino! Ahora corren ustedes; mañana correremos también nosotros, huyendo de la leva, perseguidos por esos condenados del gobierno que nos han declarado guerra a muerte a todos los pobres; que nos roban nuestros puercos, nuestras gallinas y hasta el maicito que tenemos para comer; que queman nuestras casas y se llevan a nuestras mujeres, y que, por fin, donde dan con uno, allí lo acaban como si fuera perro del mal."

Cuando atardeció, en llamaradas que tiñeron el cielo de vivísimos colores, pardearon unas casucas en una explanada que circundaban las montañas azueles. Demetrio hizo que lo llevaran allí.

Eran unos cuantos pobres jacales de zacate, diseminados en la orilla del río, entre pequeñas sementeras de maíz y frijol recién nacidos.

Cuando pusieron la camilla en el suelo, Demetrio pidió, con débil voz, un trago de agua.

En las bocas obscuras de las chozas se aglomeraron chomites incoloros, pechos huesudos, cabezas desgreñadas, y detrás, ojos brillantes y carrillos frescos.

Un chico gordiflón, de piel morena y reluciente

se acercó a ver al hombre de la camilla, luego una vieja y después las demás, vinieron a hacerle ruedo.

Una moza muy amable se acercó con una jícara de agua azul. Demetrio cogió la vasija entre sus manos trémulas y bebió con avidez.

—¿No quiere más?

Alzó los ojos y reparó en la muchacha: su rostro era vulgar, pero en su voz había mucha dulzura.

Se limpió con el dorso del puño el sudor que perlaba en su frente y volviéndose de un lado, pronunció con fatiga:

—¡Dios se lo pague!

Y comenzó a tiritar con tal fuerza, que sacudía las yerbas y los pies de la camilla. La fiebre lo aletargó.

—Está haciendo sereno y eso es malo para la calentura—dijo señá Remigia, una vieja enchomitada, descalza y con una garra de manta al pecho, a guisa de camisa.

Y los invitó a que metieran a Demetrio a su jacal Como perros fieles se echaron a los pies de la camilla, Pancracio, Anastasio Montañez y la "Codorniz," pendientes de la voluntad de su jefe.

Los demás se dispersaron en busca de comida.

Señá Remigia sirvió a sus huéspedes chile y tortillas.

—!Afigúrense.... tenía huevos, gallinas y hasta unas chivas..... pero estos maldecidos federales me limpiaron.....!

Luego, puestas las manos en bocina, se acercó al oído de Anastasio y le dijo muy quedo:

—Afigúrese.... ¡cargaron hasta con la muchachilla de señá Nieves!....

V.

La "Codorniz, sobresaltado, abrió los ojos y se incorporó.

—Montañez, oíste?.... ¡un balazo!

—¡Montañez, Montañez!... despierta.

Le dió fuertes empellones hasta conseguir que se removiera y dejara de roncar.

—¡Con un .....tal! ¡Ya estás moliendo "Codorniz"! ..... Te digo que los muertos no se aparecen.....—balbuceó despertando a medias.

—¡Un balazo, Montañez!

—Duérmete o te doy unas trompadas....

—No, Anastasio, no es pesadilla.... Ya no me he vuelto a acordar de los ahorcados. Es de veras un balazo; lo oí clarito.....

—¿Dices que un balazo? A ver, daca mi mausser......

Anastasio Montañez se restregó los ojos, estiró los brazos y las piernas con mucha flojera y se puso en pie.

Salieron del jacal. El cielo estaba cuajado de estrellas y como una uña delgada, la luna ascendía. De las casucas salió el rumor confuso de las mujeres asustadas y se oyó el riudo de armas de los que dormían afuera y se despertaban también.

—"Estúpido.... me has destrozado un pie."

La voz se oyó clara y distinta en las inmediaciones.

—¿Quién vive?

El grito resonó de peña en peña por cantiles y hondonadas hasta perderse en la lejanía y el silencio de la noche.

—¿Quién vive?—repitió Anastasio, haciendo correr el cerrojo de su mausser.

—¡Demetrio Macías!—respondió una voz ríspida.

—¡Es Pancracio!—dijo "La Codorniz" muy contento. Y ya sin zozobras, dejó reposar la culata de su fusil.

Pancracio conducía a un mozalvete cubierto de polvo, desde el fieltro americano hasta los toscos borceguíes; llevaba una mancha de sangre fresca en su pantalón, cerca de un pie.

—¿Quién es este curro?—preguntó Anastasio.

—A mí me tocó de centinela.... oí ruido entre las yerbas y grité: ¿quién vive?..... "Carranzo" respondió este vale..... "¿Carranzo?"...... No conozco yo ese gallo.... Y toma tu Carranzo... le metí un plomazo en una pata.

Y sonriendo, Pancracio volvía su cara lampiña y sucia, en solicitud de aplausos.

Entonces habló el desconocido:

—¿Quién es aquí el jefe?

Anastasio levantó la cabeza con mucha altivez.

El tono del mozo bajó un tanto.

—Pues yo soy revolucionario también. Los federales me cogieron en la leva y entré a filas; pero en el combate de antier conseguí desertarme y

FOLLETIN NUM. 4

he venido caminando en busca de ustedes.

—¡Es federal!—interrumpieron algunos, mirándolo con admiración.

—Es mocho—dijo Anastasio Montañez. —¿Y por qué no le metiste el plomo en la mera chapa?

—¡Quién sabe qué mitote trae! ¡Que quiere hablar con Demetrio; que va a decirle quién sabe cuántas cosas!..... Pero eso no le hace; para todo hay tiempo—respondió Pancracio, poniéndose en actitud de disparar su rifle.

—Pero, ¿qué clase de brutos son ustedes?....—exclamó el desconocido.

No pudo seguir hablando porque un revés de Anastasio lo derribó con la cara bañada en sangre.

—¡Fusilen a ese mocho!

—¡Ahórquenlo!

—¡Quémenlo.... es federal!

Exaltados, ululaban y levantaban sus rifles amenazadores.

—Chist.... Chist.... cállense, parece que Demetrio habla—dijo Anastasio sosegándolos.

Demetrio se informó de lo que ocurría y quiso que le llevaran al prisionero.

—¡Una infamia, mi jefe; mire usted..... mire usted!—pronunció Luis Cervantes, mostrando las manchas de sangre en su pantalón, y su boca y nariz abotagadas.

—Por eso, pues ¿quién tales ....es usted?—interrogó Demetrio mohino.

—Me llamo Luis Cervantes, soy estudiante de medicina y periodista. Por decir algo en favor de ustedes los revolucionarios, tuve graves dificultades; me persiguieron, me atraparon y fuí a dar al cuartel....

La relación que de su aventura siguió detallando Luis Cervantes, en tono patético, causó la hilaridad de Pancracio y de "El Manteca."

—Yo he procurado hacerme entender, convencerlos de que soy un verdadero correligionario.

—¿Corre.... qué?—inquirió Demetrio, tendiendo una oreja.

—Correligionario, mi jefe... es decir, que persigo los mismos ideales y defiendo la misma causa que ustedes defienden.

Demetrio se sonrió.

—¿Pues cuál causa defendemos nosotros?

Luis Cervantes, desconcertado, no encontró qué contestar.

—Mí ¡qué cara pone!.... ¿pa qué hecha tantos brincos.... estando tan parejo el suelo? ¿Lo tronamos ya, Demetrio?—interrogó Pancracio ancioso.

Demetrio llevó su mano al mechón de pelo que le cubría la oreja, se rascó largo rato, meditabundo.

—¡Ah! ya me está doliendo otra vez!... Sálganse. Anastasio, apaga la mecha. Enciérrenlo en el corral y me lo ciudan Pancracio y "El Manteca"..... Mañana veremos.....

Luis Cervantes, muy pensativo, se paseó toda la moche de largo a largo del corral.

Los gallos cantaban sonoramente llenando de alegría la mañana; las gallinas, trepadas en un arbusto, se removían, abrían las alas, esponjaban las plumas; luego, de un salto pesado, se ponían en el suelo.

Luis Cervantes se dió cuenta de sus centinelas profundamente dormidos, tirados en un estercolero. Y por un instante, su piel se puso carne de gallina. En su imaginación revivieron las fisonomías de aquellos dos hombres. Pancracio, agüerido, pecoso, con su barba lampiña muy saliente, la frente roma y oblícua, las orejan untadas al cráneo y su aspecto perfectamente bestial. Y el otro, "El Manteca," una piltrafa humana: ojos oblícuos y mirada torva, los cabellos lacios, muy largos, cubriéndole la nuca, la frente y los oídos; los labios hinchados de escrofuloso, siempre entreabiertos.

VI.

Una voz dulce y armoniosa hizo a Demetrio levantar los ojos: la misma muchacha de mirada amable, que la víspera le había ofrecido una jícara de agua deliciosamente fría, ahora, cuando los primeros rayos del sol dardeaban por entre los popotes del jacal, entraba con una olla de leche espumosa.

—¿Cómo te llamas?—le preguntó.

—Camila—contestó ella. Y como Demetrio le clavara su mirada penetrante, cubierta de rubor, salió a prisa.

—Me siento bien, compadre Anastasio—Dijo Demetrio—parece que me dieron fríos; sudé mucho y amanecí muy refrescado. Lo que no deja de dolerme es la herida. Llama a Venancio para que me cure.

—¿Y qué hacemos, pues, con el curro que agarré anoche?—inquirió Pancracio.

—¡Cabal.... hombre!..... no me había vuelto a acordar.

Demetrio pensó mucho para decidir.

—A ver, "Codorniz," ven acá. Pregunta por una capilla que hay a cinco leguas de aquí. Vas y le robas la sotana al cura.

—¿Pos qué va a hacer, compadre?—preguntó Anastasio, admirado.

—Si el curro este viene a asesinarme, es muy fácil sacarle la verdad. "La Codorniz" se viste de padre y lo confiesa. Le digo que lo voy a fusilar. Si no tiene culpa, no dice nada, y entonces lo dejo ir.

—¡Hum,—cuántos requisitos.... Yo le tronaba, y ya—exclamó Pancracio.

Por la noche regresó "La Codorniz" con la sotana.

Demetrio hizo que llevaran al prisionero.

Luis Cervantes, sin dormir ni comer en dos días, entraba con el rostro demacrado y ojeroso, los labios descoloridos y secos.

Habló con lentitud y torpeza:

—Hagan lo que quieran...... Me he equivocado......

Hubo un prolongado silencio.

—Creí que ustedes aceptarían con gusto al que viene a ofrecerles humilde ayuda, para beneficio propio.... ¿Yo qué gano con que la Revolución triunfe o no?

Poco a poco iba animándose y la languidez de su mirada desaparecía por instantes.

—La Revolución beneficia al pobre, al ignorante, al que toda su vida ha sido vida de esclavo, a los desdichados que ni siquiera saben que el rico es rico porque sabe volver oro las lágrimas de los pobres.

—¿Y eso es ya cosa de qué? ¡Cuando ni a mí me gustan los sermones!—dijo Pancracio, interrumpiéndolo.

—Yo quiero pelear por la causa de los pobres. Pero me he equivocado: creí que ustedes eran revolucionarios..... ¡Erré! ¡Hagan conmigo lo que gusten!

—Por de pronto no más te pongo un lazo en el pescuezo. ¡Y vaya que lo tienes blanco y rechonchito!

—Sí; ya sé a lo que viene usted—pronunció Demetrio con desabrimiento y rascándose la cabeza.—Lo voy a fusilar.

Luego se dirigió a Anastasio:

—Llévenlo.... pero que se confiese primero... ¿Ya vino el padre?

Anastasio, impacible como siempre, lo tomó de un brazo.

—Véngase para acá, curro.

Cuando regresó "La Codorniz," ensotanado, todos rieron a carcajadas.

—Este curro es muy pico-largo—dijo—hasta se me figura que se rió de mí cuando le comencé a hacer preguntas.

—¿Pero nada confesó?—inquirió Demetrio.

—Lo mismo que nos dijo anoche.

—Me late que no viene a lo que usted piensa, compadre—pronunció Anastasio.

—Bueno, pues; dénle de comer y ténganlo a una vista.....

Luis Cervantes, de jacal en jacal, buscó agua hervida y pedazos de lienzo usado. Camila le proporcionó todo.

Con curiosidad de serrana se sentó a verlo curar su herida.

—Oiga ¿y quién lo enseñó a curar?..... ¿Y para qué girvió el agua? ¿Y los trapos para qué los coció?...Mire, mire, ¡cuánta curiosidad para todo!..... ¿Y eso que se echó en las manos?...... ¿Aguardiente?..... ¡Ande, pos si yo creiba que el aguardiente no más para el cólico era bueno!.... ¡Ah! ¿de modo es que usted iba a ser dotor?..... ¡Ja... ja.... ja!... ¡cosa de morirse de risa!... ¿Y por qué no le revolvió aguá fría mejor?...... ¡Mire qué cuentos!... ¡Que izque animales en el agua sin gervir!.... ¡Cuando yo ni miro nada de animales!.....

Camila lo siguió interrogando, y con tanta familiaridad, que derrepente comenzó a tutearlo.

Pero Luis Cervantes no la escuchaba.

—"En dónde están esos hombres admirablemente montados y armados que reciben sus haberes en puros pesos duros de los que Villa está acuñando en Chihuahua? Una veintena de encuerados, pio-

FOLLETIN NUM. 5

josos y mugrientos: había quien llevara montura con un solo arzón y quien cabalgara en una yegua decrépita, matadura de la cruz a la cola. Entonces era cierto lo que la prensa del Gobierno decía de los revolucionarios: que sólo eran bandidos agrupados con cualquier pretexto, y mentira todo lo que de bueno contaban de ellos los simpatizadores de la revolución. Y sin embargo, revolucionarios, bandidos o como quisiera llamárseles, ellos eran los que iban a derrocar al Gobierno: los periódicos decían una cosa, los periodistas afirmaban lo contrario. Huerta clamaba todavía: "haré la paz, cueste lo que cueste" y sus parientes y sus favoritos y sus amigos llenaban los vapores hacia Europa. ¿Si me habré equivocado de veras?"

Abstraído pronunció las últimas palabras, acabando de curarse.

—¿Qué estáás diciendo?—preguntó Camila,—pos si yo creiba ya que los ratones te habían comido la lengua.

Luis Cervantes contrajo las cejas y miró con aire hostil a aquella especie de mono enchomitado, de pies descalzos, anchos y chatos.

—¿Oye, curro, tú no sabes contar cuentos?

Luis hizo un gesto de aspereza y se alejó sin contestarle.

VII.

—¿Por qué no llama al Curro para que lo cure, compadre?—dijo Anastasio Montañez a Demetrio, que a diario, por las tardes, sufría grandes calosfríos y calenturas.—Si viera.... él se cura solo y anda tan alviado que ni cojea siquiera.

Pero Venancio, que tenía ya dispuestos los botes de manteca y las planchuelas de hilas mugrientas, protestó:

—Si alguien le pone mano.... yo no respondo de las resultas.

—Oye, compa.... ¿pero qué dotor ni qué nada eres tú?.... ¿Qué ya se te olvidó por qué veniste a dar acá?—dijo "La Codorniz."

—Sí, si me acuerdo de que andas con nosotros, "Codorniz" porque te robaste un relox y dos anillos de oro—pronunció con exaltación Venancio.

—¡Siquiera!..... Peor es que tú corriste de tu tierra porque envenenaste a tu novia.

—¡Mientes!

—Sí, le diste cantáridas..... para.....

Todos prorrumpieron en carcajadas y Venancio en insolencias.

Demetrio avinagró otra vez su semblante. El dolor de la herida, a ratos, era intolerable.

—A ver, traigan pues al estudiante....

Luis descubrió la pierna, la examinó rápidamente y meneó la cabeza con desagrado.

La ligadura de manta se hundía en la piel; la pierna abotargada parecía reventar. Cada movimiento lo hacía dar un gemido. Luis Cervantes cortó la ligadura, lavó abundantemente la herida, cubrió el muslo con grandes compresas húmedas y muy calientes, y lo vendó.

Demetrio durmió toda la tarde y toda la noche y despertó otro día muy contento.

Venancio dijo: "está bueno; pero hay que saber que los curros son como la humedad, por donde quiera se meten. Por los curros se ha perdido el fruto de las revoluciones."

Y como Demetrio creía en la ciencia del barbero, cuando Luis Cervantes lo volvió a curar, le dijo:

—Oiga, cúreme bien, para que cuando me deje sano, se largue a su casa o a donde le dé la gana.

Pero un día, después de la curación, le preguntó si los soldados le daban carne y leche. Luis Cervantes tuvo que decir que sólo comía lo que las buenas viejas de los jacales le obsequiaban; y que los hombres lo seguían mirando con manifiesta hostilidad, como un advenedizo, como un intruso.

—Todos son gente buena—dijo Demetrio, rascándole la cabeza,—pero hay que saberles el modo.......

Y Cervantes salió ese día muy contento a vagar por la sierra.

Parapetado en un picacho, las piernas pendientes y la mirada soñando, lo descubrió Anastasio Montañez.

—¿Por qué está triste, Curro? ¿qué piensa tanto? Venga auá, arrímese a platicar. A usté le hace falta el ruido de su tierra. Bien se echa de ver que es de zapato pintado y de moñito en la camisa.... Mire, ahí donde me ve, yo, todo mugroso y desgarrado, no soy lo que parezco.... ¿A que no me lo cree? yo no tengo necesidad, yo soy dueño de diez yuntas de bueyes.... ¡De veras!.... ¿a que no me lo cree?.... tengo mis diez fanegas de siembra... ¡Ai que lo diga mi compadre Demetrio que me conoce!.... Pero en mi casa no hay necesidad...... Mire, Curro, yo hago repelar mucho a los federales y por eso no me quieren. La última vez, hace ocho meses ya.... los mismos que tengo de andar aquí, le metí un navajazo a un capitancillo faceto (Dios me guarde) aquí merito del ombligo.... Pero, de veras, yo no tengo necesidad... ando aquí por eso ....y por darle la mano a mi compadre Demetrio.

VIII.

Al fresco de la tarde, al pie de un angosto crestón, alagartados entre los jarales a orillas del río, Pancracio y "El Manteca" jugaban bajara.

Anastasio echa un brazo a la espalda de Luis.

—¿Cómo cree que a mi no me cuadra el juego, Curro?..... ¿Quiere usted apostar?.... ¡Andele! mire: esta viborita de cuero todavía suena—dijo

Anastasio, tocando con sus dedos el fajo que llevaba a la cintura y haciendo oír el choque de los pesos duros.

—De veras, Curro; yo no tengo necesidad.

—Tengo mis veinte yuntas de bueyes ¿a que no me lo cree?—pronunció "La Codorniz" llegando detrás de ellos.

—Moza de mi corazón—dijo luego, viendo la sota que Pancracio tiraba al lado del cinco de oros.

"El Manteca" puso diez centavos encima de la sota.

Corrió la baraja, vino la sota y se armó altercado. Jácara, gritos, insultos a granel.

Pancracio, con su cara de piedra, "El Manteca" con los ojos como de víbora y contracciones de epiléptico.

Parecía que de un momento a otro llegaban a las manos; a falta de palabras suficientemente incisivas, acudían a nombrar padres y madres en un bordado de indecencias; pero nada ocurrió. Termina el juego, se levantan, se echan el brazo a la espalda con gran indiferencia y se invitan a tomar un trago.

—Tampoco a mí me gusta pelear de lengua. ¡Es feo eso! ¿Verdad, Curro?

Pero Luis Cervantes que los ha estado festejando a carcajadas, vacila en decidir.

—¡Qué no!—pronuncia "El Manteca"—¿entonces para qué es un amigo?

Luego se vuelve a Luis Cervantes.

—¿Verdad, Curro?

—¡Claro!... habiendo conformidad.. sin intención de ofender a nadie—pronuncia Luis.

—Es meramente lo que yo digo.

—No, pos verdá de Dios que a mí naiden me ha mentado la madre.. A mí me gusta darme mi lugar ......Y por eso me verá, Curro, que nunca ando chacoteando—dijo muy grave Montañez.

Tirados en el suelo duro, a la tibia claridad de una luna tierna, Venancio refería episodios dramáticos de "El Judío Errante." Bostezaban, esperando el sueño, y y aalgunos, arrullados por la voz suave y melíflua del barbero, comenzaban a roncar.

—¡Admirable! — pronunció Luis, cuando aquél acabó la relación con extraños comentarios anticlericales.—¡Tiene usted un bellísimo talento!

¡No lo tengo malo!—pronunció, convencido, Venancio—pero mis padres murieron y yo no pude hacer carrera.

—Es lo de menos... Al triunfo de la revolución, usted va a obtener su título. Dos o tres meses de concurrir a un hospital, una recomendación de nuestro jefe Macías y usted, doctor. Tiene una facilidad tan grande, que sería un juego todo.

Y desde ese día, Venancio se distinguió de los demás soldados, dejando de llamarle Curro. Y Luisito por aquí, y Luisito por allá.

—Oiga, Curro—dijo Anastasio Montañez con una mano extendida sobre la frente—¿qué polvareda se levanta allá detrás de aquel cerrito? ¡Demonche!... ¡a poco son los mochos! Y uno tan desprevenido..... Véngase, vamos a avisarles a los muchachos.

Paso a paso, saltando piedras y por entre la maleza, dejaron la montaña.

"La Codorniz" fijó sus ojos de pupilas anchas y muy negras, en la lejanía en donde se alzaba la polvareda.

—¡Vamos a toparlos! ¡qué pueden traer que no lleven!—dijo Anastasio y se encaminó a sacar su montura del jacal.

FOLLETIN NUM. 6

Luego "El Meco," Pancracio y otros más, ensillaron con mucho regocijo.

—Yo me quedo a cuidar a Demetrio—dijo "La Codorniz," provocando risas y burlas.

Pero dando unos cuantos saltos sobre un montecillo, él fué quien rió después.

El enemigo se reducía a un atajo de burros y dos arrieros.

—Párenlos—ordenó Demetrio— y tráiganlos para acá. Estos son arribeños y han de tener noticias.

Y las tuvieron sensacionales.

Los federales tenían fortificados los cerros de "El Grillo" y "La Bufa" de Zacatecas. Se decía que era el último reducto de Huerta, y todo el mundo aseguraba la caída de la plaza. Las familias salían con precipitación hacia el sur; los trenes iban colmados de gente hasta los techos; faltaban carruajes y carretones para los que tomaban los caminos reales y, muchas gentes, sobrecogidas por el pánico, marchaban a pie, con sus equipajes a cuestas. El cabecilla Pánfilo Natera reunía su gente en Fresnillo y a los federales "les venían muy anchos los pantalones."

—La caída de Zacatecas es la caída de Huerta—aseguró Luis Cervantes con vehemencia.—Necesitamos llegar antes, con Natera.

Y hasta que vió el extrañamiento en los rostros de Demetrio y algunos de sus compañeros, se dió cuenta de que aún era "nadie" allí.

IX.

Señá Remigia, emprésteme tres blanquillos; mi gallina amaneció echada. Allí tengo unos señores que quieren almorzar.

Y en voz baja:

—¿Cómo ve al hombre?... ¿aliviado?.... Mire, y tan muchacho.... Pero está muy descolorido todavía.... ¿Y ya le cerró el balazo?

Sale una comadre y entra la otra. Todas tienen un pretexto para curiosear, a diario, a Demetrio.

—Señá Remigia, ¿no tiene unas hojitas de laurel para hacerle un cocimiento a María Antonia? Amaneció con el cólico....

Y al mismo tiempo con los ojos le pregunta por el herido.

Señá Remigia baja los párpados para indicar que está dormido y dice:

—No tengo hojitas de laurel, mi alma; pero vaya con doña Dolores..... es la única que puede conseguirlas.

—Doña Dolores desde anoche está en el otro ranchito. Según razón, vinieron por ella para que fuera a sacar de su cuidado a la muchachilla de tío Matías.

—¡Ande... no me lo diga!

—Cierto. ¡Se lo dije que estaba gorda!...

—¡Pobre criatura! ¡Mal ajo pa esos condenaos federales! ¡Allí está otra infelizada más!

Despertaron a Demetrio para que recibiera un presente: señá Fortunata traía un pollo rabón para el señor herido. Y como tenía cuita que contar, allí pasó la mañana. A ella también le habían robado una hija, y como era la única, estaba inconsolable. Al principio de su relato, "La Codorniz" y Anastasio Montañez, acochinados al pie de la camilla, levantando la cabeza y entreabriendo la boca, la oían lelos; pero a media narración "La Codorniz," aburrido, salió a rascarse los piojos al sol; y cuando ella terminó con esta imprecación: "espero de Dios y María Santísima que ustedes han de acabar con esos federales del infierno," De-

metrio, vuelta la cara al muro, pensaba en la toma de Zacatecas y Anastasio Montañez roncaba como un trombón.

—Oye, Curro, yo quiero que repases "La Adelita",—dijo Camila a Luis Cervantes, cuando éste curaba su herida.

Luis hizo un mohín de desagrado y no contestó.

—¿Sabes por qué quiero aprenderla? Para cantarla cuando ya no estés aquí.... cuando andes en tierras, lejos, muy lejos.... Para acordarme mucho de tí.

A Luis le hacían las palabras de Camila, el efecto de una punta de acero resbalando por las paredes de una redoma.

—Mira, Curro, qué bonito viene encarnando; parece un botón de rosa de castilla... ¡Anda, no te he contado! si vieras que malo es el viejo ese de Demetrio.... No quiere la comida de ña Remigia .....y que yo, y que yo le he de hacer su comida y se la he de llevar. Bueno. ¿qué te parece?, entré con el champurrado y me agarró de una mano y me apretó mucho, luego comenzó a pelizcarme las piernas. ¡Ah, pero qué buen pliegue le puse! "¡eh! ... ¡pior!... estese quieto ... ¡pior! déjeme.... le digo que me suelte..... ¡pior!,.... ¡viejo malcriado!.... ¡suélteme, viejo sin vergüenza!".... Y de un tirón me le safé y me salí a toda carrera ...... ¿Qué te parece?

—De veras?—inquirió Luis con ostensible regocijo.

Camila se turbó. Y contempló un instante los ojos glaucos de Luis, su tez blanca y pulida, su pelo ligeramente rizado y rubio, y suspiró. Luego le vinieron deseos de llorar y, sin haber contestado nada, se alejó para que él no viera sus lágrimas.

El día que Demetrio vió que su herida estaba ya cicatrizada, le dijo a Luis Cervantes:

—¿De veras quiere irse con nosotros, Curro?... Usté es de otra madera, y la verdá es que yo no entiendo cómo le puede cuadrar esta vida. ¿Que cree que uno anda en esto por su puro gusto? Mire, siéntese para contarle: ¿Sabe por qué me levanté? Bueno, pues, odiosidades que no le faltan a uno y, también, ¡por qué negarlo! porque a uno le cuadra el ruido. Antes de la revolución tenía yo ya hasta volteada mi tierra para sembrar, y si no hubiera habido el choque con don Mónico y los demás caciques de Moyahua, a estas horas andaría

Moyahua

yo con mucha priesa preparando la yunta para las siembras.

—Pancracio, apéate dos botellas de cerveza; una para mí, y otra para el Curro. Por la señal de la Santa Cruz..... Ya no me hace daño, ¿verdad?

X.

"Yo soy de "Limón," allí, muy cerca de Moya-hua, del puro cañón de Juchipila. Tenía mi casa, mis vacas y un pedazo de tierra para sembrar: es decir, que nada me faltaba. Pues, señor, nosotros los rancheros tenemos el costumbre de bajar al lugar cada ocho días. Oye uno su misa, oye el sermón, luego va a la plaza, compra sus cebollas, sus jitomates, todas las encomiendas, y después entra uno con los amigos a la tienda de Primitivo López a hacer las once. Se toma la copita, a veces es uno condescendiente y se deja cargar la mano y se le sube el trago, y le da mucho gusto, y ríe uno, grita y canta si le da la gana. Todo está muy bueno, porque no se ofende a nadie; pero comienzan a meterse con usté; que el policía pasa y pasa, y arrima la oreja a la puerta ; que al comisario o a los auxiliares se les ocurre quitarle a usté su gusto... ¡claro, hombre, uno no tiene la sangre de horchata, uno lleva el alma en el cuerpo, a uno le da coraje, y se levanta y les dice su justo precio. Si entendieron, santo y bueno; a uno le dejan en paz y ahí para todo. Pero a veces quieren hablar ronco y golpeado..... y uno es lebroncito de por sí..... y no le cuadra que le peln los eojos.... Y, sí señor, sale la daga... y sale la pistola... Y luego, vamos a correr la sierra hasta que se les olvida el difuntito."

"Bueno, ¿qué pasó con don Mónico? ¡Faceto! mucho menos que con los otros, ¡ni siquiera vió correr el gallo! Una escupida en la cara por entrometido y ya. Pues con eso ha habido para que me eche encima la federación. Usté ha de saber del chisme ese de México, donde mataron al señor Madero y a otro, un tal Félix o Felipe Díaz, ¡qué sé yo! Bueno, pues el tal don Mónico fué en persona a Zacatecas a traer escolta para que me agarraran. Que izque yo era maderista y que me iba a levantar. Pero como no le faltan a uno amigos en donde quiero, me lo avisaron, y cuando los federales llegaron a "Limón," yo ya me había pelado. Después vino mi compadre Anastasio, que hizo una muerte, y Pancracio, y "La Codorniz," todos mis amigos y conocidos. En seguida se nos juntaron otros y ya ve, hacemos la lucha como podemos.

—Mi Jefe—dijo Cervantes, después de meditar, —usted sabe que ya aquí cerca, en Juchipila, tenemos gente de Natera: nos conviene ir a juntarnos con ellos antes de que tomen Zacatecas. Nos presentamos con el General.

—No tengo genio para eso... a mí no me gusta rendirle a nadie.

—Pero usted, solo con unos cuantos hombres por acá, no deja de pasar por un cabecilla sin importancia alguna. La revolución gana indefectiblemente; luego que se acabe le dicen como les dijo Madero a los que le ayudaron: "amigos, muchas gracias, ahora vuélvanse a sus casas"....

—No quiere yo otra cosa, sino que me dejen en paz para volver a mi casa.

FOLLETIN NUM. 7

—Allá voy... no he terminado: "ustedes que me levantaron y que me hicieron presidente de la República, arriesgando la vida, con peligro de dejar viudas y huérfanos en la miseria, ahora que ya conseguí mi objeto, váyanse a coger el azadón y la pala, a medio vivir, siempre con hambre y sin vestir, como estaban antes, mientras que nosotros, los de arriba, hacemos unos cuantos millones de pesos."

Demetrio meneó la cabeza y sonriendo se rascó.

—Como decía,—prosiguió Luis Cervantes — se acaba la revolución y se acabó todo. ¡Lástima de tanta viuda, de tanto huérfano, de tanta sangre derramada! ¿Todo para qué? para que unos cuantos bribones se enriquezcan, y todo quede igual. Usted es desprendido y dice: "yo lo que quiero es volver a mi casa;" pero usted tiene mujer, hijos, hogar... hay que pensar en la familia y.... en la Patria...

Macías sonrió y sus ojos brillaron.

—¿Qué será bueno ir con Natera?

—No sólo bueno, sino necesario, indispensable. Usted me ha simpatizado, y le tengo mucho cariño. Usted mismo no sabe por qué anda en la revolución. No, no somos sino unos de tantos elementos de este gran movimiento social que tiene que acabar en el engrandecimiento de nuestra Patria. Somos instrumentos del destino para la reivindicación de los sagrados derechos del Pueblo. Usted no se ha levantado contra don Mónico, sino contra el caciquismo de toda la nación; no peleamos para derrocar a un miserable asesino, sino contra la tiranía misma.

Eso es lo que se llama luchad por principios, tener ideales. Por ellos luchan Carranza, Villa, Natera, y por ellos está usted luchando.

—Pancracio, apéate otras dos cervezas, una para mí y otra para el Curro—dijo Demetrio.

—¿Y yo no más lo miro?—respondió Pancracio.

XI.

—Si viera qué bien explica las cosas el Curro, compadre Anastasio—dijo Demetrio preocupado por lo que había podido sacar en claro de las palabras de Luis Cervantes.

—Ya lo estuve oyendo—respondió Anastasio.—La verdad, es gente que como sabe leer y escribir, entiende bien las cosas. Pero lo que yo no puedo comprender es cómo va usted, compadre, a presentarse con ese señor Natera con tan poquitos hombres.

—Hum, es lo de menos. Desde hoy vamos a seguir de otra manera. ¡Ya verás! Les vamos a caer como lo hace Crispín Robles en Juchipila, a todos los pueblitos les sacamos armas y caballos, y con los presos que echemos fuera de la cárcel, en dos por tres somos más de cien. Compadre Anastasio, la verdad es que hemos tonteado mucho. Parece a manera de mentira, que este Curro haya venido a enseñarnos la cartilla.... ¡Lo que es eso de saber leer y escribir!

Y los dos dejaron escapar un suspiro.

Demetrio anuncia la marcha para otro día.

Fué esa tarde de mucho regocijo, y se hicieron venir tres músicos del pueblito inmediato.

—Pos nos iremos; pero lo que soy yo no me vuelvo solo—exclamó Pancracio.—Tengo mi amor y me lo llevo.

Demetrio contestó que él de muy buena gana se llevaría también a una muchacha que traía entre ojos; pero que no quería ni él, ni que ninguno de los suyos dejara recuerdos como los federales.

—No hay que esperar mucho; a la vuelta se arregla todo—pronunció a su oído Luis Cervantes.

—¿Cómo?—dijo Demetrio—¿pues no dicen que Camila y usted ....se entienden?

—No es cierto; ella lo quiere a usted....pero le tiene miedo.

—¿De veras, curro?

—Sí, mas es prudente lo que usted piensa: no hay que dejar una mala impresión... Cuando volvamos en triunfo, todo es diferente: hasta le agradecerán el honor que les hace.

—¡Ah, Curro!..... .¡es usté muy lanza!—contestó Demetrio sonriendo y palmeándole la espalda.

Por la tarde, ya al meterse el sol, Camila que bajó al río, llamó a Luis que venía por la vereda.

—Oye, Curro... ven a decirme adiós siquiera... ¡Orgulloso! Tan mal te serví que basta el habla me niegas?

—Sí, sí quiero decirte adiós. Voy muy agradecido y siempre me acordaré de ti, de tus buenos servicios....

—¡Mentiroso!—pronunció ella con coquetería.—¡Si yo no te hablo!....

—Todo eso te lo iba a decir a la noche, en el baile.

—Yo no voy al baile.

—¿Por qué no vas?

—Porque no puedo ver al viejo ese... .al Demetrio.

—¡Tonta! El te quiere mucho y te pierdes de una ocasión como no volverás a encontrarla. Mira, Demetrio Macías, va a llegar a general, va a ser muy rico; muchos caballos, muchas alhajas, vestidos muy buenos, casas y dinero para gastar, Imagínate lo que tú serías al lado de él.

—Oye, Curro, no me digas esas cosas, porque entonces ya no te quiero.... ¡Bah!... ya te lo dije ....Ahora vete, porque te tengo mucha vergüenza.....

Luis se alejó perdiéndose entre los riscos.

Camila siguió la vereda del río a llenar su cántaro. El agua parecía espolvoreada de finísimo carmín; en sus ondas se removían un cielo de colores, y los picachos mitad luz y mitad sombra. Miriadas de insectos de alas luminosas parpadeaban en un remanso. Y en el fondo de guijas lavadas se reprodujo Camila con su blusa amarilla de cintas verdes, sus enaguas blancas, sin almidonar; lamida la cabeza, estiradas las cejas y la frente; tal como se atavió para gustar a Luis.

Suspiró y comenzó a tararear una canción. Y en su garganta armoniosa, una sonata vulgar surgió llena de ternura y de profunda tristeza. Parecía que hasta las cigarras y los zenzontles se habían callado un instante para escucharla.

En el baile hubo mucha alegría, y se bebió muy buen mezcal.

—Extraño a Camila—pronunció en voz alta Demetrio.

Y todo el mundo buscó a Camila con los ojos.

—Está mala... tiene jaqueca—respondió con aspereza su madre, señá Agapita, amoscada por las miradas de malicia que todas las comadres tenían puestas en ella.

Ya al acabarse el fandango, Demetrio, bamboleándose un poco, dió las gracias a los buenos vecinos que tan bien los habían atendido, y prometió que al triunfo de la revolución los tendrían presentes. "En la cárcel y en la cama se conoce a los amigos."

—Dios los bendiga y los lleve por buen camino—dijeron las viejas.

—Que vuelvan pronto—gritó María Antonia.

XII.

—¿Eh? ¿qué es eso, Camila? ¿Qué haces en el rincón con el rebozo liado a la cabeza?... ¡Huy! ¿llorando?..... ¡Mira qué ojos! Ya pareces hechicera .... No te apures, mira: no hay dolor que al alma llegue que en tres días no se acabe.

Eso dijo María Antonia que, aunque cacariza y con una nube en un ojo, tenía muy mala fama; tan mala, que se aseguraba que no había habido hombre de los de Demetrio que no la hubiera conocido entre los jarales del río.

Señá Agapita juntó las cejas, y quién sabe qué gruñó.

Las comadres estaban desazonadas por la partida de la gente, y los mismos hombres, no obstante la habladuría de sus mujeres, sentían ahora que no hubiera ya quien les llevara carneritos y terneras para comer. ¡Tan agusto que se pasa la vida comiendo y durmiendo y descansando durante el día a la sombra de las peñas, mirando el azul del cielo!

—¡Mírenlos, allá van!—clamó María Antonia;—parecen juguetes de rinconera.

A lo lejos, tramontando una cuesta, se perfilaban los hombres de Macías en sus escuetos jamelgos. Una ráfaga de aire llevó hasta los jacales los acentos cortados de la "Adelita."

Camila, que había salido a verlos por última vez, no pudo contenerse y regresó sollozando.

María Antonia la miró y lanzó una sonora carcajada, yéndose sin despedirse.

—A mi hija le han hecho mal de ojo—pensó señá Agapita, después de ver fijamente a Camila.

Se estuvo pensando algunos minutos, y cuando reflexionó bien, tomó su decisión; de una estaca clavada en un poste del jacal, entre el Divino Rostro y la Virgen de Jalpa, descolgó un barzón de cuero crudo que servía a su marido para uncir la yunta y con él, doblado, le propinó una golpiza para sacarle todo el daño.

En su caballo zaino Demetrio se sentía rejuvene-

FOLLETIN NUM. 8

cido: sus ojos recuperaban el brillo metálico peculiar y en sus mejillas cobrizas de indígena de raza pura, corría de nuevo la sangre roja y caliente.

Todos ensanchaban sus pulmones como para respirar los horizontes dilatados, la inmensidad el cielo, el azul de las montañas y el aire fresco embalsamado de los aromas de la sierra. Y hacían correr sus caballos como si en su loca carrera pretendieran posesionarse de toda la tierra. ¿Quién se acordaba ya del severo comandante de policía, del gendarme gruñón, del cacique enfatuado? ¿Quién del mísero jacal donde se vivía como un esclavo; siempre bajo la vigilancia del amo, del hosco y sañudo mayordomo, con la obligación imprescindible de estar de pie antes de salir el sol, con la pala y la canasta o con la mancera y el otate, para ganarse la olla de atole y el plato de frijoles del día?

Cantaban, reían y ululaban, ébrios de sol, de aire y de vida.

"El Meco", haciendo cabriolas y mostrando su blanca dentadura, bromeaba con payasadas.

—Oye, Pancracio—preguntó— en carta que me pone mi mujer, me noticia que ya tenemos otro hijo. ¿Cómo es eso? ¡Yo no la veo desde el tiempo del señor Madero!

—No, no es nada.....la dejaste enhuevada....

Todos ríen estrepitosamente. Luego con voz de falcete y desentonado canta:

"Yo le daba un centavo
y ella me dijo que no....
  Yo le daba medio
y no lo quiso agarrar.
  Tanto me estuvo rogando
hasta que me sacó un real.
  ¡Ay, qué mujeres tan ingratas!
¡no me saben considerar!

La algarabía no cesó sino hasta que el sol los aturdió.

Prosiguieron caminando por el cañón, sobre cerros que se tendían uno tras otro, una al lado de otro; cerros pelones, rapados y sucios como cabezas tiñosas.

Al atardecer, en la lejanía, se esfumaron las

torrecillas blancas en medio de un lomerío azul; luego se divisaron los postes del telégrafo y un camino
real ancho y polvoriento.

Procuraron algún caminante para informarse.
"La Codorniz" vió muy lejos el bulto de un hombre, reposando a la vera del camino.

Era un viejo haraposo, con un borrico car-
gado de alfalfa.

Cuando ellos se arcecaron, cogió su navaja, se
quitó un guarache y se puso a remendarlo.

eDmetrio lo interrogó. Iba al pueblo a llevar
alfalfa para su vaca....... "Sí, están allí unos
cuantos federales; pero no llegan a docena". En
seguida confirmó los díceres que corrían de boca
en boca: Obregón cerca de Guadalajara. Carrera
Tórres en San Luis, Natera en Fresnillo.

—Bueno—pronunció Demetrio—pues cuida-
do con ir a decir una palabra de nosotros al pueblo, viejo, porque te trueno..... te hallaría hasta
en el centro de la tierra".......

Cuando el viejo se alejó, Demetrio interrogó
a los compañeros.

—¡A darles...... a no dejar un mocho vivo!
—fué la exclamación general.

Contaron los cartuchos y las granadas de mano que "El Tecolote", un operario de la fundi-
ción de Aguascalientes, había fabricado con fragmentos de tubo de hierro y perillas de [latón.]

—Son pocos; pero los vamos a cambiar por
carabinas—observó Anastacio Montañez.

Y anciosos se apresuraron a avanzar, hincando
las espuelas en los hijares de sus cabalgaduras y
haciendolas galopar.

La voz imperiosa de Demetrio los detuvo.

A la falda de una loma acamparon, en el hui-
zachal dejaron sus caballos y cada un busco una
piedra para convertirla en cabecera.

XIII.

A media noche, Demetrio Macias mando en-
silar.

El pueblo distaba seis leguas y había que dar
un alabazo a los federales.

El cielo estaba nublado, brillaba una que otra
estrella y, de vez en vez, el parpadeo de un relámpago iluminaba la lejanía rojizamente.

Luis Cervantes preguntó a Demetrio si no era
conveniente, para el mejor éxito del ataque, un
guía o cuando menos los datos topográficos del
pueblito y la situación del cuartel.

—No, Curro —respondió Demetrio sonrriendo
y con un gesto de desdén—nosotros caemos cuando
ellos menos nos esperan y ya. Así lo hemos hecho
siempre. ¿Ha visto como sacan la cabeza las ardi-
llas por la boca del tusero cuando uno se los llena
de agua? Pues igual de aturdidos van a salir los
mochitos infelices luego que oigan los primeros disparos; no más salen para servirnos de blanco y ya.

—¿Y si el viejo que ayer nos dió informes nos
hubiese engañado? ¿Si en vez de veinte hombres
resultaren cincuenta? ¿Si fuese un espía de ellos
apostado en este camino?

—¡Este Curro ya tuvo miedo!—dijo Anastasio
Montañez.

—No es lo mismo poner cataplasmas y coger
una geringa que manejar un fusil—agregó Pancracio.

—¡Hum!— contestó "El Manteca" es mucha
plática....... pa una docena de ratas aturdidas..
....No va a ser ahora cuando nuestras madres se-
pan si parieron hombres o qué.......

Pero cuando llegaron a orillas del pueblito,
Venancio llamó a la primera casa.

—¿Dónde está el cuartel?—interrogó al hombre que salió, descalzo y con una garra de jorongo
cobijando su pecho y su espalda.

El cuartel está abajito de la plaza—contestó.

Más como nadie sabía donde era abajito de la
plaza, Venancio lo obligó a que caminara delante y
les mostrara el camino.

Temblando de azoro, el pobre diablo exclamó
que era una barbaridad lo que iban a hacer con él,
que era hombre sólo y tenía mujer y muchos hijos.

—¿Y los que yo tengo son perros?— observó
Demetrio.

Luego añadió:

—Mucho silencio, y uno a uno por la tierra
suelta.

Sobre el caserío asomaba la ancha cúpula cuadrangular de la iglesia.

—Al frente de la iglesia está la plaza; caminan
no más otro tantito pa abajo y allí está el cuartel.

El hombre se arrodillaba para que le permitie-
ran regresar.

Pancracio sin responderle le amenazó con el
cañón de su rifle.

—¿Cuántos son los que hay aquí?—interrogó
Luis Cervantes.

—Amo, no le miento, pero es un titipuchal.

Luis Cervantes volvió los ojos a Demetrio, quien
fingía no haber escuchado nada.

De pronto desembocaron en la plazoleta. Una estruendosa descarga de fusilería los ensordeció.

Extremecido el caballo zaino de Demetrio, vaciló sobre las piernas y cayó. "El Tecolote" dió un grito agudo, y rodó del caballo, que desbocado fué a dar a media plaza.

Una nueva descarga, y el hombre que había servido de guía abrió los brazos y cayó de espaldas.

Anastasio Montañez levantó violentamente a Demetrio, y lo puso en ancas. Los demás ya habían retrocedido y se amparaban de las paredes de las casas.

—Señores, señores —habló un hombre del pueblo, sacando la cabeza por un zaguán grande, —lléguenles por la espalda de la capilla.... Allí están todos. Devuélvanse por esta misma calle, tuercen sobre su mano izquierda, luego dan con un callejoncito, y siguen otra vez para adelante, y van ya a caer a la mera espalda de la capilla.

En ese momento comenzaron a recibir una lluvia de tiros de pistola.

Venían de las azoteas de casas inmediatas.

—¡Hum! —dijo el hombre —esos son curros..... ¡pero no son arañas que pican!.... Métanse aquí mientras se van. Esos corren: le tienen miedo hasta a su sombra.

—¿Qué tantos son los mochos? —preguntó Demetrio.

—No estaban aquí más que doce; pero anoche traían mucho miedo y llamaron por telégrafo a los de más adelante. Quién sabe cuántos serán los que llegaron. Pero no le hace que sean muchos. Los más son de leva y todo es que uno haga por voltearse y dejan a los jefes solos. A mi hermano le tocó la leva y anda aquí con ellos; yo le hago una señal, y todos se vienen de este lado. Y acabamos con los oficiales. Si el señor quisiera darme un rifle... Me tienen muy agraviado: me robaron una hija, y un oficialillo me quitó una mujer que yo tenía... ¡Hijos de.....!

—Rifle no hay, hermano; pero esto de algo te ha

FOLLETIN NUM. 9

de servir —dijo Anastasio sacando dos granadas de mano y tendiéndoselas.

El jefe de los federales era un joven rubio, de bigotes retorcidos y muy presuntuoso. Mientras no se convenció de que el número de los asaltantes se reducía a una veintena, se había mantenido callado y prudente. Pero ahora que los rechazaban con tal éxito, que ni un tiro habían podido contestarles, hacía gala de valor y temeridad: cuando todos los soldados apenas asomaban sus cabezas por detrás de los pretiles del frente de la iglesia, él, a la pálida claridad del amanecer, destacaba airosamente su esbelta silueta, su capa dragona que el aire inflaba.

—¡Ah!.... me acuerdo de cuando lo de la Ciudadela......

Como su vida militar se reducía a la aventura en que se vió envuelto por ser alumno de la Escuela de Aspirantes al consumarse la traición cometida al Presidente Madero, siempre que el caso se presentaba, la traía a colación.

—Teniente Campos —pronunció con mucho énfasis —baje usted con diez hombres a chicotearme a esos bandidos que se esconden... .¡Bribones!.... ¡sólo son valientes para comer vacas y gallinas!

En la puertecilla del caracol apareció un paisano. Llevaba el aviso de que los bandidos estaban en un corral donde era facilísimo cogerlos a todos juntos. Eso lo decían los vecinos apostados en las azoteas, que ya estaban listos para no dejarlos escapar.

—Yo mismo voy a acabar con ellos —dijo con precipitación el jefe; pero de la puerta misma se volvió.

—Es posible que esperen refuerzos y no conviene abandonar este puesto. Teniente Campos, va usted y me los coge vivos a todos, para fusilarlos hoy mismo, a medio día, delante de todo el pueblo. Ya verán los bandidos qué ejemplar voy a poner....... Pero si no es posible, Teniente Campos, acabe con todos, no me deje uno solo vivo. ¿Me ha entendido?

Satisfecho comenzó a dar vueltas meditando la redacción del parte que rendiría.

"Señor Ministro de la Guerra, General Aureliano Blanquet. —Hónrome, mi General, en poner en el superior conocimiento de usted, que en la madrugada del día... una gruesa partida de quinientos bandoleros al mando del cabecilla H.... osó atacar esta plaza. Con la violencia necesaria, me fortifiqué en las alturas principales de la población. El ataque comenzó al amanecer, durando más de dos horas el nutrido fuego. No obstante la superioridad numérica del enemigo, logré castigarlo severamente, infligiéndole una completa derrota. El número de muertos fué de veinte, y muy numeroso el de heridos, a juzgar por las huellas de sangre que dejaron en su precipitada fuga. En nuestras fuerzas tuvimos la fortuna de no contar una sola baja. —Me honro en felicitar a usted, señor Ministro, por este triunfo de las armas de la República.... ¡Viva México!"

"Y luego—siguió pensando el joven capitán,—mi ascenso a mayor."

Y se apretó las manos con regocijo, en el mismo momento que un estallido atronador le dejó con los oídos zumbando.

XIV.

—¿De modo es que si por este corral pudiéramos atravesar, saldríamos derecho al callejón?—preguntó Demetrio.

—Sí: sólo que del corral sigue una casa, luego otro corral y una tienda más adelante—respondió el paisano.

Demetrio, pensativo, se rascó la cabeza. Pero su decisión fué pronta.

—¿Puedes conseguir un barretón, una pica, algo para agujerear las paredes?

—Sí hay... pero...

El paisano vacilaba.

—¿En dónde están?—preguntó Demetrio en voz fuerte.

—Precisamente aquí están todos los avíos de mi patrón. Pero las casas que quieren romper son suyas.....

Demetrio y sus hombres entraron a un cuartito ruinoso, que aquél les había señalado como depósito, sin acabar de escucharlo.

—Ahora a mí me van a echar la culpa—seguía diciendo muy afligido el llavero.

Fué todo obra de minutos. Inmediatamente que estuvieron en el callejón, uno tras otro, arrimados a la pared, corrieron hasta ponerse detrás de la iglesia.

Había que saltar primero una tapia, en seguida el muro posterior de la capilla.

—"Obra de Dios"—pensó Demetrio, y fué el primero que la escaló.

Como monos siguieron los demás, llegando con las manos rayadas de sangre. El resto era más fácil: escalones a propósito en la mampostería, les permitieron saltar el muro de la capilla; luego, la cúpula misma los ocultaba a la vista de los soldados.

—Espérense tantito—dijo el paisano—voy a ver dónde está mi hermano. Yo les hago la señal.....
Después sobre las clases y oficiales, ¿eh?

Sólo que nadie le oía ni hacía caso de él.

Demetrio contempló un instante el negrear de los capotes a lo largo del pretil en todo el frente y parte de los lados; las torres estaban apretadas de federales, tras la baranda de fierro.

Se sonrió con satisfacción, volviendo la cara a los suyos.

—¡Hora!—exclamó.

Veinte bombas estallaron a un tiempo en medio de los federales, que llenos de espanto se yerguen con los ojos inmensamente abiertos. Mas antes de que puedan darse cuenta cabal del trance, otras veinte bombas estallan con fragor, dejando un reguero de muertos y de heridos.

—¡Todavía no..... todavía no veo a mi hermano!—implora llorando el que sirvió de guía.

En vano un viejo sargento increpa a los soldados y los injuria, en una esperanza de reorganización. Es como una correría de ratas dentro de la trampa. Unos van a tomar la puertecilla de la escalera, y allí caen en montón; otros son acribillados por los tiros de Demetrio; otros se echan a los pies de aquella veintena de espectros de cabeza y pechos obscuros como de hierro, y de largos calzones blancos que les cubren hasta los huaraches. En la torre, muchos luchan por salir de entre los muertos y heridos que han caído sobre ellos.

—Mi jefe—exclama Luis Cervantes, alarmadísimo—ya se acabaron las bombas....... y los rifles allá se quedaron en el corral.... ¡Qué barbaridad!

Demetrio se sonríe, saca un puñal de larga hoja reluciente. Instantáneos, brillan los aceros en las manos de sus veinte soldados; unos delgados y puntiagudos, otros tan anchos como la palma de la mano, otros pesados como marrazos.

—¡El espía!—dice triunfalmente Luis Cervantes, y vuelve la cara en un gesto de terror.

—No me mates, padrecito—implora el viejo sargento, echándose a los pies de Demetrio.

Levanta su cara de indio, llena de arrugas y sin una cana. Demetrio lo reconoce: es el viejo que la víspera los engañó.

La lámina tropieza con las costillas que hacen crac, crac, y el viejo cae de espaldas, con los brazos abiertos y los ojos espantados.

—¡A mi hermano no!... ¡no lo maten! clama en un grito de horror el paisano que ve a Pancracio arrojarse sobre un federal.

Pero es tarde: Pancracio, de un tajo, de ha rebanado el cuello, y como de una fuente brotan dos chorros escarlata.

—¡Mueran los juanes!—¡Mueran los mochos!

Se distinguen en la carnicería Pancracio y "El

Manteca" rematando a los heridos. Montañez deja caer su mano fatigada: en su semblante persiste la misma mirada dulzona; su impasible rostro, donde brilla la ingenuidad del niño y la amoralidad del chacal.

—Acá quedó uno vivo—gritó "La Codorniz," sin atreverse a matarlo.

Pancracio corre hacia el superviviente: es el capitancito rubio, de bigotes retorcidos, blanco como un papel, que arrimado a un rincón del caracol se ha detenido por falta de fuerza para descender.

Pancracio lo lleva a empellones al borde del pretil: un rodillazo en el abdomen, y algo como un saco de piedras que cae a veinte metros, sobre el pavimento.

—¡Qué bruto eres!—exclama "La Codorniz.""—Si lo he sabido no te digo nada. ¡Tan buenos zapatos que le iba yo a avanzar.

Los hombres ahra, inclinados, se dedican a desbalijar a los que traen mejores ropas. Y bromean y ríen muy divertidos.

Demetrio, echando a un lado los largos mechones que le han caído sobre la frente cubriéndole los ojos, empapado de sudor, dice:

—¡Ahora con los curros!

XV.

Demetrio llegó con cincuenta hombres a Fresni-

FOLLETIN NUM. 10

llo el mismo día que Natera, un cabecilla revolucionario, iniciaba el avance de sus hombres hacia la plaza de Zacatecas.

Natera acogió cordialmente a Macías:

—Ya sé quién es usted y su gente. Buena cuereada les han dado a los federales desde Tepic hasta Durango.

—Mi general—dijo animosamente Luis Cervantes—con hombres como usted y como mi coronel Macías, la Patria será pronto muy gloriosa.

Y Demetrio sintió mucha regocijo cuando Natera siguió dándole el título de coronel.

Se hicieron traer vino y cerveza. Demetrio y Natera chocaron sus vasos y Cervantes dijo: "Por el triunfo de nuestra causa que es el de la justicia; porque se realicen pronto los ideales de redención de este nuestro pueblo noble y sufrido, y sean los mismos hombres que han regado con su sangre la simiente, los que pronto cosechen los frutos."

Natera volvió sus ojos ligeramente hacia Cervantes, luego, dándole la espalda, se puso a charlar con Macías.

Poco a poco un ayudante de Natera se había acercado, fijando sus ojos insistentemente en Luis Cervantes. Era un joven de agradable aspecto.

Luis volvió su rostro, y los dos se reconocieron.

—¡Luis Cervantes?....

—¡Señor Solís!

—Desde que entré, creí que era Cervantes..... ¡Vamos! pero no puedo asegurarlo todavía!....

—Ya ve usted.....!

—¿De modo que.... Véngase por acá a tomar una copa, compañero.

Entraron a la pieza inmediata.

—¿Pues desde cuándo es revolucionario?—inquirio Alberto Solís, tomando asiento en torno de una pequeña mesa.

—Dos meses corridos.

—¡Ah, con razón viene usted con el entusiasmo y la fe que todos traemos al principio!

—¿Usted los ha perdido ya?

—Mire, compañero; no le extrañen confidencias de buenas a primas: dan tantos deseos, por acá, de encontrarse gente de sentido común con quién hablar, que las hace uno con tal ansiedad, como quien se toma una vasija de agua fría después de horas y más horas de caminar por el rayo del sol...... Pero necesito primero que usted me explique........ Francamente me maravillo de verlo por aquí, a usted, el de los furibundos artículos de "La Nación" y de "El Regional", usted que usaba para nosotros del epíteto de bandidos con una prodigialidad completa.

—¡La verdad me ha convencido!

—¿Convencido?

—¡Enteramente!

Alberto Solís dejó escapar un suspiro; llenó los vasos y bebieron.

—¿Se ha cansado ya de la Revolución?—preguntó Luis Cervantes.

—¿Cansado? Tengo veinticinco años y, usted me ve, me sobra salud......¿Desilucionado? Puede ser.

—Debe tener razones muy poderosas.

—Amigo mío: hay hechos y hay hombres que no son sino pura hiel. Y esa hiel va cayendo gota a gota.....y todo se amarga.....Y todo se acaba: entusiasmo, esperanzas, alegría...... Luego no queda más: o se encierra uno en una muralla de egoísmo impenetrable.......o desaparece.

Luis Cervantes plegó sus labios irónicamente, y como le torturara aquel tono y aquellos aires de suficiencia, lo invitó a que refiriera algo de lo que lo había conducido a tal estado de decepción, para eximirse de estar inquiriendo o replicando más.

—¡Naderías! contestó Alberto Solís—hechos insignificantes a primera vista; gestos que pasan inadvertidos; la vida instantánea de una línea que se contrae, de unos ojos que brillan, de unos labios que se pliegan; el significado fugaz de una palabra que se escapa. Pero hechos, gestos y expresiones que agrupados en su natural proporción constituyen la mueca pavorosa y grotesca de una raza irredenta!.........

Me preguntará—agregó—que por qué sigo a pesar de eso en la Revolución. Primero, porque la Revolución es un huracán, y el hombre que entra a la Revolución es una mísera hoja seca...... Segundo, porque un atavismo implacable y mi organización mental de idealista a outrance, de sentimentalista sin remedio, me han hecho creer, con toda la fuerza de una convicción, que todo mexicano que incline su cuello ante el gobierno del asesino Huerta, es un miserable y un indigno!......¡Contradicciones!

tradicciones!.........¡Tonterías! ¿Qué quiere ust d?

A ese punto fueron interrumpidos por Demetrio Macías que se retiraba ya.

Alberto Solís felicitó calurosamente al coronel, y con fácil palabra narró alguna de las aventuras que le conocía.

Y Demetrio escuchó, sorprendido, la relación de hazañas por él mismo realizadas. Cierto que las componendas y los adornos las desfiguraban; pero se oían tan bien así referidas que tanto Demetrio como Luis Cervantes las contaron en lo sucesivo en esa forma.

—¡Qué hombre tan simpático es el general Natera!—dijo Cervantes a Demetrio Macías, cuando estuvieron de regreso en el mezón. En cambio el capitancillo es muy pesado.

Y Demetrio sin escucharlo, con mucho contento, le oprimió un brazo a la vez que le decía:

—Ya soy coronel, de veras, Curro, y usted mi secretario.

Los hombres de Macías también hicieron muchas amistades nuevas esa noche, y "por el gusto de habernos conocido", se bebió mezcal y aguardiente

en abundancia. Como no todo el mundo congenia y a veces el alchohol es mal consejero, naturalmente hubo sus diferencias; pero todo se arregló muy bien afuera de la cantina, de la fonda o del billar, y sin molestar a los amigos. A la mañana siguiente amanecieron algunos muertos: una vieja prostituta con un balazo en el ombligo y dos reclutas del coronel Macías con el cráneo destrozado.

Anatstacio Montañez le dió cuenta a su jefe y éste, alzando los hombros, dijo:

—¡Pst!...... pues que los entierren....

XV.

—¡Ahí vienen otra vez los sombrerudos!—clamaron la gentes de Fresnillo, con azoro, cuando supieron que el asalto de los revolucionarios a la plaza de Zacatecas había sido un fracaso.

Volvía la turba desenfrenada de hombres requemados, mugrientos y casi desnudos, cubierta la cabeza con sombreros de palma de alta copa cónica y gran falda que les cubría hasta la nariz.

Les llamaban los 'sombrerudos.' L los "sombrerudos" regresaban tan alegremente como habían marchado al combate, saqueando cada pueblo, cada hacienda, cada rancho y hasta el jacal más miserable que encontraban a su paso.

—¿Quién me compra esta maquinaria?—gritaba uno, enrojecido y muy fatigado de la carga que se había avanzado.

Era una máquina de escribir nueva que a todos los atrajo con los reflejos brillantes de su niquelado.

La "Oliver", en una sola mañana, tuvo cinco propietarios, comenzando por valer diez pesos y despreciándose uno o dos, a cada dueño. La verdad es que pesaba mucho y nadie la soportaba más de media hora.

—Yo doy veinticinco centavos por ella—dija "La Codorniz".

—Tómala—exclamó el dueño, ofreciéndosela prontamente y como con miedo de que aquel se arrepintiera.

"La Codorniz" dió los veinticinco centavos y tuvo el gusto de tomarla entre sus manos y luego de lanzarla entre las piedras, donde cayó con gran estrépito.

Fué la señal: todos los que llevaban objetos pesados y molestos comenzaron a deshacerse de ellos estrellándolos entre las rocas: suntuosos aparatos de cristal, espejos de grueso vidrio, candelabros de latón, estátuas de porcelana y tiboreos de barro, todo el avance de la jornada.

Demetrio no participaba de aquella alegría, agena al resultado de las operaciones militares. Llamó aparte a Anastasio Montañez y a Pancracio y les dijo:

—Les falta nervio. No es tan difícil tomar una plaza. Miren, primero se abre uno así.... luego se va juntando, se va juntando...... ¡y ya!

Y en un gesto amplia abría sus brazos y luego los aproximaba poco a poco, acompañando al gesto la palabra, hasta estrecharlos contra su pecho.

Anastasio y Pancracio encontraban tan sencilla y tan clara la explicación, que no pudieron menos que contestar:

—Es la pura verdad... les falta nervio.

FOLLETIN NUM. 11

—¿Se acuerda de Camila, compadre Anastasio? —dijo Demetrio, tirado boca arriba sobre el estiércol del corral donde todos acostados bostezaban ya para dormir.

—¿Quién es esa Camila, compadre?

—La que me daba comida allá en el ranchito...

Montañez hizo un gesto que quería decir "esas cosas de mujeres no me importan a mí."

—No se me olvida—continuó diciendo Demetrio, encendiendo su cigarro. —Iba yo muy malo. Acababa de beber una jícara de agua azul muy fresca. "¿Quiere más?" me preguntó ella, una muchachilla prietita... sin gracia ¿eh? Bueno, pues me quedé rundido del calenturón y todo fué estar viendo la jícara de agua azul y oír la vocesita: "¿no quiere más?"..... pero una voz que me sonaba en los oídos como una musiquita de plata.... ¿Qué dices, Pancracio, vamos al ranchito?

—Mire, compadre Demetrio, ¿a que no me lo cree? Yo tengo mucha experencia en eso de mujeres......¿Las mujeres?......pa un rato....... ¡Y mi....... qué rato! ¡Pa las lepras y rasguños que me marcan mi cuerpo!... Mal ajo pa ellas.... ...Son el mismo enemigo malo.....De veras, compadre ¿voy a que no me lo cree?.... por eso me verá.....que ni..... Pero yo tengo mucha experencia en eso....

—¿Qué día vamos al ranchito, Pancracio?—persistió Demetrio, echando una bocanada de humo blanco.

—Usté nomás dice....ya sabe que allá dejé mi amor....

—Tu amor.... y mío—pronunció "La Codorniz."

—Y mío también.... Es bueno que seas compadecido, anda a traernoslo....—añadió "El Meco."

—¡Ah! entonces la de todos... la tuerta María Antonio—gritó "El Meco.'"

Y prorrumpieron en carcajadas. Y comenzó el torneo de insolencias y obscenidades entre Pancracio y "El Manteca."

XVI.

—¡Que viene Villa!

La noticia se propagó con la velocidad del relámpago, de boca en boca.

¡Ah! ¡Villa! la palabra mágica: el gran hombre que se esboza; el guerrero invicto que como una boa fascina ya liebres y conejos.

—Nuestro Napoleón mexicano—dice Luis Cervantes.

—El águila azteca que clava su pico de hierro en la cabeza de la bívora Victoriano Huerta!—Así dije yo en un discurso en Ciudad Juárez—agregó con una sonrisa irónica Alberto Solís, el ayudante de Natera.

Los dos montados en el mostrador de una cantina, apuraban cervezas y aguardiente.

Y los sombrerudos de bufandas al cuello, de gruesos zapatos de baqueta y callosas manos de vaquero, comiendo y bebiendo sin cesar, sólo hablaban de Villa y de sus tropas. Los de Natera hacen abrir tamaña buca a los de Macías. ¡Oh, Villa! ¡Los combates de Ciudad Juárez, de Tierra Blanca, Chihuahua, Torreón!.... Pero los hechos vistos y vividos se quedan muy por abajo de la fábula, la vieja leyenda mexicana renacía una vez más: el indomable hombre de la montaña, perseguido como una fiera por el gobierno. El hombre sin miedo que una bella noche, sin anunciarse, aparece derrepente en el despacho del industrial o hacendado millonario y, sonriendo, le dice: "Necesito diez mil pesos". El grave señor levanta la cabeza, sorprendido, y su faz se torna terrosa y mortecina.....A veces todo sale en el acto de la caja; pero a veces falta y no puede hacerse la entrega inmediata. Más el hombre de negra barba y ojos de águila, es persona que sabe fiar en la palabra de un caballero. "Mañana tal cantidad, a tal hora y en tal sitio". Y desaparece tan intempestivamente como entró. ¿Para qué quiere ese dinero? ¡Claro! para hacer caridades. A un anciano que viene en un viejo borrico reumático, le tira a las barbas un puñado de billetes de banco, a una viuda que se mantiene, con sus seis pequeños, comiendo nopales en la sierra, le alarga un talego de tostones. Y así pasa la vida del bandido-providencia: robando a los ricos para hacer dichosos a los pobres. ¡Ah; pero guay del que lo engañe! Así como es de bondadoso con el que accede a sus órdenes, es de terrible con el que no las acata. A un rico comerciante se le encontró sobre las alfombras de su recámara con la cabeza arrancada del tronco; a un vaquero, con los intestinos desparramados por el pavimento de su despacho; a un hacendado, en un potrero, picoteado por las auras, con las plantas desolladas y arenas y pedruzcos enterrados en las carnes. El Proteo que de lo sublime pasa bruscamente a lo bestial. El Gran Hombre de la turba multa!

—Porque ya sabe, amigo Montañez—decía uno de Natera—si usté le cae bien a mi general Villa, le regala una hacienda, pero si le cae mal..... no más lo manda fusilar!

—¡Ah, y las tropas de Villa! Puros hombrotes muy bien puestos, de sombrero tejano, traje de kaki siempre nuevecito, calzado americano de cuatro dolares.

Y cuando de eso hablaban los hombres de Natera, se veían unos a los otros y se daban cuenta cabal de sus sombrerotes de soyate podrido por la humedad y por el sol, de las garras de calzones y camisa que cubrían su cuerpo todo renegrido y sucio.

—Porque ahí no hay hambre..... Traen carros apretados de vacas y de carneros, furgones de comestibles y trenes enteros de ropa, armas y parque.

Y luego se hablaba de los aeroplanos de Villa. "¡Ah, los airoplanos! Abajo, así de cerca, no sabe usted qué son, parecen canoas, parecen chalupas; pero que comienzan a subir y es un ruidaso que lo aturde a uno; luego, algo así como un automóvil que va muy recio, y hagan de cuenta un pájaro, no quieran ver más sino un pájaro, grande, que camina sin que parezca que se buye siquiera. Pero aquí va lo bueno: adentro de ese pájaro, un gringo lleva miles de granadas. ¡Figúrense lo que será eso! Llega la hora del combate y como quien les riega maíz a las gallinas, el gringo comienza a tirar puños de granadas sobre el enemigo... y todo se vuelve un camposanto: muertos por aquí, muertos por allá, muertos por todas partes."

Y como Anastasio Montañez preguntara si los hombres del general Natera habían peleado alguna vez formando parte de las fuerzas del general Villa, ellos dan a entender que ni siquiera lo conocen y sólo de oídas sabían lo que con tanto calor estaban refiriendo.

—¡Hum!.... pos de hombre a hombre todos somos iguales y pa mí, nadie es más valiente que otro ... Lo que se necesita para pelear, es tener vergiienza...... ¡Yo qué soldado había de ser! Pero aquí donde ven un desgarrado, ¿voy a que no me lo creen? yo no tengo necesidad......

—Tengo mis diez yuntas de bueyes, ¿a que no me lo creen?—agrega "La Codorniz" y se aleja riendo a carcajadas a tomar copas a otro grupo.

XVI.

El atronar de la fusilería aminoró y fué alejándose. Luis Cervantes se atrevió a sacar la cabeza de su escondrijo, en medio de los escombros de fortificaciones, en lo más alto de un cerrito. Apenas se daba cuenta de cómo había llegado allí. Demetrio y su gente desaparecieron en un abrir y cerrar de ojos. De pronto, él solo, a caballo, se encontró arrastrado por una avalancha de infantería. Lo derribaron de la montura y cuando se quedó, todo pisoteado, uno de a caballo, de pañuelo rojo en el cuello y muchas estampas en el sombrero, lo levantó y lo puso en ancas. Mas, a poco, caballo y montado dieron en tierra y él, sin saber de su fusil, ni de su revólver, ni de nada, se encontró en medio de la humareda blanca y del silbar sonoro de los proyectiles; y aquel hoyanco, y aquellos pedazos de adobe amontonados, se le habían ofrecido como refugio segurísimo.

—¡Compañero!
—¡Compañero!
—Me tiró el caballo, se me echaron encima..... me han creído muerto y me despojaron de las armas...... ¿Qué podía hacer?—explicó Luis Cervantes.

—A mí nadie me tiró.... Estoy aquí... por precaución, ¿sabe usted?

La entonación festiva de Alberto Solís hizo enrojecer a Cervantes.

—¡Caramba!—exclamó aquél con entusiasmo.—Su jefe Macías es de veras un valiente...... ¡Qué temeridad y qué serenidad! La hazaña de hoy es digna de la pluma de Homero.....

Luis Cervantes, todo confuso, no supo qué decir.

—¡Ah, usted no sabe?.... Usted buscó su buen lugar desde luego.

Luis apretó los dientes.

FOLLETIN NUM. 12

—Bueno, pues so le voy a contar. ¡Yo ví todo llegué aquí con los de la última carga, y claro, ahora hago lo que usted, descanso.

Luis se ponía lívido de cólera.

—Mire, compañero—pronunció Solís que no se percataba del efecto de sus palabras, carentes de mala intención—venga acá para explicarle; vamos detrás de ese picacho. Note usted que de aquella laderita, al pie del cerro, no hay otra vía accesible que la q' tenemos al frente; de este lado, la vertiente hace imposible todo acceso, del opuesto; si no es imposible, es tan peligroso que un paso solo en falso hace desbarrancar entre las aristas cortantes de las peñas. Pues bien, una parte de la Brigada Moya nos tendimos en la ladera, pecho a tierra y resueltos a avanzar sobre la primera trinchera del enemigo. Los proyectiles pasaban zumbando sobre nuestras cabezas, y el combate era general. Durante breves minutos dejaron de foguearnos. Parecía que por otra parte los atacaban muy duro. Entonces nos arrojamos sobre la posición. ¡Ah, compañero, fíjese!... de media ladera abajo, un verdadero tapiz de cadáveres. Las ametralladoras hicieron la faena, y fué un barrido del que sólo unos cuantos escapamos. Los jefes estaban lívidos y vacilaban en ordenar una nueva carga. Entonces fué cuando Demetrio Macías, sin esperar órdenes ningunas, gritó de pronto: "arriba, muchachos." "¡Qué bárbaro!" dijimos. El caballo de Demetrio, como si tuviera garfios en las pezuñas, trepó por sobre esos peñazcos.... fíjese, compañero. "¡Arriba! ¡Arriba!" gritaban sus veinte hombres detrás de él, saltando de roca en roca, como venados: hombres y caballos hechos uno solo. Alguno perdió pisada y rodó destrozado entre las peñas; los más aparecieron aquí mismo, derribando las trincheras, acuchillando soldados. Demetrio lazó una ametralladora y la arrastró como quien tira un toro bravo. Los federales sorprendidos se desorganizaron, y de aquel desconcierto, que no podía durar sino breves momentos, nos aprovechamos nosotros y les quitamos la posición.... ¡Ah, su jefe es todo un valiente!

De lo alto del cerro se veía a un costado "La Bu-

fa" con su crestón, como la testa empenachada de algún altivo rey azteca. La vertiente de seiscientos metros estaba cubierta de muertos con los cabellos enmarañados y las ropas manchadas de sangre con tierra; y sobre el hacinamiento de cadáveres, mujeres harapasas iban y venían, como coyotes famélicos, esculcando y despojando.

En medio de la humareda blanca de la fusilería y los negros borbotones de humo de los edificios incendiados, refulgían bañadas de sol. las casas de ventanas y puertas cerradas, calles sobrepuestas, amontonadas, en vericuetos pintorescos, trepando a los cerros en cuyo fondo se levantaban; la arquería de esbeltas columnas, las torres y las cúpulas de las iglesias.

—¡Qué hermosa es la Revolución, aún en su misma barbarie!—exclamó Luis Cervantes.

—Sí, efectivamente.... Lástima que lo que falta no sea así..... Hay que esperar a que no haya combatientes, a que no se oigan los disparos de las turbas entregadas a las delicias del saqueo, a que resplandezca diáfana como una gota de agua la psicología de nuestra raza, condensada en las palabras: robar y matar..... ¡Qué chasco tan solemne, amigo mío, si los que venimos a ofrecer todo nuestro entusiasmo, nuestras esperanzas y nuestra vida misma por derrocar a un bandido y asesino, resultásemos los obreros de un monstruoso pedestal para cien o doscientos mil Victorianos Huerta .....

Unos fugitivos subían escondiéndose de algunos montados de copudos sombreros y calzones blancos. Pasó silbando una bala.

Alberto Solís, que cruzados los brazos permanecía absorto, pronunció:

—Compañero, maldito lo que me simpatizan estos mosquitos. ¿Quiere que nos retiremos un poco?

Fué la sonrisa de Luis Cervantes tan expresiva, que Alberto amoscado, buscó un cómodo asiento en un peña y se sentó.

Su mirada volvió a vagar hacia las espirales blancas del humo de los rifles y la povareda de cada casa derribada, de cada techo que se hundía. Y le pareció que había descubierto un símbolo de la revolución en aquellas nubes de humo y en aquellas nubes de polvo, que fraternalmente se abrazaban, se confundían y se borraban en la nada.

—¡Ah!—clamó de pronto.—Ahora sí.

Y regocijado señaló con su mano tendida la estación del ferocarril. Los trenes resoplando, arrojando negras columnas de humo; los carros colmados de federales, salían a toda máquina.

Sintió un golpecito seco en el vientre y como si las piernas se le hubieran vuelto de trapo, resbaló de la piedra. Luego, le zumbaron los oídos.... después obscuridad y silencio....

FIN DE LA PRIMERA PARTE

SEGUNDA PARTE

I.

Al champagne que ebulle en burbujas donde se descompone la luz de los candiles, Demetrio Macías prefiere el límpido tequila de Jalisco.

Hombres manchados de tierra, de humo y de sudor, de barbas crespas y alborotadas cabelleras; cubiertos de andrajos mugrientos, se agrupan en torno de las mesas de un restaurant.

—Yo maté dos coroneles—clama con voz ríspida y gutural un sujeto pequeño y gordo, de sombrero galonado, cotona de gamuza y mascada solferina al cuello.—No podían correr de tan tripones; se tropezaban con las piedras, y para subir al cerro, se ponían como gitomates y echaban tanta lengua!.. "No corran tanto, mochitos—les grité—párense; no me gustan las gallinas asustadas. ¡Párense, pelones, que no les voy a hacer nada! ¡están dados! ¡Ja, ja, ja! ¡La comieron los muy........! ¡Paf! ¡paf! uno para cada uno... y de veras descansaron.

—A mí se me jué uno de los meros copetones—habló un soldado que descansaba en un ángulo del salón, entre el muro y el mostrador, con las piernas alargadas y el fusil entre ellas.—¡Ah, cómo traiba oro el condenao! No más le hacían visos los galones en las charreteras y en la mantilla. ¿Y yo?.... ¡lo dejé pasar, el muy burro! Sacó el paño, me hizo la contraseña y yo me quedé nomás abriendo la boca. Apenas me dió campo de agarrarme de la esquina, y.... ¡bala y bala! Lo dejé que acabara el cargador. ¡Hora voy yo! ¡Madre mía de Jalpa, que no le jierre a este jijo......... de la mala palabra! ¡Nada! ¡Nomás dió el estampido! ¡Traiba muy buen cuaco! ¡Me pasó por los ojos como un relámpago! y otro que venía por la mesma calle me la pagó: ¡qué maroma le hice echar!

Se arrebatan las palabras de la boca y, mientras ellos refieren con mucho calor sus aventuras, mujeres de tez aceitunada, de ojos blanquiscos y dientes como de marfil, con revólvers a la cintura, cananas apretadas de tiros, cruzadas sobre el pecho, grandes sombreros de palma, van y vienen como perros callejeros entre los grupos.

Una muchacha de carrillos teñidos de carmín, de cuello y brazos muy trigueños y de burdísimo continente, da un salto y se pone sobre el mostrador de la cantina, muy cerca de la mesa de Demetrio.

Este vuelve la cara hacia ella, y choca con unos ojos lascivos, bajo una frente pequeña, entre dos bandos de pelo hirsuto.

La puerta se abre de par en par y, boquiabiertos

FOLLETIN NUM. 13

y deslumbrados, uno tras otro, penetran Anastasio Montañez, Pancracio, "La Codorniz" y "El Meco."

Anastasio da un grito de sorpresa y se adelanta a saludar al charro pequeño y gordo, de sombrero galonado y mascada solferina.

Son amigos viejos que ahora se reconocen. Y se abrazan tan fuerte, que la cara se les pone negra.

—Compadre Demetrio, tengo el gusto de presentarle al giiero Margarito.... ¡Un amigo de veras! ¡Ah como quiero yo a este giiero! Ya lo conocerá, compadre. Es reteacabado. ¿Te acuerdas, giiero, de la Penitenciaria de Escobedo, allá en Jalisco? .... ¡Un año juntos!

Demetrio, que permanecía silencioso y como meditabundo en medio de la alharaca general, sin quitarse el puro de entre los dientes, rumoró, tendien:do la mano:

—Servidor....

¿Usted, pues, se llama Demetrio Macías?—preguntó intempestivamente la muchacha, que sobre el mostrador estaba meneando las piernas y tocaba con sus zapatos de vaqueta la espalda de Demetrio.

—Al orden—le contestó éste, volviendo apenas la cara.

Ella, indiferente, siguió moviendo las piernas descubiertas, haciendo gala de sus medias azules..

—¡Eh! "Pintada" ¿Tú por acá, ahora? Anda, baja, ven a tomar una copa—le dijo el giiero Margarito.

La muchacha aceptó en seguida la invitación y con mucho desparpajo se abrió lugar, sentándose en frente de Demetrio.

Zacatecas and La Bufa

—¿Con que usté es el famoso Demetrio Macías, que tanto se lució en Zacatecas?—preguntó "La Pintada."

Demetrio inclinó la cabeza, asintiendo, en tanto que el giiero Margarito lanzaba una alegre carcajada y decía:

—¡Diablo de "Pintada" tan lista!.... ¡Ya quieres estrenar General!

Demetrio, sin comprender, volvió los ojos hacia ella: se miraron cara a cara, como dos perros desconocidos que se olfatean con desconfianza.

Demetrio no pudo sostener los ojos furiosamente provocativos de la muchacha y tuvo que bajar los suyos.

Oficiales de Natera, desde sus asientos, comenzaron a bromear a "La Pintada" con dicharajos obscenos.

Ella, sin inmutarse, dijo:

—Mi General Natera le va a dar a usté ya su aguilita...... ¡Andele, chóquela!

Y tendió su mano hacia Demetrio y lo estrechó con fuerza varonil.

Demetrio, envanecido por las felicitaciones que comenzaron a lloverle, mandó que se sirviera champagne.

—Yo no quiero vino, chico—dijo el giiero Margarito al mesero;—agua con hielo, y nada más.

—Yo, algo de comer; con tal de que no sea ni chile ni frijoles,—pidió Pancracio.

Siguen entrando oficiales y, poco a poco, se llena el restaurant. Menudean las estrellas y las barras, sombreros de todas formas y colores, mascadas escarlata, anillos de gruesos brillantes, pesadas leopoldinas de oro.

—Oye, mozo—grita el giiero Margarito—te he pedido un vaso de agua con hielo... Entiende que no quiero limosna. Mira este fajo de billetes: te compro a tí y hasta a la más vieja de tu casa!.... ¿Me entiendes, buen mozo?.... Oye, amigo, a mí no me gusta mandar dos veces... Te digo que quiero agua con hielo... No me respondas; tú no me conoces; tú no sabes con quién estás hablando... Dame agua con hielo..... Nada me importan tus explicaciones; no quiero saber si se acabó, o no.... Tú sabrás de dónde me la traes.... Dame agua con hielo, chico... Mira que soy muy corajudo... te digo que no quiero explicaciones, sino agua con hielo..... Por eso, pues, ¿me la traes o no me la traes?.... ¡Ah! ¿No?...Pues toma....

El mesero cae al golpe de una soberbia bofetada.

—Así soy yo, mi General Macías: Mire cómo ya no me queda pelo de barba en la cara. ¿Sabe por qué? Pues porque soy muy corajudo, y cuando no tengo en quién descansar, me arranco los pelos, hasta que se me baja el coraje..... ¡Palabra de honor, mi General, si yo no lo hiciera así, me moriría del puro berrinche!

—Es muy malo comerse uno solo los corajes—afirma, muy serio, uno de sombrero de petate como cobertizo de jacal.—Yo en Torreón, maté a una vieja que no quiso venderme un plato de enchiladas. Estaban de apetito. No cumplí mi antojo, pero siquiera descansé.

—Yo maté a un tendajonero en el Parral, porque me metió en un cambio dos billetes de Huerta—dice otro de estrellita, mostrando en sus dedos negros y callosos, piedras de luces refulgentes.

—Yo, en Chihuahua, maté a un tío porque a diario me lo encontraba en la misma mesa y a la misma hora, cuando iba yo a almorzar... Me chocaba mucho: ¿qué quieren ustedes?

—Yo maté......

El tema es inagotable.

A la madrugada, cuando el restaurant está lleno de alegría y de escupitajos, cuando con las hembras norteñas, de caras obscuras y cenizas, se revuelven jovencitas pintarrajeadas, de los suburbios, Demetrio saca su repetición de oro, incrustado de piedras, y pide a su vecino la hora.

Anastasio Montañez ve la carátula, luego saca la cabeza por una ventanilla y mirando el cielo estrellado, dice:

—Ya van colgadas las cabrillas, compadre: no dilata en amanecer.

Afuera no cesan los gritos, las carcajadas, las canciones de los ebrios. Pasan soldados a caballo desbocado, azotando las aceras. Por todas partes disparos de fusiles y pistolas.

Y por en medio de la calle caminan, rumbo al hotel, Demetrio y "La Pintada" abrazados y dando tumbos.

Detrás el cortejo con tres músicos de violines y guitarra que no dejan de tocar un solo instante.

II.

—¡Qué brutos!—exclamó "La Pintada," riendo a carcajadas.—¿De dónde son ustedes? Si eso de que los soldados vayan a parar a los mesones ya no se usa. ¿De dónde vienen? Llega uno a cualquier parte, y no tiene mas que escoger la casa que le cuadre y esa agarra sin pedirle licencia a naiden. Entonces, ¿pa quén fué la revolución? ¿Pa los catrines? ¡Si ahora nosotros vamos a ser los meros catrines!.... A ver Pancracio, presta acá tu marrazo....! ¡Ricos tales! Todo lo han de guardar debajo de siete llaves.

Hundió la punta de acero en la hendidura de un cajón y haciendo palanca, con el mango rompió la chapa y levantó, astillada, la cubierta del escritorio.

Las manos de Anastasio Montañez, de Pancracio y de "La Pintada," se hundieron en el montón de cartas, estampas, fotografías y papeles desparramados por la alfombra.

Pancracio manifestó su enojo de no encontrar nada que le complaciera, lanzando al aire con la punta del huarache, un retrato encuadrado, cuyo cristal se estrelló en el candelabro del centro.

Sacaron las manos vacías de entre los papeles, profiriendo en insolencias.

Pero "La Pintada," incansable, siguió desarrajando cajón por cajón, hasta no dejar hueco sin escudriñar.

No advirtieron el rodar silencioso de una pequeña caja forrada de terciopelo gris, que fué a detenerse a los pies de Luis Cervantes.

Este, que lo veía todo con aires de profunda indolencia, mientras que Demetrio, despatarrado sobre la alfombra parecía dormir, atrajo con la punta del pie la cajita, se inclinó, rascose un tobillo, y con ligereza levantó el objeto.

Se quedó deslumbrado: dos diamantes de aguas purísimas en una montadura de filigrana. Con prontitud lo ocultó en el bolsillo.

Cuando Demetrio despertó, Luis Cervantes le dijo:—Mi General, vea usted qué diabluras han hecho los muchachos. ¿No sería conveniente evitarles esto?

—No, Curro.... ¡pobres! Es el único gusto que les queda después de poner la barriga a las balas.

—Sí, mi General; pero siquiera que no lo hagan aquí.... Mire usted, eso nos desprestigia, y lo que es peor, desprestigia a nuestra causa.

Demetrio clavó sus ojos de aguilucho en Luis Cervantes. Se golpeó los dientes con las uñas de dos dedos, y dijo:

—¡No se ponga colorado!..... ¡Mire, a mí no me cuente!.... Ya sabemos que lo tuyo, tuyo y lo mío, mío. A usted le tocó la cajita, bueno; a mí, el reloj de reptición..... .

Y ya los dos en muy buena inteligencia, se mostraron sus avances.

"La Pintada" y sus compañeros, entre tanto, registraban el resto de la casa.

"La Codorniz" entró a la sala con una chiquilla de doce años, ya marcada con manchas cobrizas en la frente y en los brazos. Sorprendidos los dos, se mantuvieron absortos, contemplando los montones de libros sobre la alfombra, mesas y sillas; los espejos descolgados con sus vidrios rotos; grandes marcos de estampas y retratos destrozados; muebles y bibelots hechos pedazos. Con ojos ávidos "La Codorniz buscaba su presa, suspendiendo la respiración.

Afuera, en un ángulo del patio y entre el humo sofocante, "El Manteca" cocía elotes, atizando las brasas con libros y papeles que alzaban vivas llamaradas.

—¡Ah!—gritó de pronto "La Codorniz,"—mira lo que me jallé.... ¡Qué sudaderos para mi yegua!

Y de un tirón, arrancó una cortina de peluche que se vino al suelo con todo y galería, sobre el copete finamente tallado de un sillón.

—¡Mira, tú!....... ¡cuánta vieja encuerada!— clamó la chiquilla, divertidísima con las láminas de un lujoso ejemplar de la Divina Comedia.—Esta me cuadra mucho, y me la voy a llevar.

Y comenzó a arrancar los grabados que más llamaban su atención.

Demetrio se incorporó y tomó asiento en un muelle sillón al lado de Luis Cervantes. Pidió cerveza, alargó una botella a su secretario, y de un solo trago, apuró la suya. Luego, amodorrado, entrecerró los ojos y comenzo a dormir de nuevo.

—Oiga—dijo un individuo en el zaguán a Pancracio—¿a qué hora se le puede hablar al General?

—No se le puede hablar; amaneció crudo—respondió Pancracio,—¿qué se le ofrece?

—Que me venda unos libros de esos que de nada le sirven.

—Yo mesmo se los puedo vender.

—¿A cómo me los da?

Pancracio frunció las cejas y meditó:

—Los que tengan monitos, a cinco centavos, y los otros..... pos los otros se los doy de pilón, si me los merca todos.

Y el interesado llevó libros en canastas pizcadoras.

—Demetrio, hombre, Demetrio, despierta ya—gritó "La Pintada"—Ya no duermas como puerco gordo. ¡Mira quién está aquí! ¡El giiero Margarito! No sabes tú, todo lo que vale este giiero.

—Yo lo aprecio mucho a usted, mi general Macías, y quiero decirle que le tengo muy buena voluntad y me gustan mucho sus modales. Así es que si no lo tiene a mal, yo me paso a su brigada.

—Qué grado tiene?—inquirió Demetrio.

—Capitán primero, mi general.

—Pos aquí se viene como Mayor.

Era el giiero Margarito un hombrecillo gordo, de bigotes retorcidos, ojos azules muy malignos, que se le perdían entre los carrilos y la frente cuando se reía. Ex-mesero de "El Mónico" de Chihuahua, ostentaba ahora tres barras de latón amarillo, como capitán primero del Ejército del Norte.

Colmó de elogios a Demetrio y a su gente. Y con eso, la caja de cerveza se vació luego.

"La Pintada" apareció, de pronto, a la puerta de la sala, ostentando un espléndido traje de seda, ornado de ricos encajes.

—¡Nomás las medias se te olvidaron!—exclamó el giiero Margarito, desternillándose de risa.

La chiquilla de "La Codorniz," regocijadísima, prorrumpió también en agudos chillidos.

Pero a "La Pintada" nada se le dió, hizo una mueca de indiferencia, se tiró en la alfombra, y con los propios pies, hizo saltar las zapatillas de raso blanco, moviendo muy a gusto los dedos desnudos, entumecidos por la opresión del calzado, y dijo:

—¡Epa, tú, Pancracio!.... traeme unas medias azules de mis avances.

Mientras que la sala se iba llenando de nuevos amigos y viejos compañeros de campaña, Demetrio refería menudamente sus más notables hechos de armas.

—¿Qué ruido oigo?—inquirió sorprendido por el afinar de cuerdas y latones en las afueras.

—Mi General— pronunció solemnemente Luis Cervantes,—es un banquete que le ofrecemos sus viejos amigos para celebrar el hecho de armas de Zacatecas, y el merecido ascenso de usted a General.

III.

—Mi General—pronunció enfático Luis Cervantes, haciendo entrar a una muchacha de belleza extraordinaria al comedor—le presento a usted a mi futura esposa.

Todos volvieron sus rostros hacia ella, que abría sus grandes ojos azules con azoro.

Tendría apenas catorce años; su piel era fresca y suave como un pétalo de rosa té, sus cabellos rubios, y la expresión de sus ojos con algo de maligna curiosidad y mucho de vago terror infantil.

Luis Cervantes, con regocijo interior, vió que Demetrio clavaba su mirda de ave de rapiña en el pimpollo.

Se le abrió sitio a la muchacha entre el giiero Margarito y Luis Cervantes, en frente de Demetrio.

Entre los cristales, porcelanas y búcaros de flores, abundaban las botellas de tequila.

"El Meco," entró sudoroso y renegando, con una caja de cerveza a cuestas.

—Ustedes no conocen todavía a este giiero,—dijo "La Pintada," reparando en que Margarito no quitaba los ojos de la novia de Luis Cervantes.

—Tiene mucha sal, y no hay en el mundo gente más acabada que él.

Le lanzó una mirada lúbrica y añadió:

—¡Por eso no lo puedo ver ni pintado!

Rompió la orquesta en una rumbosa marcha taurina.

Los soldados bramaron de alegría.

—¡Qué menudo, mi General! ¡le juro que en mi vida he comido otro más bien guisado!—dijo el giiero Margarito, acordándose, seguramente, del "Mónico" de Chihuahua.

—¿Le gusta de veras, giiero?—repuso Demetrio.—Pos que le sirvan hasta que llene.

Ese es mi mero gusto—confirmó Anastasio Montañez—y eso es lo bonito, de que a mí me cuadra un guiso, como, como, hasta que lo eruto.

Siguió un ruido de bocazas y grandes tragantadas. Se bebió copiosamente.

Al final, Luis Cervantes tomó una copa de champagne y se puso en pie.

—Señor General.....

—¡Hum!—interrumpió "La Pintada"—ora va de discurso, y eso es cosa que a mí me aburre mucho. Voy mejor al corral; al cabo ya no hay qué comer.

Luis Cervantes ofreció el escudo de paño negro con una aguilita de latón, en un brindis que nadie entendió, pero que todos aplaudieron con estrépito.

Demetrio tomó en sus manos la insignia de su nuevo grado y, muy encendido, la mirada brillante, relucientes los dientes, dijo con mucha ingenuidad:

—¿Y qué voy a hacer yo ahora con este zopilote?

—Compadre—pronunció trémulo y en pie Anastasio Montañez—yo no tengo qué dicirle....

Transcurrieron minutos enteros; las malditas palabras no querían acudir al llamado del compadre Anastasio. Su cara enrojecía, perlada el sudor en su frente costruda de mugre. Por fin, se resolvió a terminar su brindis:

—Pos yo no tengo qué dicirle...... sino que ya sabe que soy su compadre.

Y como todos habían aplaudido a Luis Cervantes, el propio Anastasio, al acabar, dió la señal de aplauso con mucha gravedad.

Pero todo estuvo bien. Su torpeza fué un estímulo y brindaron hasta "El Manteca" y "La Codorniz."

Llegaba su turno al "Meco," cuando se presentó "La Pintada" dando fuertes voces de júbilo. Chasqueando la lengua, pretendía meter al comedor una bellísima yegua de color negro azabache.

—¡Mi avance! ¡mi avance!—clamaba, palmeando el cuello corvo del soberbio animal.

La yegua se resistía a franquear la puerta, pero un tirón del cabestro y un latigazo en el anca, la hizo entrar con brío estrépito.

Los soldados, embobecidos, contemplaban, con mal disimulada envidia la rica presa.

—Yo no sé qué carga esta diablo de "Pintada" que siempre nos gana los mejores avances —clamó el giiero Margarito.—Así la verán desde que se nos juntó en Tierra Blanca.

—Epa, tú, Pancracio, anda a trerme un tercio de alfalfa pa mi yegua—ordenó secamente "La Pintada."

Tomó su asiento y tendió la zoga hacia un soldado.

Una vez más se llenaron los vasos y las copas. Algunos comenzaban a doblar el cuello y a entrecerrar los ojos; la mayoría gritaba jubilosa.

FOLLETIN NUM. 15

Y entre ellos, la muchacha de Luis Cervantes, que había tirado todo el vino en un pañuelo, tornaba de una parte a la otra, sus ojos azules llenos de azoro.

—¡Muchachos!—gritó, de pie, el giiero Margarito, dominando con su voz aguda ygutural el vocerío, —estoy cansado ya de vivir, y me voy a matar. "La Pintada" ya me hartó..... Y este querubincito del cielo no arrienda siquiera a verme.

Luis Cervantes notó que las últimas palabras iban dirigidas a su novia y con gran sorpresa vino a cuentas de que el pie que sentía entre los de la muchacha, no era de Demetrio Macías, sino de giiero Margarito.

Y la indignación hirvió en su pecho.

—¡Fíjense, muchachos—prosiguió el giiero, con el revólver en alto—me voy a pegar un tiro en la merita frente.

Y apuntó al gran espejo del fondo donde se veía de cuerpo entero.

—¡No te buigas, "Pintada"!

El espejo se estrelló en largos y puntiagudos fragmentos. La bala había pasado rozando los cabellos de "La Pintada" que ni pestañeó siquiera.

IV.

Al atardecer despertó Luis Cervantes, se restregó los ojos, y se incorporó. Se encontraba en el suelo duro, entre los tiestos del huerto. Cerca de él respiraban ruidosamente, muy dormidos, Anastasio Montañez, Pancracio y "La Codorniz."

Sintió los labios hinchados y la nariz dura y muy seca; se miró sangre en las manos y en la camisa, e instantáneamente hizo memoria de lo ocurrido. Pronto se puso en pie y se dirigió hacia una recámara, empujando la puerta repetidas veces, sin conseguir abrirla. Mantúvose indeciso algunos instantes. Porque todo era cierto; estaba seguro de no haberlo soñado. De la mesa del comedor se había levantado con su muchacha, la condujo a una recámara; pero antes de cerrar la puerta, Demetrio, tambaleándose de borracho, se precipitó tras ellos. Luego "La Pintada" siguió a Demetrio y conmenzaron a forcejear. Demetrio, con los ojos encendidos como una brasa y hebras cristalinas en los burdos labios, buscaba con avidez a la muchacha. 'La Pintada' daba fuertes empellones a Demetrio para alejarlo.

—¡Peru tú qué!.... ¿tú qué....!—ululaba éste irritado.

"La Pintada" se le metió entre las rodillas, y de un tremendo empellón lo hizo caer de largo a largo, fuera del cuarto.

Demetrio se levantó furioso.

—¡Auxilio! ¡Auxilio!..... ¡que me mata!—chilló "La Pintada" cogiéndole vigorosamente la muñeca y desviando el cañón de la pistola.

La bala se incrustó en los ladrillos. "La Pintada' seguía clamando. Anastasio Montañez llegó por detrás y desarmó a Demetrio.

Este, como toro a media plaza, volvió sus ojos extraviados.

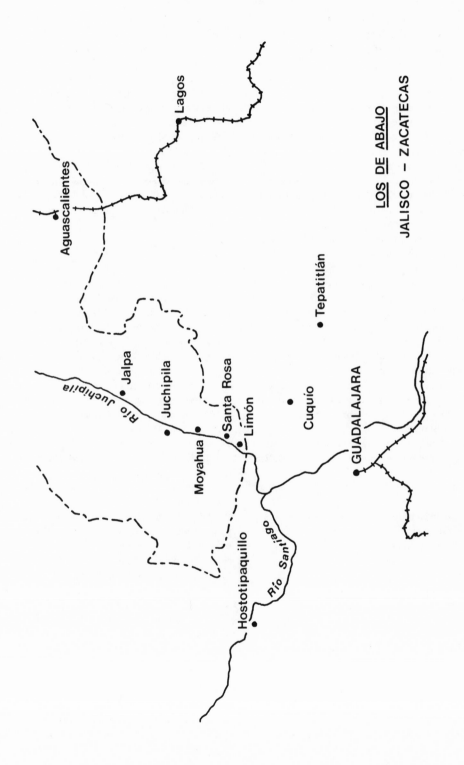

LOS DE ABAJO
JALISCO – ZACATECAS

Le rodeaban el mismo Luis Cervantes, Anastasio, "El Manteca" y muchos otros.

—¡Infelices!.... ¡Me han desarmado!.... ¡Como si pa ustedes se necesitaran armas!.....

Y abriendo los brazos, en brevísimos instantes los volteó de narices sobre el enladrillado.

Y después.... Luis Cervantes no recordaba más. Seguramente que allí se habían quedado bien aporreados y dormidos. Seguramente que su novia, por miedo a tanto ebrio, había tomado la buena precaución de encerrarse.

"Tal vez esa recámara comunique con la sala y por aquí pueda yo entrar", pensó.

A sus pasos despertó "La Pintada" que dormía cerca de Demetrio sobre la alfombra, al pie de un confidente, donde la yegua negra cenaba alfalfa y maíz.

—¿Qué busca?—preguntó la mujer.—¡Ah, sí, ya sé lo que quiere... ¡Sinvergiienza! Mire, encerré a su novia porque ya no podía aguantar a este condenado de Demetrio. Coja la llave, allí está sobre la mesa.

En vano buscó Luis Cervantes por todos los escondrijos de la sala.

—A ver, Curro, cuénteme cómo se robó esa muchacha?

Luis Cervantes muy nervioso, seguía buscando la llave.

—No coma ansia, hombre, allá se la voy a dar. Pero cuénteme. A mí me divierte mucho todo eso. Esa currita es igual a usted. No es pata rajada como nosotros.

—No tengo qué contar: es mi novia, y ya....

—¡Ja, ja, ja!.... ¡Su novia!.... Mire, Curro, a donde usté va, yo ya vengo..... ¡Tengo el colmillo duro! A esa pobre la sacaron de su casa entre el "Meco" y "El Manteca," y usté les dió por ella una estampa milagrosa del "Señor de la Villita" y unas mancuernillas chapeadas.... ¿Miento, Curro? ...¡Que los hay los hay! ..... ¡el trabajo es dar con ellos! ¿verdá?

"La Pintada" se levantó a darle la llave, pero tampoco la encontró, y se sorprendió mucho. Estuvo pensativa un rato. De repente, salió a toda carrera hacia la puerta de la recámara. Aplicó un ojo al agujero de la cerradura y ahí se mantuvo inmóvil hasta que su vista se hizo a la obscuridad del cuarto. De pronto y sin quitar los ojos, rumoró:

—¡Ah, Giiero... jijo de un.....! ¡Asómese no-más, Curro!

Y se alejó lanzando una sonora carcajada.

—Si les digo que en mi vida he visto hombre más acabado que éste!

Otro día por la mañana, "La Pintada" espió el momento en que el giiero salía de la recámara a darle de almorzar a su caballo.

¡Criatura de Dios!...¡anda, vete a tu casa! ¡Estos hombres te matan! ..... ¡Anda, corre!

Y sobre la chiquilla de ojos azules y semblante de virgen, que sólo vestía camisón y medias, echó la frazada piojosa del "Manteca"; la cogió de la mano y la puso en la calle.

—¡Bendito sea Dios!—exclamó—¡Ahora sí! ¡Cómo quiero yo a este giiero!

V.

Como los potros que relinchan y retozan, a los primeros truenos de Mayo, así van por la sierra los hombres de Demetrio.

—¡A Moyahua, muchachos!

—¡A la tierra de Demetrio Macías!

—¡A la tierra de don Mónico, el cacique!

El paisaje se aclara, el sol soma en una faja escarlata, sobre la diafanidad del cielo.

Vanse destacando las cordilleras como monstruos alagartados, de angulosa vertebradura; cerros que parecen testas de colosales ídolos aztecas, caras de gigantes, muecas pavorosas y grotescas, que ora hacen sonreír, ora dejan un vago terror, como un presentimiento de misterio.

A la cabeza de la tropa va Demetrio Macías con su Estado Mayor: el coronel Anastasio Montañez, los mayores Luis Cervantes y Margarito Aranda. Va en segunda fila 'La Pintada" a quien con mucha fineza galantea el dotor Venancio.

Cuando los rayos del sol bordearon los pretiles del caserío, de cuatro en fondo, comenzaron a entrar a Moyahua.

Cantaban los gallos a ensordecer, ladraban con alarma los perros; pero la gente no asomó en parte alguna.

"La Pintada" azuza su yegua negra y en un salto se pone codo con codo de Demetrio. Deja a Venancio con las palabras en la boca, muy poco divertida con los versos de Antonio Plaza.

Muy ufana, toma la derecha del General. Luce vestido de seda y grandes arracadas de oro; el azul pálido del talle acentúa el tinte aceitunado de su rostro, manchado por la avería. Perniabierta, su falda se remanga a la rodilla, y se ven sus medias deslavadas y con muchos agujeros. Lleva un revólver al pecho, y la cartuchera sobre la cabeza de la silla.

Demetrio también va de gala: sombrero galonado, pantalón de cuero de botonadura de plata y chamarra de gamuza, bordada de hilo de oro.

Comienza a oírse el abrir forzado de las puertas, por la gente diseminada por todo el pueblo, en busca de caballos, armas y monturas.

—Nosotros vamos a "hacer la mañana" a casa de don Mónico—pronuncia muy serio Demetrio, tendiendo las riendas de su caballo a un soldado, y apeándose.

—Vamos a almorzar en el comedor de don Mónico, un amigo mío que me quiere mucho....

Su "Estado Mayor" sonríe con risa siniestra. Y arrastrando ruidosamente las espuelas por la banqueta, se encamina con ellos a la plaza, hacia un caserón pretencioso, que no puede ser más que albergue de cacique.

—Está cerrado a piedra y cal,—dice Anastasio Montañez, empujando con toda su fuerza la puerta.

—Pero yo sé abrir—repone Pancracio, abocando prontamente su fusil al prestillo.

FOLLETIN NUM. 16

—No...no—pronuncia Demetrio—toca primero.

Tres golpes con la culata del rifle, otros tres, y nadie responde. Pancracio se insolenta y no se atiene más a órdenes. Dispara, salta la chapa y se abre la puerta.

Vense extremos de faldas, piernas de niños, todos en disperción hacia el interior de la casa.

Demetrio entra en derechura del comedor.

—¡Quero vino!.... ¡aquí vino!....—pide con voz imperiosa, dando fuertes golpes sobre la mesa.

—Siéntense, compañeros.

Una señora asoma, luego otra y otra, y entre las faldas negras aparecen cabezas de niños asustados. Una de las mujeres, temblando, se encamina hacia un aparador, saca copas y botellas, y sirve el vino.

—Qué armas tienen?—inquiere Demetrio con aspereza.

—¡Armas?...—contesta la señora, la lengua hecha un trapo—¿pero qué armas quieren ustedes que tengan unas pobres señoras solas y decentes?

—¡Ah, solas! .... ¿Y don Mónico?....

—No está aquí, señores... Nosotros rentamos la casa.... Al señor don Mónico, apenas de nombre lo conocemos.

Demetrio manda que se practique un cateo.

—No, señores, por favor... nosotros mismas vamos a atrerles todo lo que tenemos, pero, por el amor de Dios, no nos falten al respeto. ¡Somos niñas solas y decentes....!

—¿Y los chamacos?—inquiere Pancracio, brutalmente—¿nacieron de la tierra?

Las señoras desaparecen con precipitación, y vuelven a poco con una escopeta astillada, cubierta de tierra y de telarañas, y una pistola de muelles enmohecidas y descompuesta.

Demetrio se sonríe.

—Bueno.... ¿a ver el dinero?

—¡Dinero!.... ¿pero qué dinero quieren ustedes que tengan unas pobres niñas solas?

Y vuelven sus ojos suplicatorios hacia el más cercano de los soldados; pero luego los cierran con horror: han visto a Pancracio, han visto al sayón que está crucificando a Nuestro Señor Jesucristo en el viacrucis de la parroquia.

Demetrio ordena de nuevo el cateo.

A un tiempo se precipitan otra vez las señoras, y al instante vuelven con una cartera apolillada, con unos cuantos billetes de los de la emisión de Huerta.

Demetrio sonríe, y ya, sin más consideraciones, hace entrar a su gente.

Como perros hambrientos que han olfateado la carne, la turba penetra atropellando a las señoras que pretenden defender la entrada de una pieza, con su propio cuerpo. Unas caen desvanecidas, otras huyen, los chicos dan de gritos.

Pancracio se dispone a romper la cerradura de un gran ropero, cuando las hojas se abren solas, y de adentro salta un hombre con un fusil en las manos.

—¡Don Mónico!—exclaman sorprendidos.

—¡Hombre, Demetrio!...... ¡no me haga nada! ....¡No me perjudique!... ¡Soy su amigo, don Demetrio....!

Demetrio Macías se ríe socarronamente y le pregunta si a los amigos se les recibe con el fusil en las manos.

Don Mónico, confuso, aturdido, se echa a los pies de Demetrio, le estrecha las rodillas, le besa los pies:

—¡Mi mujer! .....mis hijos!...... amigo don Demetrio!

Demetrio con mano trémula vuelve el revólver a la cintura.

Una silueta dolorida ha pasado por su memoria. Una mujer con su hijo en los brazos, atravesando por las rocas de la sierra, a media noche y a la luz de la luna....... Una casa ardiendo.....

—¡Vámonos!...... ¡Afuera todos!—clama sombríamente.

Su "Estado Mayor" obedece; don Mónico y las señoras le besan las manos agradecidísimos.

En la calle la turba está esperando alegre y dicharajera el permiso del General para saquear la casa del cacique.

—El dinero, yo sé muy bien dónde lo tienen escondido, pero no lo digo—dice un muchacho con un cesto al brazo.

—¡Hum! yo ya sé—repone una vieja que lleva un costal para recoger "lo que le toque." —Está en un altito, allí hay muchos triques, y entre los triques, una petaquilla con dibujitos de concha...... Allí mero está lo giieno!

—No es cierto—repone un hombre,—no son tan guajes para dejar así el dinero. Pa mí, lo tienen enterrado en el pozo en un tanate de cuero.

Y se remueve el gentío, unos con sogas para hacer sus fardos, otros con bateas; las mujeres extienden sus delantales o el extremo de sus rebozos, calculando lo que les puede caber. Todos esperan, dándole gracias a Dios, su parte de saqueo.

Cuando Demetrio anuncia que no permitirá nada, y ordena que todos se retiren, con gesto desconsolado la gente del pueblo lo obedece, y se disemina luego; pero entre la soldadezca hay un sordo rumor de desaprobación y nadie se mueve de su sitio.

Demetrio, irritado, repite que se retiren.

Un mozalvete, de los últimos reclutados, con algo de aguardiente en la cabeza, se ríe y avanza sin zozobra, hacia la puerta.

Demetrio con la pistola humeante en las manos, inmutable, espera a que los soldados se retiren. .

—!Que se le pegue fuego a la casa!—ordenó a Luis Cervantes cuando regresaron al cuartel.

Y Luis Cervantes, con rara solicitud, sin trasmitir la orden, se encargó de ejecutarla él mismo.

Cuando dos horas después, la plazuela del pueblo se ennegrecía de humo, y de la casa de don Mónico se alzaban lenguas enormes de fuego, nadie comprendió el extraño proceder del General.

VI.

—¡Hombre, Curro!..... ¡Yo no quería eso!.... ¡Aquí casi es mi tierra!—dijo Demetrio a Luis Cervantes, que en el silencio de la noche, a la débil y rojiza luz de un aparatito de petróleo, vaciaba sobre el colchón un talego de hidalgos, resplandecientes como ascuas, de oro.

Sentados en la cama del mismo Demetrio, Luis Cervantes proponía la equitativa repartición.

—En primer lugar, mi General, esto lo sabemos sólo usted y yo, y luego, que al buen sol hay que abrirle la ventana. Hoy nos está dando de cerca, mi General. Hay que ver adelante. Una bala, un disparar del caballo, un resfrío..... y una viuda y unos huérfanos en la miseria!.... ¿El Gobierno? ....¡Ja, ja, ja!.... ¡Qué ilusiones! Vaya usted con Villa, vaya con Carranza o con cualquier otro de los jefes principales, y hábleles de su familia!.... Si le responden con un puntapié donde usted ya sabe......ya puede asegurar que le fué de perlas! Y harán bien: nosotros no nos hemos levantado para que un tal Carranza o un tal Villa sea Presidente de la República; nosotros peleamos en defensa de los sagrados derechos del pueblo, pisoteados por el cacique..... Y así como ni Villa, ni ninguno, han de venir a pedir nuestro consentimiento para pagarse los servicios que le han hecho a la Patria, tampoco nosotros tenemos que pedirle licencia a nadie.

—¡Qué pico largo es usté, Curro!

Y sus dedos negros y toscos ondularon sobre las brillantes monedas a cuenta y cuenta.

Luego, Luis Cervantes sacó un botecito de fosfatina Fallieres y volcó dijes, anillos, pendientes, y otras muchas alhajas de valor.

—¡Mire, mi General, si como parece, va a seguir "la bola," si la Revolución no se acaba, ya nosotros nos vamos a vivir al extranjero. Ya tenemos con qué vivir.

Demetrio meneó la cabeza, negativamente.

—¡Cómo!.... ¿No haría eso? ¿Pues a qué se quedaría uno ya? ¿Qué causa iríamos a defender ahora?

—Es cosa que yo no puedo explicar, Curro, pero siento que eso no sería cosa de hombres.

—Escoja lo que guste—dijo Luis Cervantes, mostrándole las joyas puestas en fila.

—¡Déjelas pa usté!.... De veras, Curro: si viera que no le tengo amor al dinero. ¿Quiere que le diga la verdá? Pos yo con vino, y una chamaca que me cuadre, soy el hombre más dichoso del mundo.

—¿Y por qué aguanta a esa sierpa de "La Pintada, mi General?

—Hombre, Curro, me tiene harto; pero así soy yo; no me animo a decírselo.... No tengo valor pa despacharla a.... Yo soy así, ese es mi genio. Mire, me cuadra una mujer y soy tan boca de palo que si ella no me dice algo, yo no me animo a nada.

Y sus piró.

—Allí está Camila la del Ranchito.... La muchachilla es fea; pero si viera cómo me llena el ojo....

—El día que quiera nos la vamos a robar.

Demetrio guiñó los ojos con malicia.

—Usté se la va a robar?.... ¿Y yo a qué voy?..

—Le juro que se la "hago buena," mi General...

FOLLETIN NUM. 17

—¿De veras, Curro?... ¡Mire, si cumple su palabra, para usted es este reloj con todo y su leontina, ya que le cuadra tanto.

Los ojos de Luis Cervantes resplandecieron.

—¡Jijo de un....tal, pal que se raje?.... ¿Qué dice, Curro?

Luis Cervantes tomó el pesado bote de fosfatina ya bien lleno, se puso en pie y sonriendo dijo:

—Hasta mañana, mi General...... Que duerma bien.......

—¿Yo qué sé? Lo mismo que ustedes saben. A mí me dijo el General: "Codorniz" ensilla tu caballo y mi yegua mora. Vas con el Curro a una comisión. "Bueno, salimos de aquí, al medio día; llegamos al "Ranchito" ya anocheciendo. Nos dió posada la tuerta María Antonia.

—Te saluda mucho, Pancracio. En la madrugada me despertó el Curro. "Codorniz," "Codorniz", ensilla las bestias.Me dejas mi caballo y te vuelves con la yegua del general otra vez para Moyahua. Te sigo dentro de un rato. Y el sol alto me alcanzó. venía con Camila en la silla, allí la apió para subirla a la yegua mora.

—Bueno, ¿y ella qué cara le venía haciendo?—preguntó uno.

—No le paraba la boca de tan contenta.....

—¿Y el Curro.?

—Callado como siempre. Igual a como es él.

—Yo creo—opinó con mucha gravedad el dotor Venancio—que si Camila amaneció en la cama de Demetrio, sólo fué por una equivocación. ¿Se acuerdan cómo bebimos?... .Se les subieron los espíritus alcohólicos y perdieron completamente el sentido.

—¡Qué espíritus alcohólicos ni qué...Fué cosa convenida entre el general y el Curro para engañar a Camila que está enamorada de éste.

—Para mí, el tal Curro no es más que un......

—No es más que un afortunado—habló el hiiero Margarito, que sólo había estado escuchando la conversación.—Dos novias ha tenido: una para mí y la otra.....para Demetrio.

Y prorrumpieron e risotadas.

Luego que "La Pintada" se dió cuenta cabal de lo sucedido, fué muy cariñosa a consolar a Camila.

—¡Pobre de tí, platícame cómo estuvo eso!....

Camila tenía los ojos altos de llorar.

—¡Me mintió, me mintió! ....Me dijo: "Camila ¿te sales con migo? No más por tí he venido aquí ¡Hum! dígame si ¿yo no tendría ganas de irme con él? De quererlo, lo quiero mucho.... Míreme tan encanijada sólo por estar pensando en él. Amanece y ni ganas de hacer nada; me llama mi ama a almorzar y la gorda se me hace hilacho en la boca. Y ¡aquella pinción...aquella pinción! A piense y piense con él.

—Bueno,te saliste con él ¿y después?

—Pos yo no sé.... Pero a mí se me afigura que lo hizo de mala intención.

Y comenzó a llorar otra vez y para que no se oyeran sus sollozos, se cubría de boca y la nariz con el rebozo.

—Mira, yo te voy a sacar de esta agrupación. No seas tonta, ya no llores. Ya no pienses en el Curro. ¿Sabes lo que es ese Curro?.... De veras, puedes creerlo. Pa eso lo trae el General aquí... ¡Qué tonta!.... Bueno, ¿queres volverte a tu casa?

—Me matará mi mamá a palos....

—Nada te hace. Vamos a hacer esto. La tropa tiene que salir de un momento a otro. Cuando Demetrio te diga que te prevengas para irnos, tú le respondes que tienes mucha dolencia de cuerpo, que estás como si te hubieran dado de palos. Y te estiras mucho, y bostezas muy seguido. Luego te tientas la frente y dices: "Estoy ardiendo en calentura." Entonces yo le digo a Demetrio que nos deje a las dos; que yo me quedo a curarte, y que luego luego que estés buena, nos vamos a alcanzarlo. Y lo que hgo es ponerte en tu casa, buena y sana.

VIII.

—Le ordenan, mi General, que aliste la gente para salir en seguida a perseguir a los orozquistas,— dijo Luis Cervantes leyendo el propio que Demetrio acababa de recibir.

—¡A Jalisco, muchachos!

—¡Aprevénganse, tapatías de mi alma, que allá voy!

Fué un momento de regocijo y de entusiasmo para toda la tropa.

Los ojos de Demetrio relampagueaban. ¡Ah! ir a batir a los Orozquistas. ¡Qué alegría! ¡Habérselas, al fin, con hombres de verdad! ¡Dejar ya de matar federales como se matan las liebres y los guajolotes!

¡Ah, si yo pudiera coger vivo al bandido ese de Pascual Orozco, le arrancaría la planta de los pies y lo haría caminar veinticuatro horas por la sierra! —pronunció exaltado el giiero Margarito.

—Qué pues? —observó desconcertado Anastasio Montañez—¿Pos luego Pascual Orozco no es de nosotros?

—Es el primero que traicionó a Madero —pronunció Venancio—¡El primer Judas de la Revolución!

—Y en el acto mismo se tomaron providencias para emprender la marcha.

—Para Camila, la yegua mora con mi silla plateada—dijo Demetrio a Pancracio.

—Camila no puede ir, habló pronto "La Pintada."

—¿Quién te pide a tí tu parecer? —pronunció Demetrio con sequedad.

—¿Verdá, Camila, que amaneciste con mucha dolencia y te siente ahora acalenturada? ¿Verdá que no quieres salir ahora?

—Pos yo..... lo que diga don Demetrio....

—¡Ah qué tonta! Dí que no, dí que no..... le sopló al oído con mucha alarma "La Pintada."

—Pos es que ya le estoy cobrando voluntá...... ¿lo cree? —contestó Camila, también muy quedo.

"La Pintada" se puso negra y los carrilos se le soplaron. Pero no dijo más y se alegó a montar la yegua que estaba ensillando el giiero Margarito.

En tierras de Jalisco, Demetrio supo ya que los Orozquistas se habían desperdigado por Michoacán. No quedaba más que un núcleo reducido al que, según noticias de última hora, se reunía un Cura con un centenar de payos, bajo la apolillada bandera de "Religión y Fueros."

Demetrio se cercioró del derrotero que llevaban y logró darles alcance. Fué un juego divertido para sus soldados. Al primero que lograron atrapar, fue al cura y luego que los devotos lo vieron suspendido de un mezquite con la lengua de fuera y los ojos muy abiertos, se desperdigaron como codornices, y así los cazaron los soldados, dejando un reguero de muertos, que ostentaban en la camisa un escudo de balleta roja con un letrerito: "Detente: el Sagrado Corazón de Jesús está conmigo."

De allí regresaban los soldados en medio de una nube de polvo; los caballos, al galope, resoplando y con las narices abiertas. Los hombres blandían sus rifles o los atravesaban sobre la cabeza de las monturas.

Entre gritos y carcajadas se referían las peripecias del combate.

—Yo ya me pagué, hasta de más, mis sueldos atrazados—dijo "La Codorniz," mostrando los relojes y anillos de oro que había extraído de la casa cural.

—¡Así siquiera pelea uno con gusto! —exclamó "El Manteca," entreverando insolencias entre cada palabra. —Ya sabe uno por qué arriezga la pelleja....

Y cogía ufertemente con la misma mano que empuñaba las riendas, un reluciente resplandor que le había arrancado de la cabeza al "Divino Preso" de la iglesia.

Cuando "La Codorniz" muy perito en la materia, examinó codiciosamente la presa de "El Manteca" lanzó un estupenda carcajada.

—¡Tu resplandor es de hoja de lata!.......¡Ja! ja, ja!......

—¿Para qué vienes cargando con esa roña, giiero? —preguntó Pancracio a Margarito, que llegaba con un prisionero.

—¿Saben por qué?.... Porque nunca he visto la cara que pone un hombre cuando se le aprieta una reata en el pescuezo.

El prisionero, muy gordo, respiraba fatigado; su cara estaba encendida, sus ojos inyectados y su frente goteaba. Lo traían atado de las muñecas y a pie.

—Anastasio, préstame tu reata; mi cabestro se revienta con este gallo.... ero ahora que lo pienso, mejor no.... —Amigo federal, te voy a matar de una vez; vienes penando mucho.... Mira, los mezquites están muy lejos todavía, y aquí no hay siquiera telégrafo para ahorcarte de algún poste.

Y el giiero Margarito sacó su pistola, puso el cañón sobre la tetilla izquierda del prisionero y paulatinamente echó el gatillo atrás.

El hombre empalideció como muerto, su cara se afiló y sus ojos vidriosos se quebraron. Un extremecimiento sacuía todo su cuerpo.

Margarito, mirándolo con júbilo, sintiendo un placer muy raro, mantuvo la pistola sobre el pecho que palpitaba tumultuosamente.

Volvió el revólver a la funda, y con una sonrisa en los labios y la mirada brillante, dijo:

—No, amigo federal, no te quiero matar todavía .... Vas a seguir como mi asistente..... Ya verás si soy hombre de mal corazón.

Y guiñó malignamente los ojos a sus inmediatos. El prisionero parecía haber embrutecido; sólo hacía movimientos de deglutición: su boca y su garganta estaban secas.

Camila, que se había quedado atrás, picó el hijar de su yegua y alcanzó a Demetrio.

—¡Ah, qué malo es el hombre ése Margarito! ¡Si viera lo que viene haciendo con un preso!—Y refirió a Demetrio lo que acababa de ver.

Demetrio frució las cejas, pero nada contestó.

"La Pintada" llamó a Camila a distancia.

—Oye, tú.... ¿qué chismes le traes a Demetrio? El giiero Margarito es mi mero amor... ¡pa que te lo sepas! Y.... ya sabes que lo que haiga con él, hay con migo! Ya te lo aviso!

Y Camila, muy asustada, fué a reunirse con Demetrio.

IX.

La tropa acampó en una llanura cerca de tres casitas que se recortaban sobre la línea roja del horizonte. En la inmensidad de la planicie rapada de árboles, parecían un milagro tres grandes fresnos de cimas redondas y verdi-negras, que se inclinaban hasta besar la tierra, enfrente de cada casa.

Demetrio y Camila se dirigieron hacia ellas.

Dentro del corral platicaban tranquilamente unos hombres, sentados en las piedras. Se levantaron muy asustados.

—Quiero alojamiento para mí y para mi mujer—dijo Demetrio.

Y cuando el dueño mismo de la casa cogió una escoba y un apaste de agua para arreglarles el sitio en el mejor rincón de la troje, donde se guardaba el maíz, el frijol, los olotes, el arado, las picas y demás útiles de campo, Demetrio lo tranquilizó, asegurándole que bastaría con que él estuviera allí para que nadie se atreviera a tocarle nada de sus bienes.

Luego que Demetrio y Camila se instalaron, el amo gritó a su sirviente:

Epifano, date priesa, acaba de desgranar para que vayas a darles agua a las bestias.

El peón se puso trabajosamente en pie. Vestía unas garras de pantalón abiertas en dos alas, que se levantaban de la rodilla hasta la cintura; una de sus piernas, deforme, remataba en un pie como pezuña de caballo. Anduvo y su paso marcó un compás grotesco.

—¿Pero ese hombre puede trabajar?—preguntó Demetrio.

—¡Pobre! le falta la juerza.... pero si viera qué bien desquita el sueldo. Trabaja desde que Dios amanece.... Dende qué ha que se metió el sol y él sigue sin parar.

—Yo no sé qué siento por acá que me dá tanta tristeza. Vamos andando—dijo Demetrio a Camila, y a Anastasio Montañez que llegaba.

Y Camila, como un perro leal, lo siguió obediente, respondiendo sí a todo lo que él le decía.

A la orilla de un riachuelo tropezaron con el peón, que tiraba rudamente de la soga de un bambilete. Una olla enorme se volcaba sobre un montón de hierba fresca en un chorro cristalino sobre la pila. Allí bebían ruidosamente una vaca, un caballo matado y un burro.

—¿Cuánto ganas diario, amigo?

—Diez y seis centavos, Jefe.

Era el peón un hombrecillo rubio, escrofuloso, de pelo lacio y ojos azules deslavados. Comenzó a decir pestes del rancho, del patrón y de su suerte.

—Desquitas bien el sueldo, hijo—dijo Demetrio con mansedumbre.—A reniega y reniega; pero a trabaja a trabaja.

—¡Siempre hay otros más pencos que nosotros los de la sierra, compadre!

Demetrio durmió mal y muy temprano se echó fuera de la casa.

"A mí me va a suceder algo," pensó.

Era un amanecer silencioso y de discreta alegría. Un tordo piaba en el fresno, las vacas removían las basuras de rastrojo en el corral, gruñían los cerdos su somnolencia.

Asomó el tinte anaranjado del sol, y la última estrellita se apagó.

Demetrio caminó paso a paso al campamento. Pensó en su casa, en su yunta de bueyes, dos bueyes prietos de dos años apenas; en sus dos fanegas de labor bien abonadas,. La fisonomía de su joven esposa se reprodujo fielmente en su memoria: aquellas líneas de infinita mansedumbre y de gran dulzura para el esposo, de indomable altivez para el extraño. Pero cuando pretendió reconstruir la imagen de su hijo, sus esfuerzos fueron vanos. Lo había olvidado por completo.

Tendidos entre el surquerío de un barbecho, los soldados dormían con las manturas de cabecera, y entre ellos, los caballos echados, caída la cebaza y cerrados los ojos.

—Están muy estragadas las remudas, compadre Anastasio; es bueno que hoy nos quedemos a descansar aquí.

—¡Uf!... ¡tantas ganas que dan ya de la sierra! —respondió Anastasio.—Si viera, compadre, que yo no me jallo por acá... Una tristeza ¡que quién sabe qué me hace falta!

—Las planicies son aplanadoras. Aquí no dan ganas más que de dormir—dijo Luis Cervantes, removiéndose. Se envolvió muy bien en su frazada, y volvió a quedarse silencio.

—¿Qué tantas horas se hacen de aquí a "Limón"?

—No es cosa de horas, compadre Demetrio, son tres jornadas muy bien hechas.

—Ya tengo ganas de ver a mi mujer.

Poco más tarde "La Pintada" fué con Camila.

—¡Ujule! ¡újule! ¡sólo por eso que ya Demetrio te va a largar! A mí me lo dijo. Va a trair a su mujer de veras. Y es muy bonita, muy blanca y...... ¡unos chapetes!..... Pero si tú no te queres ir, puede que te ocupen, tienen una criaturita que tú podrías cargar.

Cuando Demetrio regresó, Camila, llorando, se lo dijo todo.

—No le hagas caso a esa loca..... Son mentiras lo que te contó.

Y como Demetrio no fué a "Limón" ni se volvio a acordar de su mujer, Camila estuvo muy contenta y "La Pintada" se volvió una víbora.

X.

—Hoy, a Tepatitlán, mañana a Cuquío... ¡Y a la sierra!

—¡No hay como la sierra!

—A la sierra!.....

Y todos hablaron de la sierra como de la deseada amante a quien se ha dejado de ver por mucho tiempo.

—Giiero Margarito—gritó de pronto "El Manteca"—ya tu asistente quiere pelar gallo. Dice que ya no puede andar. El prisionero federal, se había dejado caer en medio del camino, exhausto.

—¡Calle!—exclamó el giiero Margarito, retrocediendo.—¿Conque ya te cansaste, simpático? ¡Pobrecito de tí! Voy a comprar un nicho de cristal para guardarte en una rinconera como niño Dios. Pero es necesario llegar primero al pueblo, y para esto te voy a ayudar.

Y sacó el sable y descargó sobre él repetidos golpes secos.

—A ver la reata, Anastasio—dijo luego, con los ojos muy brillantes.

Pero como "La Codorniz" le hicera ver que ya el federal no movía ni pie ni mano, exclamó exaltado:

—¡Qué bruto soy!..... Yo que lo estaba enseñando a no comer.....

Y lanzó una carcajada.

Muy temprano llegaron a Tepatitlán. Las escuelas municipales quedaron convertidas en cuarteles. Demetrio se alojó en la sacristía de una capilla abandonada.

Cuando acabaron de dar de almorzar a sus animales, unos salieron a buscar monturas, caballos y armamento, mientras que los otros, aflojerados y tristones, se tiraban en los patios y en las banquetas.

Después del medio día, en el atrio de la iglesia donde Demetrio se alojaba, "El Manteca," "La Codorniz" y otros, tirados al sol, se rascaban el abdomen: Pancracio, pecho y espalda desnudos, expugaba su camisa.

Un hombre pobre se acercó a la barda, pidiendo la venia de hablarle al General.

Los soldados levantaron la cabeza, sin responderle.

FOLLETIN NUM. 19

—Soy hombre pobre, siñores, vivo de mi trabajo; soy viudo y tengo nueve criaturas de familia.... ¡No sean ingratos con los pobres!....

—Por mujer no te apures, tío. Ahí traimos a "La Pintada." Te la vamos a pasar al costo.....

El hombre se sonrió con una sonrisa amarga.

—No más que tiene una maña—observó Pancracio —apenas mira un hombre, y luego, luego, se prepara.

"La Codorniz," que con un cabo de vela de cebo se embadurnaba los dedos de los pies, indicó la puerta de la sacristía al paisano.

Dijo su negocio. Los soldados le habían sacado todo su maíz para darles de comer a sus caballos.

—¿Pa qué se dejan?—respondió Demetrio con indolencia.

—Y Camila dijo:

—Ande, don Demetrio, déle una orden pa que le devuelvan su maíz.....

—¡Dios se lo pague, niña! ¡Dios le dé su santa gloria! ¡Mi cosechita de este año!....Diez fanegas .....¡Apenas para comer!....—clamó el hombre, llorando de agradecimiento.

Luis Cervantes escribió unos renglones, y Demetrio puso al calce un garabato.

El hombre cogió el papel, besó las manos de Demetrio y de Camila, que sonreían muy complacidos.

Otro día, camino de Cuquío, Anastasio Montañez se acercó a Demetrio, y le dijo:

—¡Ande, compadre, ni le he contado! ¡....Qué terrible es, de veras, el giiero Margarito! ¿Sabe lo que hizo ayer con el hombre que vino a darle la queja de que le habíamos sacado su maíz para nuestros caballos? Bueno, pos con la orden que usté le dió fué al cuartel. "Sí amigo, le dijo el Giiero, entra para acá: es muy justo devolverte lo tuyo. Entra, entra...... ¿Cuántas fanegas te robamos? ¿Diez? ¡Pero estás seguro de que no son más que diez?.... Sí, eso es, como quince, poco más o menos. ¿No serían veinte?..... Acuérdate bien..... eres muy pobre, tienes muchos hijos que mantener. .....Sí, como veinte, esas deben de haber sido... Pasa por acá: no te voy a dar diez, ni quince, ni veinte..... Tú nomás vas contando, una, dos, tres ...... Y luego que ya no quieras, me dices, ya." Y saca el sable y le ha dado una cintareada que lo hizo pedir misericordia.

"La Pintada" se caía de risa.

Y Camila, sin poderse contener, dijo:

—¡Viejo condenao, tan mala entraña! ¡Con razón no lo puedo ver!....

Instantáneamente cambió el semblante de "La Pintada." Sus ojos parecían de vaca brava.

—¿Y a tí te dá tos por eso?....

Camila tuvo miedo y adelantó su yegua.

"La Pintada" disparó la suya, y rapidísima, al pasar atropellando a Camila, la cogió de la cabeza y le deshizo la trenza.

La yegua de Camila dió un salto al empellón, y la muchacha abandonó las riendas para quitarse los cabellos de la cara, vaciló, perdió el equilibrio y cayó en un pedregal, rompiéndose la fretne.

Desmorecida de risa, "La Pintada" con mucha habilidad galopó a detener la yegua desbocada.

—Andale, Curro, ya te cayó trabajo—dijo Pancracio luego que vió a Camila en la silla de Demetrio, con la cara llena de sangre.

Cuando Luis Cervantes se presentó con sus materiales de curación listos, Camila dejó de sollozar, se limpió los ojos, y dijo con gran desdén:

—Mejor que me cure el dotor... ¿De usté?.... aunque me estuviera muriendo... ni agua...

Se comenzaba ya a ver la sierra cerca, cuando Demetrio recibió un propio.

—Otra vez a Tepatitlán..... Ahí tiene que dejar la gente, mi General. Y usté a Lagos, a tomar el tren de Aguascalientes—dijo Luis Cervantes después de leer.

Demetrio hizo un gesto de extrañeza, y los soldados de desconsuelo.

—Nadie sabe el bien que tiene hasta que lo ve perdido—exclamó desolado Anastasio Montañez.

Y todos suspiraron con mucha tristeza por la sierra.

Pernoctaron en una hacienda.

Camila, que lloró toda la noche, le dijo a Demetrio, por la mañana, que le diera licencia de volverse a su casa.

—¡Si le falta la voluntá!—contestó Demetrio, hosco.

—¡No es eso, don Demetrio, voluntá se la tengo y mucha! ... yo la ha estado viendo... pero .... ¡esa mujer!

—No se apure: hoy mismo la despacho a...... Ya lo tengo bien pensado.

—Y Camila dejó de llorar.

Otro día, cuando todos estaban esillando ya, Demetrio se acercó a "La Pintada" y le dijo en voz baja:

—Tú ya no te vas con nosotros.

—¿Qué dices?—interrogó ella, sin comprender.

—Que te quedas aquí, o te largas a donde te dé la gana, pero no con nosotros.

—¿Qué me estás diciendo?—exclamó ella con un

gesto de asombro. —¿Es decir que tú me corres?..
....¡ja, ja, ja! Pues que.... tal serás tú, si te andas creyendo de los chismes de esa.....

Y "La Pintada insultó a Camila, a Luis Cervantes, a Demetrio y a todos los que le vinieron a las
mientes. Y la tropa oyó insolencias e injurias que
jamás había escuchado.

Demetrio la escuchó largo rato con paciencia; pero
como no llevara traza de callar, con mucha calma
le dijo a un soldado:

—Echa fuera a esa borracha.

—¡Giiero Margarito! ¡Giiero de mi vida! ven a
defenderme de estos.... ¡Anda, giierito de mi corazón!... Ven a enseñarles que no son más que
unos hijos de.....

Y gesticulaba, pateaba y daba de gritos.

El giiero Margarito apareció. Acababa de levan-
tarse; sus ojos azules se perdían tras de unos párpados hinchados, y su voz estaba ronca. Se informó
del sucedido, y acercándose a "La Pintada" le dijo con mucha gravedad:

—Sí, me parece muy bien que ya te largues mucho a la..... ¡A todos nos tienes hartos....!

El rostro de "La Pintada" se granitificó. Quiso
hablar, y sus músculos estaban rígidos.

Los soldados reían divertidísimos. Camila estaba asustada.

"La Pintada" paseó sus ojos en torno. Y todo
fué en un abrir y cerrar de ojos. Se inclinó, sacó una
hoja aguda y brillante de entre la pierna y la media y se lanzó sobre Camila.

Un grito estridente y un cuerpo que se desploma
arrojando sangre a borbotones.

Nadie se atrevió a detenerla. Se alejó muda y
pasa a paso.

Y el silencio de estupefacción lo rompió la voz
aguda y gutural del giiero Margarito:

—¡Ah, qué bueno! .... ¡hasta que se me despe-
gó esta chinche!

XII.

"En la medianía del cuerpo
una daga me metió.
sin saber por qué,
ni por qué sé yo:
él sí lo sabía,
...pero yo no....."
Y de aquella herida mortal
mucha sangre me salió,
sin saber por qué,

ni por qué sé yo:
él sí lo sabía,
...pero yo no....."

Caída la cabeza, las manos cruzadas sobre la
montura, Demetrio tarareaba con tonadilla melan-
cólica aquella cancioneta que a cada instante le
obscecionaba.

Luego se quedaba mucho rato silencio y pesaro-
so.

—Ya verá cómo llegando a Lagos, le quito esa
murria, mi General. Allí hay muchas muchachas bo-
nitas para darnos gusto—dijo el giiero Margarito.

—De lo que tengo ganas ahora nomás es de ponerme una buena borrachera—contestó Demetrio.

Luego se alejó de ellos, espoleando su caballo,
como si quisiera estar solo con su tristeza.

Después de horas y más horas de caminar, se detuvo a esperar a Luis Cervantes:

—Oiga, Curro, ahora que estoy pensando ¿yo
qué pitos voy a tocar a Aguascalientes?

—A dar su voto, mi General, para el Presidente
Provisional de la República.

—¿Presidente Provisional? Pos entonces ¿qué
......tales es Carranza? La verdá yo no entiendo
esas políticas.

—Llegaron a Lagos. El giiero apostó a que esa
noche haría reír a Demetrio a carcajadas.

Arrastrando las espuelas, las chivarras caídas
abajo de la cintura, entró Demetrio a "El Cosmopolita" con Luis Cervantes, el giiero Margarito y
sus asistentes.

FOLLETIN NUM. 20

—¿Por qué corren, curros?..... No sabemos comer gente—exclamó el giiero.

Los paisanos, sorprendidos en el momento mismo
en que intentaban escapar, se detuvieron: unos
con disimulo, regresaron a sus mesas a seguir char-
lando y bebiendo, y los otros, vacilantes, se adelan-
taron a ofrecer sus respetos a los huéspedes.

—Mi General..... mucho gusto!.... Señor Mayor....

—Así me gustan los amigos, finos y decentes—
dijo el giiero Margarito.

—Vamos, muchachos—agregó sacando su pistola jovialmente—ahí les va un busca-pies para que
lo toreen.

Una bala rebota en el cemento, pasa entre las patas de las mesas y las piernas de los señoritos, que saltan asustados como una dama a quien se le ha metido un ratón bajo la falda.

Pálidos sonríen para festejar debidamente al señor Mayor. Demetrio despliega apenas sus labios, mientras que el acompañamiento lanza carcajadas a pierna tendida.

—Giiero—observa "La Codorniz"—a ese que va saliendo, le prendió la avispa; mira cómo cojea.

El giiero, sin parar mientes, ni volver siquiera la cara hacia el herido, afirma con entusiasmo que a treinta pasos de distancia y al descubrir, le pega a un cartucho de tequila.

—A ver, amigo, párese—dice al mozo de la cantina.

Luego, de la mano, lo lleva a la cabecera del patio del hotel y le pone un cartucho de tequila sobre la cabeza.

El pobre diablo se resiste, corre espantado; pero el giiero prepara su pistola y apunta.

—A tu lugar.... ¡tal!, si no quieres que de veras te meta una calientita.

El giiero se vuelve a la pared opuesta, levanta la pistola y hace puntería. El cartucho se hace pedazos, bañando de tequila la cara del muchacho, como un papel.

—Ahora va de veras—clama el giiero Margarito corriendo por un nuevo cartucho que vuelve a colocar sobre la cabeza del mozo.

Torna a su sitio, dá una vuelta vertiginosa sobre los talones y dispara.

Sólo que ahora se ha llevado una oreja en vez del cartucho.

Y apretándose el estómago de tanto reír, dice al muchacho de la cantina:

—Toma, chico, esos billetes. ¡Es cualquier cosa! ¡Eso se quita con tantita árnica y aguardiente!

Después de beber mucho vino y cerveza, dice Demetrio:

—Pague, giiero.

—No traigo nada; pero no hay cuidado por eso.

—¿Qué tanto se te debe, amigo?—pregunta al cantinero.

—Ciento ochenta pesos, mi jefe.

Margarito salta el mostrador y en dos manotadas derriba frascos, botellas y cristales.

—Ai le pasas la cuenta a tu padre Villa ¿sabes?

Y salen dando estrepitosas carcajadas.

—Oiga, amigo, ¿dónde es el barrio de las muchachas?—pregunta el giiero, tambaleándose ya de borracho, a un sujeto pequeño, correctamente vestido, que está cerrando la puerta de una sastrería.

El hombre se baja de la banqueta, atentamente, para cederles el paso.

El giiero se detiene y lo mira con mucha curiosidad:

—Oiga, amigo, ¡qué chiquito y qué bonito es usted!..... ¿Cómo que no?..... ¿Entonces yo soy mentiroso?.... Bueno, así me gusta..... ¿Usted sabe bailar los enanos?... ¿Que no sabe?...... ¡Resabe! ¡Yo lo conicí a usted en un circo! ¡Le juro que sí sabe y muy ebién! Ahora lo verá....

El giiero saca su pistola y comienza a disparar hacia los pies del sastre, que muy gordo y muy pequeño, a cada tiro da un saltito.

—¡Ya vé cómo sí sabe bailar los enanos?

Y echando los brazos a espaldas de sus amigos, se hace conducir hacia el arrabal de gente alegre, marcando su paso a balas en los focos de las esquinas, en las puertas y en las paredes del poblado.

Demetrio lo deja y regresa al hotel tarareando entre los dientes:

En la medianía del cuerpo
una daga me metió
sin saber por qué,
ni por qué sé yo......

XIII.

Humo de cigarro, olor de ropas sudadas, emanaciones alcohólicas y el respirar de una multitud, en hacinamiento mayor que el de un carro de carneros.

Predominan los de sombrero tejano, toquilla de galón y vestido de kaki.

"Caballeros: un señor decente me ha robado mi petaca en la estación de Silao. Los ahorros de toda mi vida de trabajo.... No tengo para darle de comer a mi hijo...."

La voz era aguda, chillona y plañidera; pero se extinguía a corta distancia, en el vocerío que llenaba el carro.

—¿Qué dice esa vieja?—preguntó el giiero Margarito, entrando en busca de un asiento.

—Que una petaca... que un niño decente....—respondió Pancracio, que ya había encontrado las rodillas de dos paisanos para sentarse.

Demetrio y los demás se abrían paso a fuerza de

codos. Y como los que soportaban a Pancracio pre-firieran dejar los asientos y seguir de pie, Deme-trio y Luis Cervantes los tomaron muy gustosos.

Una señora que venía parada, con un niño en las brazos, sufrió un desmayo. Un paisano se aprontó a tomar en sus manos a la criatura y dijo que la señora así venía desde Irapuato. Pero nadie se dió por entendido: las hembras de tropa ocupaban dos o tres asientos cada una, con sus maletas, perros, gatos y hasta pericos. Al contrario, los de sombre-ro texano rieron muchos de la robustez de muslos y laxitud de pechos de la desmayada.

—"Caballeros: un señor decente me ha robado mi petaca en la estación de Silao.... Los ahorros de toda mi vida de trabajo.... No tengo ni para larle de comer a mi niño...."

Habla de prisa, y automáticamente suspira y so-lloza. Sus ojos muy vivos, se vuelven de todos la-dos. Y aquí recoge un billete y más allá otro. Le llueven en abundancia.

Acaba una colecta y adelanta unos cuantos asientos:

—"Caballeros: un señor decente me ha robado mi petaca....."

El efecto de sus palabras es seguro e inmediato. ¡Un señor decente!.... ¡Un señor decente que se roba una petaca! ¡Eso es incalificable! ¡Eso des-pierta un movimiento de indignación general. ¡Oh: es lástima que ese señor decente no esté por ahí para fusilarlo cada cinco minutos siquiera!

...Porque a mí no hay cosa que me dé tanto co-raje como un curro ratero—dice uno.

—¡Robar a una pobre señora!

—¡Robar a una infeliz mujer que no puede de-fenderse!

Y todos manifiestan sus sentimientos, de pala-bra y obra: una insolencia para el ladrón y un bi-llete de cinco pesos para la víctima.

—Yo la verdad les digo, no creo que sea malo matar; pero eso de robar?....—exclama el giiero Margarito.

Todos convienen en que ciertamente es más ma-lo robar que matar, "porque cuando uno mata,—dice el giiero Margarito—lo hace siempre con cora-je."

Después de breve silencio y un momento de re-flecxión, un capitán se atreve y aventura su pare-cer:

—La verdá es que todo tiene sus asegunes. Para qué es más que la verdá. La puritita verdá es que

yo he robao...... y si digo que todos los que ve-nemos aquí hemos hecho lo mesmo se me figura que no echo mentiras.....

—¡Hum! ¡pa las máquinas de coser que yo me robé en México!—exclamó con ánimo un subte-niente.—Junté más de quientos pesos, y vaya que vendí a peso y cincuenta centavos máquina.

—Yo en Zacatecas me robé unos caballos tan fi-nos, que si no me los hubiera robao mi general Li-ma, era hora que no andaba yo por acá y ya no me apuraría pa comer los días que me quedan de vida —dijo un Mayor, desmolado y blanco de canas.

—¡Bueno! ¡Pa qué negarlo pues? Yo también he robao,—afirmó el giiero Margarito—pero ahí están todos mis compañeros que digan cuánto tengo de capital. Mi gusto es gastarlo todo con los amigos. Para mí es de más contento ponerme una papalina con todos mis amigos, que mandarles un centavo a las viejas de mi casa!

El tema de "Yo robé" se agota cuando en cada banca van apareciendo tendidos de naipes que atraen a los oficiales como la luz a los mosquitos.

Las peripecias del juego caldean más y más el

FOLLETIN NUM. 21

---

ambiente, que de todo tiene: de cuartel, de cárcel, de lupanar y hasta de zahurda.

Y dominando el barullo general se escucha, allá en el otro carro:

"Caballeros: un señor decente me ha robado mi petaca...."

XIV.

Las calles de Aguascalientes se habían vuelto basureros. Los de vestido de kaki se removían co-mo las moscas a la puerta de un panal, en las puer-tas de restaurants, fonduchos, mesas de comistra-jos y puestos de panelas, quesos, mantequillas, to-do negro de mugre y de tierra.

El olor de las fritangas abrió el apetito de Deme-trio y sus acompañantes. A empellones se abrieron paso a una fonda de última clase. Una vieja des-greñada y asquerosa les sirvió un plato burdo de caldo de chile, con un hueso de puerco y tres tor-tillas correosas y quemadas. Pagaron dos pesos por cabeza, y al salir, aseguró Pancracio que tenía más hambre que antes de haber entrado.

—Pues ahora sí—dijo Demetrio—vamos a tomar consejo de mi General Natera.

Y siguieron una calle en dirección al domicilio del jefe norteño. Un grupo de soldados en torno de un hombre de camisa y calzón blanco, les detuvo. Con un puñado de impresos en las manos, el hombre clamaba con acento uncioso y tonada de rezandero:

"Todos los buenos católicos que rezen con devoción esta oración a Cristo Crucificado, se verán libres de tempestades, de pestes, de guerras, de hambres....."

Demetrio se sonrió.

El vendedor, por un instante, desapareció entre la multitud; se había inclinado a levantar de su puesto un colmillo de víbora, una estrella de mar. esqueletos de pescados. Y con el mismo acento proclamaba ahora las propiedades medicinales y virtudes de cada cosa.

"La Codorniz," que no le tenía fe a Venancio, pidió al vendedor que le extrajera una muela; el giiero Margarito compró un núcleo negro de cierta fruta, que tiene la propiedad de librarlo a uno lo mismo del rayo que de cualquier malhora; y Anastasio Montañez una oración a Cristo Crucificado, que cuidadosamente dobló y con gran piedad guardó en el seno.

—¡Cierto como hay Dios, compañero; sigue la bola! ¡Ahora Villa contra Carranza!—dijo Natera.

Y Demetrio, sin responderle, con los ojos muy abiertos, le pedía más explicaciones.

—Es decir,—prosiguió Natera—que "La Convención desconoce a Carranza como Primer Jefe de la Revolución y va a nombrar uno nuevo...... ¿Entiende, compañero?

Demetrio inclinó la cabeza en señal de asentimiento.

—¿Qué dice de eso, compañero?—interrogó Natera.

Demetrio alzó los hombros.

—Se trata, a lo que parece, de seguir peleando—habló Macías.—Bueno, pos a darle, ya sabe, mi General, que por mi lado, no hay portillo.

—Bueno, ¿y de parte de quién se va a poner?

Demetrio, muy perplejo, se llevó las manos a los cabellos, y se rascó breves instantes:

—Mire, a mí no me haga preguntas, que no soy escuelante. La aguilita que traigo en el sombrero

usté me la dió..... Bueno, pos ya sabe que nomás me dice: —"Demetrio, haces esto y esto y esto..... y se acabó el cuento".....

FIN DE LA SEGUNDA PARTE

TERCERA PARTE

I

"El Paso, Tex., Mayo 16 de 1915
"¡Muy estimado Venancio:

"Hasta ahora puedo contestar su grata del cuatro de enero del corriente año, debido a que mis atenciones profesionales absorben todo mi tiempo. Me recibí en Diciembre pasado, y ejerzo mi profesión en esta ciudad, como usted lo sabe. Lamento la suerte de Pancracio y de "El Manteca." Pero no me extraña que después de una partida de juego, se hayan apuñaleado. ¡Lástima.... eran unos valientes!"

"Me parece difícil, amigo Venancio, que pueda usted obtener el título que ambiciona aquí en los Estados Unidos, por más que haya reunido suficiente oro y plata para comprarlo. Yo le tengo estimación, Venancio, y creo que es muy digno de mejor suerte. Ahora bien, me ocurre una idea que podría favorecer nuestros mutuos intereses y las ambiciones justas que usted tiene por cambiar de posición social. Si usted y yo nos asociáramos, podríamos hacer un negocio muy bonito. Cierto que por el momento yo no tengo fondos de reserva, porque todo lo he agotado en mis estudios y en mi recepción, pero cuento con algo que vale mucho más que el dinero; mi conocimiento perfecto de esta plaza, de sus necesidades y de los negocios seguros que pueden emprenderse. Podríamos establecer un restaurant netamente mexicano, apareciendo usted como el propietario y repartiéndonos las utilidades a fin de cada mes. Además, algo relativo a lo que tanto le interesa: su cambio de esfera social. Yo me acuerdo que usted toca bastante bien la guitarra, y creo fácil, por medio de mis recomendaciones y de los conocimientos musicales de usted, conseguirle el ser admitido como miembro del "Ejército de Salvación," sociedad respetabilísima, que le daría a usted mucho carácter."

"No vacile, querido Venancio, véngase con los

fondos y podremos hacernos ricos en muy poco tiempo.

"Sírvase dar mis recuerdos afectuosos al General, a Anastasio y a todos los amigos!"

"Su amigo que lo estima:

Luis Cervantes."

Venancio acabó de leer su carta y muy triste se puso a meditar.

—Este Curro de veras que la supo hacer—dijo Anastasio Montañez.—Porque lo que yo no puedo hacerme entrar en la cabeza es, por qué tales peleamos ya?........ ¿Pos no acabamos ya con la Federación?

Asomó Juchipila a lo lejos, blanca y bañada de sol, en medio del frondaje verde, al pie de un cerro elevado y altivo, plegado como albornoz.

Juchipila, cuna de la Revolución de 1910. Juchipila regada con la sangre de los primeros revolucionarios. aL huella queda en todos sus contornos y cercanías: cruces negras recién barnizadas, cruces formados con rústicos leños atravesados, cruces de piedra en montón, cruces pintadas con la cal en los adobes de casucas arruinadas, y hasta humildísimas cruces marcadas con un carbón sobre el canto de las peñas... Cruces regadas por caminos y veredas, en las encrespaduras de las rocas, en los vericuetos de los arroyos, en las márgenes del río.....

Soldados mancos, cojos y reumáticos, ven las torrecillas de Juchipila, suspiran y comienzan a decir mal de sus jefes. Advenedizos de banqueta, causan alta, con barras de latón en el sombrero, antes de conocer un fusil; mientras que el veterano fogueado en cien combates, inútil ya para el trabajo, el veterano que entró soldado razo, soldado razo sigue todavía.......

Y sotto voce los oficiales dicen pestes del General Macías, que está cubriendo las bajas de su Estado Mayor con puros señoritos perfumados y presuntuosos.

Y peor todavía: ¡oficialillos que pertenecieron al ejército federal!

Y el mismo Anastasio Montañez, que de ordinario encuentra muy bien hecho todo lo que su compadre Demetrio hace, ahora dice:

—Miren, compañeros, yo soy muy claridoso.... y yo le digo a mi compadre que si vamos a tener aquí a los federales, malamente andamos, ¡de veras! ¿a que no me lo creen?..... Pero yo no tengo pelos en la lengua, y por vida de mi madre que se lo digo a Demetrio.

Y se lo dijo.

Demetrio lo escuchó con mucha benevolencia, y luego que acabó de hablar le contestó:

Compadre, es cierto lo que usté dice. Malmente andamos; los soldados hablan de las clases y las clases de los oficiales y los oficiales de nosotros y nosotros, estamos ya por despachar a Villa y a Zapata y a Carranza a la..... a que se diviertan ellos solos..... Pero se me afigura que nos está

FOLLETIN NUM. 22

sucediendo lo que a aquel peón que conocimos en Tepatitlán. ¿Se acuerda? No paraba de hablar de su patrón, pero no paraba de trabajar tampoco. Y así estamos nosotros: a reniega y reniega y a mátenos y mátenos...... Pero eso no hay que dicirlo, compadre, porque.... pos porque nó, ¿me entiende? Lo que ha de hacer es dármele ánimo a la gente. Dentro de muy poquitos días tenemos que darnos un encontronazo con los carranclanes y necesitamos pegarles hasta por debajo de la lengua.

Entraban ya a las calles de Juchipila y les llamó mucho la atención un ruidoso repique en la iglesita.

—Se me afigura, compadre, que estamos allá cuando apenas iba comenzando la revolución, cuando llegábamos a un pueblito y nos repicaban mucho, y salía la música a encontrarnos, y la gente con banderas, y nos echaban muchos cohetes y vivas.......

—Ahora ya no nos quieren—repuso Demetrio.

—¡Cómo nos han de querer, compadre?.......

Desembocaron en una plazoleta, en frente de la iglesia de torre octagonal, burda y maciza, reminiscencia del régimen colonial.

La plaza debía haber sido jardín, a juzgar por unos naranjos escuetos y rofiosos, entreverados entre restos de bancas desquebrajadas.

El repique volvió a escucharse sonoro y alegre; luego, dentro de la iglesia un coro de robustas voces femeniles. Los misterios cantados por las doncellas del pueblo, con acopañamiento de guitarra y tonada de canción.

—¿Qué fiesta tienen, señora?—preguntó Demetrio a una vieja que pasaba a toda prisa hacia la iglesia.

—La del Sagrado Corazón de Jesús.

Y Demetrio se acordó de que hacía un año ya de la toma de Zacatecas, y suspiró.

Como todos los pueblos que vienen recorriendo desde Tepic, Jalisco, Aguascalientes y Zacatecas, Juchipila es una ruina. La huella negra de los incendios en las casas destechadas, en los pretiles ardidos. Casas cerradas y casi todas las tiendas lo mismo. Una que otra permanece con sus puertas entreabiertas y es para mostrar sus armazones vacías y desnudas, que recuerdan los blancos esqueletos de los caballos diseminados por todos los caminos. La mueca pavorosa del hambre está ya en las caras pálidas y terrosas de la gente, en la llama luminosa de los ojos que cuando se detienen sobre un soldado, queman con el fuego de una maldición.

Y los soldados que recorren en vano las calles en busca de comida, se muerden la lengua, ardiendo de ira. Un sólo fonducho está abierto, y en seguida se apretó de gente. No hay frijoles, no hay tortillas, puro chile picado y sal. En vano los jefes gritan amenazadores y muestran sus bolsillos reventando de billets.

—Papeles, sí....eso es todo lo que train...... ¡pos eso coman!.....—dice la fondera, una viejota con una cicatriz enorme en la cara, quien cuenta que "ya durmió en el petate del muerto" para no morirse de un susto.

Y en la tristeza y desolación del pueblo, los pajarillos no cesan de piar en las arboledas, ni el canto de las carrucas deja de oírse en las ramas secas de los naranjos.

II.

La mujer de Demetrio Macías salió, loca de alegría, a encontrarlo por la vereda de la sierra, llevando de la mano al niño.

Casi dos años de ausencia.

Se abrazaron y permanecieron mudos, ella embargada por los sollozos y las lágrimas.

Demetrio, pasmado, veía a su mujer envejecida, como si diez o veinte años hubieran pasado ya. Luego miró al niño que clavaba en su padre los ojos con azoro. Y su corazón dió un vuelco, cuando reparó en sus mismos ojos flamantes y las mismas líneas de acero de su rostro. Y quiso atraerlo y abrazarlo; pero el chico muy asustado, se refugió en el regazo de su madre.

—¡Es tu padre, hijo!.... ¡es tu padre!.....

El muchacho metió la cabeza entre los pliegues de la falda, y se mantuvo huraño.

Demetrio, que había dado su caballo al asistente, caminaba a pie y poco a poco, con su mujer y su hijo por la estrecha vereda de la sierra.

—¡Hora sí, bendito sea Dios que ya veniste! ¡Ya nunca nos dejarás! ¿verdá? ¿Verdá que ya te vas a quedar con nosotros?

La faz de Demetrio se ensombreció.

Y los dos estuvieron silenciosos, angustiados.

Una nube negra se levantaba tras de la sierra, y se oyó un trueno sordo.

Demetrio ahogó un suspiro. Los recuerdos afluían a su memoria como una colmena de abejas.

La lluvia comenzó en gruesas gotas, y tuvieron que refugiarse en una covacha rocallosa.

El aguacero se desató estruendoso y sacudió las blancas flores de San Juan, que parecían manojos de estrellas prendidos en los árboles, en las peñas, entre la maleza, en los pitayos y en toda la serranía.

Abajo, en el fondo del cañón y a través de la gasa de la lluvia, se miran las palmas rectas y cimbradoras. Lentamente se mecen sus cabezas angulosas, y al soplo del viento se despliegan las hojas como abanico. Y todo es serranía: ondulaciones de cerros que suceden a cerros, más cerros circundados de montañas y éstas encerradas en una muralla de sierra de cumbres tan altas, que su azul se pierde en el zafir.

—¡Demetrio, por Dios! .... ¡Ya no te vayas!.... ¡El corazón me avisa que te va a suceder algo!....

Y se deja sacudir por los sollozos otra vez.

El niño, asustado, llora a gritos y ella tiene que refrenar su pena para contentarlo.

La lluvia va cesando; una golondrina de plateado vientre y alas angulosas, cruza oblícuamente los hilos de cristal, repentinamente iluminados por el sol vespertino.

—¿Por qué pelean todavía, Demetrio?....

Demetrio, las cejas muy juntas, toma una piedrecilla y la arroja con fuerza por el desfiladero hacia el fondo del cañón:

—Mira esa piedra, cómo ya no se para.

III.

Fué una verdadera mañana de nupcias. Había llovido la víspera toda la noche y el cielo amanecía entoldado en blancas nubes. Por la cima de la sierra, trotaban potrillos brutos de crines alzadas y tensas colas, gallardos con la gallardía de los picachos que levantan su cabeza hasta besar las nubes.

Los soldados caminan por el abrupto peñascal contagiados de la alegría de la mañana. Nadie piensa en la artera bala que puede estarlo esperando más adelante. La más grande alegría de la partida estriba cabalmente en lo imprevisto. Y por eso los soldados cantan y ríen y charlan locamente. En su alma rebulle el alma de las viejas tribus nómadas. Nada importa saber a dónde van ni de dónde vienen. Lo necesario es caminar, caminar siempre, no estacionarse jamás, ser dueños del valle, de las planicies, de la sierra y de todo lo que la vista abarca.

Arboles, cactus y helechos, todo parece acabado de lavar. Las rocas, que llevan su ocre como el orín las viejas armaduras, vierten gruesas gotas de agua trasparente.

Los hombres de Macías hacen silencio un momento; parece que han escuchado un ruido conocido; el estallar lejano de un cohete, pero pasan minutos y nada se vuelve a oír.

—En esta misma sierra—dice Demetrio—yo, solo con veinte hombres, les hice más de quinientas bajas a los federales.... ¿Se acuerda, compadre Anastasio?

Y cuando Demetrio comienza a referir aquel famoso hecho de armas, la gente se dá cuenta del gran peligro que va corriendo. ¿Conque si el enemigo, en vez de estar a dos días todavía de camino, les fuera resultando escondido en las malezas de aquel formidable barranco, por cuyo fondo se han aventurado? ¿Pero, quién sería capaz de revelar su miedo? Cuando los hombres de Demetrio Macías dijeron: "por aquí no caminamos."

Y cuando comienza un tiroteo lejano, donde va la vanguardia, ni siquiera se sorprenden ya. Los reclutas vuelven grupas en carrera desenfrenada hacia la salida del cañón.

Una maldición se escapa de la garganta ronca de Demetrio.....

—Fuego.... Fuego sobre los que corren.....

—A quitarles las alturas—ruge después como una fiera.

Pero el enemigo, escondido a millaradas entre la maleza, desgrana sus ametralladoras y los hombres de Demetrio caen como las espigas tronchadas por la hoz.

Demetrio derrrma lágrimas de rabia y de dolor cuando Anastasio resbala lentamente de su caballo, sin exhalar una queja, y se queda tendido inmóvil.

FOLLETIN NUM. 23

móvil. Venancio cae a su lado, con el pecho horriblemente abierto por la ametralladora, y "El Meco" se desbarranca y rueda hasta el fondo del abismo. Demetrio se encuentra sólo derrepente. Las balas zumban en sus oídos como una granizada. Desmonta, arrástrase por las rocas hasta encontrar un parapeto, coloca una piedra que le defienda la cabeza, y pecho a tierra, comienza a disparar.

El enemigo se disemina, persiguiendo a los raros fugitivos que quedan ocultos entre los chaparros.

Demetrio apunta y no hierra un solo tiro..... ¡Paf!.... ¡Paf! ... ¡Paf!...

Su puntería famosa lo llena de regocijo; donde pone el ojo, pone la bala. Se acaba un cargador y mete otro nuevo. Y apunta....... ....
....

El humo de la fusilería no acaba de extinguirse. Las cigarras entonan su canto imperturbable y misterioso; las palomas cantan con dulzura en las rinconadas de las rocas; ramonean apasiblemente las vacas.

La sierra está de gala; sobre sus cúspides inaccesibles cae la niebla albísima como un crespón de nieve sobre la cabeza de una novia.

Y al pie de una resquebrajadura enorme y suntuosa, como pórtico de vieja catedral, Demetrio Macías, con los ojos fijos para siempre, sigue apuntando con el cañón de su fusil .....

FIN

CHAPTER 4

The Underdogs

My rendition of *Los de abajo* into English has as its basis the texts that Fernando Gamiochipi published for Mariano Azuela in El Paso late in 1915. Two translations into English have preceded it. The first was prepared by Enrique Munguía, Jr., with the title *The Underdogs* (New York: Brentano's, 1929; 225 pp.). It has long been unavailable. It has been reprinted, however, by the New American Library as a Signet Classic (New York, 1963; xi, 149 pp.), although this edition is likewise no longer in print. Frances Kellam Hendricks and Beatrice Berler have since made another translation, which appeared in their *Two Novels of the Mexican Revolution: The Trials of a Respectable Family and The Underdogs* (San Antonio, Texas: Principia Press of Trinity University, 1963, pp. 163–261). Both earlier translations are based upon the text of *Los de abajo* as it was generally known after the Razaster edition of 1920.

Los de abajo has never been an easy novel to translate. Azuela's Spanish is colloquial, even when it comes from the mouths of relatively sophisticated characters, but more often he is writing about soldiers, farmers, townspeople, and other figures from the less learned realms of Mexican society. Their speech is not that of the social, intellectual, or political elite, and consequently it presents definite problems for the translator. There are, in addition to popu-

lar terms and construction, others that were peculiarly of the revolutionary period or earlier. Two specific examples may be cited here. One is *pelón,* a strongly pejorative term applied to the hated federal soldier of the Díaz period, who wore his head shaved as a sanitary measure. Another is *mocho,* a similarly opprobrious name for the government soldier, although in the mid-nineteenth century and even earlier it designated political conservatives and reactionaries. These forms have no true equivalent when taken outside the framework of the political and ideological climate contemporary to *Los de abajo.* Azuela's language admirably reflects the spirit and atmosphere of the Mexican revolutionary scene, yet his use of popular vocabulary and grammatical construction presents a formidable challenge to the translator.

A standard feature of Mexican speech is the use of nicknames in informal social situations. Azuela supplies most of his characters with at least a Christian name, Camila, Venancio, Pancracio, Agapita, and María Antonia. Demetrio's wife alone is left without any kind of designation. Others have a Christian and a family name: Anastasio Montañez, Demetrio Macías, and Alberto Solís. None of these people acquires a nickname during the course of the novel, but others do. Luis Cervantes, whose urban origin is unchallenged, is usually addressed as Curro or referred to as *el curro* 'dude'

169

or 'tenderfoot.' Margarito Aranda for nearly all his comrades is El Güero Margarito or simply *el güero*. In Mexican Spanish *güero* is the usual designation for a blond person, so an equivalent in English would be 'Blondie.' His Christian name is unusual, certainly to non-Mexican speakers of Spanish, in that it is derived from a name that is applied to women exclusively, but here it is inflected in *-o* so that it may refer to a man.

Five of Azuela's people are known to the reader only by their nicknames. These labels usually are determined by some real or fancied attribute of the possessor or are based upon some incident in which he has been involved. Only in one case does Azuela explain the reason behind the nickname. The character involved here is La Pintada, the camp follower who is addicted to gaudy, showy clothing and uses lipstick, rouge, face powder, and other cosmetics in profusion. Thus Azuela identifies her as La Pintada 'the painted woman.'

The remaining characters are relatively minor, all of them soldiers under Demetrio's command, and Azuela does not bother to identify them except by nicknames: Codorniz 'quail', Meco 'lout' or 'roughneck,' Manteca 'lard,' and El Tecolote 'owl.'

In handling these forms in the translation I have preferred to leave them as Azuela first named them. The men and women thus preserve their Mexican identity, and it is preferable not to translate their names into English and perhaps place them, linguistically at least, in an alien environment. For those readers who demand English equivalents for these Mexican nicknames, these introductory comments to the translation should suffice.

INSTALLMENT NO. 1

FROM

"EL PASO DEL NORTE"

Mariano Azuela

THE UNDERDOGS

*VIEWS AND SCENES
FROM THE
PRESENT REVOLUTION*

FIRST PART

I.

"I tell you it's no animal. Just listen how Palomo is barking. It must be a person."

The woman peered into the blackness of the sierra.

"And what if they turned out to be soldiers?" replied a man who was squatting in a corner eating, holding a clay pot in his right hand and three tortillas rolled up in the other.

The woman did not answer. Her thoughts were on what was happening outside the shack.

Then came the clatter of hooves on the stone of the outcropping down the road and Palomo barked more furiously than ever.

"You'd better hide, Demetrio, just in case."

The man finished eating without showing any signs of being concerned. He picked up a jug and drank from it noisily. Then he stood up.

"Your rifle is under the cradle," she whispered to him.

A single oil wick dimly lit the tiny room. A yoke, a plow, a goad, and other farm implements were piled up in a corner. A rope suspended from the ceiling held up a well-worn mould for making adobes, and on this improvised cradle in a pile of blankets and faded rags a child was sleeping.

Demetrio strapped a cartridge belt around his middle and picked up his gun. He was tall, well built, of ruddy complexion, with only a few stray hairs on his face. He was wearing a shirt and trousers of white cotton, a broad-brimmed hat of palm fiber, and coarse sandals.

He went out deliberately, disappearing into the impenetrable gloom of the night.

Palomo, furious now, had jumped over the wall of the corral.

Suddenly a shot rang out. The dog gave out a howl and then barked no more.

Several men arrived amid curses and shouts. Two of them got down from their horses and a third remained behind to care for the animals.

"Women! ... Let's have something to eat! Eggs, milk, beans, whatever you've got! We're about starved."

"Damned sierra! Only the devil himself wouldn't get lost here!"

"He'd get lost too, sergeant, if he were as drunk as we are."

One of them wore braid on his shoulders; the other had red stripes on his sleeve.

"Say, woman, what's the name of this place? Do you mean to tell me there's no one in this house? Then what about that light and that kid? Hurry up, we want something to eat and be quick about it. Are you coming out? Or do we have to make you come out?"

The woman appeared, dragging the dog, who had turned very white and was swollen now, his eyes bright and his body limp.

"Just look at those cheeks, sergeant. Don't get upset, my love, I'm going to turn you house into a love nest and I'll even get down on my hands and knees to do things for you. But by God ...

> Don't look at me with angry air
> If you are only vexed with me.
> Show love instead when I am near,
> For you're the apple of my eye."

The officer sang with a tipsy voice.

"Lady, what's the name of this place?" the sergeant asked.

The woman, who was fanning the coals on the cooking hearth and adding more firewood, answered hoarsely but with no fear in her voice, "Limón."

"So this is Limón? The home country of the famous Demetrio Macías. Do you hear, lieutenant? We are at Limón."

"Limón? Good! I don't care where we are. Sergeant, if I have to go to hell, I want to go there on a good horse. But you've never seen pink cheeks like these. Why, they look like a rosy apple that's ripe, good enough to bite."

"You must know the bandit then. I met him years ago. We used to be in the penitentiary together."

"Sergeant, bring me a bottle of tequila. I've decided to spend the night here with this cute little brunette. ... The colonel? He can go to hell! And if the colonel gets sore, I don't care. Say, girlie, let the sergeant fry the eggs and heat the tortillas. You come over here with me. Look, this pocketbook stuffed with bills is just for you. That's the way I want it. I've had a little something to drink, and my voice is a little husky. In Guadalajara I left half my gullet, and along the way I've been spitting out the rest of it. Well, who cares? Sergeant, my bottle of tequila! Girlie, you're too far away. Come up closer and have a drink. What's the matter? Are you afraid of your husband ... or whatever he is? If you're keeping him hidden in some nook or cranny like a rat, tell him to come out. I don't care. He won't make any difference to us."

A luminous shadow filled the dark opening of the doorway.

"Demetrio Macías!" the terrified sergeant shouted as he staggered back.

The lieutenant stood up and could not speak, frozen like a statue.

"Kill them, Demetrio!" the woman cried out, her throat dry with emotion.

Demetrio stood looking at them, with a devil-may-care, scornful smile.

"Not only do I respect them. I really admire them with affection. Here, take the hand of a real friend. That's all right, Demetrio Macías, if you snub me. It's because you don't know me, because I have this miserable job. What else would you expect, my friend? I'm poor, I've a family to support. Sergeant, let's get out of here. I always respect the home of a brave fellow, a real man."

As soon as they had left, the woman squeezed Demetrio tightly.

"Holy Mother of Talpa! What a scare! I thought you were the one they had shot!"

"You'd better go to my father's house just as soon as you can," Demetrio told her.

She was about ready to cry and tried to dissuade him, pleading, but he pushed her away gently, adding ominously, "I have a hunch the whole gang's going to come back."

"Why didn't you kill them?"

Demetrio shrugged his shoulders and answered philosophically, "I guess their turn hadn't come yet."

They left together, with her carrying the child in her arms, but just outside the door of the house they turned in different directions.

The moon's rays clothed the mountainside with confused shadows. And on every crag and every tree, wherever Demetrio looked, he could see the disconsolate figure of a woman carrying a child in her arms. Finally, after hours of climbing up the wall of the gorge, he looked back into the depths of the canyon. Near the river, columns of flame were rising. His house was burning.

II.

The day broke when Demetrio began to descend to the bottom of the gorge again. The narrow ledge along the edge of the cliff served as a path, between the rocky mountainside streaked with enormous clefts and the sheer slope hundreds of feet down, as if it had been sliced by a single stroke.

Supporting himself against clumps of bushes, he pulled on the horn that was hanging from his shoulder. He put it to his lips and blew three times, puffing up his cheeks. Three long whistles came as an answer from beyond the neighboring summit. Then with quick, nimble movements he continued his descent.

"Surely," he thought, "the government soldiers will pick up our trail now, and they will come after us as if we were a pack of dogs. At least they don't know the trails or how to get in and out. They could only if someone from Moyahua came along as a guide, because the people from Limón and Santa Rosa and all the other places around here would never turn us in. The political boss in Moyahua is the one who is hounding me through these mountains, and he's the one who would really like to see me strung up to a telegraph pole with my tongue hanging out."

He reached the bottom of the gorge while it was still cast in shadow. He crawled between some large rocks, stretched out, and went to sleep.

The river rushed along in tiny musical cascades. Birds hidden in the pitahaya trees chirped away, and with their monotonous rhythms the cicadas filled the shadowy solitude of the mountain scene.

Demetrio woke up with a start. Then he forded the river and started up the opposite wall of the canyon. Like a laborious ant

Installment no. 2

he climbed up the ridge, his hands clutching the rocks and branches that clung to the slopes,

the soles of his feet grasping the stones of the trail.

When he finally reached the top, sunlight bathed the high flatland, turning it into a lake of gold. The rim of the gorge was lined with enormous crags that seemed to have been sliced off, thrust up like fantastic African heads. The pitahaya trees were like the gnarled fingers of some colossus, reaching toward the bottom of the chasm. And against the dryness of the crags and the thirsty branches, the white of the Saint John's roses shone out like an offering to the heavenly orb whose golden threads were beginning to unfold, skipping from one crag to another.

Demetrio halted when he reached the top and blew three times on his horn. Another signal answered. Off in the distance from out of a heap of rotten straw came men, many men, one after another, with naked shanks and chests, polished like ancient bronze pieces.

They came to meet Demetrio.

"They burned my house down," he replied to the questioning stares.

There were curses, threats, coarse insults.

Demetrio let them vent their anger, then took a bottle from underneath his shirt and drank from it. He wiped it off with the back of his hand and passed it on to the man next to him. The bottle made its way from one mouth to another, and soon it was empty. The men smacked their lips.

"If God wills it," Demetrio explained to them, "tomorrow or maybe even tonight we'll get to see again what those government soldiers look like. What do you think? Shall we let them figure out our paths and trails?"

The half-naked men jumped around in glee, shouting with joy. And then the stream of insults, curses, and threats started over again.

"We don't know how many of them there will be," Demetrio remarked, looking carefully into their faces.

Julián Medina in Hostotipaquillo with a half a dozen nobodies with knives whetted on the metate in the kitchen stood up against all the cops and soldiers in the town and whipped them. What do Medina's followers have that we don't have?" said one fellow who wore a beard and had black bushy eyebrows. This strong, well-built man nevertheless had a gentle countenance.

"All I can say is that my name won't be Anastasio Montañez any more if tomorrow I don't pick up a revolver, cartridge belts, a pair of pants, and some shoes. Really! Look, Codorniz, I'll bet you don't believe me. I have a half a dozen bullets in my hide. If you don't think so, just ask Demetrio. But I'm about as afraid of a hail of bullets as I am of a piece of candy. I'll bet you don't believe me."

Manteca yelled, "Hooray for Anastasio Montañez!"

"No," Anastasio countered. "Hooray for Demetrio Macías! He is our leader and praise God in Heaven and most holy Mary!"

"Hooray for Demetrio Macías!" they all yelled.

They built a fire out of grass and dry branches and on top of the coals they laid out strips of newly butchered meat. They squatted around the fire, eagerly sniffing the meat as it sizzled over the flames. Not far away, lying in a heap on the damp bloody ground, was the golden hide of a steer. From a rope stretched between two huisache trees they had hung up the rest of the meat, letting the sun and the breeze dry it out.

"Good!" said Demetrio. "Aside from my thirty-thirty we have only twenty weapons. If there are only a few federals, we'll let them have it and not leave one soldier alive. If there are a lot of them, then we'll at least give them a good scare."

He loosened the cloth sash around his waist and untied the knot, the proceeded to share the contents with his fellows.

"Salt!" they shouted, and each of them reached in and took a few grains between finger and thumb.

They ate greedily and when at last they had had enough they stretched out full length with their bellies showing to the sun. Then they burst into song, sad and monotonous tunes that they punctuated with raucous whoops after each verse.

III.

The twenty-five men of Demetrio Macías bedded down in the underbrush of the sierra, and there they slept until a signal from the horn woke them up. Pancracio had blown from the highest point of one of the mountain peaks.

"This is it, boys! Get ready!" called out Anastasio Montañez, inspecting the springs of his rifle.

But an hour went by without their hearing anything but the constant singing of the cicadas in the grassy uplands and the croaking of the frogs in the river.

When the last of the moon's rays faded away before the light rosy streak of daybreak, the first silhouette of a soldier stood out at the topmost part of the trail. And behind him appeared another and then ten more and after those still a hundred more, but almost immediately they moved into the shadow and were lost from view. Not until the sun came forth in its brilliance could one see the base of the precipice covered with humans, tiny men riding on little horses that looked like toys.

"Look how pretty they are!" Pancracio commented. "Let's go down and have some fun with them!"

Those shifting, moving figures crept along, sometimes losing themselves in the thickets of the underbrush, then standing out black against the ocher of the canyon walls.

The voices of the officers and their men carried distinctly in the morning air. Demetrio gave the signal and immediately the bolts and locks of the rifles clattered.

"Fire!" he ordered in a low voice.

Twenty-one men fired all at the same time, and a like number of federal soldiers fell from their mounts.

Surprised, they stood motionless, as moulded in relief against the cliffs.

Then a new volley and twenty more men fell, rolling down from one boulder to another with their heads split open.

"Come on out, you bandits, you famished curs!"

"Kill the cowards!"

"Kill the poor devils!"

The federal officers kept bawling at their enemy, who remained out of sight and kept their mouths shut while they continued to show off the marksmanship for which they were already famous.

"Look, Pancracio," said Meco, a man who had traces of white only in his teeth and his eyes, "this shot is for the one who's getting ready to pass under that big cactus. ... The bastard! Take that! Right in the noggin! Did you see? Now the one that's on the gray horse!"

"I'm going to give a bath to the one who is at the crest of the trail... If you don't fall into the water, you wretch, at least you'll be pretty close! Did you see him?"

"Please, Anastasio, don't hog it. Let me have your rifle for just one shot!"

"Come out of there if you're real he-men!"

"Just show your heads, you lousy trash!"

Manteca, Codorniz, and two more who were without weapons pestered the others, asking as a supreme favor the privilege of taking one single shot at the hated federal soldiers.

From one mountain height to the other the yells were as sharp and clear as if they had been heard from the other side of the street.

Codorniz appeared out of nowhere, stark naked and holding his cotton drawers in front of him as if fighting a bull and the soldiers below were that bull.

Soon a rain of bullets began to pour in on Demetrio's men.

"Codoroniz, you son of a bitch!" Demetrio growled.

"They turned loose a hive of bees on top of my head," said Anastasio Montañez without daring to raise his eyes.

"Go to where I told you," Demetrio roared out.

And they dragged themselves between the rocks to new positions.

The federals began to celebrate their victory and stopped firing, but a new volley brought confusion to them.

And overcome by a sudden panic, some tried to turn their horses around. Others abandoned them and climbed up among the rocks seeking a secure hiding place. Their officers had to open fire on the fleeing soldiers to restore order.

"Fire on the ones down there, down there!" exclaimed Demetrio, pointing his thirty-thirty toward the crystalline thread of the river. A soldier fell into the waters of the river itself, and one by one without fail they continued to drop with each bullet that he fired. But he was the only one who continued to shoot in the direction of the river and for every one who fell, ten, twenty, or more were able to ride on unscathed.

"Fire on the ones down there, down there!" he continued to shout in rage.

His men lent one another their weapons and while taking aim made new bets among themselves.

"I'll give you my leather belt if I don't bean the one that's riding the black horse! Hand me your rifle, Meco."

"Twenty Mauser shells and half a yard of sausage if you'll let me knock out the one on the dapple mare."

"Did you see how he jumped? Just like a deer!"

"Don't run, you bald heads! Come and meet your father Demetrio Macías!"

But now his men began to insult the others. Pancracio shouted, stretching out his hairless face, with a fixed expression as if it were of stone. And Meco bawled away, drawing up the tendons in his neck and stretching the lines of his countenance with its fierce eyes, like those of a murderer.

Installment no. 3

Demetrio kept shouting and warning the others of the danger they were in. But they were unable to hear him until they began to notice the zip of the bullets on one of their flanks.

"They hit me!" Demetrio groaned and gritted his teeth. "The bastards ...!" And he slid down into a hollow between the rocks.

IV.

Two were missing, Serapio the candymaker and Antonio, the fellow who handled the cymbals in the band in Juchipila.

"We'll hope they join us later," Demetrio said.

They were downcast. Only Anastasio Montañez was able to maintain the usual gentle look, in his sleepy eyes and his bearded face. Pancracio was as repulsive as ever.

The federal forces had pulled back, and Demetrio was on his way to gather up all his horses, which he had hidden away safely in the sierra.

Suddenly Codorniz, who was walking along ahead of the others, gave out a yell. He had come upon the missing companions, dangling from the limbs of a mesquite tree.

They were Serapio and Antonio. The men proceeded to identify them and Montañez recited aloud: "Our Father who art in heaven ...."

"Amen," they all answered with bowed head and each with his hat held to his heart.

Hastily they started off in the direction of the canyon of Juchipila, heading toward Moyahua, traveling without stopping until well into the night.

Codorniz did not leave Anastasio's side for a single moment. The figures of the hanged men with their limp necks, their hands hanging down, their stiff legs swinging slightly in the breeze. He could not get them out of his mind.

The next day Demetrio complained bitterly about his wound and was unable to climb on his horse. They had to carry him on a stretcher that they had put together from branches from an oak tree and bundles of soft grass.

¡You're losing a lot of blood, Demetrio," said Anastasio Montañez, and with a single tug he tore a sleeve from his shirt and knotted it tightly around Demetrio's thigh above the gunshot wound.

"Good," said Venancio. "That will stop the blood and ease the pain."

Venancio was a barber, and in his home town he pulled teeth and applied blister plasters and leeches. He enjoyed a certain prestige because he had read *The Wandering Jew* and *May Sun*. They called him "doctor" and he had become very conceited about his knowledge and very stingy with his words.

Taking turns four at a time, they bore the stretcher between bare, rocky hills and up the steepest slopes.

At midday when the haze from the lime-laden earth was stifling and their eyesight was beclouded, through the incessant chanting of the cicadas one could hear the rhythmic monotonous groans of Demetrio.

At each hut, hidden among the tremendous, abrupt rocks, they stopped to rest.

"Thank God that everywhere we have found compassionate souls and tortillas heaped high with chile and beans," said Anastasio Montañez.

And the people who lived in the mountains when they saw them get ready to continue their journey, clasping their calloused hands, exclaimed, "God bless you! May God assist you and guide you along your way! Now you are the ones who are on the run. Tomorrow we shall have to flee, to escape military conscription, hounded by those damned government soldiers who have declared war to the death against all of us poor people. They steal our pigs, our chickens, and even the little bit of corn that we have to eat. They burn our houses and carry off our women, and then when at last they catch up with one of us, they finish him off as if he were a mad dog."

When late afternoon came, with the sky aflame with radiant colors, they came to some drab huts on a level clearing surrounded by high mountains. Demetrio had his men carry him there.

They were just a few miserable thatched huts scattered along the river bank, among small fields planted with corn and beans that had just come up.

When the men had set the stretcher on the ground, Demetrio asked for some water to drink, hardly making his faint voice heard.

In the lightless openings of the huts were crowded together faded homespun dresses, bony chests, disheveled heads of hair, and behind them, shining eyes and ruddy cheeks.

A chubby little boy with dark, shiny skin came up to see the man who was lying on the stretcher. Soon an old woman approached and stood near him.

A pleasant young girl came forward with a gourd filled with fresh, clear water. Demetrio took the gourd in his trembling hands and drank eagerly.

"Do you want some more?"

He raised his eyes and looked at the girl. Her face was plain, but there was a gentleness in her voice.

With the back of his fist he wiped away the perspiration that had come out in beads on his forehead and then, turning on one side, he said, "May God reward you for it."

He began to shiver so violently that he caused all the grass that was on the stretcher to shake and even the base on which it was standing. Then, because of the fever, he fainted.

"The cool evening air is coming on and that isn't good for his fever," said Remigia, an old hag dressed in homespun, barefoot, and across her chest a scrap of coarse muslin that served as a blouse. And she invited them to carry Demetrio into her hut.

Like faithful dogs, Pancracio, Anastasio Montañez, and Codorniz hastened to pick up the corners of the stretcher, ever alert to the wishes of their leader. The rest of the men scattered, going to look for something to eat.

"Just imagine. I had eggs, some chickens, and even a few goats, but those cursed federal soldiers completely cleaned me out."

Then cupping her hands she came close to Anastasio's ear and whispered in it, "Why they even ran off with Señora Nieves's little girl."

V.

Codorniz, startled, opened his eyes and sat up.

"Montañez, did you hear that? A shot! Montañez, Montañez, wake up!"

He shoved him violently several times until at last he made Montañez stir and stop snoring.

"Dammit! You're making me sore, Codor-niz! I tell you dead men don't come back!" as he began to awaken.

"A shot, Montañez!"

"Go back to sleep or I'll punch you!"

"No, Anastasio, I'm not having a nightmare. I haven't thought about those fellows who were hanged any more. It was really a shot I heard, ever so clear."

"A shot, you say? Then hand me my rifle."

Anastasio Montañez rubbed his eyes, lazily stretched his arms and legs, and then stood up.

They left the hut and went outside. The sky was still studded with stars and, like a slender trimming from a fingernail, the moon was rising. From the shacks one could hear the fluster of the frightened women and then the clatter of the weapons of the men who were sleeping outside and were beginning to wake up.

"You fool! You've smashed my foot!"

The voice could be heard clearly and distinctly from not far away.

"Who goes there?"

The words reverberated from one mountainside to the other, across the lowlands and the cliffs until they became lost in the distance and the silence of the night.

"Who goes there?" Anastasio repeated, closing the bolt on his rifle.

"Demetrio Macías!" replied a gruff voice.

"It's Pancracio," Codorniz said, with a tone of gladness in his voice. Then, relieved, he let the butt of his rifle drop.

Pancracio was pushing a young fellow who was covered with dust from his felt hat all the way down to his rough high top shoes. A spot of fresh blood marked his trouser leg near one of his feet.

"Who is this dude?" asked Anastasio.

"I was on sentry duty and I heard a noise out there and I yelled 'Who goes there?' 'Carranzo,' this guy answered. 'Carranzo? I don't know that bird, so, take your Carranzo!' I winged him in the hoof."

And smiling, Pancracio turned his beardless, dirty face toward the others, in anticipation of their approval.

Then the stranger spoke up, "Who is your commander here?"

Anastasio raised his head with an air of extreme haughtiness.

The young man began to speak less arrogantly. "Well, I'm a revolutionary too. The federal army picked me up and conscripted me. I came into military service, but in the battle the day before yesterday I was able to desert and

Installment no. 4

since then I have been walking trying to find you."

"He's a federal!" some of them burst out, looking at him admiringly.

"He's one of those short-haired bastards!" said Anastasio Montañez. "While you were at it, why didn't you let him have it in the head?"

"Who knows what sort of business he's up to. He says he wants to talk to Demetrio, that he's got something he wants to tell him. But let's not worry about that. There's plenty of time," Pancracio answered while getting ready to fire his rifle.

"But what kind of ignorant brutes are you people?" the newcomer blurted out.

His sentence was interrupted because a blow from Anastasio knocked him down and bloodied his nose.

"Shoot the cur!"

"Hang him!"

"Burn him! He's one of the federals!"

Carried away, they shrieked and raised their rifles in a menacing fashion.

"Sshh! Be quiet! I think Demetrio is trying to say something," said Anastasio, calming them down.

Demetrio had found out what was going on and wanted them to take the prisoner to him.

"This is a disgrace, chief! Just look! Look!" Luis Cervantes proclaimed, pointing to the blood stain on his trousers and his swollen mouth and nose.

"Well, who in the devil are you?" asked Demetrio in a fretful mood.

"My name is Luis Cervantes, and I have

been a medical student and a writer for a newspaper. Because I said something in favor of you revolutionaries, I got into real trouble. They harrassed me, arrested me, and I ended up in the barracks."

The story that Luis Cervantes kept telling, spouted out in great detail and in touching terms, amused Pancracio and Manteca so much that they burst out in peals of laughter.

"I have tried to make myself understood, to convince you that I am a true coreligionary."

"Corre ... what?" inquired Demetrio, stretching his neck and turning his ear toward the newcomer.

"Coreligionary, chief. By that I mean that I pursue the same ideals and defend the same cause that you people are defending."

Demetrio smiled.

"Well, what cause are we defending?"

Luis Cervantes, who was baffled by the question, was unable to answer.

"Just look at him! Why does he go through all this palaver when everything is so clear? Can we take him out and shoot him now, Demetrio?" asked Pancracio anxiously.

With his hand Demetrio pushed away the lock of hair that had fallen down over his ear. Then he scratched himself while he tried to think.

"Ouch! This thing is hurting me again! Get out of here! Anastasio, put out the candle. Shut him up in the corral and have Pancracio and Manteca guard him. Tomorrow we'll decide what to do about him."

Luis Cervantes, absorbed in thought, spent the whole night walking back and forth in the corral.

The roosters were crowing lustily, filling the dawn with joy. The hens, still in their refuge in the trees and bushes, were beginning to move about, opening their wings and ruffling their feathers. Then with a clumsy leap, they dropped to the ground.

Luis Cervantes became aware of his guards, who were sound asleep stretched out on a pile of manure. For a moment the sight caused him to have gooseflesh. In his thoughts he went over again the countenances of those two men. Pancracio, fair of complexion and freckled, with his scanty yet prominent beard, his low, slanting forehead, his ears plastered against his skull, and his general appearance, which was completely brutal. And the other, Manteca, who was a mere scrap of flesh with slanting eyes and a fierce look on his face, his long straight hair reaching down to cover the nape of his neck, his forehead, and his ears, his lips always partly open and swollen from the scrofula that afflicted him.

VI.

A pleasant, agreeable voice caused Demetrio to raise his eyes. The same girl with the kind appearance who the night before had offered him a gourd full of delightfully cool water, now, when the first rays of the sun were finding their way between the reeds of the walls of the hut, came with a bowl of goat's milk covered with foam.

"What's your name?" he asked her.

"Camila," she answered. And because Demetrio began to stare as if he were looking through her, she began to blush and left as fast as she could.

"I feel a lot better, Anastasio," Demetrio said. "I had a chill, then I sweat a lot, and I woke up feeling cooler. This wound keeps hurting me, though. Call Venancio in so he can patch me up."

"And what do you want us to do with the city slicker I picked up last night?" Pancracio asked.

"I'd completely forgotten. I hadn't thought about that until this minute!"

Demetrio reflected a while before making up his mind.

"Say, Codorniz. Come here. There's a chapel five miles or so from here. I want you to go and steal the cassock from the priest who is there."

"Well, what do you plan to do, friend?" asked Anastasio in wonder.

"If this city guy has come here to murder me, it won't be very hard to get the truth out of him. Codorniz is going to dress up like a priest and hear his confession. I'll tell him that I'm going to line him up and shoot him. If he hasn't done anything, he won't have anything to say and then I'll let him go."

"Hm, what a lot of bother. I'd shoot him and get it over with," Pancracio exclaimed.

That night Codorniz came back with the cassock.

Demetrio had the prisoner brought in.

Luis Cervantes had not slept or eaten in two days. He looked haggard, and he had circles under his eyes, with his lips pale and chapped.

He spoke slowly and haltingly.

"Do with me whatever you wish. I made a mistake …."

There was a lengthy silence.

"I thought that you would accept gladly someone who came to offer his humble assistance, for your own good…. What advantage do I get out of the revolution, whether it succeeds or not?"

Slowly he began to get fired up, and the listlessness that had been noticeable in his face began to leave him.

"The revolution benefits the poor, the unlearned, those who have spent all their lives as slaves, those unfortunate ones who don't even know that the rich man is rich because he is able to turn the tears of the poor into gold."

"And what's that got to do with it? I'm not going to put up with sermons!" Pancracio remarked, interrupting him.

"For the time being I'm just going to put a noose around your neck. And just look how white and chubby it is!"

"Yes, I know what you have come here for," Demetrio declared harshly, scratching his head. "I am going to shoot you."

Then he turned toward Anastasio. "Take him away, but first let him confess. Has the priest come yet?"

Anastasio with his usual impassive nature took him by the arm.

"Come this way, dude."

When Codorniz came back wearing the cassock everyone burst out laughing.

"This slicker is quite a talker," he said. "I kind of think he laughed at me when I began to ask him questions."

"But did he confess anything?" Demetrio questioned.

"Only what he told us last night."

"I have a hunch that he didn't come here for the reason that you suspect, my friend," Anastasio declared.

"Well, give him something to eat and keep your eye on him."

Luis Cervantes, going from one hut to another, sought out boiling water and strips of cloth. Camila was able to provide him with all this.

With her curiosity, common to the mountain women, she sat down to watch him dress his wound.

"Say, who taught you to cure people? Why did you go and boil the water? And why did you cook the rags? And what was that you put on your hands, alcohol? Come on, I use to think it was good only for the colic. Ah, so you was going to be a doctor? Ha, ha, that's enough to make a person laugh. And why didn't you use cold water instead of that? Just listen to those stories.... They say there are critters in the water if it isn't boiled! And I can't see any kind of critters."

Camila kept on questioning him and became so friendly that even in her speech her familiarity could be noticed.

But Luis Cervantes wasn't even listening to her.

"Where are those men so wonderfully mounted and armed and paid with solid silver pesos that Villa is minting in Chihuahua? Maybe there are twenty naked,

Installment no. 5

lousy, filthy creatures."

"There were even men who had only one saddletree for their saddles, and one of them rode on a decrepit old mare, covered with sores from her withers to her tail. So what the government press said about the revolutionaries was true after all, that they were bandits who had gotten together for no good reason at all, and everything good about them that the sympathizers with the revolution said was nothing but lies. But just the same, revolutionaries, bandits, or whatever you want to call them, they were the ones who were going to bring down the government. The newspapers printed one thing, the newspaper writers said just the opposite. Huerta still cried out: 'I shall impose peace, whatever the price.' But his relatives and his favorites loaded the passenger ships that were leaving for Europe. I wonder if I really have done the wrong thing."

Absorbed in his thoughts, he uttered these final words while he finished dressing his wound.

"What were you saying?" Camila asked him. "Why, I thought the mice had gnawed your tongue away.

Luis Cervantes drew his eyebrows together in a frown and glared coldly at that kind of homespun-clad monkey, barefoot with wide stubby feet.

"Say, Curro, you don't know how to tell stories, do you?"

Luis gave her a mean look and then went off without answering her.

VII.

"Why don't you call the Curro to take care of you, my friend?" said Anastasio Montañez to Demetrio, who every afternoon chattered from tremendous chills which were followed by a fever. "You ought to see what he does. He takes care of himself, and now he's better and doesn't even limp any more."

But Venancio, who had already brought out cans of grease and compresses of dirty rags, protested. "If anyone lays a hand on him, I'll not be responsible for what happens."

"Say, but tell me. You're no sawbones at all. Have you already forgotten how you came to end up in his outfit?" said Codorniz.

"Yes, yes, I remember that you came to

join us because you sneaked off with a watch and two gold rings," Venancio declared, becoming excited.

"Why even .... You did worse because you had to run off after you poisoned your girl friend!"

"You're a liar!"

"You did too! You gave her Spanish fly ... so that ...."

The rest burst out in guffaws and Venancio in a string of insults.

Demetrio's expression became peevish again. The pain of his wound was occasionally more than he could stand.

"All right, then. Bring on the student ...."

Luis uncovered the limb, examined it quickly, and shook his head as a sign of displeasure.

The muslin strip that bound the leg cut into the flesh. The swollen leg looked as if it were about to burst. The slightest movement caused Demetrio to groan. Luis Cervantes cut loose the binding, then washed the wound thoroughly. He placed over it some compresses as hot as Demetrio could stand them and then bandaged it.

Demetrio slept all that afternoon and the night as well and the next morning woke up feeling much better.

Venancio said, "All right, but you've got to remember that those slickers are like moisture. They can get in anywhere. Because of the *curros* the fruits of our revolutions have always been lost."

Because Demetrio had faith in the learning of the barber, when Luis Cervantes came to treat him again he said to him, "Say, take good care of me so when I am all in one piece again you can go back home or wherever you feel like."

But one day after the treatment, Demetrio asked him if the soldiers gave him meat and milk. Luis Cervantes had to tell him that he only got to eat whatever the generous old women who lived in the huts felt like giving him. Also that the men treated him with undisguised hostility, like a newcomer or an intruder.

"They are all well-meaning fellows," said Demetrio, scratching his head, "but you've got to know how to figure them out."

Then Cervantes went out in a good humor to take a walk in the sierra.

Lying on an eminence with his legs hanging over the edge with a dreamy look on his face, Anastasio Montañez found him.

"Why are you feeling sad, "Curro? What's on your mind? Come over here, come over and talk a while. You miss what's going on in your hometown. It's easy to see that you're one of those who likes to keep his shoes shiny and wear a pretty bow on his shirt. Look, just look at me, filthy and with my clothes in shreds. But I'm not what I seem to be. I'll bet you don't believe me! I'm not hard up. I own ten yoke of oxen. Really! I bet you don't believe me! I still have my ten acres of land to sow. You can ask Demetrio about it. He knows. But in my home we aren't poor. Look, Curro, I've given the government soldiers a rough time. That's why they are after me. The last time ... it's been eight months now ... I ran a knife through a foolish little captain, right here in the belly button. But really, I'm not bad off. That's the reason I'm here ... and to lend a hand to my friend Demetrio."

VIII.

At the base of a ledge that jutted out, Pancracio and Manteca were playing cards, stretched out full length among the reeds of the river bank.

Anastasio threw an arm around Luis's shoulder. "What makes you think I don't like to gamble, Curro? Do you want to bet too? Go ahead! Look, this little leather snake that I use for a belt still has something in it," said Anastasio, touching the wad that he wore around his middle and causing the silver pesos inside to clink.

"Really, Curro, I'm not hard up for money."

"I have my twenty yoke of oxen. I bet you don't believe it," declared Codorniz, coming up behind them.

"Oh, my sweet little damsel!" he exclaimed, when he laid eyes on the jack that Pancracio laid out beside the five of diamonds.

Manteca placed a nickel on the five.

The deck was shuffled, but then another jack came up and a fierce argument broke out, marked by squabbling, shouting, and generously sprinkled with insults.

Pancracio, with his stony impassive face, stared sullenly at Manteca. Manteca stared back through his snaky eyes and jerked from time to time like a epileptic.

The two were on the verge of blows. They ran out of terms that were expressive enough for the situation and resorted to mention of fathers and mothers woven into a tapestry of obscenities, but nothing came of it. The game ended, and they got up. They slapped their arms around each other's shoulders as if nothing had happened and went off to have a drink together.

"I don't like to brawl with my tongue! That doesn't look good. What do you say, Curro?"

But Luis Cervantes, who had been urging them on with wild bursts of laughter, was hesitant about giving an answer.

"No!" declared Manteca. "Then what is a friend for?"

Then he turned toward Luis Cervantes.

"Isn't that right, Curro?"

"Of course! If they are on good terms … and don't really mean to offend anyone," Luis Cervantes agreed.

"That's exactly what I say."

"No. Well, really no one has ever called me a son of a bitch. I like to have people respect me. That's why, Curro, I never go around making a lot of noise," said Montañez in a serious mood.

Stretched out on the hard ground, by the warm light of a soft moon, Venancio recounted incidents of *The Wandering Jew*. The men yawned, knowing that sleep would come sooner or later, and some of them, lulled by the soft, easy-flowing voice of the barber, were already snoring.

"Wonderful," exclaimed Luis Cervantes, when the barber had finished his narrative after tacking on a number of unconnected anticlerical observations. "You have exquisite talent!"

"I'm pretty good at that," Venancio declared, convinced by the flattery, "but my par-

ents died when I was small, and I didn't get any schooling."

"That doesn't really matter. When the revolution is triumphant, then you will be able to get a degree. Two or three months of service in a hospital somewhere backed up by a recommendation from our leader Macías and you will be a doctor. You have such great ability and ease in doing things that it would be child's play."

And from that day on Venancio was no longer like the other soldiers and stopped calling him 'Curro.' So it was Luisito here and Luisito there and it wasn't 'Curro' any more.

"Say, Curro," said Anastasio Montañez as he held his hand to his forehead to shield his eyes, "what's that cloud of dust over the hill there? What if it's those lousy government troops and here we are, not ready for them yet? Come, let's go tell the rest of the boys."

Slowly they made their way down the mountainside, leaping from one stone to the other and beating their way through the brush.

Codorniz kept his big dark eyes looking off into the distance where the dust cloud was rising up over the hill.

"Let's go after them! What do you suppose they have that we'll take away from them?" said Anastasio, and he went off to the shack to get his saddle.

Installment no. 6

Then Meco, Pancracio, and a number of others saddled their horses, all in a great humor.

"I'm going to stay behind to look after Demetrio," said Codorniz. His statement gave rise to an outburst of laughter and jeers. But he hopped on to a mound and from there into his saddle and then laughed at the others.

The enemy turned out to be nothing more than a string of burros and a couple of drivers.

"Stop them," Demetrio ordered, "and bring them here. Those fellows are from the up-country and they must have some news."

And what they had was really sensational.

The federal army had dug in on El Grillo and La Bufa, hills that overlooked the city of Zacatecas. It was supposed to be Huerta's last stronghold, and everyone was certain that before long it would fall. Entire families were fleeing helter-skelter toward the south. The trains were crammed with people, and they covered even the roofs of the cars. There were not enough carriages and wagons for all those who had taken to the roads, and many people overcome by panic streamed out of the city, carrying their possessions and baggage on their backs. The revolutionary chieftain Pánfilo Natera was concentrating his troops in Fresnillo, and the federal soldiers were really in a tough spot.

"The fall of Zacatecas is the fall of Huerta," Luis Cervantes assured him enthusiastically. "We ought to go join Natera just as soon as we can."

And when he saw the puzzled look on the faces of Demetrio and some of his men he realized that he was still nobody as far as they were concerned.

IX.

"Señora Remigia, can you let me have a few eggs? My hen has decided to set this morning. Some of the men are waiting to eat breakfast."

And she added under her breath, "How does the man look to you? Better? But he still looks awfully pale. Has the bullet wound healed up yet?"

One of the gossipy women left, and another one came in. They all had figured out some pretext to come in every day to satisfy their curiosity about Demetrio.

"Señora Remigia, don't you have a few laurel leaves so I can cook up a brew for María Antonia? She woke up with an upset stomach."

And with her eyes she inquired about the wounded man.

Señora Remigia lowered her eyes to let her know that he was sleeping. Then she said, "I don't have any laurel leaves, my dear, but try Señora Dolores. She is the only one who can get them for you."

"Señora Dolores went away last night to the other ranch. They say they came after her to go care for uncle Matías's little girl."

"Come now, don't tell me!"

"I swear it's true! I told you she was big with child."

"Poor thing! Curses on those damned federals! There's another wretched girl and they are the ones who did it."

They woke up Demetrio so he could receive a gift. Señora Fortunata had brought a short-tailed chicken for the ailing man. And since she had many woes to tell, she spent the whole morning at it. She too had lost a daughter to the federals, and because it was her only child she was beside herself with grief. When she began her account, Codorniz and Anastasio Montañez were in their wallows at the foot of Demetrio's stretcher. They raised their heads and, with their mouths half-open, listened to her like stupid dolts, but Anastasio got bored when she was only half-finished and went out into the sun to scratch the bites from his lice. Finally she wound up her recital with a fulmination: "I hope by God and most holy Mary that you and your men will wipe out those hellish federals." By that time Demetrio, with his face turned to the wall, was trying to figure out how to capture Zacatecas, and Anastasio Montañez was making snoring noises like a trombone.

"Say, Curro, I want you to sing 'La Adelita' again," Camila said to Luis Cervantes while he was treating his wound.

Luis screwed up his face in dissatisfaction, but he did not answer.

"Do you know why I want to learn it? So I can sing it when you aren't here any more, when you are off in places far, far away. So I can keep remembering you ...."

When Luis heard Camila's words, they felt like the sharp point of a piece of steel as it scrapes the surface of a metal flask.

"Look, Curro, how pretty and pink it is. It looks like a wild rose bud. Say, I haven't told you about it! If you could only see how mean that old Demetrio is. He doesn't want the food Señora Remigia fixes for him ... and I'm supposed to get his meals and take them to him.

Well, what do you know! I went in with the cho-
colate for him and he grabbed me by the hand
and he squeezed me tight. Then he began to
pinch my legs, but I really socked him a good
one. There! You! Be still! You old brute, let me
go! Immoral old man! Let me go, shameless old
fool! And I gave a jerk and tore myself loose
and ran out of there as fast as I could. What
do you think about that?"

"Really?" Luis Cervantes asked with undisguised joy.

Camila got mixed up. For a moment she
gazed at Luis, with his greenish eyes, his smooth,
fair skin, his wavy blond hair. And then she
heaved a sigh. Then suddenly she was moved
to weep, and without saying anything further to
Luis she got up and went away so that he would
not notice her tears.

The day that Demetrio saw that his wound
had healed over, he said to Luis Cervantes:

"Curro, do you really want to stick with us?
You're made of different stuff and I really can't
figure out how you can take to this way we have
to live. Do you think that I'm in this business
because I like it? Come here, sit down so I can
tell you about it. Do you know why I rebelled?
Well, because of hard feelings you always come
up against and also, why shouldn't I say it, because I like to be where the noise is. Before the
revolution I had already turned over my fields
and was ready to sow my crops, and if it hadn't
been for my run-in with don Mónico and the
other political bosses in Moyahua right now I
would be hurrying around getting my two oxen
ready for sowing."

"Pancracio, get out two bottles of beer, one
for me and another one for Curro. By the sign
of the Holy Cross ... it won't hurt me, will it?"

X.

"I'm from Limón, not far from Moyahua,
right in the Juchipila canyon. I had my own
house, my cows, and a piece of land that I could
plant with crops. When you get down to it, I
had everything I wanted. Well, we country people are in the habit of going in to town once a
week. One goes to mass, listens to the sermon
and when it is over heads for the market to buy
his onions, his tomatoes, and takes care of all his
errands. After that he gets together with his
friends in Primitivo López's store for a midday
snack. He has a drink or two. Sometimes he
gives in a bit and goes too far and the drinks
go to his head. Then he gets to feeling good and
he laughs, shouts, and sings if he feels like it.
That's all right because no one gets offended
over it. But then they really start to bother you.
The police keep coming by, and they stick their
ears in the door to see what's going on. Then the
police chief or the assistants decide to put a stop
to the fun. But one has real blood in his veins
and some spirit in his body. So he gets mad
and stands up and tells them what's what. If
they understood, everything was all right. They
left me alone, and the whole thing stopped
there. But sometimes the boys got to talking
loud and threatening, and of course a person
can get a little too smart and doesn't like to have
anyone scare him. So, out comes the knife and
out comes the pistol. And then we have to run
off to the mountains and hide for a while until
things blow over and they forget about the dead
fellow."

"Well, what happened to don Mónico? He
was a stupid old fool, but he was a lot less
stupid with me than with other people. He never
got any fun out of it. I spit in his face because
he didn't mind his own business. Well, that was
enough for them to sick the government on me.
You must have heard about that business in
Mexico City where they killed Mr. Madero and
another guy, some bird named Félix or Felipe
Díaz, and so forth. Well, that dirty don Mónico
went personally to Zacatecas to bring back a
squad of soldiers to pinch me because I was supposed to be for Madero and was getting ready to
rebel. But since one always has pals, they came
and warned me, and when the soldiers finally
got to Limón, I'd already flown the coop. After
that my good friend Anastasio came along. He
had killed somebody, and then Pancracio, and
Codorniz, all of them my friends and fellows
I had known. Before long others joined us, and
so you see, we keep on fighting the best we can."

"Chief," said Luis Cervantes, after sitting

and thinking for a while, "you must know that not far away from here in Juchipila there are people who support Natera. It would be a good idea if we went to join them before they take Zacatecas. We can go and join up with the general."

"I don't like that idea. I don't like to give in to anybody."

"But you, all by yourself with just a few men, if you stay around here you can never amount to more than an insignificant little rebel leader who will never get anywhere. The revolution eventually gains, and when it is over they can say to you what Madero said to those who helped him, 'Boys, thanks a lot! Now you can all go home.' "

"I don't want anything but for them to leave me alone so I can go home in peace."

Installment no. 7

"But I'm getting around to that. I'm not through yet. 'Those of you who rebelled against Díaz and risked your lives in making me president of the republic, with the chance of leaving widows and orphans in poverty, now that I have reached my goal, you can pick up your hoe and your shovel and go back to your miserable existence, hungry and in rags, while those of us who are on top can get around to making millions of pesos.' "

Demetrio nodded his head and with a smile scratched himself.

"As I was saying," Luis continued, "when the revolution ends, then it's all over. It's a dirty shame that it leaves so many widows, so many orphans and so much blood spilled. And all for what? Just so a few crooks can get fat and have everything the way it was before. But you are honest and so you say, 'what I want is to go home.' But you have a home, wife, and children."

"You've got to think about your family ... and about our country."

Macías smiled and his eyes shone.

"So you think it would be a good idea to join up with Natera?"

"Not only a good idea but necessary, absolutely indispensable. I have taken a liking to and I am really quite fond of you. You don't really know why you are in the revolution. No, we are really only one of the many features of this great social movement that can only end in the exaltation of our fatherland. We are the instruments of destiny for the recovery of the sacred rights of the people. You have not taken up arms against don Mónico but against the system of bosses in this whole nation of ours. We are not fighting to overthrow a wretched murderer but against tyranny itself. That is what you call a struggle for principles, for one's ideals. Those are what Carranza, Villa, and Natera are fighting for, and you are fighting for them too."

"Pancracio, bring a couple more beers, one for me and one for Curro," Demetrio said.

"And am I just supposed to stand around and look at him?" Pancracio said.

XI.

"If you could only see how well the Curro explains everything, Anastasio," said Demetrio, who was upset by what he had been able to comprehend out of all of Luis Cervantes's words.

"I was listening to him, too," Anastasio answered. "Because he knows how to read and write he understand things pretty well. But my trouble is how are you, my friend, going to join up with that guy Natera when you have so few men?"

"Oh, that doesn't make any difference. From now on we're going to handle things in a new way. You'll soon find out. We're going to do it the way Crispín Robles does it in Juchipila. We'll take weapons and horses from all the small towns and with all the prisoners that we rescue from the jails, in no time there'll be a hundred of us. The truth is, Anastasio, that we've really been pretty stupid. It doesn't seem possible that this Curro fellow has come here and shown us how. That's what reading and writing can do for you!"

Demetrio announced that the next day they would leave.

That afternoon every one was excited and happy, and they brought in three musicians from the town nearby.

"Well, we may be leaving but as far as I'm concerned I'm not going alone," Pancracio exclaimed. "I have my love and I'm taking her with me!"

Demetrio answered that he would like very much to take along a girl that he had his eyes on, but he did not want to nor did he want any of his men to leave behind souvenirs like those the federals had left.

"You won't have to wait long. When you get back you can fix everything up," Luis Cervantes whispered in his ear.

"What?" said Demetrio. "Haven't they been telling me that you and Camila ... had something together?"

"That isn't true. The one she cares for is you ... but she's afraid of you."

"Really, Curro?"

"Yes, but it's better to do it your way. One shouldn't leave a bad impression. When we come back in triumph, everything will be different. The women will even appreciate the honor that you show them."

"Oh, Curro, you're really a smart guy," Demetrio replied, smiling and slapping him on the back.

Late in the afternoon when the sun was about to set, Camila was going down to the river. She called to Luis as he came along the path.

"Hey, Curro, at least come and say good-bye to me. Stuck up! Did I treat you so badly that you won't even speak to me?"

"Yes, yes, I was going to say good-bye. I am very grateful, and I shall always keep you in my memory. I'll always remember what you have done for me."

"You're fibbing," she said, flirting with him. "Why I don't even speak to you."

"I was going to say all that to you tonight at the dance."

"I'm not going to the dance."

"Why aren't you going?"

"Because I can't stand that old guy ... Demetrio."

"You're silly! He loves you a lot, and you're losing a chance that may not come your way again. Look, Demetrio Macías will someday be a general. He's going to be very rich, with a lot of horses, jewels, a lot of fine dresses, houses, and money to spend. Just think what you would be if you were with him!"

"No, Curro, don't tell me these things, because then you won't be the one I love. Now I've said it. Well then, you'd better leave because you make me feel ashamed."

Luis walked off and was soon lost among the cliffs.

Camila followed the path down to the river to fill her pitcher. The water was flicked with tiny bits that were bright carmine in color. In its ripples flickered all the colors of the rainbow, and the mountain peaks were half bathed in sunlight and half in shadow. Swarms of insects with shiny wings blinked and flickered over a pool. And reflected against the smooth pebbles of the bottom of the stream was Camila in her blue blouse with green ribbons, her white, unstarched skirt, her hair carefully combed, her wide eyebrows and her forehead, just as she had brightened herself up in order to please Luis.

She sighed and began to hum a tune. And from her pleasant throat there burst forth a popular melody, charged with tenderness and intense sadness. It seemed that even the cicadas and the mockingbirds had become still for a moment to listen to her.

At the dance there was a lot of gaiety and some very good mescal was consumed.

"I miss Camila," Demetrio blurted out in a loud voice.

And immediately everyone looked around, trying to locate Camila.

"She isn't well. She's laid up with a headache," her mother doña Agapita answered impatiently, annoyed by the sly glances that all the other old women were casting at her.

When the dance was about over, Demetrio, tottering a bit, expressed his thanks to the good residents who had treated them so graciously and promised them that when the revolution ended in victory he would keep them in mind. "In jail and in bed one finds out who his friends are."

"May God bless you and guide you on your way," replied the old women.

"Come back soon," María Antonia shouted.

XII.

"Hey! What's the matter, Camila? What are you doing in the corner with your shawl tied over your head? Oh, you're crying? Just look at those eyes! You look like an old witch. Don't get so upset. Listen, there is no pain that afflicts the soul that doesn't go away in three days."

That was the advice of María Antonia and she, despite her pockmarks and a cast over one eye, enjoyed a very bad reputation, so bad, in fact, that some said there was not a single one of Demetrio's men who had not lain with her among the reeds that grew along the river bank.

Señora Agapita drew her eyebrows together in a frown and growled something to her daughter.

The women of the community were gloomy over the departure of all the people, and the men themselves, despite all the gossip and chatter from their own women, realized now that there would no longer be anyone to bring them mutton and veal to eat. How pleasant it is to spend one's time eating, sleeping, and resting, lying in the shadow of the mountain crags, looking upward into the blue of the sky!

"Look at them, there they go!" María Antonia cried out. "They look just like those little toys that you put in the cupboard in the corner."

Far in the distance, climbing up a mountain slope, the men of Macías on their thin nags could be seen in profile. A gust of wind that reached the huts carried the brief strains of "La Adelita."

Camila, who had come out for one last look at them, could not restrain herself and burst into sobs, before going back to the houses.

María Antonia looked at her and then laughed loudly. Then she left without saying good-bye.

"Someone with the evil eye has harmed my daughter," thought Señora Agapita after staring fixedly at Camila.

She thought the matter over for several minutes before she reached a decision. From a peg driven into the wall between the Divine Countenance and the Virgin of Jalpa she took down a yoke strap of uncured leather that her husband used to harness his oxen and after folding it beat Camila in order to drive out the evil.

On his chestnut horse, Demetrio felt that he had been made young again.

Installment no. 8

His eyes had recovered their peculiar metallic luster and in his copper-colored cheeks, those of a pure Indian, hot, red blood was flowing again.

All the men expanded their lungs as if to breathe in the vast horizons, the immense expanse of the blue sky, the azure of the mountains, and the fresh scented air that bore the perfume of the sierra. And they made their horses gallop as if in their wild ride they were attempting to take possession of the whole earth. Who recalled any longer the harsh police commander, the grumbling patrolman, the conceited political boss? Who remembered the wretched shack where he lived like a slave, always under the watchfulness of the landowner, of the sullen, stern foreman, with the indispensable obligation of being on the job before the sun came up, with the shovel and the basket or the plow handle and the goad for the oxen and the daily plate of beans?

They danced, laughed, and whooped it up, intoxicated with sun, air, and life itself.

Meco, cutting capers and showing his white set of teeth, kept joking and clowning away. "Say, Pancracio," he asked, "my wife has sent me a letter saying that we have another kid. How can that be? I haven't even seen her since when Madero was president."

"Oh, that's nothing special. You left her sitting on the eggs."

They all laughed boisterously. Then in a falsetto voice that was off key he started to sing:

I gave her a penny.
She said she didn't want it.
I gave her a nickel.
She didn't want to take it
But she kept imploring
Until she pried a quarter out of me.
Oh, such ungrateful women,
They're not considerate at all!

The racket did not stop until the hot sun came out and made them feel lethargic.

They continued their journey through the canyon, across hills strung out one after the other and one beside the other, barren hills, shorn and dirty, like heads with the ringworm.

In the late afternoon in the distant haze they could make out a pair of white church towers against the blue of the mountain range. Then they spotted the poles of the telegraph line and a highroad that was broad and dusty.

They sought out some traveler in order to obtain information. Codorniz saw in the distance the figure of a man who was taking a rest at the side of the road.

He was a ragged old fellow with a burro carrying a load of alfalfa.

When they approached, he picked up his sharp pointed knife, took off one of his sandals, and began to repair it.

Demetrio questioned him. He was going to town taking alfalfa for his cow. "Yes, there are several federals in the town but there aren't more than a dozen." Then he confirmed immediately the rumors that were making the rounds, that Obregón was approaching Guadalajara, Carrera Torres had taken San Luis Potosí, and Natera was in Fresnillo.

"Good!" Demetrio concluded. "But be careful not to say a word about us in the town, old man, or I'll blow your brains out. I'd track you down to the center of the earth."

After the old man had gone on, Demetrio consulted with his men.

"Let's go after them, and not leave a single bastard alive!" This was the expression of most of them.

They counted out the rifle shells and the hand grenades that El Tecolote, a machinist from the foundry in Aguascalientes, had manufactured using sections of iron pipe and brass ornaments from a bedstead.

"There aren't many of them, but we'll trade them for rifles," Anastasio Montañez commented.

The commanding voice of Demetrio halted this activity.

They made camp on the slope of a hill. They left their horses among the huisache brush, and each man sought out a rock to use as a pillow.

XIII.

At midnight Demetrio Macías ordered every one to saddle.

The town was six miles away, and he had planned a surprise for the federal soldiers.

The sky was clouded over but occasionally a star shone through, and from time to time the flicker of a lightning bolt in the distance reddened the sky.

Luis Cervantes asked Demetrio if it wouldn't be a good idea to have a guide to the town or at least some idea of the arrangement of the streets and where the barracks were situated. Having that information, the attack might more likely succeed.

"No, Curro," Demetrio answered with a smile and a scornful gesture. "We'll catch them unawares when they least expect us and it will all be over. That's the way we've always done it. Have you seen how ground squirrels stick their heads out of their holes when you fill their tunnels with water? Well, those damned wretches are going to come out just as bewildered when they hear our first shots. They'll be sitting ducks for us and that's it."

"And if it turns out that the old fellow we saw yesterday afternoon has tricked us? If instead of twenty men they turn out to be fifty? If that fellow was one of their spies posted on this road?"

"That Curro's a real coward," Anastasio Montañez spoke up.

"Putting on a poultice and grabbing a syringe isn't the same thing as handling a gun," Pancracio added.

"That's too much gab to waste on a dozen stupid rats," Manteca answered. "Our mothers already know whether their sons are men ... or something else."

But when they reached the edge of the village Venancio knocked on the door of the first house.

"Where's the barracks?" he asked of the man who came out, a chap barefoot and wearing a torn poncho that covered his chest and back.

"The barracks are just below the square," he answered.

But since no one knew where "below the square" was, Venancio forced him to march ahead and show them the way.

Shaking with terror, the poor devil complained that they were being overly cruel with him, that he was but one man against many and that he had a wife and many children.

"And the ones I have are dogs?" Demetrio remarked.

Then he added, "Everyone keep still. Go on one by one and keep to the side of the road where the loose dirt is."

The ample square dome of the church loomed over the houses of the village.

"Right in front of the church is the main square. You keep going just a little ways on below and that's where the barracks are."

Then the man knelt down, pleading with them to let him go home.

Without saying anything, Pancracio threatened him with the barrel of his rifle.

"How many soldiers are there here?" questioned Luis Cervantes.

"I'm not lying to you, old man, but there's a lot of them."

Luis Cervantes glanced toward Demetrio, but he pretended not to have heard what the man had said.

Suddenly they came out into a small square. A tremendous blast of gunfire deafened them.

Demetrio's chestnut horse shook, wobbled on its feet, and then fell. Tecolote uttered a shriek and rolled off his horse, which kept on going, wild and riderless, into the plaza.

Another volley, and the man who had been their guide flung his arms apart and fell over on his back.

Anastasio Montañez hurriedly lifted Demetrio up on the horse behind him. The others had already retreated and were seeking protection against the walls of the houses.

"Say, fellows," shouted one of the town's residents, sticking his head out of a large doorway, "why don't you get at them from the back part of the chapel? They are all cooped up there. Go back down this same street, turn to your left and then you come right away to an alley and then again you keep going straight ahead and you'll end up right behind the chapel."

At that moment pistol fire began to rain down on them.

It came from the roofs of the nearby houses.

"Oh," the man remarked, "those are town dudes. They aren't anyone to be afraid of. Come in here until they go away. They'll take off and run. They're afraid of their own shadows!"

"How many soldiers are there?" Demetrio inquired.

"There were only twelve, but last night they began to get scared and sent word down the line for more. I don't know how many more came, but it doesn't make any difference. Most of them have been rounded up in the draft, and they'd just as soon desert and leave their officers on their own. My brother was picked up in the conscription, and he's come here with them. I'll give him a signal, and they'll all come over to your side. Let's get rid of the officers. Could you let me have a rifle? I'm really sore at them. They ran off with my daughter. Some nasty little officer got away with a woman that I had, the bastard!"

"I don't have a rifle, my friend, but these may be

Installment no. 9

useful to you," answered Anastasio Montañez as he pulled out two hand grenades and held them out to the townsman.

The commander of the federal soldiers was a blond young officer with a pointed moustache, very arrogant. Until he finally found out that there were only twenty or so attackers, he said little and was cautious, but as soon as he beat them off so easily, and they had not been able to fire one shot in return, he showed off his bravery and rashness. Even though his soldiers scarcely dared to peek out from behind the stone railing in front of the church, in the pale light of dawn he showed off gracefully his slender figure and his officer's cape with insignia on the shoulders, letting it puff out in the wind.

"Ah, I remember what happened at the Ciudadela!"

His military experience was limited to the adventure in which he had participated when he was a cadet in the officers' candidate school at the time when the betrayal of President Madero was plotted and carried out, so whenever the opportunity came along he made the most of it and mentioned the incident.

"Lieutenant Campos," he ordered emphatically, "take ten men and go wipe out those bandits who are hiding somewhere. The rascals! They are brave only when it comes to eating cows and chickens!"

A civilian appeared in the doorway of the spiral stairway that led to the church tower. He brought the news that the bandits had taken refuge in a corral where it would be very easy to trap all of them together. At least that was the word from the residents of the town who had taken up positions on the housetops. They were prepared not to let a single one get away.

"I'll go myself to wipe them out," the officer said hastily. But scarcely had he passed through the door when he turned back.

"It may be that they are waiting for reinforcements, and it wouldn't be proper for me to leave my post. Lieutenant Campos, go capture all of them alive so that we can execute them at midday in full view of the town. Those bandits will soon see what kind of example I'm going to make of them. But if that isn't possible, Lieutenant Campos, do away with all of them. Don't leave a single one alive. Do you understand?"

Satisfied with these orders, he turned around and began to think how he would word the report that he expected to submit.

"Honorable Minister of War General Aureliano Blanquet, Mexico.

I have the honor of reporting to you, General Blanquet, that at daybreak today a strong contingent of five hundred brigands under the command of the leader named H. was foolhardy enough to attack this place. With the necessary urgency I and my men fortified ourselves in the highest points of the town. The attack began at dawn, the heavy fire lasting for more than two hours. Despite the numerical superiority of the enemy, I was able to inflict severe punishment on him and to defeat him soundly. The number of dead reached twenty and the wounded were many, judging from the traces of blood that they left in their hasty flight. Among our forces we were fortunate not to have suffered a single casualty. I have the honor to congratulate you on the occasion of this victory of the armed forces of the Republic. Long live Mexico!"

"And then," the young captain kept on thinking, "I'll be promoted to major."

And he clasped his hands together with joy, at the precise moment when a deafening explosion left him with his ears ringing.

XIV.

"So, if we can get across this corral we'll come out right on the alley?" Demetrio asked.

"Yes, except that on the other side of the corral there's a house, then another corral, and a store beyond that," the villager replied.

Demetrio scratched his head while he thought. It did not take him long to make up his mind.

"Can you get hold of a crowbar or a pick, something we could use to make holes in the walls?"

"Yes, I have them, but ...."

The villager was confused.

"Well, where are they?" Demetrio asked, speaking loudly.

"All my boss's tools are right here, but the houses that you want to cut through belong to him."

Demetrio and his men broke into a miserable little room that the man had pointed out as a storeroom. They paid no attention whatever to his attempted explanation.

"Now they'll really blame me for this business," the man lamented, for he was the keeper of all his boss's keys.

It was all over in a matter of minutes. As soon as they reached the corral, one after another and hugging the wall, they ran at full speed to reach their positions in the rear of the church.

First they had to climb over an adobe wall and just beyond it the back wall of the chapel.

"God's will be done!" Demetrio thought, and he was the first to scale the wall.

Like monkeys the others followed him, and in the rough climb their hands became streaked with blood. The rest of the task was easier. Steps that had been hacked in the masonry made it easy to climb the wall of the chapel. Once they were across it, the cupola hid them from the view of the soldiers.

"Wait just a minute," the villager said. "I want to see where my brother is. I'll give you the sign and then you can go after the non-coms and the officers."

But in all the movement and bustle no one listened or paid any attention to him.

For a moment Demetrio gazed upon the dark mass of the army coats along the stone railing, stretching across the front of the church and part way down the sides. The church towers were jammed with federal soldiers, crowded behind the iron railing.

He smiled, satisfied with what he saw, and then turned to face his men.

"Let 'em have it!" he yelled.

Twenty bombs exploded simultaneously in the midst of the federal soldiers. In terror they rose up, their eyes opened full wide. But before they could realize the nature of their predicament twenty more bombs burst among them with a crash, leaving dead and wounded scattered over the churchyard.

"Wait a minute! I haven't found my brother yet!" the guide begged Demetrio with distress in his voice.

An old sergeant scolded and insulted his soldiers in a futile attempt to reorganize them. It was like chasing down rats who are caught in a trap. Some hurried to reach the little door that led to the stairway, and there they fell in a heap. Others were riddled by Demetrio's bullets. Still others cast themselves at the feet of those twenty ghosts whose heads and chests were the dark color of iron, their long white trousers reaching all the way to their crude sandals. In the church tower, many struggled to make their way out from under the dead and wounded who had fallen on top of them.

"Chief," Luis Cervantes exclaimed in great alarm, "the bombs are all gone and we left the rifles back there in the corral. What do we do now?"

Demetrio smiled and pulled out a knife with a long, shiny blade. Immediately knives began to shine in the hands of his twenty soldiers, some slender and pointed, others as broad as the palm of one's hand, and still others as heavy as machetes.

"The spy!" Luis Cervantes shouted victoriously and turned his face away with a look of terror on it.

"Don't kill me, dear father!" the old sergeant begged, throwing himself at Demetrio's feet.

He lifted up his Indian face, crossed with wrinkles but still without a single gray hair. Demetrio recognized him. He was the old man who had deceived them the night before.

The knife blade crunched into his ribs, and they splintered under the impact. The old man fell on his back, his arms spread out and his frightened eyes wide open.

"Not my brother! Don't kill him!" the villager cried out in horror as he saw Pancracio leaping upon one of the federal soldiers.

But it was too late. Pancracio with one single stroke sliced open his neck, and from it as from a fountain two scarlet streams gushed out.

"Kill the federals! Kill the bald heads!"

Pancracio and Manteca distinguished themselves in the butchery, finishing off the wounded. Montañez let his hand drop. It was exhausted from the slaughter. He still retained the gentle look on his face and his countenance showed no expression, where he combined the innocence of a child and the utter lack of moral spirit found in the jackal.

"Here's one that's still alive," Codorniz shouted, although not venturing to kill him.

Pancracio rushed over to the survivor. It was the little blond captain, as white as a sheet, who had stopped to cling to an edge of the spiral staircase, lacking the strength to go down.

Pancracio grabbed him and dragged him, pushing him to the edge of the railing. There he gave him a shove in the stomach, and the captain fell like a bag of stones to the pavement sixty feet below.

"You're sure stupid!" Codorniz exclaimed. "If I'd known you were going to do that I wouldn't have said anything! I was going to take charge of those fine shoes that he was wearing!"

The men bent over and went about stripping those who were wearing the best clothing. They joked with one another and laughed with amusement.

Demetrio was bathed in sweat. He pushed back the long locks of hair that had fallen down over his forehead, covering his eyes. Then he said, "Now let's go after the city dudes!"

XV.

With fifty men Demetrio arrived in Fresni-

Installment no. 10

───────────────────────────

llo on the same day that Natera, one of the revolutionary chieftains, was beginning the advance of his forces on the city of Zacatecas.

Natera greeted Macías cordially:

"I already know about you and your men. You've given the federals a good licking all the way from Tepic to Durango."

"General," Luis Cervantes broke in spiritedly, "with men like you and Colonel Macías, our nation will soon be covered with glory!"

And Demetrio was overjoyed to hear that Natera kept referring to him by the rank of colonel.

Wine and beer were brought in. Demetrio and Natera touched their glasses together and Cervantes toasted, "To the triumph of our cause, which is that of justice. May the ideals of redemption of this noble and long-suffering country of ours soon be fulfilled, and may those same men who have sprinkled their blood on the seeds of liberty be the ones who will harvest its fruits!"

Natera glanced briefly toward Luis Cervantes and then, turning his back on him, began to converse with Macías.

All the while one of Natera's assistants had been approaching the group, with his eyes fixed persistently on Luis Cervantes. He was a young man of pleasant appearance.

"Luis Cervantes!"

"Mr. Solís!"

"The moment I came in I thought you were Cervantes. Come! I still can't be sure of it!"

"But you see me!"

"So .... Come on over and have a drink, my friend!"

They went into the next room.

"Since when did you turn into a revolutionist?" Alberto Solís asked, drawing up a chair at one of the small tables.

"Five months ago."

"So that's why you still have all the enthusiasm and faith that those of us all had at the beginning of the revolution."

"Have you lost them already?"

"Look, my friend. Don't be surprised if right off the bat I start telling you my innermost thoughts. Around here you get starved for someone else to talk to, someone who shares the same ideas, so one blurts them out eagerly. It's just like a man who gulps down a glass of cold water after he has walked hour upon hour with the burning sun beating down on him. But first of all I want an explanation from you. Frankly I am amazed to find you here, you, the author of furious articles in *La Nación* and *El Regional,* you, the fellow who pinned on us the tag of 'bandits' every chance you had."

"The truth convinced me!"

"Convinced?"

"Absolutely!"

Alberto Solís gave out a deep sigh. The two men filled their glasses and drank.

"Have you gotten tired of the revolution already?" Luis Cervantes asked him.

"Tired? I'm twenty-five years old, and just look at me. I'm in the best of health. Disillusioned? That may be."

"You must have good reasons for feeling that way."

"My friend, there are deeds and there are men that are nothing more than gall itself. And that gall keeps dripping away, one drop after another. And everything turns to bitterness. Everything wastes away and is gone, enthusiasm, hopes, joy. Nothing is left. One either shuts himself off behind a wall of impenetrable self-ishness ... or he perishes."

Luis Cervantes pursed his lips in an ironic smirk and since the tone of voice and the looks of self-sufficiency tortured him inside, he begged Solís to recount what had led him into such a state of deception, so as to keep him from asking more questions or from contradicting him.

"Mere trifles," Alberto Solís answered. "Actions that were outwardly insignificant. Looks that pass unnoticed, the momentary flicker on a face of a line that contracts, a pair of eyes that shine, of lips that purse up, the fleeting meaning of a word that is uttered. But they are words, actions, and expressions that when they are arranged and related to one another produce the grotesque and dreadful grimace of a damned race."

"You may want to ask me," he added, "why in spite of everything I keep on fighting in the revolution. First, because the revolution is a hurricane, and any man who is swept up in it

is a wretched, helpless dry leaf. Second, because a stubborn primitive streak and my mental attitude of a confirmed idealist and a hopelessly sentimental person have caused me to believe with every ounce of my conviction that any Mexican who bows down to the government of the murderer Huerta is despicable and contemptible! Contradictions! ... Rubbish! What more do you want?"

At this point they were interrupted by Demetrio Macías, who was getting ready to leave.

Alberto Solís greeted the colonel enthusiastically and with eloquent expression he recounted some of the exploits that he had heard about.

Demetrio listened in surprise to the account of feats that he himself had accomplished. Of course the accretions and adornments altered them somewhat, but they were so well told that thereafter both Demetrio and Luis Cervantes told them in that same fashion.

"What a pleasant fellow General Natera is," Cervantes said to Demetrio Macías, when they were back in the inn where they were lodged. "On the other hand, that little captain of his is a real bore."

But Demetrio wasn't paying attention to what he was saying and squeezed his arm with joy as he said:

"Curro, now I'm really a colonel and you are my secretary."

That night Macías's men made all kinds of new friends and they consumed mescal and other kinds of alcohol in quantity in order to celebrate the new acquaintances. Since not everyone gets along well with others and sometimes alcohol does not give good advice, naturally certain differences arose. But everything was taken care of very well, outside the saloon, or the restaurant or the pool hall and without inconveniencing one's friends. The next morning it turned out that several had died in the process, an old prostitute with a bullet in her belly and two of Colonel Macías's new recruits with their heads bashed in.

Anastasio Montañez reported the situation

to his superior, who with a shrug of his shoulders said:

"Well, have them buried."

XV.

There come the big hats again," the people of Fresnillo shouted in terror when they learned that the attack by the revolutionaries had failed. The reckless mob was reeling back from Zacatecas, men bronzed by the sun, filthy and almost naked, their heads hidden by enormous straw hats with a high cone-shaped crown and a wide brim that reached down as far as the nose.

They called them the "big hats." The big hats were as gay coming back as they had been when they marched away to battle, looting each village, each hacienda, each farm, and even the most wretched hut that they found along the way.

"Who will buy this piece of machinery from me?" shouted one, flushed and weary from carrying the burden that he had "liberated."

It was a new typewriter whose shiny nickel trim gave off sparkles that attracted everyone's attention.

In one single morning the Oliver had gone through the hands of five owners, starting out with a value of ten pesos or so and dropping one or two with each new owner. The truth was that it was too heavy, and no one was willing to put up with it for more than half an hour.

"I'll give you twenty-five cents for it," said Codorniz.

"Take it! shouted the owner, handing it over rapidly, almost afraid that the purchaser would change his mind.

Codorniz gave him the twenty-five centavos and had the enjoyment of taking it in his hands and then tossing it on a pile of rocks were it fell noisily.

That was the signal that started it. All those who were carrying heavy or bothersome objects began to get rid of them by smashing them against the rocks—costly objects of crystal, thick glass mirrors, brass candelabra, porcelain figurines and chinaware, all the booty of the day's action.

Demetrio took no part in all that gaiety, which had little to do with the outcome of the military operations. He called Anastasio Montañez and Pancracio aside and said to them:

"Look, those fellows don't have any nerve! It isn't so hard to take a town. Look, first you open up like this, then you keep coming together, coming together ... and that's it!"

And with a broad gesture he opened his arms wide and then gradually brought them together, explaining his movements, until finally he brought his arms across his chest.

Anastasio and Pancracio found the explanation so simple and so clear that they could only answer:

"That's the plain truth. They don't have any nerve!"

"Do you remember Camila, Anastasio?" Demetrio asked, stretched out on his back on the manure of the corral where they were all lying, yawning before going to sleep.

"Who is this Camila you're talking about, friend?"

"The girl that used to bring in my food when we were back on the ranch."

Montañez made a gesture that seemed to say, "As far as I'm concerned, women just don't count."

"I can't get her out of my mind," Demetrio kept on saying as he lit a cigarette. "I was real sick. I had just downed a cup of cool, clear water. 'Do you want some more,' she asked me, a dark little girl, not really cute. Well, I was all worn out from the fever, and the only thing I could see was that cup of water and hear that sweet little voice, 'Don't you want some more?' but that voice sounded in my ears like the tinkling of a silver bell.... Pancracio, what do you say? Do we go back to the ranch?"

"Look, Demetrio, I bet you don't believe it. I've had a lot of experience in handling women. But women? They're all right for a time. But, what a time! Think of all the sores and scratches that mark my body! Damn them! They are the devil himself! Really, Demetrio, I bet you don't believe it! That's why you will see I don't .... But I've had all kinds of experience with them."

"What day do we go back to the ranch, Pancracio?" Demetrio kept on asking, blowing out a cloud of light-colored smoke.

"Just tell us when. You know I left my love back there."

"Your love ... and mine," Codorniz remarked.

"And mine too. I'm glad you're generous. Go bring her for us!" Meco added.

"Well, then, bring the one for all of us .. that one-eyed gal María Antonia," Meco shouted.

And they burst out in guffaws. Then began a competition in insults and obscenities between Pancracio and Manteca.

XVI.

"Villa is coming!"

The news spread like lightning from one mouth to another.

Ah, Villa! The magic word, the great man who stands out over all others, the invincible warrior who like a serpent hypnotizes hares and rabbits.

"Our Mexican Napoleon," Luis Cervantes says.

"The Aztec eagle who thrusts his beak into the head of the snake Victoriano Huerta! That's what I said in a speech in Ciudad Juárez," added Natera's assistant Alberto Solís, with an ironic smile.

The two of them were seated at the counter of a saloon downing beer and liquor.

And the big hats, with scarves around their necks, heavy leather shoes, and calloused cowboy hands, eating and drinking constantly, could talk about nothing but Villa and his troops. Natera's men told stories that caused the newcomers of Macías to gape in wonder. Oh, Villa! The victories at Ciudad Juárez, Tierra Blanca, Chihuahua, Torreón! But those deeds that were witnessed or experienced could in no way approach the marvelous tales, the ancient Mexican legend that was born again, the indomitable man of the mountain, pursued by the government as if he were a beast. The fearless fellow who one fine night appears unannounced at the office of a millionaire industrialist or hacienda owner and with a smile says to him, "I need ten thousand pesos." The solemn-faced owner raises his head in surprise, and his face turns the color of earth and deathly pale. Sometimes the funds come out of the cashbox immediately, but occasionally there isn't enough on hand and the delivery cannot be made on the spot. But the man with the black beard and the eagle eye is a person who is able to trust in the word of a gentleman. "Tomorrow you have ready such and such an amount at such and such a time and at such and such a place." And he disappears as suddenly as he has entered. Why does he want that money? To give it away as charity, of course! To an old man who comes along on a worn-out, rheumatic donkey he tosses a bundle of bank notes. To a widow who keeps herself and her six little ones alive by eating cactus leaves on the mountainside he hands over a sack of silver coins. And that is how the bandit savior goes through life: robbing the rich to make the poor happy. But woe to anyone who deceives him! As he is generous toward those who give in to his commands, so is he vengeful toward those who do not heed them.

A wealthy businessman was found lying on the carpet of his bedroom with his head torn off his body, a banker with his intestines strewn across the tile floor of his office, an hacendado found in a pasture, pecked by the buzzards, with the skin torn from the soles of his feet and sand and stones embedded in his flesh. Proteus, who from the sublime suddenly reverts to the brutal. The great man of the rabble.

"Because you know, my friend Montañez," one of Natera's men was saying, "if you hit General Villa just right he will give you a whole hacienda, but if you get on the wrong side of him he'll have you shot!"

"Ah, and Villa's soldiers! Nothing but big

well-dressed fellows, wearing Stetson hats, new khaki uniforms, and four-dollar American shoes."

And when Natera's men talked about all that they glanced at one another and took stock of their own coarse hats of straw made rotten by moisture and the sun, of their tattered trousers and shirts that covered their bruised and dirty bodies.

"No one is hungry there. They have rail-road cars jammed with cows and calves, freight cars loaded with food and whole trainloads of clothing, arms, and ammunition.

And then they talked about Villa's air-planes.

"Oh, those airplanes! Down on the ground when you look at them from up close, you don't know what they are. They look like dugout canoes or maybe rafts, but then they sort of rise up into the air, and they make a racket that frightens you, something like an automobile that moves real fast. Just imagine it's a bird, don't think about anything but a great big bird that travels, yet it hardly seems to move at all. But now comes the best part. Inside the big bird there's a gringo who's got a lot of hand grenades. Can you imagine what that's like? When it comes time to fight it's just like scattering corn out for the chickens. The gringo starts flinging handsful of grenades on top of the enemy ... and then the whole place looks like a cemetery, dead men here, there, and all over."

And when Anastasio Montañez finally asked whether General Natera's men had ever fought among the troops that General Villa had commanded, they informed him that they did not know him, and what they had been describing in such glowing terms had come to them only through hearsay.

"Well, as far as I'm concerned, among us men we're all alike and no one is braver than anyone else. What you really need to fight is to be ashamed. I was never meant to be a soldier! Here you see me ragged like this. I'll bet you don't believe it, but I'm not poor."

"I have my ten yoke of oxen, I'll bet you don't believe it," Codorniz adds and goes off laughing uproariously to have some drinks with another band of soldiers.

XVII.

The roar of gunfire lessened and moved away into the distance. Luis Cervantes screwed up his courage and poked his head out from his hiding place in the middle of a pile of rubble from some fortifications on the highest point of a hill. He scarcely realized how he came to be there. Demetrio and his men disappeared all of a sudden, and before he knew it he was all alone on his horse, but then he was swept away by an onslaught of infantry. They knocked him off his horse, and then when he had been trampled and scratched, a man on horseback with a red bandana around his neck and with many religious prints on his hat came along, picked him up, and put him on behind. But before long the horse and its rider stumbled and crashed to the ground and Cervantes lost all idea of his rifle, his revolver, and everything else. Then he found himself in a cloud of white smoke and the whistling of the shells, and the hole and those piled up chunks of adobe looked to him like a very safe refuge.

"Comrade!"

"Comrade!"

"My horse threw me. ... They set upon me. They left me for dead and stole my weapons! What could I do?" Luis Cervantes explained.

"Nobody threw me off. Here I am ... just as a precaution. Do you understand?"

The light-hearted tone of Alberto Solís caused Cervantes to blush.

"Confound it!" Solís shouted enthusiastically. "That leader of yours, Macías, is really a brave fellow! What daring and what calmness! His feat today is worthy of the pen of Homer."

Luis Cervantes, completely confused, did not know what to reply.

"Oh, you hadn't heard about it? You must have looked for a safe place right away."

Luis gritted his teeth.

Installment no. 12

"Well, I'll tell you about it. I saw the whole thing. I got here with the last wave of the infantry, and of course now I'm doing what you are doing. I'm resting."

Luis turned purple with rage.

"Look, partner," Solís said, without being aware of the effect of his words, which lacked any evil intent. "Come here and I'll tell you about it. We were behind that peak over there. You can see that from that slope, at the foot of the mountain there is no way up except for the one that is right in front of us. On this side the slope is so steep that it's impossible to get to the top. It's so dangerous that one false step would make you fall over the cliff and into the sharp edges of the rocks. Well, anyway, a part of the Moya Brigade was stretched out on the slope, determined to advance on the first row of trenches of the enemy. Shells passed whizzing over our heads, and there was fighting all over. For a few minutes they quit firing on us, but everywhere else they seemed to be attacking us fiercely. Then we charged their position. But my friend, you should have seen it. The lower half of the slope was like a carpet of corpses. The machine guns did the job, and they swept us up with only a few getting out alive. The officers were enraged and were hesitant to order a new assault. That was the moment when Demetrio Macías, without waiting for orders from anyone, shouted out 'Come on, men!' "

" 'What does he think he's doing?' we all said."

"Demetrio's horse, almost as if it had hooks on its hooves, scrambled up the slope strewn with boulders."

"Can you imagine it, comrade? 'Up, up!' shouted his twenty men and they followed him, leaping like deer from one rock to another, as though man and horse were one single being. Sometimes one of them lost his footing and broke his bones as he fell between the crags, but most of them were able to reach this place where we are now, overrunning the trenches and knifing the soldiers in them. Demetrio tossed his rope around a machine gun and dragged it along as you would a wild bull. The onslaught caught the federals by surprise and their discipline broke down, but all this could not have lasted more than a few minutes. But we took advantage of their lapse and took the position from them. Your leader is truly a fearless man!"

From the top of the hill, to one side was La Bufa with its crest, like the feathered headdress of some haughty Aztec king. Its slope for several hundred yards was covered with dead soldiers, their hair matted and their clothing stained with blood and dirt, and among the piles of corpses, tattered women kept moving about, like starved coyotes, searching and looting.

Amid the white smoke of the gunfire and the thick black clouds that issued from the burning buildings there were spots that were bathed in sunlight — houses whose windows and doors were closed tight, streets in layers, piled one on top of another in a maze of patterns, climbing up the mountainsides, and against these stood out arches between graceful columns, the towers and domes of the churches.

"How beautiful the revolution is, even in its own barbarity!" Luis Cervantes exclaimed.

"Yes, it really is. It's a shame that what we have left to do isn't like that. We have to wait until there are no longer any combatants, until we no longer hear the shots of the mob that is given over to the delights of looting, until the psychology of our race will shine as limpid as a drop of water, condensed into two words: rob and kill. What a terrible disappointment it would be, my friend, if those of us who are putting into this all our enthusiasm, our hopes, and our very lives to overthrow a bandit who is a murderer should turn out to fashion a monstrous pedestal for a hundred or two hundred scoundrels of the likes of Victoriano Huerta."

A number of federal stragglers still were trying to hide from some cavalrymen wearing white breeches and high-topped hats. A bullet whistled above their heads.

Alberto Solís, who had remained with his arms crossed and absorbed in thought, remarked, "I'll be damned if I like these mosquitoes! What do you say we get out of here?"

Luis Cervantes's smile was so scornful that Alberto sat down comfortably on a boulder.

His gaze again wandered toward the white spirals of rifle smoke and the cloud of dust that rose from each demolished building, from each roof that collapsed. And it seemed that he had discovered a symbol of the revolution in the billowing smoke and the clouds of dust that embraced one another in brotherly fashion, which mixed together and became lost in nothingness.

"Ah!" he suddenly cried out. "That's it!"

And joyfully with his arm outstretched he pointed toward the railroad station. The trains, snorting, coughing out great columns of black smoke, with the cars overflowing with federal soldiers, were pulling out at full speed.

He felt a sharp pain in his belly and as if his legs had suddenly become as limp as a rag, he slipped down off the rock. Then his ears buzzed, and all was darkness and silence.

END OF THE FIRST PART

SECOND PART

I.

Rather than champagne that bubbles as it gushes out, diffusing the light of the candles, Demetrio Macías prefers the limpid tequila of Jalisco.

Men smeared with dirt, smoke, and sweat, with curly beards, disheveled heads of hair, wearing filthy rags, were clustered around the tables of a restaurant.

"I killed two colonels," shouted in a harsh, guttural voice a fat little fellow who wore a hat trimmed with braid, a leather jacket, and a red handkerchief around his neck. "They were so pot-bellied they couldn't even run. They kept stumbling over the stones, and to get up the hill they turned as red as tomatoes and their tongues hung out. 'Don't run so fast, you hairless brutes!' I yelled at them. 'Stop, I can't stand flustered chickens like you. Stop, you bald bastards. I'm not going to do anything to you!' They gave up. Ha, ha! Those birds swallowed it. Bang, bang! One shot for each one ... and then they really got to rest."

"One of the big shots got away from me," spoke up a soldier who was resting in a corner of the large room between the wall and the counter, with his legs stretched out and his rifle lying between them. "That son of a bitch was really loaded with gold! The gold braid on his epaulets and his cape was enough to knock your eyes out. And what did I do? I let the big dummy go on by! He took out his handkerchief and gave the password, and I just stood there with my mouth open. He barely gave me time to get around the corner and then he started shooting, one bullet after another! I let him use up all the shells in his clip. And then I said, 'Now it's my turn.' Holy Mother of Jalpa, don't let me miss this son of a ... dirty word. I didn't get him! He got away. He was riding a good nag. He passed in front of me like a bolt of lightning! But another bird that was coming along the same street made up for it. I sure made him do a flip flop!"

Words rush furiously from their mouths, and while the men give heated accounts of their adventures, olive-skinned women, with prominent whites in their eyes and teeth the color of ivory, carrying revolvers at their waists and crossed belts stuffed with cartridges over their chests and shoulders and wearing wide-brimmed straw hats, move here and there among the groups like dogs in the street.

A girl with cheeks bright with carmine, very dark neck and arms, and with a very coarse bearing took a leap and jumped up on the counter of the saloon, close to the table where Demetrio was seated.

He turned and looked at her and faced a pair of lustful eyes beneath a low forehead between two thick bands of hair.

The door opened wide

Installment no. 13

and one after another Anastasio Montañez, Pancracio, Codorniz, and Meco made their way in, each with his mouth agape and dazzled by the sight.

Anastasio cried out in surprise and rushed over to greet the fat little charro with the hat trimmed with braid and wearing the bright red handkerchief.

They are old friends who now recognize one another. They go into a bear hug so tight that their faces turn black.

"Demetrio, I want you to meet Margarito. A real friend! Oh how I'm glad to be with Blondie! You'll get to know him, partner. He's real smart. Do you remember, Blondie, when we were in the Escobedo Penitentiary, down in Jalisco? We were together a whole year."

Demetrio, who remained quiet and even thoughtful amid the general hubbub, without removing the cigar from between his teeth, stuck out his hand and mumbled:

"Pleased to meet you."

"Then you are Demetrio Macías?" the girl asked abruptly. She was still sitting on the counter, swinging her legs and touching Demetrio's shoulder with her leather shoes.

"At your service," he replied, hardly moving his head to look at her.

She paid no attention and kept swinging her uncovered legs, showing off her blue stockings.

"Hey, Pintada, what are you doing here? Come on down and have a drink with us," Margarito yelled to her.

The girl accepted the invitation immediately and boldly made a place for herself, placing her body in a chair opposite Demetrio.

"So you are the famous Demetrio Macías who won the day in Zacatecas?" Pintada asked.

Demetrio nodded his head affirmatively, while Margarito burst out laughing and said to her:

"You're a slick one, Pintada! Now you want to try a general on for size!"

Demetrio, who didn't catch on, turned and looked at her. They stared face to face, like two strange dogs who sniff at one another in distrust.

Demetrio was unable to stand up under the furiously provocative eyes of the girl and had to look away.

Some of Natera's officers from where they were sitting began to make fun of Pintada and shouted obscene remarks at her.

Her expression did not change and she commented:

"General Natera is getting ready to give you your eagles to make you a general. Go ahead, shake!"

And she held her hand out to Demetrio and grasped his with the strength of a man.

Demetrio, swelled with pride by the congratulations that were beginning to pour in on him, ordered champagne for everyone.

"I don't want any wine, boy," said Margarito to the waiter, "just water with some ice in it, that's all."

"I want something to eat, just so it isn't chile or beans," Pancracio ordered.

Officers continued to come in, and soon the restaurant was filled. Many of them wore insignia of stars and bars, hats of all shapes and colors, scarlet-colored handkerchiefs, rings with fat diamonds, heavy gold watch chains.

"Say, boy," Margarito shouted, "I asked you for some water with ice in it. Understand I'm not asking for charity. Do you see this wad of bills? I can buy you and even the old woman that lives in your house. Do you understand me, boy? You know, I don't like to have to ask for something a second time. I tell you I want some water with ice in it. Don't answer me. You don't know me. You don't know who you're talking to. Give me some ice water. I don't want to hear your explanations. I don't want to know if you're out of it. You can find a way to get me some. Look, I'm likely to fly off the handle! I tell you I don't want your explanations. Just some ice water. Well then, are you going to bring it or not? Oh, you aren't? Then take that ...."

The waiter goes down under a magnificent smash.

"That's the way I am, General Macías! Look how I don't have a single hair left on my face. Do you know why? Because I get mad easily, and when I don't have anyone to take it out on, I just pull out one whisker after another until I get over my angry fit. I tell you, general, if I hadn't done it that way I would have died from all that rage."

"It's hard to keep it bottled up inside of you when you're angry," agreed a soldier who was wearing a straw hat that looked like the thatch on an old hut. "In Torreón I killed an old woman because she didn't want to sell me a plateful of enchiladas. I could have eaten them. I didn't get what I wanted, but at least I felt better afterwards."

"I killed a storekeeper in Parral because in the change he gave me he gave me two of Huerta's bills," commented another who was wearing a star, showing at the same time on his dark, calloused fingers precious stones that shone.

"Up in Chihuahua I killed a guy because every day we came together at the same table and at the same time when I went to have lunch. That really griped me! But what could I do?"

"I killed ...."

The subject is inexhaustible.

At daybreak, when gaiety as well as raucous spitting reached their height in the restaurant, when gaudily painted young girls from the outskirts of the town mixed with the women from the north, women with dark faces the color of ashes, then Demetrio took out his watch that struck the hours, inlaid with precious stones, and asked his neighbor what time it was.

Anastasio Montañez looked at the face, then poked his head out of a window and scanning the star-studded sky, remarked:

"The Pleiades are hanging pretty low. It'll be daylight before long."

Outside wild shouts, bursts of laughter, songs of drunken soldiers still go on. Soldiers on runaway horses race headlong, beating the sidewalks with their hooves. Everywhere one hears shots of rifles and pistols.

And down the middle of the street on the way to the hotel, Demetrio and Pintada stumble along, their arms around each other.

Following up the procession are three men who provide music, playing violins and guitar without stopping.

II.

"How stupid you are!" burst out Pintada in loud laughter. "Where have you been? Who ever hears of soldiers going to stay in a hotel any more? Where are you from? When you get somewhere all you do is pick out the house you like best, and then you take it over and don't ask no one whether you can or not. So, who is the revolution for? For the city dudes? Now we're going to be the real dudes. Hey, Pancracio, let me have your bayonet! Rich bastards! They have to keep everything under lock and key!"

She thrust the steel point in the crack of a drawer and prying with it, with the handle she broke open the lock and lifted up the splintered top of the desk.

Anastasio Montañez, Pancracio, and Pintada ran their hands through the pile of letters, prints, photographs, and other papers that were in a heap on the rug.

Pancracio was peeved because he found nothing that he took a fancy to, and with the toe of his sandal he kicked a framed photograph which sailed through the air and crashed noisily against the chandelier in the center of the room.

They drew their empty hands from among the papers, muttering curses.

But Pintada was tireless and kept breaking open drawer after drawer until there was no cranny she hadn't looked into.

They failed to notice the noiseless roll of a tiny container covered with gray velvet that came to rest at the feet of Luis Cervantes.

He pretended to glance at it with an extreme lack of concern, while Demetrio, stretched out on the rug, seemed to be asleep. Cervantes drew the container close to him with the toe of his shoe, then leaned over, scratched his ankle, and quickly picked up the object.

He was dazzled. Two diamonds with the purest sparkle in a filigree mounting. Quickly he hid them in his pocket.

When Demetrio woke up, Luis Cervantes said to him, "General, have you seen the mess the boys have been making? Don't you think something should be done to stop it?"

"No, Curro. Poor fellows! After they've had bullets whiz by their bellies it's the only fun they have left."

"Yes, general, but at least they shouldn't do it here. Look, that runs us down and, worst of all, it makes our cause look bad."

Demetrio fixed his eagle eyes on Luis Cervantes. He tapped his teeth with his fingernails and said:

"Don't blush! Look, don't come to me with stories. We know that what's yours is yours and what's mine is mine. Well, you got the little box, right? Well, I got the watch."

And the two of them having reached an understanding showed one another their booty.

Installment no. 14

Meanwhile Pintada and her companions searched the rest of the house.

Codorniz entered the room with a twelve-year-old girl, who already bore copper-colored spots on her forehead and her arms. The two stopped in surprise and then, lost in thought, looked at the piles of books lying on the rug,

tables and chairs, mirrors torn from the walls with the glass smashed, great frames of prints and portraits shattered and broken, furniture and whatnots splintered. With eager eyes, stopping his breathing, Codorniz sought out his prey.

Outside, in a corner of the patio and in a cloud of suffocating smoke, Manteca was cooking ears of corn, keeping the fire going with books and papers that gave off lively flames.

"Hey," Codorniz shouted suddenly, "look what I found! These are good saddle cloths for my mare."

And with a jerk, he yanked on a plush curtain that came crashing down with its rod upon the finely carved finial of an armchair.

"Look here! I've never seen so many naked women!" exclaimed the girl, enthralled with the illustrations from a luxurious copy of the *Divine Comedy*. I really like this, and I'm going to take it with me."

And she began to tear out the illustrations that most attracted her attention.

Demetrio got up and sat down in a large easy chair beside Luis Cervantes. He ordered some beer. He handed a bottle to his secretary and with one single swallow downed his. Then he became drowsy, half closed his eyes, and went to sleep again.

"Say," said a man to Pancracio in the entrance, "what time of day can I talk to the general?"

"You can't see him. He woke up with a hangover," Pancracio answered. "What's your business?"

"I want him to sell some of those books that he hasn't any use for."

"I can sell them to you myself."

"How much do you want for them?"

Pancracio wrinkled his eyebrows and then thought a bit.

"The ones that have pictures for a nickel and the others ... well if you want to buy all of them I'll give you the others for nothing."

The man carried away books in baskets used for harvesting corn and fruit.

"Demetrio, hey! Demetrio, wake up!" yelled Pintada. "You don't want to sleep like a fat old hog. Look who's here! Margarito! You don't know what a fine fellow this Blondie is."

"I respect you, General Macías, and I want you to know that I like you and your way of doing things. So if it's all right I'd like to come over to your brigade."

"What is your rank?" Demetrio inquired.

"Captain of the first grade, general."

"Well, over here I'll make you a major."

Margarito was a fat little man with a pointed moustache and cruel blue eyes that were hidden by his cheeks when he laughed. Formerly a waiter in El Mónico's in Chihuahua, he now boasted three bars of yellow metal as a captain of the first grade in the Army of the North.

He heaped praise on Demetrio and all his men. And while he was doing that the case of beer disappeared in no time.

Pintada suddenly appeared in the doorway of the parlor, showing off a splendid silk dress, trimmed with exquisite lace.

"You forgot to put on your stockings," shouted Blondie, his sides splitting with laughter.

The little girl who came in with Codorniz, in great glee, burst out in piercing shrieks.

But it made no difference to Pintada. She made a face showing her indifference, then threw herself down on the rug and with her own feet flipped off the white satin slippers, wiggling pleasantly her bare toes that had become numb because of the tightness of her footwear and then said:

"Hey, Pancracio! Bring me some of my blue stockings from my bundle of booty!"

While the room kept filling up with new friends and friends from previous campaigns, Demetrio recounted in detail his most outstanding military exploits.

"What's that racket I hear?" he inquired, surprised by the tuning up of stringed instruments and brasses outside.

"General," Luis Cervantes solemnly reported, "it's a banquet that your old friends are giving for you to celebrate the battle of Zacatecas and your well-deserved promotion to general."

III.

"General," Luis Cervantes spoke up clearly, as he led into the dining room a strikingly beautiful girl, "I want you to meet my bride-to-be."

They all turned to look at the girl, who opened wide her startled blue eyes.

She could scarcely have been more than fourteen. Her skin was far and soft, like a petal from a tea rose, her hair golden, and the expression in her eyes was a combination of perverse curiosity and an undefined childish terror.

Luis Cervantes, who felt an extreme satisfaction inside, saw that Demetrio was staring like a bird of prey at the attractive girl.

They made room for her between Blondie and Luis Cervantes, facing Demetrio.

Scattered among the goblets, crystal and cut glass dishes, china dinner plates, and clay vases of flowers were enormous bottles of tequila.

All sweaty and cursing under his load, Meco staggered in carrying a case of beer on his shoulder.

"You don't know yet what this Blondie is like," Pintada said when she noticed that Margarito did not for a single moment take his eyes off Luis Cervantes's fiancée. "He's got a way with him and there's no one in the world more expert than he is."

She cast a lascivious glance in his direction and added:

"That's why I can't stand him, not even looking at him in a picture."

The orchestra burst out in a magnificent bullfighting march.

The soldiers roared in exhilaration.

"What wonderful tripe, General! I swear I've never eaten any prepared better than this!" said Blondie, recalling certainly El Mónico's in Chihuahua.

"Do you really like it, Blondie? answered Demetrio. "If you do, then have them serve you until you're filled up."

"That's the way I like things," Anastasio Montañez agreed. "And that's the fine part of it, because if I like a dish I keep eating and eating until it comes up in belches."

Then came the noisy opening of mouths and great swallowing. Great drinking went on.

Finally Luis Cervantes took a glass of champagne and stood up.

"General ...."

"Oh, oh," Pintada broke in, "now they're getting ready for the speeches, and I get bored as hell listening to them. This is a good time for me to go out to the corral. There's nothing else to eat here anyway."

Luis Cervantes presented the emblem of black cloth with its little metal eagle in a toast that no one understood but all applauded thunderously.

Demetrio took in his hands the insignia of his new rank, and with blushing face and a gleaming look, his teeth shining, he said ingenuously:

"And now what do I do with this buzzard?"

"Friend," Anastasio Montañez said in a quavering voice as he stood up, "I don't have anything to say ...."

Whole minutes went by. The cursed words refused to come out when Anastasio tried to call them to mind. He turned as red as a beet, beads of perspiration came out on his forehead streaked with grime. Finally he decided to bring his toast to an end.

"Well, I don't have anything to say ... except that you know I'm your pal."

And as they had applauded Luis Cervantes, Anastasio Montañez when he finished with great seriousness gave the signal to applaud.

But everything worked out. His awkwardness was a stimulus and even Manteca and Codorniz offered toasts.

It was Meco's turn when Pintada appeared amid great shouts of glee. Clicking with her tongue, she was trying to lead an excellent jet black mare into the dining room.

The mare refused to pass through the door, but a tug on the halter and a lash of the whip on her haunch caused her to enter with some spirit and considerable noise.

The soldiers, stupefied, looked with ill-concealed envy upon the choice booty.

"I don't know how this damned Pintada does it. She always turns up with the best loot," yelled Margarito. "She's been doing this ever since she joined up with us in Tierra Blanca."

"Hey, Pancracio, go bring me in a bundle of alfalfa for my mare," Pintada ordered curtly.

She sat down and handed the reins to a soldier.

Once again goblets and glasses were filled. Some were beginning to lean over and their eyelids wanted to go shut but most of them continued to shout merrily.

Installment no. 15

And among them the little girl whom Luis Cervantes had brought in, having poured all her wine into a handkerchief, looked first in one direction and then another, her blue eyes charged with terror.

"Fellows," shouted Blondie as he stood up, shouting above the hubbub with his shrill voice, "I'm tired of living and I've decided to kill myself. I'm fed up with Pintada. And this little angel from heaven here doesn't even want to look at me."

Luis Cervantes realized that these last words were meant for his fiancée and was astounded when he realized that the foot whose presence he noted between those of the girl was not Demetrio's but Margarito's.

And resentment began to boil inside him.

"Look, fellow," Blondie went on, holding his revolver straight up, "I'm going to shoot myself right in the forehead."

And he pointed right at the great mirror at the end of the room where he appeared full length.

"Don't budge, Pintada!"

The mirror shattered into long, pointed slivers. The bullet grazed Pintada's hair but she didn't even blink.

IV.

Luis Cervantes woke up toward evening. He rubbed his eyes and straightened up. He was on the hard ground among the flower pots of the garden. Nearby, breathing noisily, were Anastasio Montañez, Pancracio, and Codorniz, still sound asleep.

He could feel that his lips were swollen, and his nose was stiff and dried out. He could see blood on his hands and spots on his shirt, and then he remembered suddenly what had happened. Quickly he got up and headed for one of the bedrooms. He pushed on the door several times, but was unable to open it. Then he hesitated for a few moments. It was all true. He was sure that he had not dreamed it. He had gotten up from the table with the girl. He took her to a bedroom, but before he could close the door, Demetrio rushed after them, stumbling in his drunkenness. Then Pintada followed Demetrio, and they struggled together. Demetrio, his eyes gleaming like two coals and with light-colored hairs on his coarse lips, pursued the girl with ardent desire. Pintada pushed Demetrio as hard as she could to drive him away.

"But you! ... What are you trying to do?" he howled.

Pintada thrust her leg between his knees and with a tremendous shove tripped him and sent him sprawling full length outside the room.

Demetrio got up raging mad.

"Help! Help! He's going to kill me!" squealed Pintada, gripping his wrist as tightly as she could and turning away the barrel of the pistol.

The bullet became embedded in the bricks. Pintada continued to scream. Anastasio Montañez came up behind Demetrio and disarmed him.

Demetrio, like a bull newly arrived in the middle of the ring, looked around, his eyes wandering.

Standing around him were Luis Cervantes, Anastasio, Manteca, and many others.

"Damn! You've taken my gun! As if I needed a gun to take care of you bastards!"

And flailing away, in a few brief moments he sent them tumbling face down on the brick pavement.

And afterward ... Luis Cervantes remembered no more. Surely they lay there asleep after the beating they had received. Certainly his fiancée, out of fear of all those boozy soldiers, had been foresighted enough to lock herself up.

"Perhaps that bedroom opens on the parlor and I can get in that way," he thought.

The footsteps awakened Pintada, who was sleeping near Demetrio on the rug at the foot of a settee, where the black mare was eating alfalfa and corn.

"What are you after?" the woman asked. "Oh, now I know what you're trying to find. You damn fool! Look! I locked up your girl friend because she couldn't take any more of that damned Demetrio. Get the key. It's there on the table."

Luis Cervantes looked for the key in every nook and cranny of the parlor but without success.

"Say, Curro, tell me how you got your hands on that girl."

Luis Cervantes nervously kept looking for the key.

"You don't have to get so hot and bothered. I'm going to give it to you. But tell me. This whole thing amuses the hell out of me. That fancy kid is your kind of girl. She's not a country hick like the rest of us."

"I don't have anything to tell. She's my fiancée, and that's all there is to it."

"Haw, haw, haw! Your fiancée! Look Curro, whatever you're up to I know all about it. I'm damn sharp. Meco and Manteca dragged her out of her house, and they traded her to you for a print of the Lord of the Villita and a set of plated cufflinks. Am I lying, Curro? There are smart people around here, but it's hard work to find them. Isn't that right?"

Pintada got up to get him the key, but she couldn't find it either and she was greatly surprised. She stopped and thought a bit. Then suddenly she rushed over to the bedroom door. She leaned over and peeked through the keyhole and stayed there motionless until her eyes grew accustomed to the darkness of the room. Then with her eye still glued to the keyhole she murmured abruptly:

"Oh, Blondie, you son of a bitch! Come look, Curro!"

And she moved away laughing raucously.

"Never in my life have I seen a faster man than this one!"

The morning of the next day Pintada waited for the moment when Blondie left his bedroom to go out to feed his horse.

"You poor child! Hurry up! Get out of here and go home! These monsters are likely to kill you. Hurry up, run!"

And over the little girl with blue eyes and the appearance of a Virgin, who was wearing only a slip and stockings, she draped the louse-infested blanket that belonged to Manteca. She took the girl by the hand and led her to the street.

"God be praised!" she exclaimed. "Well! How I love that Blondie!"

V.

Like colts that whinny and caper when the first claps of thunder come in May, so do Demetrio's men travel through the sierra.

"To Moyahua, fellows!"

"To the country of Demetrio Macías!"

"To the country of don Mónico the tyrant!"

The landscape becomes bright and clear. The sun comes out in a scarlet band upon the transparency of the sky.

The mountain ranges began taking the shape of monsters that resembled lizards, with angular backbones, mountains that remind one of the heads of colossal Aztec idols, with faces of giants, frightful and grotesque expressions that at first seem to smile, then leave one with an undefinable terror, like a foreboding of mystery.

At the head of the band is Demetrio Macías accompanied by his staff: Colonel Anastasio Montañez, Majors Luis Cervantes and Margarito Aranda. Right behind them comes Pintada, who is expertly flirting with Doctor Venancio.

When the sun's rays flickered on the walls of the town, four abreast they began to come into Moyahua.

The cocks made a great fuss with their crowing, and all the dogs barked in alarm but not a single human being appeared.

Pintada spurred on her black mare and leaped forward to ride at Demetrio's side. She left Venancio with a sentence still unfinished, for she was not greatly inspired by the verses of Antonio Plaza.

Very self-confident she establishes herself on the general's right hand. She has on a silk dress and prominent gold earrings. The pale blue of her outline brings out the olive color of her face with its syphilitic spots. With her legs spread apart, her skirt is rolled up to her knee, revealing her faded stockings that are full of holes. She carries a revolver in her bosom and a cartridge belt over the horn of her saddle.

Demetrio also is all dressed up, wearing a hat trimmed with braid, leather trousers with rows of silver buttons, and a deerskin jacket, embroidered with gold thread.

Before long the silence is broken by the noise of doors being forced upon, by men who have fanned out through the town in search of horses, arms, and saddles.

"We are going to make a morning visit to don Mónico's house," Demetrio remarked very seriously as he handed the reins of his horse to a soldier and dismounted.

"We'll have breakfast in don Mónico's dining room. He's a friend of mine who thinks a lot of me."

His staff smiles with a sinister grin. And scraping his spurs noisily along the sidewalk, he heads for the plaza, toward a pretentious house that can only be the residence of a political boss.

"It's sealed up with stone and mortar," says Anastasio Montañez, pushing as hard as he can against the door.

"I know how to open it," replies Pancracio, aiming the muzzle of his rifle at the lock.

Installment no. 16

"No," Demetrio orders. "Go ahead and knock first."

Three blows with the butt of the rifle, then three more, and no one answers. Pancracio begins to curse in impatience and pays no attention to orders. He fires, the latch flies off, and the door finally opens.

There is a hurried movement of hems of skirts, limbs of children, all scurrying off toward the interior of the house.

Demetrio heads straight for the dining room.

"I want something to drink! Here, bring me some wine!" He gives his order in a domineering tone, pounding loudly on the table.

"Sit down, comrades!"

A woman comes out, then another and still another, and between the ample folds of thin black skirts appear the heads of frightened children. One of the women with trembling body goes over to a cupboard, takes out a number of glasses and bottles, and serves wine to the men.

"What weapons do you have?" Demetrio inquires gruffly.

"Weapons?" answers the woman, so frightened she can hardly put words together. "What kind of weapons do you expect a bunch of poor, respectable women all alone to have?"

"Alone? What about don Mónico?"

"He isn't here. We rent the house from him. We hardly know don Mónico except by name."

Demetrio orders a thorough search of the house.

"Oh, no! Please don't! We'll bring you everything we have, but for God's sake don't harm us. We are respectable women all alone!"

"And those kids," Pancracio inquires brutally, "were they born out of the ground?"

The women disappear hastily and return with an old shotgun whose butt is in splinters, covered with dust and cobwebs, and a pistol whose springs are all rusted and out of order.

Demetrio smiles.

"Well, where is the money?"

"Money? What money would we poor unprotected women have?"

They cast a glance with pleading eyes at the soldier who is nearest to them, but then they close them in horror. They have caught sight of Pancracio. They have seen in him the executioner who is crucifying our Lord, Jesus Christ, in the stations of the cross in the parish church.

Demetrio again orders his men to ransack the house.

The women all rush out again and immediately they return with a moth-eaten old wallet that contains a few bills put out by the Huerta government.

Demetrio smiles and without any further discussion has his men come in.

Like hungry dogs that have at last sniffed meat, the mob pushes in, trampling the women who with their own bodies try to prevent them from entering one of the rooms. Some of them fall in a faint, others flee, while the children shriek.

Pancracio is preparing to force open the lock of an enormous clothes closet when suddenly the doors swing open by themselves and a man jumps out carrying a rifle in his hands.

"Don Mónico!" they shout in surprise.

"Demetrio! Don't do anything to me! Don't hurt me! I'm your friend, Demetrio."

Demetrio Macías laughs slyly and asks if he receives his friends with his rifle in his hands.

Don Mónico, confused, stunned, falls at Demetrio's feet, hugging him around the knees. He kisses his feet.

"My wife! My children, friend Demetrio!"

With trembling hand Demetrio replaces his revolver in its holster.

A plaintive image has come to his memory. A woman with his child in her arms, fleeing among the crags of the sierra, at midnight by the light of the moon.... A house burning ....

"Come on! Everybody out!" he yells ominously.

His staff obeys. Don Mónico and all the women kiss his hand in extreme appreciation.

In the street the mob stands by, making jokes and comments while it awaits the general's permission to ransack the house of the town boss.

"Talking about money, I know exactly where they've got it hidden, but I'm not going to tell," says a boy who is carrying a basket on his arm.

"Well, I already know," replies an old woman who has brought a large sack in which to stuff whatever comes her way. "It's in an attic with all kinds of stuff, and in among all that stuff there's a little suitcase with some designs made of shells. That's where the good stuff is."

"That isn't true," a man replies. "They're not dumb enough to leave money around like that. I think they've wrapped it up in a cowhide and buried it in the well."

And the people stir around, some with ropes to tie up their bundles, others with trays. Women hold out their rebozos or open up their aprons, trying to get an idea about how much they might hold. All of them wait, giving thanks to God for whatever they may get from the pillaging.

When Demetrio makes it known that he will not permit any of it, he orders them all to leave. With an expression of disappointment, the townspeople obey him, and before long they melt away. But in the ranks of his soldiers there is grumbling, a murmur of dissatisfaction and no one moves from where he is standing.

Demetrio is upset and again orders them to draw back.

A youth, one of the most recent recruits, who has had too much to drink, laughs and with no anxiety heads for the door.

Demetrio, his expression unchanged, stands holding his smoking pistol, waiting for his soldiers to leave the house.

"Set fire to the house!" he ordered Luis Cervantes when they had returned to the barracks.

And Luis Cervantes, with solicitude that he rarely displayed, without handing down the order to anyone else, carried it out himself.

When two hours later the little plaza of the town was engulfed in smoke and enormous tongues of flame were rising from don Mónico's house, nobody still had been able to fathom the strange procedure the general had followed.

VI.

"Hey, Curro! That isn't what I wanted to happen! This is almost my hometown," Demetrio said to Luis Cervantes, who in the silence of the night by the weak reddish light of a kerosene lamp was emptying out a bag of gold coins bearing the figure of Hidalgo, gleaming like embers.

Seated on Demetrio's bed, Luis Cervantes was suggesting that they divide them in equal parts.

"In the first place, general, only you and I know about it, and then when the sun shines favorably on your house, you've got to open the window and take advantage of the sunlight. Right now it's shining right over us, but we've got to look ahead. A bullet may come along, a runaway horse, a bad cold ... and a widow and children are left in poverty. The government? That's a joke. Don't you be fooled. For example, if you go to see Villa, Carranza, or any of the big leaders and you speak to them about your family. If they reply with a kick on the you know where, you can be sure that you got off easy. And they are right. We haven't taken up arms so that some guy named Carranza or Villa can get to be president of the country. We are fighting to defend the sacred rights of the people, that have been trampled upon by the political boss. And so since neither Villa nor anyone else ought to come and ask our permission to be paid for the services they have given to the country neither do we have to ask permission from anyone."

"What a gabber you are, Curro!"

And his rough black hands moved back and forth over the shiny gold coins, counting and counting away.

Then Luis Cervantes pulled out a medicine box that had contained Fallières phosphate and poured out a stream of trinkets, rings, earrings, and many other jewels of value.

"Look, General. If the revolution keeps on, and it looks as if it will, if the revolution does not come to an end, we can go outside the country to live. We have enough to live on."

Demetrio nodded his head negatively.

"What? You wouldn't do that? Why would one stay here? What cause would we be defending then?"

"That's something I can't explain, Curro, but it wouldn't be the thing for a man to do."

"Take what you like," said Luis Cervantes, showing him the jewels all lined up in a row.

"You keep them! Really, Curro. You know, I'm not really wild about money. Do you want me to tell you how I really feel? Well, if I have a little wine and a girl that I like, I'm the happiest man in the world."

"And why do you put up with that snake in the grass, Pintada?"

"Well, Curro, I'm fed up with her. But that's the way I am. I can't screw up enough courage to tell her. I don't have the nerve to run her off. That's how I am. That's my nature. Look, when I like a woman I get so tongue-tied that if she doesn't speak up, then I can't get up my courage."

And he sighed.

"There's Camila back on the ranch. The girl is ugly but she sure pleases me."

"Whenever you want us to we'll go and get her for you."

Demetrio winked slyly.

"You're going to steal her? Why should I go?"

"I swear I'll do a good job for you, General."

"Really, Curro? Look, if you carry through on your word, I'll give you this watch and throw in its chain to boot, since you like it so much."

Luis Cervantes's eyes glistened.

"Son of a bitch! What do you say, Curro?"

Luis Cervantes took the heavy phosphate box which was by now quite full, he stood up and said with a smile, "I'll see you tomorrow, General. Sleep well."

"What do I know about it? The same as all the rest of you. The general said to me, 'Codorniz, saddle up your horse and my mulberry mare. You're going on an errand with Curro.' Good, we left here around midday. We got to the ranch when it was getting dark. That one-eyes María Antonia put us up."

"She sends you warm greetings, Pancracio. At daybreak Curro woke me up: 'Codorniz, saddle the animals. Leave me my horse and you head back for Moyahua. I'll follow you a little later.' When the sun was up high he caught up with me. He had Camila in the saddle with him, and then he put her down so she could get on the mulberry mare."

"O. K., and how did she act?" someone asked.

"She was so happy that she couldn't stop talking all the way."

"And Curro?"

"King of quiet, the way he always is."

"I think," Doctor Venancio observed in a serious tone, "that if Camila woke up in bed with Demetrio it was all a mistake. Do you remember how much we all drank? The alcoholic spirits went to our heads and we passed out completely."

"What do you mean, alcoholic spirits? The whole thing was cooked up between the general and Curro to put something over on Camila because she is in love with Luis."

"As far as I'm concerned that Curro is just a pimp."

"He's happened to be very fortunate," spoke up Margarito, who had been listening to the conversation. "He's had two fiancées. I got one of them and Demetrio got the other."

They all burst out in snorts of laughter.

As soon as Pintada realized just what had happened she went affectionately and tried to console Camila.

"Poor thing, tell me how it happened."

Camila's eyes were swollen from weeping.

"He lied to me! He lied to me! He said, 'Camila, will you come with me? For you alone I've come here.' Well, don't you think I'd go away with him? As for loving him, I love him a lot. Just look at these gray hairs of mine just from thinking about him. I get up in the morning and I don't feel like doing anything. My mamma calls me to breakfast and in my mouth the tortilla tastes like an old piece of rag. And all that worry, worry, just from thinking about him."

"Well, you went away with him. And after that, what happened?"

"Well, I don't know. But I have the notion he did it on purpose."

And she burst into tears again and in order to stifle her sobs she covered her mouth and her nose with her rebozo.

"Look, I'm going to get you out of this pickle. Don't be foolish. Don't cry any more. Don't think about Curro. Do you know what that Curro is? Really, you can believe it? The general keeps him here for good reasons. Well, do you want to go back home?"

"My mamma would beat me to death."

"She won't hurt you. Let's do this. The soldiers are supposed to leave here any minute. When Demetrio comes around and tells you to get ready, that we're about to go, you answer him that your body hurts all over, that you feel as if they had beat you with a club. And you stretch and yawn a lot when he comes around. Then you touch your forehead and say, 'I'm burning up with fever.' Then I'll tell Demetrio to leave the two of us here, that I'll stay around to look after you, and later when you're feeling

better we'll catch up with him. But what I'll really do is take you home, safe and sound."

VIII.

"You have orders, General, to get your men ready immediately to go after Orozco and his men," said Luis Cervantes, reading the message that Demetrio had just received.

"Let's head for Jalisco, men!"

"Get ready you lovely gals from Jalisco! I'm heading your way!"

It was an enthusiastic and exuberant moment for all the soldiers.

Demetrio's eyes sparkled. To go fight Orozco's men! What an opportunity! To take on real men at last! No more of this business of killing federal soldiers the way you kill rabbits and turkeys!

"If I could catch that bandit Pascual Orozco alive I'd tear the soles off his feet and make him tramp for twenty-four hours through the sierra!" Margarito announced spiritedly.

"What do you mean?" Anastasio Montañez questioned in a puzzled tone. "Then Pascual Orozco isn't on our side?"

"He was the first one who betrayed Madero," declared Venancio. "The first Judas of the revolution!"

And immediately they put their things in order to get under way.

"For Camila, the dappled mare with my silver-plated saddle," Demetrio said to Pancracio.

"Camila can't go," Pintada spoke up suddenly.

"Who asked for your opinion?" Demetrio asked harshly.

"Isn't that right, Camila? You woke up hurting all over and you feel like you've got a fever now? Isn't it true you don't want to leave now?"

"Well, she faltered. "I'll do whatever Demetrio wants ...."

"How stupid you are! Tell him you don't

want to! Tell him no," Pintada, upset and flustered, whispered in her ear.

"Well, the fact is I'm taking a liking to him. Do you see?" Camila answered softly.

Pintada's face clouded and her cheeks puffed up. But she said nothing more about it, and she went off to get on the mare that Margarito was saddling for her.

When he reached Jalisco, Demetrio learned that the band of Orozco's men had scattered and was headed for Michoacán. Only a small group was left and, according to up-to-date reports, it was being joined by a priest and a hundred or so bumpkins under the moth-eaten banner of "Religion and Law."

Demetrio made inquiry and after determining what route they were taking succeeded in overhauling them. For his soldiers it was simply a sport. The first one caught was the priest himself and as soon as his devotees saw him hanging from a mesquite tree with his tongue hanging out and his eyes bulging, they scattered like partridges and the soldiers hunted them down as if they were game, leaving a sprinkling of dead, who displayed on their shirts an emblem of red baize with the wording, "Halt! The Sacred Heart of Jesus is with me."

The soldiers came back from the chase in a tremendous cloud of dust, the horses galloping, snorting with their nostrils opened wide. The men carried their rifles high or carried them across the saddle horn.

Amid shouts and bursts of laughter they related the details of the battle.

"I got caught up and more too on my back pay," said Codorniz, holding up the gold watches and rings that he had looted from the priest's house.

"I like fighting like that," yelled Manteca, tossing in insults between every other word. "At least I know damn well why I'm risking my hide!"

And he held high in the same hand that grasped the reins a glistening golden halo that he had torn loose from the head of the "Divine Prisoner" in the village church.

When Codorniz, who was an acknowledged expert in such matters, examined carefully Manteca's booty, he gave out a roar of laughter:

"Your damned halo is just a piece of tin! Ha, ha, ha!"

"Why are you hanging on to that filthy trash, Blondie?" Pancracio asked Margarito, who had brought along a prisoner.

"Do you know why? Because I've never been able to see what a fellow's face looks like when you tighten a noose around his neck."

The prisoner, who was excessively fat, breathed heavily with exhaustion. His face was flushed, his eyes bloodshot, and large drops of perspiration stood out on his forehead. They had him tied by the wrists and he was dragged along on foot.

"Anastasio, hand me your lariat. My halter rope is about to snap with this guy. Now that I think it over, maybe I'd better not. My federal friend, I'm going to kill you and get it over with. You've been through a lot. Look, the mesquites are still a long way off and around here there isn't even a telegraph line where I can hang you to a pole."

And Margarito took his pistol, put the muzzle to the prisoner's left nipple, and slowly pulled back the trigger.

The man turned as pale as death. His face sharpened, and his glassy eyes broke. A shudder agitated his entire body.

Installment no. 18

_____

Margarito, looking at him joyfully, feeling a very strange satisfaction, held the pistol over the man's heart, which beat violently.

He put the revolver back in its holster and with a smile on his lips and a bright gleam in his eye said:

"No, my federal friend. I guess I won't kill you just yet. You can stay on as my assistant. You will get to see whether I'm hardhearted or not."

And he smiled maliciously at those who were standing around nearby. The prisoner seemed to have become stupefied. He could do nothing but swallow; his mouth and throat were completely dry.

Camila, who had stayed behind, spurred the flanks of her mare and caught up with Demetrio. "What a beast that man Margarito is! You ought to see what he has been doing to a prisoner." And she told Demetrio what she had just seen.

Demetrio frowned but he did not answer.

Pintada called Camila to one side.

"Say, you! What kind of gossip are you peddling to Demetrio? Margarito is my man. I want you to get that. And whatever is his business is my business too. I'm warning you!"

And Camila, badly scared, went off to join Demetrio again.

IX.

The troops camped for the night on a plain not far from three modest houses that stood against the red line that marked the horizon. In the broad expanse of the plain shorn of trees the three tall ash trees seemed almost a miracle. With rounded tops of greenish black foliage, they leaned down to kiss the earth, one in front of each house.

Demetrio and Camila headed toward them.

Inside the corral three men, seated on large stones, were chatting calmly but they stood up, frightened.

"I need a place to stay for myself and my wife," Demetrio explained.

And when the owner himself picked up a broom and a pail of water to put in order for them the best part of the barn, where he stored the shelled corn, beans, corn on the cob, the plow, picks, and other farm equipment, Demetrio tried to calm him down, assuring the man that his presence there was sufficient to prevent anyone from daring to touch any of his property.

As soon as Demetrio and Camila were settled down, the owner shouted to his servant:

"Epifanio, hurry up. Finish shelling the corn so you can go water the animals."

The peon stood up laboriously. He wore two strips of trousers, open in two flaps, that went from his waist to his knees. One of his legs was misshapen and at its lower extremity ended like a horse's hoof. When he walked he moved up and down with a grotesque rhythm.

"But can that man really work?" Demetrio asked.

"Poor fellow. He ain't very strong, but you ought to see how well he earns his pay. he starts to work as soon as God gets up in the morning. And long after the sun has set he's still going strong."

"There's something I feel around here that makes me feel so sad. Let's go on," Demetrio said to Camila and to Anastasio Montañez, who came up at that moment.

And Camila, like a faithful dog, followed him obediently, answering "yes" to everything that he said to her.

At the bank of a small stream they came across the peon, who was pulling awkwardly on the rope of a windlass. An enormous jar turned water on to a pile of fresh hay and in a clear stream poured into a trough. A cow, a scrawny old horse, and a burro drank noisily.

"How much do you get a day, friend?"

"Sixteen cents, boss."

The peon was a little fellow of fair complexion, covered with tumors, with straight hair and pale blue eyes. He began a bitter tirade against the farm, its owner, and his own sad state of affairs.

"You sure earn your pay, my man," Demetrio said gently. "You grumble and complain, but you keep working away."

"There are always people who don't have it so good as we do in the sierra, my friend."

Demetrio didn't sleep very well, and early in the morning he got up and went outside the barn.

"I have a hunch something's going to happen to me," he thought.

It was a quiet morning with subdued notes

of joy. A thrush sang in the ash tree, the cows turned over the scraps of straw in the corral, and the hogs grunted sleepily.

The orange sun came into view, and the last faint star faded away.

Demetrio walked slowly back to the encampment. He thought about his house, his yoke of oxen, two black oxen scarcely two years old, his two acres of fertile cultivated land. The features of his young were drawn clearly in his memory, those lines of infinite gentleness and tender feeling toward her husband, of indomitable pride toward the outsider. But when he attempted to recall and reconstruct the picture of his son, he was unable to do so. He had forgotten him completely.

Stretched out between the parallel furrows of a fallow field the soldiers were trying to sleep, with their saddles for pillows. Between them lay the horses, their heads down and their eyes closed.

"The horses are all worn out. We ought to stay here and rest today."

"Oh, how I'd like to go back to the sierra!" Anastasio replied. "You know, friend, I just don't feel at home here. I feel so sad ... I just don't know what I miss!"

"These plains make me feel so sad. Down here I only feel like sleeping," remarked Luis Cervantes, turning over. He wrapped himself up snugly in his blanket, and then silence took over again.

"How many hours does it take to get to Limón from here?"

"It isn't hours you're talking about, Demetrio. It would take a long three days of riding."

"I'd like to go see my wife."

Later in the day Pintada went to talk to Camila.

"Hey, whatta you know! Demetrio is getting ready to throw you off. He told me so himself. He's going to bring his real wife. She's real pretty. She's white, and what rosy cheeks! But if you don't want to leave they might have a job for you. They have a baby you could carry around."

When Demetrio came back, Camila, in a tearful state, told him what had happened.

"Don't trouble your head about that wacky woman."

As it turned out, Demetrio did not go to Limón nor did his thoughts turn again to his wife. Camila was very happy about that and Pintada became as hostile as a rattlesnake.

X.

"Today we'll get to Tepatitlán, tomorrow to Cuquío, and then on to the sierra!"

"There's no place like the sierra!"

"On to the sierra!"

And they all kept speaking of the sierra as if she were the long-awaited lover from whom a man has been separated for an eternity.

"Margarito," Manteca yelled suddenly, "your assistant wants to turn up his toes. He says he can't walk any more."

The federal soldier taken prisoner had collapsed from exhaustion in the middle of the road.

"Well, well!" exclaimed Blondie, turning back to where the prisoner was. "So you got tired, my fine friend? Poor little fellow. I'm going to buy a glass case so I can keep you in a corner just like Jesus Christ. But you've got to get into town first and that's why I'm going to help you."

He drew out his sword and rained blows repeatedly on the prisoner as hard as he could.

"Let me have your lariat, Anastasio," he said, his eyes shining.

But when Codorniz called to his attention that the prisoner no longer moved either hands or feet, he yelled excitedly.

"How stupid I am! Just when I was teaching him not to eat!"

And he guffawed.

Early in the morning they reached Tepatitlán. The schools of the town were turned into barracks. Demetrio was quartered in the sacristy of an abandoned church.

Tepatitlán

As soon as they had fed the animals their morning ration, some set out to hunt out saddles, horses, and weapons, while the others, feeling indolent and cheerless, lolled in the patios and on the sidewalks.

In the afternoon in the yard of the church where Demetrio was quartered, Manteca, Codorniz, and others were sprawled out in the sun, scratching their bellies. Pancracio, with his chest and back bare, was picking fleas out of his shirt.

A poor man came up to the railing, asking permission to speak to the general.

The soldiers raised their heads but did not answer him.

Installment no. 19

"I'm a poor man, mister. I've got to work hard to make ends meet. My wife's dead and I've got nine kids to take care of. Don't be mean to us poor ones."

"Don't worry about not having a woman. We've got Pintada here. We can let you have here at cost."

The man forced a bitter smile.

"Except she's got one bad habit. Just as soon as she catches sight of a man right away she starts getting ready for action."

Codorniz, who with the stub of a tallow candle was daubing his toes, directed the man to the door of the sacristy.

He explained his business. The soldiers had come and taken all his corn to feed their horses.

"Well, why'd you let them do it?" Demetrio answered indifferently.

Camila spoke up:

"Come now, Demetrio. Give him a signed order so they can give him back his corn."

"God bless you, my child! May God grant His glory to you! It was my whole year's crop. Ten bushels. Just enough to feed us," the man burst out, weeping in appreciation.

Luis Cervantes wrote out a few lines on a sheet of paper and at the bottom Demetrio added his chicken tracks.

The man took the paper and kissed the hands of both Demetrio and Camila, who smiled in satisfaction.

The next day, on the way to Cuquío, Anastasio Montañez came to Demetrio and said to him:

"Say, I haven't told you about this yet. That Blondie is really something fierce! You know what he did yesterday with that poor guy who came to complain that we'd run off with all his corn for our horses? Well, with the order that you gave him he came to the barracks. 'Yes, my friend, come right in,' Blondie told him. 'It's quite right we should return what is yours. Come in! Come in! How many bushels did we steal from you? Ten? But are you sure it wasn't more than ten? Yes, that's it. It's more like fifteen. Wasn't it around twenty? Think carefully. You're so poor, you've got a lot of kids to feed. Yes, around twenty, that's what it must have been. Come in here. I'm not going to give you ten, or fifteen, or twenty. You just keep counting, one, two three .... And then when you don't want any more, just tell me.' So he pulls out his sword and hits him so hard the poor guy begs for mercy."

Pintada doubled up with laughter.

Camila, unable to contain an expression, burst out:

"What a mean old beast! What a rotten heart! I can't stand his looks!"

Immediately Pintada's expression changed. Her eyes were like those of an angry cow.

"And what business of yours is it?"

Camila became afraid and made her horse go faster.

Pintada spurred hers on and in a flash as she went by bumping into Camila, she snatched at her head and undid the braids of her hair.

With the bump, Camila's horse jumped. At the same time she let go the reins to push the hair away from her eyes. She wavered an instant, lost her balance, and fell to the stones of the road, cutting a gash in her forehead.

Overcome with laughter, Pintada raced

ahead and skillfully took the runaway horse under control.

"Come, Curro. You've got work to do," Pancracio yelled out as soon as he saw Camila in Demetrio's saddle, her face covered with blood.

When Luis Cervantes made an appearance with his first aid materials all ready to use, Camila stopped sobbing. She wiped the tears from her eyes and commented as haughtily as she could:

"I'd rather have Venancio take care of me. Even if I were dying I wouldn't take a drop of water from you!"

They were beginning to see the sierra not far away when a messenger came with an order for Demetrio.

"It's back to Tepatitlán. You've got to leave your men there, General. And you have to go on to Lagos to take the train to Aguascalientes," Luis Cervantes said after he had read the message.

Demetrio's face looked puzzled and the soldiers were disappointed.

"Nobody appreciates what he's got until he finds out he's lost it," Anastasio Montañez remarked disconsolately.

And they all sighed sadly, wishing they could go on to the sierra.

They spent the night at a hacienda.

Camila wept all night long, and when morning came she asked Demetrio to allow her to return home.

"If you don't care for me, all right," Demetrio answered sullenly.

"That isn't the point, Demetrio. I care for you a lot. You can tell that. It's that woman!"

"Don't let that worry you. I'll get rid of her today. I've got that all figured out."

So Camila stopped weeping.

The next morning when they were all saddling up, Demetrio went up to Pintada and whispered in her ear:

"You're not going along with us!"

"What's that?" she questioned, still not understanding.

"You're going to stay here or you can take

off to wherever you want, but you're not going with us."

"What in hell are you trying to tell me?" she bellowed in surprise. "Are you telling me you're getting rid of me? Ha, ha! Well, you're a son of a bitch if you believe the cock and bull stories of that ...."

Pintada insulted Camila, Luis Cervantes, Demetrio, and anyone who came to mind. The soldiers heard oaths and insults that they had never heard before.

Demetrio was patient and listened to her for a long time, but when she showed no signs of shutting up, he calmly gave an order to a soldier:

"Get that drunk woman out of here!"

"Blondie, my darling Blondie! Come show them they're nothing but a bunch of sons of bitches!"

And she waved her arms, stamped her feet, and shouted.

Margarito finally put in an appearance. He had just gotten up. His eyes peered out from behind swollen eyelids, and his voice was hoarse. He found out what had happened, and going up to Pintada said to her grimly:

"Yes. It would be a good idea if you got the hell out of here. We're all damn sick and tired of your dirty tricks!"

Pintada's face turned to stone. She tried to speak, but her muscles were taut and nothing came out.

The soldiers laughed in great amusement. Camila was alarmed.

Pintada glanced at those who were around her. And it all happened in the space of a fleeting moment. She bent over and extracted a sharp gleaming blade from between her stocking and her leg. Then she leaped at Camila.

A piercing shriek and a body that collapsed with blood gushing from it. No one had the courage to stop her. She retreated silently, moving slowly.

Finally the sharp, throaty voice of Margarito broke the stunned silence:

"That's great! At last I got rid of that louse!"

XII.

Deep into my flesh
Someone thrust a blade.
He didn't know just why
And I never knew.
He really did know, he did,
But I never knew.

And from that mortal wound
My blood flowed in a stream.
He didn't know just why
And I never knew.
He really did know, he did,
But I never knew.

With his head bowed, his hands clasped on his saddle, Demetrio kept humming with a mournful tune the song that constantly kept going through his mind.

Then for a long time he remained quiet and sorrowful.

"Once we get to Lagos, General, I'll get you out of the dumps. They've got good-looking girls there who'll give us a good time," Blondie told him.

"What I'd really like to do now is just go on a good drunk," Demetrio answered.

Then he rode away from the rest, spurring his horse as if he wanted to be alone with his sadness.

After hours and still more long hours of riding he stopped to wait for Luis Cervantes.

"Say, Curro, I've been thinking about it. Just what am I supposed to do in Aguascalientes?"

"Cast your vote, General, for provisional president of the republic."

"Provisional president? Well then, what about Carranza? I sure don't get the hang of politics."

They finally reached Lagos. Blondie wagered that he would make Demetrio burst out laughing that night.

Dragging his spurs, his chaps hanging below his waist, Demetrio entered El Cosmopolita Bar with Luis Cervantes, Blondie, and his aides.

"Why are you running away, you dudes? We aren't going to eat anybody," Margarito yelled.

The townspeople were taken by surprise at the very moment when they were trying to leave. Some nonchalantly returned to their tables to keep on chatting and drinking. Others hesitatingly came forward to offer their regards to the guests.

"General, ... Pleased to meet you. ... Yes, major."

"That's the kind of friends I like to have, polite and dignified," Blondie commented.

"Here, boys," he added as he pulled out his pistol playfully, "here goes a foot-chaser for you to play with."

A bullet ricocheted off the concrete, passed among the legs of the tables and the town dandies, who skittered around as frightened as a woman who has found a mouse under her skirt.

They smiled palely to humor the major properly. Demetrio scarcely opened his mouth but the rest of the party was doubled up with laughter.

"Blondie," Codorniz observed, "that fellow that's going out the door must have got stung. Look how he's limping."

Blondie paid no attention and didn't bother to turn around to look at the wounded man. He declared that at thirty paces and from the draw he could hit a bottle of tequila.

"Look, my friend, stand up," he said to the waiter in the bar.

Then he led him to the far end of the patio and carefully placed a bottle of tequila on the youth's head.

The poor wretch protested; he tried to run in fright but Blondie got his pistol ready and aimed.

"Stay put, you son of a ... if you don't want me to put a hot slug of lead in you."

Blondie hurried back to the opposite wall,

raised his pistol, and aimed. The bottle was shattered into pieces, bathing with tequila the young man's face, which was as white as a sheet of paper.

"This time it's for real," Blondie cried out, running for another bottle of tequila that he again set up on the youth's head.

He went back to the firing place, turned dizzily on his heels and fired.

Only this time he clipped off an ear instead of shattering the bottle.

And holding his hands to his stomach as he went into a fit of laughter, he said to the waiter:

"Here, young fellow, take this roll of bills. It isn't anything serious. You can fix it up with a little arnica and some alcohol."

After having consumed great amounts of wine and beer, Demetrio said:

"You pay for it, Blondie."

"I haven't anything left, but that's no reason for worry."

"How much is the bill, my friend?" he asked the waiter.

"A hundred eighty pesos, boss."

Margarito jumped over the counter and with two strokes of his arm swept away flasks, bottles, and glasses.

"You can send the bill to your father Villa. O. K.?"

And they left amid bursts of raucous laughter.

Outside Blondie staggered and reeled, finding it difficult to walk in the street. "Say, friend, where are the whorehouses here?" he asked, directing himself to a dapper little man who, with the key in the lock, was closing the door of a tailor shop.

The man stepped down off the sidewalk to let the soldiers go by.

Blondie stopped and scrutinized him.

"Say, my friend, how dainty and pretty you are. What do you mean? Well then, am I a liar? Good, that's the way I like it. Do you know the dance of the dwarfs? You don't? Yes, you do too! I met you once at a circus. I'll swear you know how and very well. I'll show you!"

Blondie drew out his pistol and began to fire at the tailor's feet. With each shot the rotund little man gave a hop.

"There you see you do know the dance of the dwarfs!"

And throwing his arms around the shoulders of friends, he had them carry him to that point of town where the daughters of joy held forth, blazing his route by taking pot shots at the lights on each street corner, at the doors of houses, and the walls on either side of the street.

Demetrio left them and went back to the hotel, humming all the way,

> Deep into my flesh
> Someone thrust a blade.
> He didn't know just why
> And I never knew ....

XIII.

Cigarette smoke, the sour stink of sweaty clothing, fumes from liquor that has been drunk, and the foul breath of a throng crowded together as if they were in a cattle car.

Most of them wear Texan hats, with braid to indicate their ranks, and khaki shirts and trousers.

"Gentlemen, a well-dressed man stole my suitcase in the station at Silao. The savings of my life's labors .... I have nothing to feed my child ...."

The voice was sharp, shrill, and mournful, but it could not be heard at any great distance over the uproar that filled the railway coach.

"What's that old woman talking about?" asked Margarito as he came in, trying to find a place to sit down.

"Something about a suitcase ... a well-dressed kid ...," answered Pancracio, who had found the laps of two civilians to sit on.

Demetrio and the others propelled themselves forward by using their elbows. Since those who were putting up with Pancracio preferred to leave their seats and continue the journey standing, Demetrio and Luis Cervates willingly took them.

A woman who had to stand, carrying a child in her arms, fell over in a faint. A civilian quickly took the child in his arms and observed that the woman had been traveling standing like that all the way from Irapuato. But no one took the hint. The soldiers' women occupied two or three seats apiece, with their valises, dogs, cats, and even parrots. On the contrary, the men wearing the Texan hats jested at length about the firmness of the thighs and the flabby breasts of the woman who had swooned.

"Gentlemen, a well-dressed man stole my suitcase in the station at Silao.... The savings of my life's labors ... I don't even have anything to feed my child."

She speaks hurriedly and automatically sighs and sobs. Her quick eyes turn and glance in all directions. Here she picks up one piece of paper money and further on another. They rain down on her abundantly.

She finishes her collection in one spot and then moves a few more feet down the coach:

"Gentlemen, a well-dressed man stole my suitcase...."

The effect of her words is unfailing and immediate. A well-dressed man! A well-dressed man who would stoop to stealing a suitcase! That is unspeakable! That awakens a feeling of general indignation. Oh, what a shame it is that the well-dressed man isn't here so he could be shot every five seconds or so!

"Because there's nothing that makes my blood boil more than a well-dressed dude that's a low-down thief," one of them says.

"Stealing from a humble woman!"

"Stealing from a poor woman who has no way to defend herself!"

And all of them express their feelings, either by word or by deed: an insult for the thief and a five-peso bank note for the victim.

"I'll tell you how I feel. I don't think it's so bad to kill, but stealing, that's something else!" exclaimed Margarito.

They all reach a consensus that certainly it is more evil to rob than to kill, "because when you kill someone," explains Margarito, "you always do it when you're in a temper."

After a brief silence and a moment of thought a captain speaks up and ventures his opinion!

"The truth of the matter is that it all depends on the circumstances. You've got to know the reason why. The naked fact is, I've stolen ... and if I say that all of us who are riding along here have stolen, I don't think I'm telling any lie."

"Hell! You should have seen all the sewing machines I stole in Mexico!" a second lieutenant exclaims enthusiastically. "I got together more than five hundred pesos and just think. I only sold them for a peso and a half apiece."

"In Zacatecas I stole some horses, pretty fine horses, and if General Limón hadn't run off with them I wouldn't be doing what I'm doing now, and I wouldn't have to worry about feeding myself the rest of my days," volunteered a major, toothless and gray-haired.

"Good! Why should I deny it? I've stolen things in my time," asserted Margarito, "but there are all my buddies, and you can ask them how much I've got on me. I'd rather spend it all with my friends. I'm happier going on a binge with my friends than sending any of it to the old hens at home to use up."

The "I stole" theme finally peters out when decks of cards start appearing at each seat. These attract the officers the way light draws a swarm of mosquitoes.

The ups and downs of the cards games cause the

Installment no. 21

atmosphere to become more and more heated. It has something of everything, barracks, jail, bawdyhouse, and even a pigsty.

And over the hubbub one can hear, coming from the next coach:

"Gentlemen, a well-dressed man stole my suitcase ...."

XIV.

The streets of Aguascalientes had turned into garbage heaps. Those who wore khaki uniforms swarmed like bees at the entrance to their hive, crowded around the doors of restaurants, cheap eating places, tables that sold a variety of unattractive eatables, and open-air stands for coarse sugar, cheeses, and butter, all black with filth and dirt.

The smell of frying food whetted the appetites of Demetrio and his companions. By pushing and shoving they made their way up to a restaurant of the lowest grade. A filthy, disheveled old woman in a crude dish served them soup generously seasoned with chile, a pork bone, and three tough burned tortillas. They paid two pesos each, and as they left Pancracio expressed the opinion that he was hungrier than before he went in.

"Well," Demetrio announced, "let's go find out what General Natera has to say.

They took a street that led to the home of the chieftain from the North. A group of soldiers crowded around a man dressed in a white shirt and trousers blocked their way. With a sheaf of printed sheets in his hand, the man addressed them in unctuous tones and monotonous intonation:

"All good Catholics who say this prayer to Christ Crucified with devotion will be delivered from storms, the plague, war, famine ...."

Demetrio smiled.

For a moment the seller disappeared among the multitude. He had stooped down to pick up from his booth a snake's tooth, a starfish, and fish skeletons. And in the same tone of voice he now proclaimed the medicinal properties and virtues of each item.

Codorniz, who had little faith in Venancio as a doctor, asked the street vendor to pull a tooth for him. Margarito bought the black seed of a certain fruit that has the property of delivering one from being struck by lightning or any other misfortune, and Anastasio Montañez purchased a prayer to Christ Crucified which he folded carefully and with great piety stowed away in his bosom.

"As sure as God's in heaven, my friend, the revolution is going to drag on. Now it's Villa against Carranza," explained Natera.

And Demetrio, without answering him,

with his eyes wide open, demanded further enlightenment.

"That is to say," Natera continued, "the Convention does not recognize Carranza as the First Chief of the revolution and is going to name a new one. Do you understand, comrade?"

Demetrio nodded his head to indicate that he did.

"What do you say to that, comrade?" asked Natera.

Demetrio shrugged his shoulders.

"From what I can tell, it means that we keep on fighting," Macías responded. "All right, we'll go after them. You know, General, as far as I'm concerned you can count on me."

"Good, but whose side are you going to take?"

Demetrio, thoroughly baffled, ran his hands through his hair and scratched himself for a minute.

"Look, don't ask me any more questions. I never got no learning. The eagle I wear on my hat I got from you. All right, well you know that all you have to do is to say to me, 'Demetrio, do this and this and this and that's all there is to it.' "

END OF THE SECOND PART

THIRD PART

I.

El Paso, Texas, May 16, 1915

My dear Venancio:

Not until now am I able to answer your kind letter of January 4 of this year, because my professional obligations take up all my time. I was admitted to practice last December and I am now engaged in my profession in this city, as you know. I was certainly sorry to hear what happened to Pancracio and Manteca. But I am not surprised that they stabbed each other after a card game. What a shame, they were a couple of brave men.

I think it would be difficult, Venancio, for you to obtain the degree that you so anxiously desire here in the United States, no matter how much gold and money you may have brought together to buy it. I am very fond of you, Venancio, and I think that you deserve a better fate. So then, I have an idea that could favor our mutual interests and your own just ambitions to change your social position. If you and I went into partnership, we could do a very fine business. Of course, at this moment I haven't any reserve funds because I have used them all up on my studies and in getting my degree, but I do have something that is worth much more than money. That is my perfect knowledge of this city, of its needs, and surefire businesses that can be undertaken. We could set up a Mexican-style restaurant with you as the proprietor, distributing the profits at the end of each month. Also, relative to something that interests you greatly, a change in your social sphere. I remember that you play the guitar quite well and I think that it would be easy, because of my recommendations and your own knowledge of music, to get you accepted as a member of the Salvation Army, a highly respectable organization that would provide you with considerable prestige.

Don't hesitate, dear Venancio. Come with your funds and we can both get rich in a very short time.

Please give my affectionate greetings to the General, to Anastasio, and all my friends.

Your friend who esteems you,

Luis Cervantes.

Venancio finished reading his letter and sadly began to think about it.

"That Curro really knew how to put it together," said Anastasio Montañez. "Because what I can't get straight in my head is why we're still fighting. Didn't we get rid of the federals?"

Juchipila showed up in the distance, white and bathed by the sun, amid green foliage, at the foot of a high and haughty mountain, folded like coarse cloth.

Juchipila, cradle of the revolution of 1910. Juchipila, sprinkled with the blood of the first revolutionaries. It is evident in the town and its surroundings: recently painted black crosses, crosses formed of two rough tree branches, crosses of piled up stones, crosses painted in whitewash on the walls of houses in ruins, and even the most humble of crosses marked with charcoal on the faces of boulders. Crosses scattered along high roads and paths, on the folds of the rocks, in the rough ground along the streams, on the banks of the river.

One-armed, lame, and rheumatic soldiers see the spires of Juchipila. They sigh and begin to speak bitterly of their officers. Newcomers just off the sidewalks enlist and are given officers' bars to wear on their hats before they have ever handled a gun, while the veteran who has been under fire in a hundred battles, unable to work any longer, the veteran who joined the ranks as a common soldier, still remains a common soldier.

And in an undertone they grumbled and complained about General Macías, who was filling the vacancies on his staff with vain and perfumed dandies.

And what was worse, with cute little officers who had belonged to the federal army.

Anastasio Montañez himself, who ordinarily is in perfect agreement with what his close friend Demetrio does, now says:

"Look friends, I speak my mind ... and I tell my partner that if we are going to have federals among us, we are in a bad way. Really! Don't you think so? But I speak out and say what I think and I swear by the life of my mother that I'll tell him so."

And he did.

Demetrio listened to him sympathetically, and when he finished speaking he answered.

"Partner, what you say is true. We are in a bad way. The soldiers gripe about the non-coms, the non-coms about the officers, and the officers about us. And we are fed up and ready to send Villa and Carranza off to hell ... so they can amuse themselves all alone. But I got the notion that we are

Installment no. 22

in the same fix as that peon we met in Tepatitlán. Do you remember? He was always bitching about his boss but he didn't stop working either. And that's the way we are, complaining and complaining. But that isn't what needs to be said, partner, because ... because it shouldn't. Do you understand? What you ought to do is give our men some spirit. Within a day or two we're likely to run into the Carrancistas and we've got to beat the hell out of them."

They were already coming into the streets of Juchipila, and they could not help being aware of the noisy pealing of bells in the village church.

"It reminds me, pal, of when the revolution was just beginning. When we came into a little town like this, they used to ring the bells for us and they sent the band out to meet us and the people were all waving flags, and they shot off skyrockets and cheered us.

"But now they don't like us any more," Demetrio answered.

"Why should they like us, partner?"

They came out into a small square, facing a church with an octagonal tower, coarse and well built, mindful of the colonial period.

In times past the plaza must have been a garden, judging from a few bare and scrubby orange trees, mixed among the remains of broken down benches.

The pealing of church bells again sounded, clear and cheerful, and then from within the church a chorus of sturdy female voices. The liturgy, sung by the young women of the town, is accompanied by a guitar and has the melody of a song.

"What fiesta is it, lady?" Demetrio asked an old woman who was hurrying as fast as she could toward the church.

"The Sacred Heart of Jesus."

And Demetrio recalled that the taking of Zacatecas had occurred exactly one year previously, and he sighed.

Like all the towns that they had been traveling through in Tepic, Jalisco, Aguascalientes, and Zacatecas, Juchipila lies in ruins. The black marks left by fire on the roofless houses, on their burned walls. Houses that are boarded up and almost all of the business establishments likewise. Occasionally the doors of one of these are partly open, revealing their bare and empty shelves that remind one of the white weather-beaten skeletons of horses that are scattered along the country roads. The frightful grimace of hunger is present on the pale dirty faces of the people, in the luminous gleam in their eyes, which when they rest upon a soldier burn with the fire of a curse.

In vain the soldiers search through the streets trying to find something to eat. They bite their tongues and burn with wrath. Only one miserable eating place is open, and throngs of people gather around it. There are no beans, no tortillas. Just chopped chile peppers and salt. To no purpose do the officers shout threats and show their pockets overflowing with bank notes.

"Paper, just paper! That's all you've got! Well, that's what you can eat," says the owner of the place, an old hag who has a tremendous scar across her face who tells how she already went to bed with death himself so she won't be frightened when her time comes.

But despite the sadness and devastation of the town, the birds never stopped singing in the grove of trees nor does the song of the warblers in the dry limbs of the orange trees fade away.

II.

The wife of Demetrio Macías, overcome with joy, comes out to meet him along the path through the sierra, leading her child by the hand.

Almost two years of absence.

They embraced one another and then remained silent, while she could not speak for her sobs and tears.

Demetrio, dumbfounded, noticed that his wife had grown old, as if ten or twenty years had already gone by. Then he glanced at his son, who held his fearful eyes fixed on his father. And his heart jumped when he observed his own penetrating eyes and the same lines of steel in his face. And he wanted to draw him close and embrace him, but the child was frightened of him and sought refuge in his mother's skirts.

"He's your father, son! He's your father!"

The boy thrust his head between the folds of the skirt and remained fear-stricken.

Demetrio, who had handed over his horses to an aide, walked slowly with his wife and his son along the narrow mountain path.

"Thanks be to God that you've come! Now you'll never leave us. Will you? You're going to stay here with us, aren't you?"

Demetrio's face became gloomy.

And the two of them remained silent, overcome with anguish.

A black cloud surged up beyond the range of mountains, and they could hear a dull clap of thunder.

Demetrio held back a sigh. Memories swarmed into his mind like bees into a hive.

The rain began to fall in big drops and shook the white flowers of the Saint John's roses, which looked like clusters of stars pinned on the trees. It fell on the crags, among the underbrush, on the pitahaya cactus, and upon the entire range of mountains.

Below on the floor of the canyon and through the transparency of the rain are visible the upright swaying palms. Slowly they nod their angular heads and with the gusts of wind they open up their leaves like a fan. And everywhere there is nothing but mountains: great waves of mountains that follow behind other mountains, more hills surrounded by mountains and these surrounded by the wall of a mountain range so high that its azure is lost in the sapphire of the heavens.

"Demetrio, for God's sake! Don't ever go away again! My heart warns me that something is going to happen to you."

And she is again shaken by a fit of sobbing.

The child, frightened, bursts out crying and she has to keep her own grief in check in order to calm him.

The rain begins to slacken. A swallow with a silver belly and angular wings cuts across the crystal clear rays of light, suddenly illuminated by the evening sun.

"Why do they keep on fighting, Demetrio?"

Demetrio, his eyebrows brought together in thought, picks up a stone, and as hard as he can throws it along the narrow trail and into the bottom of the canyon.

"Look at that stone, how it never stops."

III.

It was a splendid morning. It had rained all through the night and in the morning the sky had a canopy of white clouds. Across the highest part of the sierra trot wild colts with flying manes and stiff tails, elegant with the grace of the peaks that raise their heads until they kiss the clouds.

The soldiers moved across the rocky terrain, drinking in the brightness of the morning. No one has his mind on the treacherous bullet that can be waiting for him farther on. The troops' greatest merriment lies precisely in the unforeseen event. So the soldiers sing, laugh, and chatter like madmen. In their hearts stirs the soul of the ancient nomadic tribes. They are not concerned with where they are going or where they have come from. The essential point is to travel, to keep constantly moving, never to stop, to be masters of the valley, of the plains, the sierra, and as far as the eye can see.

Trees, cacti, and ferns all look as if they were newly bathed. From the rocks, whose ocher looks like the rust from ancient armor, drip trickles of transparent water.

Macías's men are silent for a moment. It appears that they have heard a familiar sound, the distant explosion of a rocket, but minutes go by and the sound is not heard again.

"In this same sierra," says Demetrio, "with only twenty men I killed four hundred federals. Do you remember, Anastasio?"

And when Demetrio begins to recount that famous military feat, the men realize the great danger they may be facing. What if the enemy, instead of being a two days' march away, should turn out to be hiding in the brush of that tremendous chasm into whose depths they have ventured? But, who could dare to make known his apprehension? When did Demetrio Macías's men ever say "we refuse to press on?"

And when a skirmish starts up in the distance where the advance guard is moving forward, they are not even surprised. The raw recruits turn around in mad flight toward the outlet of the canyon.

From Demetrio's hoarse throat a curse slips.

"Fire! ... Fire on those cowards that are turning tail!"

"Take the heights away from them!"

But the enemy, hidden by the thousands in the brush, empties his machine guns and Demetrio's men fall like stalks of grain chopped off by the sickle.

Demetrio sheds tears of anger and grief when Anastasio slips slowly from his horse, without uttering even a moan, and lies stretched out

Installment no. 23

---

motionless. Venancio falls beside him, with his throat split open in a dreadful wound by a machine gun, and Meco falls down the slope and rolls to the bottom of the abyss. Suddenly Demetrio finds himself all alone. Bullets buzz by his ears as in a hailstorm. He dismounts and crawls among the boulders until he finds an escarpment. He sets up a large stone to protect his head and stretched out prone he begins to fire.

The enemy scatters in pursuit of the handful of fugitives who remain hidden in the brush.

Demetrio aims and not a single shot misses its mark. Bang! Bang! Bang!

His superb marksmanship fills him with joy. Where he aims, there the bullet strikes. He empties one clip and puts in another. And he aims ....

The smoke of the rifle fire has not yet disappeared. The locusts chant their constant mysterious song. The doves sing softly in the nooks of the crags. The cows browse peacefully.

The sierra is wearing its bright colors. Upon its inaccessible peaks falls the pure white mist like a veil of snow upon the head of a bride.

And at the foot of an enormous, sumptuous fissure in the canyon wall, like the portico of an ancient cathedral, he continues to aim with the barrel of his gun ....

E N D

Appendix

THE VILLISTAS IN SAN MIGUEL

Various of Mariano Azuela's close military friends took part in the battle between Villistas and Carrancistas at San Miguel el Alto, Jalisco, on June 6, 1915. Foremost among these were General Leocadio Parra and Colonel Manuel Caloca. The latter, by the time of the battle, had become the model for Demetrio Macías in the novel that was gestating in Azuela's mind.

On July 23, 1960, I interviewed José de Jesús Delgado Román, who as a young man was an eyewitness to the battle. Delgado Román knew the participants and was able to trace their roles in the fighting in the town. This he did in a running account of the battle, which he proceeded to record with great detail and expressions of the townspeople's reactions to the events and those who participated in them.

The performances of the men of Parra and Caloca in battle have often been carried over into the pages of Mariano Azuel's novel. For that reason, Mr. Delgado Román's narrative has been transcribed and the text included here. It documents the actions, procedures, and the personalities of these soldiers during the month immediately prior to those weeks when the novelist was making notes while he was escaping to northern Mexico with the wounded Caloca. It contributes, therefore, to Azuela's process of creating *Los de abajo*.

José de Jesús Delgado Román,
San Miguel el Alto, Jalisco, July 23, 1960.

Pos, si yo recuerdo, es que tenían los villistas aquí en San Miguel un mes. Entraron ellos el cinco de mayo, que lo celebraron, pos no recuerdo si ese mismo día fue, con una fiesta para los niños de las escuelas, algo así como circo o no sé qué festival. Ellos empezaron a tener amistades aquí en el pueblo. El coronel Baca estaba en lo que es ahora el colegio de, de la primaria de los religiosos, en el portal que era el Mesón de San Pedro, el coronel Caloca en el mesón que era de los, de don Encarnación de la Torre, y otros de los jefes estaban en el mesón que era de Lupe Padilla.

Pos, ya teniendo ciertas amistades aquí los jefes villistas, se captaron cierta simpatía con los vecinos, cierta confianza que, pos, ya eran muy conocidos y dondequiera los llamaban. Unos y otros los llamaban para platicar pero no previendo que los carrancistas se preparaban para venir a atacarlos. En el transcurso de un mes o sea del cinco de mayo al cinco de junio hubo una fiestecilla de teatro en el salón parroquial y se invitaron a los jefes. Fue Caloca, Baca, el teniente coronel Avilés y no recuerdo qué otros jefecillos. Asistieron de buena voluntad y se dio un sainete que se llamaba *Juan Soldado*. El muchacho que representaba el dicho Juan Soldado era un muchacho fogoso y que empezó a...en su papel que le correspondía...pos hacerles ciertas muecas allí a los jefecillos aquellos al grado de que dice que los revolucionarios que dizque son muy feos y se dirigía a ellos. ¡Bueno! Ellos estaban encantados [Laughter] porque la ocurrencia de aquel.... Entonces estaba el señor cura Retolaza aquí. A él se acompañó y otros de los sacerdotes y estaba lleno el salón. Total que pasamos la fiestecita muy contentos. No más la fecha no la recuerdo. Pasó aquella dicha fiesta y fueron ellos muy bien impresionados por la fiestecilla y hasta haciéndole resaltar aquel, aquel dato de ese muchacho que dondequiera que se encontraban: —¡Oye! Que dizque los revolucionarios que son muy feos. —Di, Pos tú serás el feo, respondió, responde el otro.

Eran algo simpáticos los fulanos, los fulanos esos. Caloca era un muchacho altote, mucho muy alto, delgado, que hasta encorvado, hasta el corral, se veía porque, ¡bueno!, era una estatura casi extraordinaria. El coronel Baca le falla una pierna. Sería de años o sería del mismo tiempo de la revolución. Ya andaba medio renco. Pos, ahí tienen ustedes.

El día cinco de junio a eso de las ocho o nueve de la mañana se empezó a rumorar que venían los carrancistas por el lado de Tepatitlán precisamente. Los trajo el coronel Silverio López que era de aquí que fue quien le insinuó la conveniencia al coronel que era entonces Miguel Guerrero, de que vinieran, porque había aquí una cría de, de caballos finos, hermosísimos, de lo mejor que había en la región, según se sabía. Entre esos caballos estaba El Tirano, que fue famosísimo y todavía las crías existen. La misma señal que tenía el caballo ese, frente blanca y la pata, no recuerdo cuál, si la derecha o la izquierda, blanca también, ésa era, diremos la característica de todas las crías del Tirano. Y hasta la fecha creo que existen algunos todavía, hijos de aquél. Entonces viendo, pues, el coronel Guerrero que tal vez convendría, porque parece que dicen algunos que se negaba, pero:

—¡Hombre! ¿Qué vamos a hacer?

—Es tu tierra.

Dice: —No le hace.

Y él que: —Vayamos a mi tierra.

Pues se vinieron, ese mismo día, el cinco de junio. Y a eso de las diez o once de la mañana todavía en la torre andaban algunos de los villistas, que no recuerdo.... Creo que fue el coronel Baca que andaba allí arriba y algunos de los otros jefes que lo acompañaban, pero la demás tropa ya estaba lista para....

Here there was a brief interruption in the narration. Consequently the reader will miss the explanation for certain events that are reported when Mr. Delgado Román resumes his story.

Serían las ocho de la mañana del domingo seis de junio. Salieron unos soldados carrancistas de su cuartel. Se dirigieron a la parte que ocupa ahora el pozo artesiano con el fin de recoger forraje para sus bestias pero sin darse cuenta que la columna central que había bajado de la Mesa de los Rábago de los villistas, andaban en el río que está contiguo o donde desemboca el agua de ese, de esos baños, o de ese manantial, y por allí viniendo los villistas. Se dan cuenta que los carrancistas estaban amanojando su pastura y se les ocurrió hacerles unos tiros si con intención de matarlos o no más para asustarlos. El hecho es de que eso fue el principio del combate en esta población de San Miguel el Alto. Las horas más o menos trans-

curridas de cuando ellos salieron y que empezaron a recoger su forraje y la proximidad de las tres columnas de los villistas, ya ésa, como digo, dentro de la población, eran las diez quince de la mañana, hora en que sonando el reloj fueron esos disparos.

Los soldados dejaron aquella pastura regada. Salieron corriendo por la calle. Se vinieron inmediatamente y entonces como los flancos de los villistas, una por el oriente y otra por el poniente oyeron aquellos disparos. Pensaron que se había dado la contraseña para generalizar el tiroteo. Los carrancistas inmediatamente tomaron posiciones, unos en el atrio, otros en la torre, y por falta de reflexión o por falta de conocimiento de la situación topográfica de la población. El coronel Guerrero subió con algunos de ellos a la torre.

Los villistas empezaron a cerrar el cerco, tanto los del oriente como del poniente, para el lado sur de la población para evitar una salida de los carrancistas, para poder decir ellos aquello que generalmente se dice, —los enratonamos, y no dejar salir uno solo. Cuando generalizado el tiroteo hubo momentos en que, como vulgarmente se dice, no se oía más que un disparo. Momentos de preocupación para los habitantes. Momentos de indecisión, por no saber por parte de quién iría a quedar el triunfo. Temeroso el poblado de que los carrancistas fueran a triunfar por los informes obtenidos de otras partes que donde triunfaban cometían barbaridad y media, como se dice, tanto en las familias como en las propiedades de los ricos. En una palabra, hacían y deshacían, y temeroso el pueblo, no sabía qué partido tomar, pero sí en todos los hogares, según informes, postrados unos de rodillas, otros aclamando a Dios, a la Virgen, sobre todo a San Miguel Arcángel, que es el patrono del pueblo, de quien se cuenta una leyenda que muchos le damos crédito. Otros no le darán pero por los grandes prodigios que ha obrado se sabe que antes del combate un joven montado en un caballo blanco recorría las filas de los villistas, estando todavía en la Mesa, y los urgía a que pronto estuvieran en la población porque los carrancistas tenían un plan muy negro para todos los habitantes de San Miguel. Aquel joven recorría las filas de los villistas y no supieron al fin quién sería aquel joven. Sí, dieron detalles de él, como un joven extraordinario, a caballo, y que por fin se les perdió. La creencia de todo el pueblo, de los creyentes, es que fue nada menos San Miguel, que en ocasiones pasadas de hace muchos años se dieron casos iguales de esos prodigios y no pudieron menos que apoyar la creencia firme de que había sido San Miguel quien había favorecido al pueblo de lo que hubiera pasado en caso de triunfo por parte de los carrancistas.

Siguiendo, pues, la narración. Ya la columna del centro, en la cual venía un muchacho de esta población llamado Francisco Alcalá, encabezando un grupo de soldados, se estacionó en la esquina de un señor llamado Aristo Alcalá, que era de las últimas casas que formaban la población. Allí estuvo, llamándoles la atención a los carrancistas que estaban en el atrio, posesionados en los barandales con piedras de cantera como mampuesto o defensa y no les permitió darse cuenta de lo que el general Parra que empezó a taladrar desde esa casa del señor Alcalá, las paredes, para introducirse de una casa a otra hasta pasar toda la cuadra y luego de allí, estando ya frente a lo que era una cochera (pertenecía al curato) salen sin temor de ser vistos por los enemigos, desquician la puerta cochera porque era molinete con unas barras.

Hacen modo de entrar y en el pasillo ya del curato que comunica la parte del curato con la parte que conducía al salón de la escuela de niñas parroquial o aquella que queda en el atrio, entonces ellos, o sea el general Parra, se dirige a la puerta del corredor y como estaba con los pasadores no pudo abrir, pero la criada del curato se da cuenta y entonces le dice: —¿Podemos abrir?

—Hay soldados ya aquí adentro y no sabemos qué clase de soldados sean.

El señor cura Benito Retolaza que era el que estaba entonces de párroco le dice al ama de llaves: —Pueden abrir mientras yo me voy a hacer un acto de contrición al santuario ante la Virgen, porque creo que son los carrancistas. Vendrán a matar.

Muy asustado el señor cura. Se fue. Se arrodilló ante la Virgen. Mientras acá al general Parra le abrían la puerta del, que comunicaba el pasillo con el corredor del curato. Entonces él, para tranquilizarlas, les dice: —No teman,

señoritas. Somos los villistas. Unicamente venimos a pedir permiso que si nos dejan pasar al salón de la escuela, pero necesitamos siempre el permiso del señor cura para poderlo hacer.

Van y lo comunican al señor cura: —Díganle que puede entrar, les dijo. —Díganle que puede entrar.

Entonces ellos con toda confianza se van repegados a la barda que divide el curato del patio segundo que comunicaba allí al salón de la escuela parroquial para no ser vistos por los que estaban en la torre. Una vez entrados en el salón de la escuela, el general les hace luego observaciones a sus soldados: —Posesiónense tantos soldados en cada ventana. A la orden que yo les dé, se abren las ventanas al mismo tiempo y entonces (como vulgarmente decían ellos) riata con ellos, a acabarlos.

Entonces ya posesionados los soldados, el general da la orden, abren las puertas de las ventanas del salón y entonces tendiendo sus rifles, aquellos soldados villistas desalojan a los carrancistas que estaban en todo el barandal del atrio. Desalojados de allí, empieza el descontrol en las filas de los carrancistas. Por verse ya amagados de tal manera que dijeron: —Andamos ya revueltos.

Ya están en el centro los villistas. En ese intermedio mientras el general Parra hacía aquellos movimientos se dice que de la parte poniente, en una casuchilla de la orilla, arriba de un mezquite estaban dos villistas. Aquéllos veían al coronel Guerrero que paseaba de un lado a otro, tal vez dándoles órdenes a los soldados que estaban en la torre, pero sin precauciones, absolutamente ningunas. Se dice que uno de aquéllos a cual más se disputaba el haberle pegado el tiro de muerte al coronel, el hecho es que el coronel fue herido, parece, no estoy bien cierto, que dijeron que le habían dado el tiro en la cabeza. Cayó el coronel en las bóvedas del templo. Una vez ya dándose cuenta los soldados que estaban arriba que todavía no eran heridos, empezaron a gritar a todos los demás: —¡Murió Guerrerito! Y —¡Guerrerito! ¡Lo mataron! Y —¡A Guerrerito lo mataron!

Y entonces entra el desconcierto, diremos universal, entró a todas las filas de los carrancistas y los clarines empiezan a tocar a reunión.

Estando yo con mi señor padre en la ventana de la casa, me daba cuenta por la rendija de la ventana, porque por allí por esa calle de Francisco I. Madero era ciertamente la calle central por donde andaban, iban y venían los carrancistas, entonces le digo yo a mi padre: —Creo que éste es toque de reunión. No los conozco bien pero creo que sí.

Mi acierto se vino confirmando cuando oigo yo galopar de muchos caballos y entonces me dice: —Hijo. Ve cuáles son los que van a salir.

Como eran tan conocidos por tener su distintivo, un listón rojo en el sombrero, el sombrero caído a la espalda y con los rifles ya con la trompetilla hacia abajo, entonces veo que el grueso de la columna de los que hayan sobrado sale por esa calle hacia el lado que le llaman las Olas Altas. Una vez ya saliendo como quien dice el último de los que alcancé a ver, le dije: —Papá, son los carrancistas los que van de salida.

En seguida veo ya villistas que van sobre de ellos. Estos pobres, el número que haya sido no nos damos cuenta. Encuentran con que el cerco estaba ya dispuesto para recibirlos. En un potrero que hora es donde están los filtros del agua potable, un potrero que vulgarmente se le llamaba de doña Jesús, allí los traían a los pobres carrancistas por todo el potrero como se dice vulgarmente, como agua en batea. No hallaban estos hombres por donde salir, porque los recibían a tiros por todos los lados donde se cercaban. Una vez ya hecho el ánimo de ellos se proponen y rompen el sitio. Brincan siempre con dirección al camino de Atotonilco por el Callejón Antiguo que era el camino de herradura.

Y entonces el coronel Baca y el coronel Caloca juntamente con otros soldados de los aguerridos, compañeros de uno y otro, se fueron revueltos con aquella, aquella bola de soldados carrancistas y ellos mismos los iban, pos, ciertamente espantándolos más de lo que iban, porque empezaron a gritar: —¡Y córranle que nos alcanzan! Y —¡Córranle que vienen sobre nosotros!

Pero ellos con pistola en mano a quemarropa matando soldados carrancistas hasta no sé qué parte en el callejón aquel por el camino de la Cruz Verde, que cuando ya volvieron con intención de saber el resultado también del teniente coronel Avilés que era el ayudante de el coronel Caloca que se le habían tomado prisionero desde el día anterior. Se vinieron rápidos por la calle Francisco I. Madero. Entraron ya en son de triunfo mientras otros soldados villistas subieron a la torre y de una manera muy destartalada unos sonaban una campana, otros sonaban otra, con un repique muy maltrecho pero dándole ya, como quien dice, la nueva al pueblo de que habían triunfado. Los habitantes empezaron a asomarse por las ventanas, por las puertas de sus casas, y se dieron cuenta que los villistas eran los que dominaban la situación. Uno que otro se encontraba en la plaza, allí les daban el tiro de gracia.

Caloca inmediatamente se va a la cárcel y al entrar le echa un grito a su teniente coronel: —¡Avilés! ¿Está vivo?

—Sí, mi coronel. Aquí estoy. No se preocuparon por mí porque tal vez la sorpresa fue tan grande que ni siquiera ya hicieron mención y aquí me tiene a sus órdenes.

Estaban él y otros dos o tres de los mismos soldados villistas pero el interés hasta de la gente, hasta de los habitantes de que a Avilés no le hubiera pasado algo, porque era un muchacho simpático, un muchacho que se dio a querer, por lo correcto que se portó con el pueblo y todos lo apreciaban. Una vez que le abren las puertas sale. Se lo llevan y entonces ellos empezaron a contar la narración del alcance aquel. Dice: —Llegamos, que traemos los brazos cansados de tanto matar.

Así se cuenta que por todo el camino en cuevas, en el camino, en los campos, quedaron heridos. Unos se aliviarían de las heridas. Otros fueron pasto de los animales, de los coyotes o de esos animales que les gusta comer carne de gente. Sí. El caso es que terminó el combate a la una quince de la tarde o sea tres horas, casi exactamente, duró el combate. Una vez ya tranquilizado el pueblo ordenó el general Parra que se recogieran todos los difuntos que quedaron en las cercanías del pueblo. Empezaron a llevar gente del pueblo para que les ayudara a traer. Casi todos más bien desnudos, que semidesnudos. Los tapaban con cualquier costal, como se dice, de raspa, para que no vinieran de a tiro desnudos. Los recogieron todos al portal que ocupa ahora lo que es donde está el Mesón de San Pedro. Se contaron sesenta y tantos muertos allí tendidos y entre ellos estaba un soldado villista.

El Coquito, que así le decían al asistente de, de Baca, ése quedó herido. Lo ponen en una capilla y a eso de las cinco y media o seis de la tarde da la orden el general Parra de salida de todos los soldados, con rumbo a San Juan de los Lagos. Se llevan al Coquito por delante con esperanzas de poderlo poner en curación, a ver si no se moría, porque lo estimaba mucho el coronel Baca. Era su asistente.

Cuando ya salen todos los soldados quedó el pueblo ciertamente, como quien dice, como si lo hubiera arrastrado Judas. Se suelta un vientecillo, algo fuerte, y por las rendijas de las ventanas silbaba aquel, aquel viento y que contribuía a lo tétrico, a lo, diremos, al espectáculo que presentaban todos aquellos difuntos tendidos en el portal, a quienes al día siguiente se les dio sepultura, pos en montón, porque no era posible darles fosa a cada uno. Pero se contaron sesenta y tantos, de todos los que se recogieron, quedando de ochocientos que se dice, que combatieron por una parte y otra, aunque los villistas después recibieron más refuerzos que fueron mil y tantos, pero ya no entraron en acción. De esos muy pocos sobraron de los carrancistas y que de los primeros disparos, no más por saber la proximidad de los villistas, fueron y dieron informe falso a la Jefatura de Operaciones a Guadalajara.

Y entonces se dice, porque un pariente mío me contaba, que vieron el regimiento que venía a quemar a San Miguel, que dizque porque aquéllos informaron que hasta las mujeres por las ventanas y puertas con pistola en mano les ayudaban a los villistas y que los habían acabado.

Y no fue así porque los heridos que atendieron en el hospital y de otros que fueron que realmente entraron en acción y se dieron cuenta del combate, éstos se libraron en casas particulares poniéndose ropa de algunos campesinos y de algunas personas que los defendieron, y aquél fue el testimonio real y verdadero de la actitud que el pueblo observó en cuanto al informe falso que habían dado aquéllos, porque aquéllos llegando, veían que salían todos aquellos soldados: —¿A dónde van?

—Vamos a quemar a San Miguel, porque San Miguel se portó de una manera que acabó con los nuestros.

Entonces dice: —No. Vamos a que reciban ustedes las informaciones tal y cual fue.

Llegan a Jefatura de Operaciones que expiden informaciones y ellos dicen: —Si no ha sido por el pueblo que nos defendió, no habíamos quedado uno solo.

Esa fue la información que ellos dieron y el testimonio que vino desbaratando aquella intención que traían en contra de San Miguel.

Una vez, como digo, pasado el combate, salieron todos los soldados. Nos quedamos en el pueblo todos espantados. ¡Ah! Pero antes como quisieron llevarse al coronel Guerrero se reúnen todos los soldados, los más que pudieron entrar a caballo al atrio, y entonces dispusieron que lo arrojaran de arriba de la torre por el lado donde se encuentra una noria antigua que es cerca del portalito que está pegado al lado oriente del templo. Entonces lo toman de los pies y de los brazos y lo arrojan desde arriba, un espectáculo algo bochornosos.

Se vio aquello como algo que no caía, no caía, porque siempre supongo yo que ya estaba muerto, pero siempre debería haberse respetado. Total, que a él lo aventaron. Otros los aventaron de la torre también y cayeron cerca de la puerta del coro. Quedaron dos o tres tendidos allí cerca de la puerta del coro.

A Guerrero lo levantaron y entonces, según algunas personas, dicen que el general Parra se puso a los pies de Guerrero cuando estaba tendido allí en el portal. Se quedó contemplándolo y que dijo: —Te miro, muerto, y te respeto.

Ésa, ésa fue la frase que según dicen pronunció el general Parra. Aquí termino el relato porque nos quedamos solos con los muertos y espantados por algún tiempo.

Los villistas por el tiempo que duraron o sea el mes que permanecieron en la población muchos de ellos continuamente se les veía ir a visitar al Santuario que está frente al templo parroquial donde se venera una Purísima muy linda. Y ellos con cierta devoción, con cierta confianza, a la hora del combate le gritaban con la fuerza de sus pulmones: —¡Tú, la de la puerta azul, defiéndenos! ¡Ayúdanos, porque San Miguel perece!

Como la puerta estaba pintada de azul, ellos no tenían otro medio de comunicarse con ella porque no sabían qué, qué advocación era de la imagen. Pero no más con eso demostraron su religiosidad y demostraron su confianza donde tenían la seguridad de que ésa de la puertita azul los defendía y como que así pasó. Fueron muy pocos los villistas que murieron y en cambio los carrancistas casi terminaron. Ésa es otra de las partes, diremos, esenciales porque en el combate de seguro que ellos vieron el peligro en que andaban. Y no pudieron más que dirigirse a aquélla de la puertita azul con la confianza de que los defendía.

Bibliography

WORKS OF MARIANO AZUELA

Andrés Pérez, maderista. Mexico: Imprenta de la Librería de Andrés Botas y Miguel, 1911.

Epistolario y archivo. Recopilación, notas y apéndices de Beatrice Berler. Mexico: Centro de Estudios Literarios, Universidad Nacional Autónoma de México, 1969.

"José María." In *Bandera de Provincias* (Guadalajara), I, 7 (August 15, 1929), pp. 3, 5.

Los de abajo. Cuadros y escenas de la revolución actual. In *El Paso del Norte,* Época II, Tomo IX, October 27–November 21, 1915.

Los de abajo. Novela (Cuadros y escenas de la Revolución Mexicana), El Paso: Imprenta de "El Paso del Norte," 1916.

Los de abajo. Cuadros y escenas de la Revolución Mexicana. Mexico: "Razaster," 1920.

Los de abajo. Cuadros y escenas de la Revolución Mexicana. Mexico: Publicaciones Literarias Exclusivas de "El Universal Ilustrado," 1925.

Los de abajo. Novela mejicana. Cuadernos Populares Biblos, Colección Quincenal Literaria, No. 1, 15 de agosto de 1927. Madrid: Ediciones Biblos, 1927.

Los de abajo. Novela de la Revolución Mejicana. Madrid, Barcelona, Bilbao: Espasa-Calpe, 1930.

Los de abajo. Novela de la Revolución Mexicana. Mexico: Editorial Pedro Robredo, 1938.

Los de abajo. Novela de la Revolución Mexicana. Edited with Introduction, Notes and Vocabulary by John E. Englekirk and Lawrence B. Kiddle. New York: F. S. Crofts and Co., 1939.

Los de abajo. Novela de la Revolución Mexicana. Mexico: Ediciones Botas, 1941.

Los de abajo. In *Obras completas.* 3 vols. Mexico: Fondo de Cultura Económica, 1958–1960, I, 320–418.

Los de abajo. Mexico and Buenos Aires: Fondo de Cultura Económica, 1958.

Los fracasados. Mexico: Tipografía y Litografía de Müller Hermanos, 1908.

Los fracasados. In *Obras completas,* I, 3–12.

Mala yerba. 3d ed. Mexico: Ediciones Botas, 1937.

Maria Luisa. Lagos de Moreno: Imprenta López Arce, 1907.

Maria Luisa. In *Obras completas,* II, 707–763.

Las moscas. 2d ed. Mexico: Ediciones de "La Razón," 1931 (followed by *Los caciques*).

Obras completas. Prólogo de Francisco Monterde. 3 vols. Mexico: Fondo de Cultura Económica, 1958–1960.

Precursores. Santiago de Chile: Editorial Ercilla, 1935.

Sin amor. Mexico: Tipografía y Litografía de Müller Hermanos, 1912.

Sin amor. In *Obras completas,* I, 225–319.

Two Novels of Mexico. The Flies. The Bosses. Translated by Lesley Byrd Simpson. Berkeley and Los Angeles: University of California Press, 1956.

WORKS CONSULTED

de Alba, Alfonso, *Antonio Moreno y Oviedo y la generación de 1903.* Prólogo de Mariano Azuela. Mexico, 1949.

Almada, Francisco R. *La Revolución en el Estado de Chihuahua.* Biblioteca del Instituto Nacional de Estudios Históricos de la Revolución Mexicana. 2 vols. Mexico, 1965.

Azuela Arriaga, María. *Mariano Azuela, novelista de la revolución mexicana.* Tesis (maestra en letras españolas), Universidad Nacional Autónoma de México. Mexico, 1955.

Boletín Militar. Diario Constitucionalista. Guadalajara. Various issues between Tomo II, Núm. 129 (Sunday, December 13, 1914) and Tomo V, Núm. 364 (Friday, January 7, 1916).

Brambila, Alberto. *Detalles de mi vida íntima.* Guadalajara, 1964.

Calzadíaz Barrera, Alberto. *Hechos reales de la Revolución.* 3 vols. Mexico: Editores Mexicanos Unidos, S. A., 1965.

Camacho, P. J. *Breve narración de los datos*

recogidos acerca del fusilamiento del sacerdote D. David Galván. Guadalajara, 1927.

Cornejo y Mejía, Ana María. "Un viaje en el
año de 1915." Manuscript. Teocaltiche, Jalisco, 1963.

Davis, Will[iam] B[rownlee]. *Experiences and
Observations of an American Consular Offi-
cer during the Recent Mexican Revolutions.*
Los Angeles: Wayside Press, 1920.

Delgado, Ricardo. *Las monedas jaliscienses durante la época revolucionaria.* Guadalajara:
Talleres "Gráfica," 1938.

Delgado Román, José de Jesús. Tape recorded
interview, San Miguel el Alto, Jalisco, July,
1960.

*Diccionario Porrúa de historia, biografía, y geo-
grafía de México.* 3d ed. 2 vols. Mexico: Editorial Porrúa, S. A., 1971.

Englekirk, John E. "The Discovery of *Los de
abajo* by Mariano Azuela." *Hispania,* 18
(1935), 53-62.

Estados Unidos Mexicanos, Departamento de la
Estadística Nacional. *Censo general de habi-
tantes. 30 de noviembre de 1921. Estado de
Zacatecas.* Mexico: Talleres Gráficos de la
Nación, 1928.

F. L. y D. *La reina occidental. Guía del viajero en Guadalajara.* Guadalajara: Taller
Tip. del Orfanatorio del S. C. de Jesús, 1900–
1901.

Figueroa Torres, J. Jesús. *Biografía de Caloca.
El cuentista parlamentario.* Mexico: Costa
Amic, Editor, 1965.

García, Pedro. *Con el cura Hidalgo en la Guerra
de Independencia.* Mexico: Empresas Edito-
riales, S. A., 1948.

Gavira Castro, Gabriel. *General de Brigada
Gabriel Gavira. Su actuación político-militar
revolucionaria.* 2d ed. Mexico: Talleres Tipo-
gráficos de A. del Bosque, Impresor, 1933.

González, Manuel Pedro. "Bibliografía del novelista Mariano Azuela." *Revista Bimestre
Cubana,* 48 (July–August, 1941), 50-72.

———. *Trayectoria de la novela en México.*
Mexico: Ediciones Botas, 1951.

González Dávila, Amado. *Diccionario geográfico, histórico, biográfico y estadístico del Estado de Sinaloa.* Culiacán, Sinaloa, 1959.

González de Mendoza, J. M. "Mariano Azuela
y lo mexicano." *Cuadernos Americanos,* 11:3
(1952), 282-285.

Guevara, Emilio. *Historia y estadística particu-*
lar de la Villa de Zapotlanejo, cabecera de
departamento del 1er Cantón de Jalisco,
México.* Guadalajara: Imp. de la Escuela de
Artes y Oficios del Estado, 1919.

Guzmán, Martín Luis. *El águila y la serpiente.*
4th ed. Mexico: Editorial Anáhuac, 1941.

Jones, Dewey Roscoe. *El doctor Mariano Azuela,
médico y novelista.* Mexico: Universidad Nacional Autónoma, Escuela de Verano, 1960.

Kercheville, Francis M. "El liberalismo en Azuela." *Revista Iberoamericana,* 3:6 (May 1941),
381-398.

Langford, Walter M. *The Mexican Novel Comes
of Age.* Notre Dame and London: University
of Notre Dame Press, 1971.

Langle Ramírez, Arturo. *El ejército villista.*
Mexico: Instituto Nacional de Antropología
e Historia, 1961.

Leal, Luis. *Mariano Azuela, vida y obra.* Mexico: Ediciones de Andrea, 1961.

León, J. Jesús. "Vida y hazañas de Julián Medina." Guadalajara, 1939. Broadside.

Magdaleno, Mauricio. *Ritual del año.* Los presentes. Mexico, 1955.

Medina de la Torre, Francisco. *Apuntes geo-
gráficos, estadísticos e históricos del Municipio de San Miguel el Alto, Estado de Jalisco, México.* 3d ed. Guadalajara: Tip. C. M.
Sainz, 1935.

Menton, Seymour. "La estructura épica de 'Los
de abajo' y un prólogo especulativo." *Hispania,* 50:4 (1967), 1001-1011.

Monterde, Francisco, ed. *Mariano Azuela y la
crítica mexicana. Estudios, artículos y reseñas.*
Mexico: Secretaría de Educación Pública,
1973.

Moore, Ernest R. *Bibliografía de novelistas de la
Revolución Mexicana.* Mexico, 1941.

———. "Biografía y bibliografía de don Mari-
ano Azuela." Part 1, "Obras y artículos,"
Ábside, 4:2 (February, 1940), 53-62; Part 2,
"Crítica," *Ábside,* 4:3 (March, 1940), 50-64.

———. "Novelists of the Mexican Revolution:
Mariano Azuela." *Mexican Life,* August,
1940, pp. 21-28, 81-87.

Moreno Ochoa, J. Ángel. *Semblanzas revolucionarias. Compendio del movimiento de li-
beración en Jalisco.* Guadalajara, 1965.

Morton, F. Rand. *Los novelistas de la Revolución Mexicana.* Mexico: Editorial Cultura,
1949.

Muñoz, Ignacio. *Verdad y mito de la Revolución*

Mexicana. 2 vols. Mexico: Ediciones Populares, 1960.

Naranjo, Francisco. *Diccionario biográfico revolucionario.* Mexico: Imprenta Editorial "Cosmos," 1935.

Obregón, Álvaro. *Ocho mil kilómetros en campaña.* Estudio preliminar de Francisco L. Urquizo y Francisco J. Grajales. Apéndice de Manuel González Ramírez. 3d ed. Mexico: Fondo de Cultura Económica, 1960.

Olea, Héctor R. *Breve historia de la Revolución en Sinaloa (1910–1917).* Biblioteca del Instituto Nacional de Estudios Históricos de la Revolución Mexicana. Mexico, 1964.

Páez Brotchie, Luis. *Jalisco. Historia mínima.* 2 vols. Guadalajara, 1940.

El Paso del Norte. El Paso, Texas. Época II, Tomo IX, Núm. 1733 (October 27, 1915) to Época II, Tomo IX, Núm. 1755 (November 21, 1915).

Pérez Arce, Enrique. "Los de abajo." In *El Paso del Norte,* December 10, 1915, p. 2.

Puente, Ramón. *Villa en pie.* Mexico: Editorial "México Nuevo," 1937.

Quirarte, Clotilde Evelia. *Nochistlán de Zacatecas. Cuatro siglos de su vida.* Mexico, 1960.

Quirk, Robert E. *The Mexican Revolution, 1914–1915. The Convention of Aguascalientes.* Bloomington: Indiana University Press, 1960.

Ramírez, Agustín. *Apuntes históricos sobre el Señor de la Misericordia y su culto.* Guadalajara, 1938.

Ramos, Roberto. *Bibliografía de la Revolución Mexicana.* 3 vols. Mexico, 1931–1940.

Reed, John. *Insurgent Mexico.* New York, 1914.

Robe, Stanley L. "Dos comentarios de 1915 sobre *Los de abajo.*" *Revista Iberoamericana,* 41 (1975), 267–272.

Romero Flores, Jesús. *Anales históricos de la revolución mexicana.* 3 vols. Mexico: Libro Mex Editores, S. de R. C., 1959.

Ross, Stanley R., et al. *Fuentes de la historia contemporánea de México. Periódicos y revistas.* Vol. I. Mexico: Colegio de México, 1965.

Rulfo, Juan. *El llano en llamas.* Mexico: Fondo de Cultura Económica, 1953.

Rutherford, John. *An Annotated Bibliography of the Novels of the Mexican Revolution in English and Spanish.* Troy, N. Y.: Whitston Publishing Company, 1972.

Spell, Jefferson Rea. *Contemporary Spanish American Fiction.* Chapel Hill: University of North Carolina Press, 1944.

Texas Newspapers, 1813–1939. A Union List of Newspaper Files Available in Offices of Publishers, Libraries, and a Number of Private Collections. Houston: San Jacinto Museum of History Association, 1941.

Torres Rioseco, Arturo. *Grandes novelistas de la América Hispana.* Berkeley and Los Angeles: University of California Press, 1949.

Valadez, J. Jesús. *"Los de abajo."* In *El Paso del Norte,* December 21, 1915, pp. 2–3.

Villegas G., Jesús Gerardo. *Cosas de Tlajomulco. Sucedidos que parecen cuentos.* Guadalajara: Editorial Occidental, 1965.

La voz del pueblo. Semanario político de información (Guadalajara). Época primera, Tomo I, Núm. 14 (February 6, 1939).

Yáñez, Agustín. *Genio y figuras de Guadalajara.* Mexico, 1942.

———. *Yahualica.* Mexico, 1946.

Zuno, José Guadalupe. *Historia de la Revolución en el Estado de Jalisco.* Biblioteca del Instituto Nacional de Estudios Históricos de la Revolución Mexicana. Mexico: Talleres Gráficos de la Nación, 1964.

———. *Reminiscencias de una vida.* Biblioteca de Autores Jaliscienses. Guadalajara, 1956.